The Cursed Fortress

The Fifth Carlisle & Holbrooke Naval Adventure

Chris Durbin

Chris Durbin

To

Beth

our teacher

The Cursed Fortress

Chris Durbin

Visit my website at:

www.chris-durbin.com

First Edition: 2019

***

Chris Durbin

CONTENTS

Chris Durbin

LIST OF CHARTS

NAUTICAL TERMS

Throughout the centuries, sailors have created their own language to describe the highly technical equipment and processes that they use to live and work at sea. This holds true in the twenty-first century.

When counting the number of nautical terms that I've used in this series of novels, it became evident that a printed book wasn't the best place for them. I've therefore created a glossary of nautical terms on my website:

https://chris-durbin.com/glossary/

My glossary of nautical terms is limited to those that I've used in this series of novels, as they were used in the middle of the eighteenth century. It's intended as a work of reference to accompany the Carlisle and Holbrooke series of naval adventure novels.

Some of the usages of these terms have changed over the years, so this glossary should be used with caution when referring to periods before 1740 or after 1780.

The glossary isn't exhaustive. A more comprehensive list can be found in Falconer's Universal Dictionary of the Marine, first published in 1769. I haven't counted the number of terms that Falconer has defined, but he fills 328 pages with English language terms, followed by a further eighty-three pages of French translations. It is a monumental work.

An online version of the 1780 edition of The Universal Dictionary (which unfortunately does not include all the excellent diagrams that are in the print version) can be found on this website:

https://archive.org/details/universaldiction00falc/

***

PRINCIPAL CHARACTERS

Fictional

Captain Edward Carlisle: Commanding Officer, *Medina*

Lady Chiara Angelini: Captain Carlisle's wife

Joshua Carlisle: Captain Carlisle's father

Charles Carlisle: Captain Carlisle's brother

Barbara Dexter: Captain Carlisle's cousin

Cranmer Dexter: Barbara's husband

Patrick Moxon: First Lieutenant, *Medina*

John Hosking: Sailing Master, *Medina*

David Wishart: Master's Mate, *Medina*

Enrico Angelini: Midshipman, *Medina*. Cousin to Lady Chiara

Able Seaman Whittle: a follower of Captain Carlisle's from his home in Virginia

Black Rod: Chief-of-Household of the Angelini family, real name unknown

***

Historical

Admiral Edward Boscawen: Naval Commander-in-Chief at the siege of Louisbourg

Rear Admiral Sir Charles Hardy: Commander of the Louisbourg blockade squadron

Commodore Alexander Colville (7th Viscount Colville of Culross): Commander of the squadron at Halifax

Major General Jefferey Amherst: Land Forces Commander at the siege of Louisbourg

Brigadier-General General James Wolfe: Commander of the assault force for the Louisbourg landings

Joannis-Galand D'Olabaratz: Port Captain Louisbourg

Jean D'Olabaratz: Son of Joannis-Galand, Commanding Officer *L'Aigle*

Augustin de Boschenry de Drucour: French Governor of Louisbourg

Marquis des Gouttes: French Naval Commander at Louisbourg

***

Chart: Western Atlantic

Chart: Nova Scotia & Île Royale

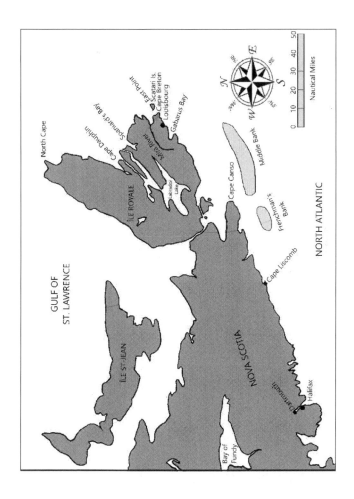

Chart: Cape Dauphin

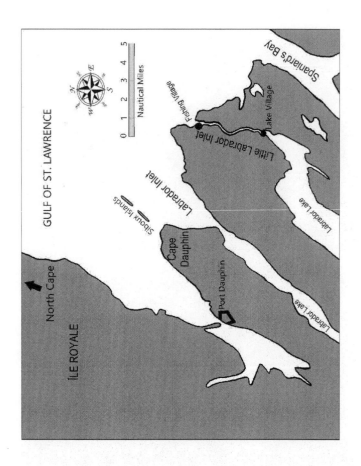

Chart: Louisbourg & Gabarus Bay

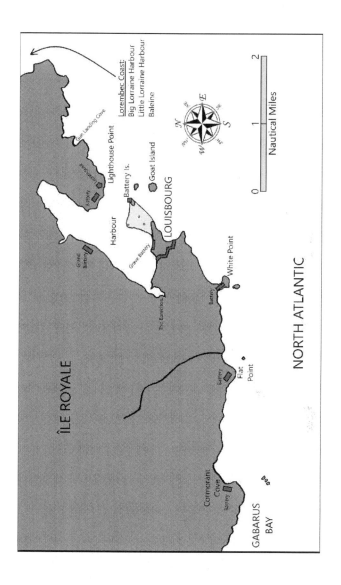

Chris Durbin

'It is more difficult to defend a coast than to invade it.'

***

Sir Walter Raleigh when confronted with pessimism and delay in the planning of an attack on Fayal in the Azores, 1597.

From: Lives of the British Admirals Volume IV, Robert Southey.

***

INTRODUCTION

The North American Strategy

Pitt's strategy for the new year was to unleash a three-pronged attack on the French possessions in North America that would last through 1758 and 1759 and culminate in the surrender of New France. A naval squadron would carry an army up the St. Lawrence River to Quebec and Montreal while two further armies would march up the Ohio Valley and across the wilderness to Lake Ontario.

The path to the St. Lawrence, however, was guarded by the French fortress of Louisbourg on Île Royale. A poorly planned expedition in 1757 had been defeated by a combination of the weather and a buildup of French naval forces. Pitt was determined that the 1758 attempt would be successful, and he planned that Louisbourg should fall early enough in the season to allow the fleet and army to move on up the St. Lawrence before the autumn weather could set in.

Hawke with the Channel Fleet and Osborn in the Mediterranean were tasked with preventing the French navy and French supply ships from crossing the Atlantic. Pitt and Anson knew that it was impossible to effectively blockade the whole of the European Atlantic coast, from Brest to Gibraltar, and they needed to have a substantial naval squadron cruising off Louisbourg as soon as the ice should melt in the Spring. That required the ships to be over-wintered as close to Louisbourg as possible. Halifax was selected for this grand gamble, even though it had been established as a naval yard only a few years before and the facilities were rudimentary. No squadron had ever before been maintained under such conditions.

***

Carlisle and Holbrooke

The start of the year of 1758 brought new horizons for our two heroes. They had served together in the Mediterranean and the Caribbean, first in the small frigate *Fury* and then in the larger *Medina*, but that was all about to change.

Holbrooke was promoted to commander and given the sloop *Kestrel* with orders were to report to the Admiralty in London. Holbrooke's story in the first half of 1758 is told in *Holbrooke's Tide*, the fourth of this series of naval adventures.

Carlisle resumed command of *Medina*, having recovered from his injuries received in a fight with a Dutch pirate. He'd been expecting to stay on the Jamaica Station, but orders to escort a convoy to Hampton, Virginia and then to join the Louisbourg blockading squadron threw his plans – and those of his wife, Chiara – into disarray.

The story continues…

***

PROLOGUE

Louisbourg Fog

Saturday, Fourteenth of January 1758.
L'Aigle, at Sea. Off Louisbourg, Île Royale.

The Île Royale fogs were notoriously impenetrable; thick as pea soup and horribly persistent. Jean d'Olabaratz had given up trying to stare through this one, and now he confined himself to watching the compass and the luff of the main tops'l that could just about be discerned through the murk. He was looking and listening with the utmost concentration, for all their lives depended upon his skill. After all, he'd mostly grown up at Louisbourg, his father was the Port Captain, and he'd lived half of his life on that wild and inhospitable shore.

'A point to larboard,' he ordered the *maître de manoeuvre*, 'and let there be silence on the upper deck so that we can hear the surf on Goat Island or White Point.'

The quartermaster nodded to the steersman, who eased the wheel a few spokes, watching the compass to avoid overshooting his mark. All hands were on deck and at their sail handling stations; the tension was as thick as the fog.

L'Aigle had left Rochefort at the end of November escorting four merchant ships with supplies for Louisbourg. She had been built as a fifty-gun two-decker but now, armed *en flute*, she carried almost eight hundred tons of food, clothing and infantry weapons. The merchant ships carried a further seven hundred tons. It represented a timely relief for the isolated and beleaguered town and fortress.

Things had started to go wrong as soon as *L'Aigle* and her charges were at sea. Shortly after they left Rochefort, they'd been sighted by British privateers who'd haunted them through the night, looking for an opportunity to pounce. They didn't know that all but four of *L'Aigle's* guns were struck down into the bottom of the hold and

3

D'Olabaratz had been careful to avoid opening any of the blind gunports. If the privateers had known, they'd have pounced immediately. The uneasy night passed, and somehow the dawn found d'Olabaratz with all four of his merchantmen still under his lee. However, as the cold winter sun rose, it revealed a horizon to windward broken by the topmasts of three ships, men-of-war. His worst fears were confirmed; it was a British squadron, cruising for just this kind of opportunity. All that he could do was to run to the south and leave the merchantmen to their fates.

D'Olabaratz swore at the wind and muttered his disdain for King Louis and his cursed fortress. He knew what an easterly wind meant at this time of year, days or weeks of fog. The cold current that ran south from the frozen lands of the Labrador country met the warmer water of the Atlantic stream over the Grand Banks two hundred miles to the east of Louisbourg. The warm air that attended the Atlantic stream was cooled by the Labrador current and condensed, forming a fog that this easterly wind carried undiminished to Île Royale. It meant misery for the French garrison and extreme danger for any ship approaching the coast.

'Furl the courses, we'll stand in under tops'ls and the jib,' he said to the sailing-master. There was a silent rush as the topmen swarmed up the shrouds. Everyone knew the danger of approaching a lee shore in thick weather.

It wasn't just the weather that concerned d'Olabaratz – poor weather was taken for granted off Louisbourg in January – it was the British navy. Halifax was only a day's sailing southwest along the coast, if the wind was fair, perhaps no more three days even in this easterly wind. He knew that a squadron had over-wintered in the harbour and although he didn't fear any of the ships-of-the-line getting out this early in the season, it was quite likely that a frigate or sloop would be waiting off Louisbourg to snap up just such a prize as *L'Aigle*. He was confident that he knew this coast better than any English sea-officer, but he'd still prefer not to meet one with his guns stowed below.

The meagre light of dawn seeped reluctantly through the moisture-heavy air, offering no real illumination; if anything, it intensified the fog. Nevertheless, D'Olabaratz was confident of his position. The sailing master had positively established their latitude the previous day from a noon sight before the visibility had deteriorated, and they had been casting the lead throughout the night. He knew the soundings and the nature of the seabed in these waters as well as he knew the steps to his childhood bedroom. *L'Aigle* was a league southeast of the harbour entrance. If he was wrong, they would have the devil's own job to make an offing when his error became obvious, when instead of the tall lighthouse on their bow they would see an uninterrupted wall of surf-beaten rocks. He knew the light would be lit, his father wouldn't omit such a basic navigational aid when he and the few thousand soldiers and civilians depended upon ships from France to keep them alive through the winter.

***

D'Olabaratz opened his mouth to make a remark, but the sailing master held up his hand, his ear cocked to starboard.

'I hear something to windward,' he whispered, 'a bell!'

The decks of *L'Aigle* were deathly silent. The light wind hardly raised a murmur in the rigging, and the noise of the sea was muted with the wind so far abaft the beam. D'Olabaratz strained to hear what the master had reported, but he heard nothing. He looked quizzically at the older man.

'I heard it, sir,' a midshipman said in a low voice. 'Eight bells in four groups of two.'

The steersman nodded. He'd heard it too.

Eight bells, the change of the watch in an English ship! They were careless to make so much noise in the fog a league off Louisbourg.

D'Olabaratz motioned to the midshipman to come closer. 'Go quietly over the deck and remind everyone to keep absolute silence, their lives and liberty depend upon it. Go now. Quickly, but quietly!'

Somewhere to windward was a British man-of-war. In *L'Aigle's* present state of disarmament, it hardly mattered what size of vessel it was, anything bigger than a schooner could batter them into submission before they could reach safety under the guns of Battery Island.

'There she is!' said the master, pointing to the ghostly outline of a vessel crossing their stern. It was very close, only a cable or so on their starboard quarter.

***

Robert Hathorn, master and commander of the brig-sloop *Hawke* had called all hands to put the sloop about twenty minutes before the turn of the watch. He'd completed his mission to look into Spanish Bay a week ago and had decided to watch the approaches to Louisbourg for a few days before returning to Halifax. Only a few days, because this was no weather to be tacking backwards and forwards off an enemy port, and his men were already starting to show the first signs of sickness. It was unlikely that the watch would be resumed until February, the wear on the ships and the men was just too much to justify it. His presence here was over and above his orders, and now that this fog had set in, he'd decided that he'd done all that an excess of zeal for his duty demanded.

Eight bells had just been struck, and the sloop was settled on its new course of south-southwest to make its offing, and with this quartering wind he'd be back in Halifax by tomorrow afternoon.

'Sail! Sail on the starboard beam!'

Hathorn glanced quickly to starboard. Nothing. Then he saw it, a darker patch in the fog, a ship! He knew instantly that it must be French. Whether a man-of-war or merchantman he couldn't yet tell, but she was making for Louisbourg.

'Beat to Quarters,' he shouted and almost instantly heard the drum roll.

'Stand by to veer ship, up helm,' he ordered.

These brig-sloops with their gaff mains'l veered quickly and *Hawke* put her stern through the wind without any fuss. They were now on the same tack as the chase, astern and to leeward.

The sloop was already cleared for action and the people were all on deck, so it was a matter of moments before his first lieutenant was reporting the starboard guns loaded and run out.

Hathorn was prepared to have a go at anything less than a ship-of-the-line. He knew that the garrison at Louisbourg was so short of stores that the French navy was forced to convert its frigates to store ships, with only a few guns left to protect themselves. It was worth the risk.

'Bear away two points, Quartermaster.'

The steersman eased the wheel to leeward, and the French frigate appeared as a spectral shape on the starboard bow. Hathorn could see the enemy but not well enough. He was caught in that age-old dilemma of the stern-chase, whether to bear away and try a few broadsides to slow the enemy down or to wait for the chase to be so close that he could finish it out of hand. In this case, the dilemma was even more acute because the frigates home port was less than a league to leeward. If he waited, the frigate could make the safety of the port before he was close enough for a decisive stroke.

'Captain, sir! I hear breakers to leeward!'

That ended the dilemma, he needed to risk everything on a crippling blow at long range. He couldn't follow the chase into the surf.

'Stand by the starboard broadside,' he called to the first lieutenant. 'Two more points, Quartermaster.'

Now the frigate could be seen by the whole starboard battery.

'Fire when you're ready,' Hathorn shouted.

The guns erupted in smoke and flame. *Hawke's* broadside of three-pounders wasn't meant to take on the heavy timbers of a frigate, but nevertheless, at only a few cables range the destruction to the stern gallery and the taffrail was impressive. There would be casualties on the quarterdeck, but fewer on the upper deck than would normally be expected, with a bare minimum of men at the guns.

Veering ship would take too long, so Hathorn held his course while the gun crews were worked feverishly to reload.

'We'll have the devil's own job clawing off this shore if we stand in any further,' said the old quartermaster who had taken upon himself the role of sailing master. 'Even I can hear that surf now.'

'Mind your damned business!' snapped Hathorn.

He knew well enough the peril of becoming embayed off Louisbourg in an easterly wind with visibility down to two cables. He knew the peril, but so desperately wanted to distinguish himself that he was prepared to accept it. There was almost no chance of taking the Frenchman. If a lucky shot should dismast her, she'd drift inshore under the guns of the island at the entrance of the harbour. Even if she was grounded, there was nothing *Hawke* could do to complete her destruction, so close to the French batteries. However, a report that he'd driven a French frigate ashore was a long way better than nothing.

'One more broadside, First Lieutenant,' he called.

The starboard battery fired again. This time the range was greater, and the frigate had almost disappeared in the fog. Hathorn would never know the effect of his last broadside, which was perhaps just as well because every ball fell harmlessly in *L'Aigle's* wake.

It was a nervous forty minutes before *Hawke* was clear of Goat Island and White Point. With Gabarus Bay under her lee, Hathorn breathed easily again, and the easterly wind allowed him to set a course south-southwest for Halifax.

***

CHAPTER ONE

Chiara's Secret

Wednesday, Fifteenth of February 1758.
Medina, at Sea. Grand Cayman East-Southeast 22 leagues.

With the trade wind broad on her starboard beam and under tops'ls alone, *Medina* made her pedestrian way northwest-by-west towards the Yucatan Channel. There was no need – in fact, no possibility – of haste, as she was convoying a mixed bag of twenty merchantmen from Jamaica towards the American colonies. With all sail spread they barely reached the speed that the frigate achieved with her much reduced canvas.

Carlisle had stationed himself at the rear of the convoy – to windward – so that he could rapidly intervene if the merchantmen were threatened or if there was an emergency that needed his intervention. The snow-rigged sloop *Shark*, John Anderson in command, was at the head of the convoy, to starboard, so that she too had the advantage of a windward position. Carlisle had disposed his escorts in the most scientific manner, to foil any attack by French privateers. Although the seas west of the Caymans were Spanish and Spain was – so far – neutral in this war, there was still a distinct possibility of French incursions from St. Domingue or their colony of Louisiana in the Gulf of Mexico.

Carlisle stared intently at his convoy as the sun rose over his right shoulder. They were behaving well so far, even keeping in close company with each on the three nights since they'd sailed from Kingston. He counted them, out of habit rather in the fear that any had gone astray. An even twenty, principally carrying sugar and molasses to the colonies to feed the growing demand for luxury foods and to be turned into the rum that fueled the budding industries of these new lands.

'I believe I'll take breakfast with Lady Chiara, Mister Moxon. Call me if any sails are sighted,' he said to the first lieutenant.

Taking one last look around the horizon, letting the sheer beauty of the Caribbean on this crystal-clear morning sink into his soul, he turned away for the cool of his cabin. The sun wouldn't have heated it yet, but its early rays would already be dispelling the overnight gloom and twinkling on the silverware that Black Rod had laid out. His personal servant had been burned in an accident the previous year and repatriated to England. So, after a fruitless search for a replacement in Kingston, his wife Chiara had offered the Angelini family chief-of-household as a substitute, the enigmatic Black Rod. To this day, Carlisle didn't know the man's real name. Even the ship's muster book didn't help; the Purser was utterly intimidated by the tall, forbidding Italian and rather than quiz him had merely entered his surname as *Black* and his Christian name as *Rod*. Carlisle could imagine all kinds of trouble when the clerks at the navy board saw *that*. But they were used to captains acquiring crew members from all corners of the globe, and his nationality would probably reassure them. For generations they'd been forced to accept the sometimes-bizarre attempts to anglicise names that really didn't lend themselves to translation. No, on reflection, *Black Rod* may raise an eyebrow but no more.

***

The cabin was indeed cool, and Black Rod had laid out a substantial breakfast that would have satisfied half a dozen men. Only three days out of Port Royal and all the luxuries of the shore were still available. Fresh eggs and ham of course, but also soft, white bread and cow's milk. Carlisle had spent half his life at sea, so the prospect of a lack of fresh cow's milk disturbed him not at all, but it was a real delight while it was available. It would be goat's milk for the next three or four weeks until they reached Hampton in his home colony of Virginia.

Carlisle had grown used to waiting for his wife. It seemed that time moved at a different pace for Chiara – perhaps it was the same for all wives – and nothing in this world would cause her to hasten her preparations to face the day. He was used to it, but he still wondered how she could be so unhurried in domestic matters and yet, as he'd seen for himself, so rapid and decisive when the need arose. Carlisle paced the few yards across the spread of the cabin windows, trying not to look longingly at the dining table while attempting to assume the air of a man who was entirely at his leisure. He'd been on deck since before dawn some three hours before, and his stomach was reminding him that he hadn't eaten since supper the night before. Black Rod, like the polished servant that he was, busied himself in the tiny scullery until his mistress should appear.

The minutes passed. Carlisle was on the point of committing the cardinal sin of sending a message to ask when his wife may be ready to join him when her maid pushed open the door from the sleeping cabin and Chiara made her entrance. *Medina* may have been a mere frigate, but Lady Chiara's presence in the great cabin lent an air of grace and nobility that would have flattered a flagship. Chiara looked radiant in a silver-grey dress that combined style with practicality. Even her maid looked well turned-out.

'Good morning, my dear,' said Chiara, not waiting for Carlisle to speak first. 'I trust all is well with the ship and the convoy. You were about long before dawn; I wonder that you look so spruce.'

Now, wasn't that just like her to get her compliment in first, before he'd recovered from seeing her enter the cabin? Carlisle stammered a conventional response as he held a chair for his wife.

Breakfast was much quieter than usual. On most mornings, Carlisle invited the off-going officer-of-the-watch and midshipman to join them, and often the first lieutenant even if he'd not had the watch. But yesterday at supper Chiara had particularly asked that they breakfast alone, 'so that she could enjoy his company,' she'd said. Carlisle was happy to agree; there would be plenty of time to socialise with his new officers on this long passage north.

Chiara picked at her breakfast while Carlisle demolished eggs, toast, buttered rolls and spread the hot English mustard liberally on his ham. The coffee was excellent. Jamaican coffee cultivation had only been started a generation before, yet the beans from the Blue Mountain region, between Kingston and the north coast, were truly superb. In the hands of Black Rod, they produced coffee with a mild flavour entirely lacking the bitterness that he was used to. Chiara had laid in enough of the Blue Mountain coffee to last for an extended cruise.

As the first edge of his hunger was satisfied, and he was able to give more of his attention to his wife, Carlisle noticed that she was watching him with peculiar intensity as she talked away about domestic affairs. When he'd removed his napkin, and Black Rod had refilled his coffee cup, Chiara paused in her flow of conversation.

'Would you leave us, please?' Chiara asked Black Rod and cast a meaningful glance at Susan her maid, who also left the cabin.

***

Carlisle was mystified. In this much, they had completely different attitudes: Chiara, having been bred into a noble Sardinian family, was perfectly comfortable with discussing almost anything in front of the servants. Carlisle was more reticent and would generally only discuss innocuous domestic matters unless they were alone. It was unprecedented for Chiara to ask the servants to withdraw, particularly Black Rod who knew all the Angelini family secrets.

'Edward, I have something to tell you,' Chiara started, 'although I expect you may have guessed it already.'

Carlisle had guessed nothing, but his concern showed immediately. It could only be some illness that his wife had discovered and was now ready to reveal.

Chiara looked at him with an amused expression.

'I am expecting our child,' she said with typical abruptness, now smiling broadly.

Carlisle froze, his cup halfway between saucer and lip. Chiara almost laughed out loud, his expression of astonishment was so comical. Clearly, he hadn't suspected anything. How could a person who shared her bed have been so unobservant?

'Are you not happy, husband?' she asked when a full two seconds had passed without any sound leaving Carlisle's mouth.

'I... I'm delighted,' he eventually managed to stammer, looking more confused than entirely happy. Edward Carlisle may have been decisive in seamanship and in battle, but after less than a year of marriage, he was still unsure of himself in domestic matters, and more particularly anything that involved his headstrong wife. However, he recovered quickly and had just enough presence of mind to push back his chair and walk around the table to hold his wife's hand.

'Nothing, nothing could give me more pleasure,' he said, feeling more confident now and managing to smile. For he *was* delighted but caught off his guard. His mind was already starting to turn over the practicalities of an expectant woman committed to a long sea passage.

'How do you feel,' he asked lamely, not knowing what else to say.

'Oh, I'm perfectly well, thank you,' replied Chiara. Many women would have taken offence at Carlisle's awkward manner, but Chiara knew her husband much better than he knew her. She'd expected a much lengthier period of dumb astonishment, which is why she'd dismissed the servants. From her close study of Edward Carlisle over the past year, Chiara thought it quite likely that he hadn't really considered that a child may be a consequence of marriage. A man's mind worked in a different way she'd concluded.

'May I ask when we can expect the happy event,' he

asked.

It was curious, thought Chiara, how he found ways to refer to her pregnancy in indirect terms. She knew very well that he'd never utter the words *pregnancy* or *birth*, and definitely no words that could be construed to refer to the medical issues around her confinement. *The Happy Event*, it would be between them, she knew, and all-in-all she was content with that. Chiara had her maid to share the more intimate details.

'During September I expect,' Chiara replied, turning to watch the range of expressions on her husband's face as he digested this information. She wouldn't miss this for the world, and Carlisle didn't disappoint as he mentally calculated the months that had passed and those to come. He reached the conclusion that his child must have been conceived in December, while *Medina* was being repaired after the action off Cape François.

'I have, of course, known for a few weeks,' Chiara added, still observing her husband carefully.

'But...you need never have come on this voyage! You could have been safe in Kingston with doctors who are used to...to this sort of thing. Why in God's name didn't you tell me before?' Carlisle realised he was in danger of becoming angry when the occasion called for tenderness. But all the same, to wilfully embark on a man-of-war in Chiara's condition! It beggared belief.

'I didn't tell you, Edward, because I knew this would be your reaction. I intend to follow you to the ship's new station at Halifax and to find accommodation ashore. I assume we will be there in good time, won't we?'

'Why, yes, I suppose we will, but a man-of-war is no place for you. I can't turn the convoy around, but I can put into Savannah or Charleston and put you ashore there.'

'No, sir. I will not be left behind nor put ashore like so much baggage,' Chiara replied, becoming heated herself. 'My place is with my husband. Who knows when you will come back to Georgia or Carolina? This war leaves you without the ability to control your own destiny, and I will not be left behind to await your coming at the damned Admiralty's pleasure.'

Carlisle was shocked. Chiara rarely if ever swore and her use of profane language now showed the depth of her feeling and the extent of her determination like nothing else could. He was tempted to walk over to the stern windows where he could think clearly, but in a flash of intuition realised how that would be taken. Instead, he moved his chair beside Chiara's and held her hand tightly.

'Well, we have some practicalities to consider,' he said as gently as he could. 'Does the doctor know of this?'

Carlisle was in an awkward position to look at his wife's face, and it was with surprise and concern that he saw that she was crying, a thin trickle of tears running down the cheek which she now turned to him.

'Only Susan knows, Edward. It's difficult to keep these things from one's maid. But I'm certain of the facts. You wouldn't want me to go into the details, I believe.'

Carlisle most certainly would not. He suppressed a shudder at the very thought.

'Will you then allow Carlton to examine you? I'm afraid he's the best professional advice that you'll have until we reach Hampton, and that could be three weeks, perhaps a month if the winds turn foul.'

'If it will set your mind at rest, Edward. Yes, Carlton may examine me, but I'd assumed that you would prefer to keep this information secret until – until it can no longer be hidden.'

'Carlton will keep the secret, or he'll answer to me,' Carlisle replied with an *I'm in command of this ship, if not of my wife* look in his eye. 'Don't worry, you won't have to muster at the foremast when the loblolly boy strikes his triangle. I assume it won't, er, show, for a month or so.'

'Oh, I can keep it hidden for a long time yet. The modern styles can hide anything, you know,' Chiara said, regaining some of her spirit, 'and I'm sure Carlton will agree that I'm quite safe until we reach Halifax. When will that be, dear?'

'Well, I have to call at Hampton and Boston before Halifax. We'll have to brave my family at Hampton, but I'm sure we'll manage.'

Chiara hadn't failed to notice the way that Carlisle was starting to use *we* rather than *you*. He was taking a share in this partnership and she was grateful, too grateful to let it show.

'I expect we'll be in Hampton in early March and Boston in the middle of March. Halifax depends on how much we're delayed at Boston. I'll be master of our destiny at Hampton, but there'll be an admiral at Boston, I expect, and he'll say when we make the last leg to Halifax, or whether he sends us somewhere else entirely. I'm afraid we'll need to be somewhat flexible in our planning.'

'Well, Halifax in April won't be too bad. I'll still have five months to go, and spring will be in the air,' she said brightly.

Carlisle looked thoughtful. Spring would hardly have touched Halifax in April; the inhabitants didn't rely upon good weather until June. In fact, where *Medina* was going, the forbidding fortress of Louisbourg on Île Royale, they would probably still be contending with ice and freezing fogs well into May.

'Then it's settled. Tell me when you're ready for Carlton to come to the cabin and I'll call him. The secret will be ours until you are safely ashore in Halifax.'

***

Carlisle didn't escape from the cabin until the forenoon watch was half over and the quartermaster was watching the glass to strike four bells. He had some thinking to do. Chiara's motives were admirable in wishing to say close to her husband for as long as possible, but she really hadn't taken the conditions in Halifax into account. The town had been established less than ten years and its facilities were little better than a makeshift border settlement. In fact, a long-running war with the Mi'kmaq tribe had only ended in 1755 when Monckton defeated the French and their native allies at Fort Beausejour. The whole Nova Scotia area was unstable and hardly the place for a member of Sardinian nobility – and the wife of a post-captain – to be giving birth.

Carlisle knew there was nothing to be gained, and much to be lost, by arguing with his wife. Privately he'd concluded that the best solution was for Chiara to stay in Boston, where a more normal existence could be maintained. The New England winters were cold, but the worst would be over by the end of March, and she'd have the temperate summer for the latter months of her confinement. Boston had proper doctors also, and that was an important consideration. He'd have to talk privately to Carlton and determine the scope of his experience of the care of expectant ladies. It was quite possible that, as a naval surgeon, he had absolutely no first-hand experience and little knowledge of the subject.

Of course, *Medina* would probably make Hampton Roads in three weeks, and his home in Williamsburg was only thirty miles by land from Hampton. On the face of it, that would be the ideal place for Chiara to stay for the next months, but Carlisle had never seen eye-to-eye with his father, and his older brother Charles was growing into a facsimile of the father, Joshua. And then there was the plantation which his father and brother operated – none too gently – with a few hundred African slaves. Carlisle understood the economic need; no Virginia plantation could survive without slave labour, but he'd rather Chiara didn't see too much of that side of his family. No, if it could be avoided, he'd keep his wife away from the Williamsburg Carlisles except for a brief visit as they passed through. Now all he needed was a plan to persuade Chiara to take up residence in Boston.

***

As it turned out, Carlton was quite familiar with the medical aspects of childbirth. He'd been an assistant to a moderately fashionable physician in Bristol before the wanderlust had taken him and he'd applied for a naval surgeon's warrant. When he reported to Carlisle after Chiara's examination, he was quite relaxed at the prospect of the captain's wife spending part of the second trimester on board a man-of-war.

'The worst discomfort will soon be over, sir, and the risks to the mother and child are reducing with each day that passes. I can't imagine how Lady Chiara kept the inevitable sickness from you for those months at Kingston, but women have ways of their own, I find…'

He'd have continued in that vein, but for the forbidding look on Carlisle's face.

'…however,' he continued hurriedly, 'I can see no reason why Lady Chiara shouldn't remain with us for the next two months…'

Carlisle interrupted to prevent any more details.

'What is your opinion of my wife spending the last months of her confinement in Halifax Doctor?'

'Halifax? I had assumed she'd be leaving us in Boston, if not in Hampton. I know little of the facilities in Halifax and nothing whatsoever of the medical expertise that may be available. I would advise a more, how shall I put it? *civilised* city. Boston is as good as Portsmouth or Bristol with fine physicians and a new hospital if it's needed.'

'Thank you, doctor. It's possible that I may require you to state that opinion to her ladyship, but for now, keep that between ourselves.'

'Aye-aye sir. And of course, nothing of these matters will escape my lips. If her ladyship requires any potions, I'll prepare them myself. Neither my assistant nor the loblolly boy will be involved.'

***

CHAPTER TWO

A Curious Incident

Thursday, Twenty-Third of February 1758.
Medina, at Sea. Cape Florida West 12 leagues.

The lookout had sighted the schooner to windward just after sunset. It was Whittle, of course, Nathaniel Whittle, the acknowledged best eyes in the ship and a volunteer from Carlisle's home city of Williamsburg in Virginia.

'She's veered, sir, she's on the same course as us now and I'm just losing sight of her.'

The night fell with its usual abruptness at this latitude, and suddenly it was fully dark to the east. To the west, towards Cape Florida, the twilight lingered but in a few moments that would also be in blackness.

'She's gone, sir,' said Whittle, 'last I saw she'd settled on a northerly course and looked set for the night.'

'Mister Moxon, relieve Whittle at the masthead, if you please, and send him to the quarterdeck.'

'Aye-aye sir,' replied the first lieutenant. *Medina,* being a twenty-eight-gun sixth rate, had only one lieutenant, called the first lieutenant by courtesy. In fact, he had all the duties of the premier in a larger ship but less opportunity to delegate. To make matters worse, there was no hope of taking him out of the watchbill until the new master's mate had settled in; he had to stand his four-on, eight-off with the master and the best of the mates.

Moxon leaned back and projected his voice to the masthead. He was old for his seniority, probably around thirty, Carlisle guessed, only a few years younger than his captain. He'd passed for lieutenant years ago but had only been commissioned with the huge expansion of the navy since 1756. He hadn't yet had a real chance to prove himself. *Medina* had encountered no enemies since leaving Port

Royal with the convoy, and only the steady north-easterly trade wind to test his seamanship. Well, that would end in a day or two, thought Carlisle, as *Medina* followed the Atlantic stream out into the wide ocean and the winds became more variable. They could expect squalls off Georgia and Carolina.

Carlisle watched Whittle slide down the backstay and run onto the quarterdeck, apparently without pausing for breath.

'Well, Whittle, what did you see?' he asked. Not only was Whittle from his hometown, but he'd been raised on the Carlisle plantation. His father had come to Virginia as an indentured servant – a time-limited, voluntary slave in effect – and he'd stayed on when he'd worked out his servitude.

'A two-masted schooner, sir. She was before the wind when I first saw her, but she veered in a hurry, I think as soon as she saw us. Anyhow, she's snugged down for the night two leagues to windward of us, and if they're honest men they'll head reach on us and be out of sight in the morning.'

Carlisle wondered. It was odd behaviour, and yet a schooner of that size could hardly be contemplating an attempt on the convoy, at least not in the daylight.

'There was one other thing, sir. Just an impression, but she looked jury-rigged, her size was all wrong.'

'Go on, Whittle, what exactly did you see?'

'Well, sir, her sides look too high for her length, and her masts and spars looked bulky, too heavy for her rig and size.'

Carlisle looked thoughtfully at the able seaman.

'Very well, Whittle. If you think of anything else, let me know.'

'Mister Hosking,' he said to the sailing master, 'make more sail. I'd like to speak to *Shark* as soon as possible.'

He looked around at the fading light.

'I don't want to sneak up on Mister Anderson in the dark, so we'll show a top light. Please make it so.'

'Aye-aye sir,' Hosking replied and busied himself with

the necessary orders to set the t'gallants. That should give the frigate an extra two knots of speed to move them rapidly up the windward flank of the lumbering convoy.

'Mister Angelini!' Carlisle called over his shoulder.

The midshipman of the watch ran for'rard from where he'd been stowing the log after the half-hourly cast. Enrico Angelini had a curious status in *Medina*. He was the captain's cousin by marriage, being the immediate cousin of Lady Chiara. He'd come with his cousin to Antigua, and when she'd married Edward Carlisle, he'd been offered a place on *Medina's* quarterdeck as a midshipman. This was quite an ordinary arrangement, the appointment of midshipmen being almost entirely in the gift of the captain of a man-of-war. What was most unusual was that Enrico, like his cousin, was a Catholic; how could he be anything else as a member of Sardinian nobility? This placed Enrico in an anomalous position. The whole purpose of being a midshipman was to gain enough sea-time and experience to pass the lieutenant's examination and so be one step closer to a King's commission. However, as everyone knew, the acceptance of a commission was dependent upon taking an oath of allegiance which, in protestant England, included a repudiation of the Pope and all his works. Enrico was in a promotional dead-end. At some point, he'd have to resume his service in King Charles Emmanuel's army, a service that he had temporarily set aside in frustration at his nation's refusal to be involved in this war.

'Pass the word for my servant, Mister Angelini, and then tell the master-at-arms to check that we're showing no lights other than the binnacle and the top light.'

'Aye-aye sir,' replied the midshipman, replacing his hat and turning fast to find Black Rod.

Carlisle could never bring himself to refer to his temporary servant as *Black Rod*. It seemed to confirm that he, the captain under God of this frigate, had no more idea of his servant's real name than did the poor intimidated purser, and that would never do.

***

Carlisle watched Black Rod as he made his stately way up the quarterdeck ladder. He was a most un-seamanlike figure: tall, ramrod straight (that was the origin of his nickname) and with an imperious air. Carlisle had to resist the urge to defer to him. At one time, in the Mediterranean, Carlisle had suspected this same Black Rod of being in league with a corsair from the Barbary Coast, but he was proved wrong. The corsair was an innocent Tunisian trader and a lost acquaintance of the Angelini family; Chiara's Godfather in fact. And yet, there was an air of mystery surrounding Black Rod that extended beyond his apparent lack of a name. Chiara wouldn't discuss it, and yet she trusted him completely.

'You sent for me, sir?' he said in his precise but accented English.

'Yes. Would you tell Lady Chiara that I will need to spend the night on deck? There's nothing to concern her and pray advise her not to endanger herself by coming on deck and subjecting herself to the falling damp.'

'Very well, sir,' replied Black Rod, as he bowed slowly and returned the way he came. The tall, urbane Sardinian may have mastered English, but he saw no need to adopt a seaman's speech.

'Mister Moxon, would you join me for a moment?' Carlisle said into the blackness. The first watch had hardly started, the air was warm, and yet it was now totally dark. The moon, just a day past full, had risen an hour before but was completely obscured by high cloud that scudded before the wind.

'I don't like the sound of this schooner. If she was planning to cross the channel, she'd have stood on and passed astern of us. If she was on passage to the north, why stand so far into the channel before turning? Now, I'm not saying that she's a French privateer, but there's something not right about her. I'm going to tell *Shark* to beat up to the east of her. If I'm wrong, she'll already be far to the north of us on her lawful occasions and there'll be no harm done. But if I'm right, we'll have her between *Shark* and *Medina*, and then we'll know what she's about.'

Carlisle watched his second-in-command's face in the meagre light from the binnacle. He could have wished that it showed more understanding of the situation, just some spark of intelligence rather than this dumb acquiescence. Oh, for the days when George Holbrooke stood beside him on the quarterdeck! Holbrooke was almost ten years younger than Moxon but far, far older in intelligence and initiative.

***

Carlisle could feel *Medina* gathering speed. Hosking had shaken out the reef in the fore tops'l and that, combined with the t'gallants, brought a new lively feeling to the frigate. She sped through the dark night, the barely visible shapes of the convoy to leeward appearing to be stationary, so great was the disparity in speed.

'*Shark's* top light is visible now, sir,' said Enrico. 'A point on the larboard bow.'

'Very well, Mister Angelini.'

Like many convoy commanders, Carlisle had issued a list of signals that they would use on the passage. The signals detailed in the Admiralty's Sailing and Fighting Instructions were meant for manoeuvering fleets and squadrons in battle, not for the subtleties of defending against nimble and aggressive commerce raiders. In any case, naval signalling was in its infancy and still relied largely upon getting two men-of-war close enough so that instructions could be shouted across. Carlisle needed *Medina* to be at pistol-shot distance from *Shark* – about twenty-five yards – to be sure of communicating effectively. He just hoped that Anderson had an alert lookout astern. A frigate looming unexpectedly out of the black night on his starboard quarter could be tragically misconstrued. He knew there was no need to tell Hosking what to do. The sailing master knew the situation perfectly, and what Carlisle knew of Anderson – a smart and lively young commander, eager to do well – reassured him.

Shark could be seen easily now, and the people on her quarterdeck must be aware of *Medina's* presence. As Carlisle watched, Anderson backed his main tops'l, and the sloop lost way, her speed dropping to little more than a knot.

'Back the fore and main tops'ls,' shouted Hosking, and the deck became a hive of activity as the waisters hauled on sheets and guys. *Medina's* speed decreased rapidly until she closely matched the speed of the slower, smaller snow-rigged sloop. The trick now was to keep the two vessels close enough together so that Carlisle could shout his instructions across the twenty-odd yards of water that separated them. It would be difficult in any circumstances, but on a black night with two very different rigs – a ship and a snow – it was a task that called for the highest level of seamanship.

Carlisle was aware of the flow of orders from Hosking to the teams of men on deck, but he could see that it was in good hands. Thankfully the first lieutenant was leaving this to the sailing master; at least he knew his own limitations and curiously didn't appear to resent the fact that he was being sidelined.

'Good evening Mister Anderson,' shouted Carlisle through the copper speaking trumpet. A wave of the hand confirmed that Anderson could hear him.

In rapid but deliberate short sentences Carlisle outlined the situation. It appeared that the lookouts in *Shark* hadn't seen the schooner, perhaps because their masthead was so much lower than *Medina's*. Anderson quickly grasped the situation, and with a final exchange of wishes of good fortune, *Shark* let draw her main tops'l and moved rapidly ahead while *Medina* waited for the sloop to clear the frigate's bow. The last that Carlisle saw was *Shark* hard on the wind beating up to north-northeast. With her top light now extinguished she rapidly disappeared into the enveloping darkness.

'We'll drop back to our old station, Mister Hosking. I

guess that the schooner will strike at the rear of the convoy if indeed she has evil intent.'

'Aye-aye sir,' replied the sailing master. 'I'll just keep her as she is until we see the tail of the convoy abeam.'

***

The first and middle watches passed slowly under the darkness of the cloud-covered night. Naturally, there was no sign of either *Shark* or the schooner. When the morning watch came on deck, they found it as silent as when they'd left it four hours before. The vigilance of the officers had been communicated to the ship's company, sensitive as always to the mood on the quarterdeck, and the watch below didn't leave the deck when they were relieved. Carlisle remembered other times when he had waited for the light; it was always a dangerous time for King's ships. The darkness lent a false sense of security, but when the light of either the sun or moon was suddenly cast on the scene, it could reveal an enemy so close that an engagement was started with none of the usual preamble. That was why King's ships often cleared for action before dawn and the hands were ordered to their quarters. In this case, the order was unnecessary; they were at their stations already.

Over to the east, the sky was just starting to lighten with the pre-dawn glow. The marine sentry struck four bells. Every idle pair of eyes was staring out to starboard.

'Sail ho!' It was difficult to know who spotted it first as a dozen voices shouted simultaneously.

'Two points for'rard of the beam, sir.'

That was Whittle, helpful as ever. Now that he knew where to look, Carlisle could just see the fore-and-aft sails of a two-masted schooner shimmering in the first light. God, she was close! Only a mile or so to windward of *Medina*, and another half mile from the nearest ships of the convoy. There was no question now, his convoy was being stalked. If the schooner's master had been bolder, if he'd arranged to be amongst the convoy at moonrise, he may have succeeded in boarding and carrying away one of

Carlisle's valuable charges. Carlisle wouldn't have dared to chase too far to leeward for fear of leaving the remainder of the convoy unprotected.

'I can see *Shark* now, sir,' called Whittle from the main topmast head, 'about two miles beyond the schooner.'

'Hold your course, Mister Hosking. We'll let *Shark* run down to take possession, she can't escape now.'

Carlisle looked carefully at the schooner. He could see what Whittle meant by her over-high sides and her heavy masts and spars. She looked almost as though she'd been cut down from a larger vessel, shortened as well. No regular privateer then. Perhaps a local fisherman or trader with an eye for a quick profit, but that was piracy, and that scourge had been eliminated decades ago from these waters.

'That funny quarterdeck reminds me of Mister Holbrooke's sloop,' remarked Hosking looking through the telescope. 'Just the same sort of slope from aft to for'rard.'

'Mister Angelini, my telescope if you please,' said Carlisle, a sense of foreboding rising within him. It only took a quick look to confirm his fears.

'Harden up, Mister Hosking,' he said urgently. 'Make all sail and close that schooner as quickly as possible.'

He turned to the waist and shouted to the first lieutenant.

'Mister Moxon. A broadside to windward, as fast as you can.'

The whole quarterdeck was staring at him now. Why was he reacting in this way to this mere schooner? It couldn't harm even the small *Shark*.

'That schooner, Mister Hosking, is the second Dutch pirate! They must have sailed her through the Old Straits of Bahama until they found a deserted island to careen. Then they cut her down to a schooner. If Mister Anderson's lieutenant gets on board he'll be cut to pieces. They've nothing to lose with the noose awaiting them!'

The word spread across the deck like wildfire. Even the new members of the crew had heard of the desperate fight in the Caicos passage where *Medina* had taken on two ship-rigged Dutch privateers-turned pirates. Carlisle had been incapacitated at the height of the battle and his first lieutenant George Holbrooke had taken command. Holbrooke had boarded and captured the lead ship but the second had escaped with severe damage. She'd last been seen running down the Old Straits of Bahama. By cutting the ship down to a schooner, they'd taken to the sea again and now were behaving like out-and-out pirates. The dimmest intellect could see the danger to *Shark*, thinking they were dealing with a legitimate privateer and at the last moment being confronted with a horde of desperate fugitive pirates.

'*Shark*'s hauled her wind, sir,' said Enrico.

Sure enough, Anderson had taken the hint. A full broadside for no apparent reason was unusual enough, but when *Medina* crowded on sail and started beating up towards the schooner, he'd realised that something must be very wrong. Now *Shark* was holding a few cables to windward of the schooner, her guns run out and her crew alerted.

***

In the end, reflected Carlisle, it had all turned out well. There had been a scuffle on the deck of the schooner between those who wanted to surrender and those who were for fighting it out, but the cooler heads won the day. After all, it was unlikely that any Admiralty court would hang more than two in ten of them, just the ringleaders if they could be identified. The rest could expect a measure of leniency if only to avoid too gross a spectacle of public execution.

Carlisle watched as a good number of muskets, pistols, swords, boarding pikes and axes had been thrown into a boat. Enough at least in proportion to the probable size of the crew to make it unlikely that they would cause trouble. When Carlisle was satisfied, he sent the longboat over with a nervous-looking Moxon and the indomitable Sergeant Wilson and almost all of *Medina's* marines. That brought an end to any thought of resistance. The pirates were manacled and divided between *Medina* and *Shark* to be delivered to the vice-admiralty court in Virginia. There were few enough of them left, just fifty-four of whom six were wounded in the scuffle before they were taken. Five bodies were quietly slipped over the side, the fatalities from the fight. By the end of the forenoon watch, the schooner had been scuttled – she was worthless and wouldn't have survived an Atlantic blow – and the convoy and its escorts were underway for Hampton Roads.

***

CHAPTER THREE

Williamsburg

Tuesday, Seventh of March 1758.
Medina, at Anchor. Hampton Roads, Virginia.

*M*edina anchored to the west of the Hampton Bar, dropping her best bower into the fine dark sand that lay under twelve fathoms of water. She'd embarked a pilot off Cape Henry, and all twenty merchant ships had followed the frigate obediently, like beads on a string. It was wonderful to see the results of three weeks of convoy discipline. When they left Kingston, it had been a significant achievement just to keep the assortment of ships and brigs in sight, but now they looked for all the world like the Western Squadron at drill. Three weeks of discipline had done that, and of course the salutary lesson of the pirate in the Florida Strait. If the convoy hadn't been in good order and if *Medina* hadn't been watchful, the Dutchmen would have certainly picked off a straggler in the night.

'Well, my dear, this is my home, more-or-less. Williamsburg is thirty miles from here and Jamestown is just five miles further. Isn't it beautiful?'

It *was* beautiful if you discounted the lowering grey sky and the occasional light drizzle. The shores of the James River were clothed in virgin forest, petering out to marshy coastal fringes. Here and there a homestead or small cluster of houses dipped their toes into the muddy water. Hampton was almost out of sight up a tree-lined creek to the north, and the infant settlement of Newport News on the point of land to the west hardly intruded on the scene. It was difficult to believe that this estuary had been colonised by the English for a hundred and fifty years.

'How long will we stay here?' asked Chiara, looking dubiously at the shoreline. It looked wild and inhospitable compared with Kingston or her home in the sunny

Mediterranean. 'You were speaking of four or five days before we left Jamaica.'

'Five days, I believe. There's sugar to be unloaded and tobacco embarked before the convoy can sail for Boston. We'll weigh on Sunday and then it's only a four-day passage.'

'I'm so much looking forward to meeting your father and brother,' said Chiara with a roguish look. 'I can't believe the awful tales you have told me about them. I know I will love them tremendously.'

'Well, you may choose to make game of me, my dear,' Carlisle replied, 'but I can see no way of avoiding a meeting. The news of our anchoring at Hampton Roads will be in Williamsburg within the day, and I imagine it's well known that *Medina* is my ship. I'm the only Virginian on the post-captain's list, so they have no other sea-officer to talk about. In any case, I'd like to see the old city again. It's quite an important place you know, it's the capital of the colony.'

'Then we must go to Williamsburg. Where can we hire a carriage?'

'There'll be a carriage in Hampton, I hope. We'll be no more than five hours on the road, and we can stop for refreshment at York. Or the longboat can carry us up the James River. It's a longer journey, but we'll be clear of the swamps.'

'Oh, the carriage, if you please Edward. Much as I've enjoyed this pleasant cruise, it's time for me to step onto dry land. We'll stay overnight, I suppose.'

'Yes. At least one day, two if the lieutenant-governor should detain us. Lord Loudoun's been recalled after last year's debacle of an attempt on Louisbourg, so we won't see him. The last that I heard he was still the governor of the colony, but he's no longer the commander-in-chief. I expect we'll see his deputy Dinwiddie. He may be only a lieutenant-governor but he's the real power in Virginia, although I heard that he's ripe for replacement.'

'Then I'll need to take Susan and a trunk,' said Chiara,

mentally itemizing the clothes that she'd need in case of an invitation to the governor's palace. She had to consider the dignity of both her husband's rank and her family in Sardinia.

'Just so, my dear, and we'll take Mister Carlton and Mister Angelini. In fact, I'll send Enrico ashore now to secure a carriage and send a message to my father.'

Chiara favoured her husband with her most dazzling smile. She could never quite understand Carlisle's determination that her cousin should be treated the same as any of the other midshipmen. There was much more respect for the nobility in her home, and if an Angelini were to be given the rank of *guardiamarina* in the Sardinian navy, it would in no sense override the rank of his birthright. She was still coming to terms with this peculiar service that so much valued professional competence over natural rank.

'That's very thoughtful of you, dear, but you know Carlton's not at all necessary. I have six months to go and I'm feeling very well,' she said, without much hope of changing her husband's mind. Carlisle was becoming increasingly protective as the weeks passed and he'd spare nobody – and certainly not his surgeon – to secure his wife's comfort and health. He pretended that he hadn't heard.

***

By two o'clock, Chiara and Carlisle were comfortably seated in a rather smart two-horse carriage that had been rushed out of its winter storage in a barn adjacent to the inn. Carlton sat opposite them, looking pleased to have the opportunity for a few days away from the frigate. The owner of the carriage was delighted to have Captain Carlisle's business and had spent the two hours since agreeing the fare in dusting and polishing. He hadn't expected to bring his best carriage out of storage for another month at least, not until the weather had improved sufficiently for people to want to spend their time on the road. Enrico and Susan followed with the baggage in the usual sort of public wagon that plied the roads of the peninsula between the York and

James rivers, between Hampton and Richmond. The roads were good for the time of year and the thin drizzle had stopped, allowing pale sunshine to brighten the journey. The carriage far outpaced the wagon as they bowled along the well-kept road. They passed the Halfway House shortly after three o'clock, and at five they passed the first buildings of the small town of York.

'Would you like a short stop for refreshment?' asked Carlisle. 'We still have two hours on the road before we reach Williamsburg.'

Carlton nodded discreetly. Clearly, he also considered it a wise precaution.

'If you please, Captain Carlisle,' Chiara replied. She'd become more formal when addressing her husband in the presence of his officers. How she missed Holbrooke and the easy relationship they had!

'Do you know a good inn at York where the lady would be comfortable for twenty minutes?' Carlisle shouted to the driver. It was difficult to be discreet under these conditions, but the driver, an old and experienced family man, understood the situation.

'Perhaps not an inn, sir, but my sister has a good house right on the road and she'll make the lady comfortable. For a few pennies, she'll put some bread, ham and beer on the table, although she'll have no wine. The wagon can't fail to see us as they pass, no doubt the young people will also welcome a break.'

The familiar Virginia tones pleased Carlisle and when Chiara nodded her acceptance, he readily agreed. Not five minutes later the carriage drew up beside a decent wooden cabin – it would have been called a respectable cottage in England – where they were greeted by a surprised but welcoming woman who looked so like the carriage driver that it was comical.

'This is better than an inn, my dear,' Carlisle said as he handed Chiara down from the carriage. 'In these parts, inns are very male affairs, and this looks altogether better for our needs.'

Better it certainly was, even though the close relatives of their luncheon could be heard squealing and squabbling in their sty outside the window of the small room where they were offered seats. Twenty minutes later they were underway again, and in an hour, they passed another of the ubiquitous halfway houses. The driver had to squint into the setting sun now as he whipped up the two horses for the final run into the city. It was all cultivated land here, except for a few strips of marshland and pines alongside the frequent creeks which they crossed by indifferently built wooden bridges. There was tobacco of course, but there was also a surprising amount of homely vegetables, and everywhere the evidence of a slave economy in full swing. Most of the field hands were Africans with just a few presumably indentured white men and women working in tight clusters.

Chiara could sense her husband's growing excitement as he recognised the sights of his youth. The outlying cabins soon gave way to more substantial houses as the roofs and chimneys of the capitol building came into view. Their arrival was at least noticed by someone, because a ragged boy leapt to his feet on seeing the carriage and ran fast in the direction that they were heading, cutting through the little alleys that ran between the houses. The carriage swung around the south side of the capitol and into Duke of Gloucester Street.

'There's Shield's Tavern,' said Carlisle, pointing to the two-story brick and clapboard building on the left just a hundred yards from the iron gates of the capitol.

It was a broad street, very wide by English or Sardinian standards. The surface was crushed shells from the York and James Rivers, and the residual moisture from an earlier shower and their natural lustre made them sparkle and shine in the last rays of the setting sun. Mature trees lined the road and if everything that Chiara had heard of the Virginian summers was true, their shade would be needed before another month had passed. Most of the businesses were already closed on this Tuesday evening, but Chiara could see a tailor's shop, a printer, a haberdasher and two or three taverns or coffee houses.

The carriage came to a halt outside their tavern. Evidently, Carlisle's message had been received – thanks to the ragged boy presumably – and here was the innkeeper, his wife and two servants bustling through the doors. They were shepherded by the boy, now puffed up with pride at having discharged his duty of giving warning of their arrival.

As they dismounted, a small crowd started to gather. Familiar and half-remembered faces turned to Carlisle greeting their returning hero, for Carlisle's exploits had reached his hometown, gaining in their glory as the stories were passed from mouth to mouth. His fights with *Vulcain* and *L'Arques* were common knowledge, and the more informed even knew about Minorca, Cape François and the Dutch pirates. With the war on the American continent still in the balance and with no notable British victories to boast of yet, either in Europe or the Americas, a true naval hero and a local boy at that was very welcome. Lady Chiara acknowledged the crowd before turning for the inn's door, and Carlisle raised his hat in salute. They passed from the twilit street into the candlelit interior pursued by a hearty cheer.

***

'Tomorrow we'll take the carriage down to my home. It's just five miles from here, on the James River, close to where the first settlers landed a hundred and fifty years ago,' said Carlisle over supper with his wife. Carlton and Enrico had sought their supper in a livelier tavern a few hundred yards down the main street of the city. 'I'd half expected my father or my brother to meet us here this evening, but perhaps they haven't yet heard that we've arrived.'

Chiara looked carefully at her husband; she knew very well that he was putting on a brave face. It was certain that his family had known of his imminent arrival since about midday, the time that Carlisle's messenger would have ridden from Hampton into Williamsburg, shouting the news to all and sundry. She knew that all was not well between Edward and his father and older brother, but this was the first sign that she'd seen that he felt in any way uncomfortable about it.

'I shall look forward to meeting them, Edward. What a good idea to hire the carriage for four days; at least we have the freedom to come and go as we please.'

Carlisle looked thoughtful. Chiara was correct, of course. It would have been devilishly embarrassing to be reliant upon his family if this was the kind of welcome that they'd be subjected to.

The door to their chambers opened tentatively. It wasn't the maid bringing more dishes, but the innkeeper's wife with a message.

'Begging your pardon sir, but Miss Barbara Dexter is down in the hall, asking whether you are at leisure for a visit.'

Barbara Dexter! Who the devil is that? thought Carlisle. His confusion must have shown on his face, and the innkeeper's wife offered an explanation.

'You may remember her as Barbara Carlisle, but she married Mister Dexter from the city. She's your cousin, sir,' said the innkeeper's wife, smiling at Carlisle's confusion.

'Oh, cousin Babs!' exclaimed Carlisle, almost knocking over his wine glass as he pushed back his chair. He was on the point of rushing to the door to hail her when he remembered his wife.

'Ah. I perhaps haven't mentioned cousin Babs. We should have been close when we were young, but my father didn't get on with his brother, Babs' father, so I rarely saw her. But we got along well when we did meet. Do you feel rested enough to meet her, dear?'

Chiara sighed. When would her husband understand how long it took to prepare to meet people after five hours in a carriage? Evidently, the customs here were different, less formal than Sardinia or even Jamaica. If this lady were ready to meet her then it would be churlish to refuse. In any case, she was starting to believe that she'd like anyone whose family didn't agree with Edward's father and brother.

'You can entertain her for a few moments, Edward. I'll be no more than ten minutes, just straightening my hair and my dress.'

By the time that Chiara returned to the dining room, her husband and Barbara were deep in conversation in the strongly accented form of English that Barbara spoke naturally, and Carlisle had easily slipped back into. Chiara was a little taken aback by the other woman's appearance. She was tall – very tall for a woman – painfully lean and had a face to match, long and cadaverous. She was dressed in clean but dull clothing of predominantly brown tones with a bright shawl that looked as though it had been brought out of storage for this occasion. However, it was her eyes that captured the attention, they were laughing eyes and they instantly transformed her from a middle-aged frump into one of the most open and welcoming people that Chiara had ever met. She'd been prepared to *try* to like this woman, even though she'd come unbidden and at such an inconvenient time, but she found that no effort was required.

'My dear, may I present my cousin, Barbara Dexter? Barbara, this is my wife, Lady Chiara.'

Barbara made her awkward courtesy. A woman of her build could never aspire to elegance, she was all elbows and knees, but Chiara returned the gesture with all the grace of the Sardinian court, yet without giving the impression that she was upstaging the older woman. Had Chiara known Barbara better she'd have known that the Virginian was immune to any attempts at upstaging. Barbara had long ago come to terms with the limits that her ungainly shape placed upon her aspirations to social grace.

'Welcome to Williamsburg, Lady Chiara,' she said in a voice that could scare the rooks out of the trees. 'I've just been giving Captain Carlisle the latest news of the capitol. I can't believe how long it is since I last saw him, but here he is with a beautiful wife! I heard news of your arrival just after noon, and I hope you don't mind me being so forward in rushing up to your door!'

'Not at all, Mrs Dexter,' replied Chiara. She was rapidly learning the social conventions of this outpost of the British Empire and realised that her native formality just wouldn't do. In any case, there was something very charming about this cousin of Edward's that made for either instant dislike or immediate intimacy, 'Would you do me the honour of calling me Chiara, and perhaps I may call you Barbara?'

***

They were interrupted by another knock on the door, a letter this time, addressed formally to Captain Edward Carlisle and sealed in wax with an impressive device. Carlisle excused himself and stepped over to the window, leaving the two women deep in conversation. It was from the lieutenant governor, a new man named Francis Fauquier; clearly Dinwiddie had been superseded. They were bidden to dinner the following day, a fashionably late dinner at six o'clock, in the Governor's Palace. Evidently the lieutenant governor had been informed of the number and quality of Carlisle's party because the invitation included Mister Enrico Angelini, without mention of his naval rank, but didn't include the surgeon.

Barbara stayed an hour, and it was late by the time that Carlisle and Chiara had a moment alone.

'Are all your relatives as unusual as Barbara?' asked Chiara, after they had discussed the preparations for tomorrow's dinner party. 'It's just that I think you should warn me in future.'

Carlisle looked at his wife with concern.

'Oh, I thought you were getting along well together. I do apologise if you've had an awkward time of it.'

Chiara laughed at her husband's concerned expression.

'You mistake me, Edward, I very much like Barbara and it was a pleasure to meet her. I feel we could be good friends.

But you must admit that she's a little … *unique*, shall we say?'

Carlisle relaxed when he realised that he hadn't offended his wife.

'Yes, she was always different. I believe it may be her shape that's to blame. She suffered a fair amount of ribaldry when she was young and developed an ability to shrug off personal slights and a character that allowed her to march boldly into any social situation. When I was last home, she had no suitors that I was aware of, and I only vaguely remember this Dexter fellow; Cranmer Dexter, I believe, named after an Archbishop of Canterbury. His father owned the printing press and book shop. Perhaps Cranmer does now.'

'An appropriate name for a printer and bookseller,' commented Chiara. 'You look surprised,' she continued, teasing a little. 'I've had little to do on this passage while you were on deck, so I read Foxe's Martyrs from cover to cover. I'm aware of Cranmer and his Book of Common Prayer.'

'You continually amaze me, my dear,' said Carlisle.

'Did you hear Barbara offer me a confinement haven in her home? She wasted no time in observing my condition. In anyone else I'd have resented her indelicacy, but not Barbara!'

'Did she now? While I was reading the invitation no doubt. Well, that's mighty generous of her,' said Carlisle slipping into his native jargon. 'However, I know you're determined to follow me to Boston, so I guess she'll be disappointed.'

Chiara said nothing, but stared thoughtfully at the darkened window, stroking the slightest of swellings that indicated where their baby was entering its third month of growth.

***

CHAPTER FOUR

The Carlisle Family

Wednesday, Eighth of March 1758.
Williamsburg, Virginia.

The visit to the Carlisle Plantation was a disaster. A deep gloom had settled over the two passengers as the carriage rolled through the five miles of cultivated fields and morasses that lined the neglected road from the present colonial capital to its abandoned predecessor at Jamestown. Chiara had a cat-like sensitivity to her husband's moods, and she could feel his increasing tension. He'd grown steadily more withdrawn, and for the last mile he'd perched himself stiffly on the edge of his seat, staring right ahead at the small oval window that gave a view of the coachman's legs. Carlton and Enrico had been given the day to explore Williamsburg, so Edward and Chiara were alone in the carriage.

The plantation was a depressing place. Over fifty years old and built to the standards of comfort that a previous generation had found acceptable, by 1758 it looked old-fashioned, dark and sinister. There were no formal gardens, but the worked fields lapped right up to the weather-stained brick walls of the house. African slaves were everywhere, and yet there were no white indentured servants in evidence. The slaves were mostly in small and large groups among the growing tobacco while some were moving in a lacklustre way about the long line of huts that were their quarters. It looked like something out of a bygone age and it was hard to see how happiness could exist in such a place, either for the slaves or for their masters.

Joshua Carlisle had met them at the steps of the house. He'd never forgiven his younger son for joining the King's navy, rather than settling down to his studies at the College of William and Mary in Williamsburg and eventually strengthening the Carlisle family's position in the colony. Charles Carlisle had stood a few paces behind his father, a heavy riding crop in his hand and a scowl on his face. The elder brother suspected the younger of having designs on the plantation when the father should die. It was beyond his imagination that anybody couldn't wish to inherit a brutal, antediluvian business that sat precariously between the growing sophistication of Virginian society and an ancient slave-owning, agricultural lifestyle.

There was no female influence at all in the house. Joshua's wife had died when Edward was young and he'd never re-married. The passage of years had hardened and coarsened him so that although Edward had been partly prepared, it still came as a shock to have such a hostile reception. Father and elder son openly sneered at Edward's Catholic wife and were barely civil to the youngest Carlisle son.

They had stayed only an hour and the relief of their parting was shared equally by both parties. Joshua and Charles could withdraw into their cruel and self-consuming industry and feed their paranoia with recollections of how the younger son had grown in stature and consequence. Edward Carlisle and Chiara could breathe the free air that seemed to become sweeter with each mile that passed under the carriage's wheels.

'Are you quite well, Edward?' asked Chiara laying her hand on her husband's knee, 'you look pale.'

Carlisle *was* pale and he could feel his heart racing erratically as he fought to recover from that appalling family meeting.

'I'll survive, Chiara, but how you'll ever forgive me for subjecting you to *that*, I cannot tell.'

'It wasn't so bad,' she lied. 'We weren't offered physical violence, at least,' she added, smiling encouragingly.

'No, they stopped short at that. But had I known just how hostile my brother had become I'd have brought Enrico with us. The midshipman who fought the

Dutchmen toe-to-toe on the decks of *Medina* and *Torenvalk* would have been a useful man to have at our backs.'

Chiara was pleased at this acknowledgement of her cousin's value; it was the first time that her husband had praised him in her presence.

'Well, I gather we won't need to repeat that meeting, and we have a few hours before I'll have to prepare for the governor's palace. Shall we have a stroll through the city?'

Chiara had quickly taken the measure of Williamsburg. The fashions were understated in comparison to Kingston and she'd dressed accordingly, so when the carriage set them down at Shields Tavern, it took only a few minutes to freshen up before she was ready.

***

'You're uneasy, try to look more relaxed,' said Chiara as they left the tavern and headed west along Duke of Gloucester Street.

'Remember, dear, that I haven't been to my hometown for six years. The last time I visited I was a mere lieutenant, a man of little consequence. I feel that everyone's watching me now.'

'Let them, Edward. You're an important man in this colony, one of the few to be born and bred here and hold a post-captain's commission. They're all wondering whether you plan to return and who's position you'll put at risk.'

'The only post-captain from Virginia, I believe,' Carlisle added proudly. 'There's no particular bar to anyone from the colonies being posted, but it's difficult to marshal the right level of influence to make that jump. I've been lucky.'

'Nonsense, luck had nothing to do with it. You're a man of parts, Edward, and now your own people will inevitably regard you in a new light.'

They walked on past the shops and businesses. It was surprising how many people remembered him because much had changed in the nearly two decades since Edward had first gone to sea. The colony had grown both in size and self-confidence – very much in self-confidence – and the balance of power between Virginian families had shifted with new people coming in from the country to live in the capital. There were familiar faces, acquaintances of his family and men who'd been boys at school with Carlisle, a few of whom remembered his ignominious departure from the grammar school and the less-than-flattering tales of his early years at sea. Nevertheless, he was greeted with the respect that his rank – and the beautiful wife on his arm – demanded.

They walked as far as the College of William and Mary before turning and walking back on the other side of the road.

'There's the Governor's Palace,' said Carlisle, pointing to the imposing building set back at the end of an avenue three or four hundred yards from the road. 'We'll take the carriage this evening; it's no great distance but perhaps the roads are too dusty to risk your gown by walking.'

Chiara gave her husband a sideways glance. Was he jesting? Had he seriously considered walking? Walking to dinner at the governor's palace, of all places? Even if it were next door to the tavern, she'd have insisted on the carriage. Chiara had a much more heightened perception of the dignity of their social rank.

'There's a respectable coffee house opposite the tavern. After we've seen the capital, we can take some refreshment,' he continued, oblivious to his wife's amused consternation.

They didn't get as far as the coffee shop. Carlisle was just about to point out the printer's workshop and bookstore that Cranmer Dexter – he now knew – had inherited from his father, when a small, round figure bounded out of the door. Making a ball of his hastily removed leather apron, he threw it behind him and danced – that seemed the best description of his energetic gait – towards Carlisle and Chiara. Carlisle had just enough wit to recognise Barbara's husband before the compact bundle of energy was upon them.

'Captain Carlisle, you remember me, I hope? Cranmer

Dexter, we used to be acquainted when we were much younger.'

The small man looked up at Carlisle much as a faithful hound would look at his master, hoping for recognition.

'Indeed, I do, Mister Dexter, and we had the honour of meeting your wife last night. I confess that I had no idea that you had married my cousin; my belated congratulations.'

The two men shook hands and looked each other up and down. It was difficult to imagine a starker contrast. Carlisle was tall and slim, and dressed in his best uniform frock coat, while Dexter stood a good six inches shorter and at least the same wider and was in rolled-up shirtsleeves, clearly having just left the printing press. There were smudges of ink on his fingertips and his quick, nervous gestures had transferred a fair amount of it to his forehead and chin.

'Can I tempt you inside for a moment? Barbara saw you walking this way and sent me out to hold you, if possible, while she washes her hands. She helps at the press, you know.'

Carlisle opened his mouth to decline the invitation when a gentle pressure on his arm from Chiara made him pause. He interpreted the gesture correctly; his wife thought it impolite to refuse.

'With pleasure, sir,' he replied. 'We were only taking the air with no particular destination in mind,' he lied glibly.

Cranmer Dexter's appearance suggested a chaotic character. Both Carlisle and Chiara were prepared for the worst when they were ushered into the workshop and store that was the entrance to his home.

What a surprise! The sparkling-clean windows let in the afternoon light, illuminating the broad polished wood countertops on their right-hand side. Behind, the cases of books that were his stock-in-trade were neatly displayed, and on the counters were wooden trays holding the broadsheets that came from the press. The presses – there were two of them – were on the left, and they were illuminated by the side windows that caught the afternoon sun as well as the store-front south-facing bow windows. It was a model of an orderly workshop with shelves for bottles of ink and reams of paper waiting to be printed. A young man, an apprentice perhaps, grinned at them as he leaned all his body weight into the handles of the press, releasing them with a flourish so that they sprang upwards when the page was finished. It was a quite delightful room, smelling of printing ink, solvent and book-binder's leather.

'Here's Barbara,' said Dexter quite unnecessarily as his wife appeared through a door at the back of the room which evidently led to the family's living areas. 'My wife has the extraordinary skill of working the press without transferring any ink to her person; none whatsoever! As you can see, I've never learned that art,' he said looking at his hands, apparently oblivious to the war-paint on his face.

If the working area was clean and tidy, the living quarters were spotless and squared away to an extent that would gladden the heart of any first lieutenant of a King's ship. Evidently, the Dexter business was flourishing because the furniture, the silverware and the furnishings were of the very best.

'Would you prefer chocolate or coffee? Or perhaps tea is more to your taste,' asked Barbara as the maid waited for instructions. 'I recommend the chocolate if you haven't had it in the true Virginia style, Chiara.'

'Certainly, chocolate if you please, Barbara. And for you, Edward?'

'I haven't had real chocolate for six years,' he replied. 'That would be perfect.'

The maid bustled away into the kitchen, taking a swipe at an imaginary speck of dust as she left the room.

'Welcome to our home, Edward and Chiara,' said Barbara. 'I hope you'll consider this an open invitation while you're in Williamsburg.'

The drinks came, two steaming cups, each with a stick of solid brown chocolate slowly melting into the boiling water. The four of them sipped it in companionable silence for a few minutes.

'Would you like a tour of the house?' asked Barbara. 'You may find it somewhat different to Sardinia, England or even Jamaica.'

'Yes, if you please,' said Chiara, clearly delighted at the prospect, 'although I can hardly compare it to England, as I spent only a few days there on my way to Antigua.'

'You have a fine establishment here,' said Carlisle after the ladies had left the room.

'Thank you,' said Dexter. 'It's been a struggle as my old father – you remember him – left it in rather a sad state. I really have Barbara to thank for our success. In only four years she's transformed the business and our home.'

'Is this the only printing business in Williamsburg?' asked Carlisle. He dimly remembered that there had been two or three when he was last at home.

'Yes, it is now. I bought out Harris a year ago, and I use his premises for the book printing and binding.'

**

The sun had left the avenue and the trees cast long shadows as Carlisle and Chiara set out for the Governor's Palace. Their coachman at least understood the gravity of the situation. He'd never been on such an exalted mission, but he'd spoken to some who had. In consequence, the carriage from Hampton sparkled as it had never done before, drawing an admiring crowd as it waited outside the tavern.

Enrico had dressed in the uniform of an ensign in the Sardinian cavalry, a gorgeous outfit of yellows and reds that made the humble blue-and-gold of Carlisle's suit look dull and ordinary. Carlisle was not at all sure that it was appropriate and was on the verge of ordering the young man to change into his midshipman's uniform, but luckily, he caught the look of family pride in his wife's eyes and wisely held his peace. Enrico held the door for his cousin and then took a seat beside the coachman. With a snap of his whip, the horses moved off at a steady walking pace, followed by a horde of children, too excited for any sense of decorum.

The dinner was a lively affair, served in the modern style with a variety of dishes following each other in an almost endless procession. The well-to-do of Williamsburg were delighted to meet their very own post-captain – many of them had known Carlisle as a child – and they were even more delighted to meet his beautiful and exotic wife, a Lady no less! Neither Carlisle nor Chiara thought it right to point out that her title was only by courtesy, and that it would never be inherited.

Carlisle spoke to a good many people and began to realise at least part of the reason for his brother's mistrust. There was a general assumption that Carlisle would return to Williamsburg when the war was over, that he'd be in contention for his father's estate and that he'd be a man to be reckoned with in the colony. Only a day ago, Carlisle would have openly declared his determination to settle elsewhere, probably in England. This reminder of the advantages of Williamsburg, where he was *someone*, a potentially important person, had given him pause for thought. Perhaps settling in Williamsburg wouldn't be such a bad idea. Chiara, as far as Carlisle could tell, was enjoying the city. He could see her now, in animated conversation with a group of well-dressed ladies sat on a group of chaise longues and chairs, beneath the portraits of King George and Queen Caroline.

Yes, there was a lot to be said for settling in Virginia, if he could only make a few thousand more in prize money.

***

At first, Carlisle watched his wife with one eye as he spoke to the lieutenant governor and the lawmakers of the colony. Not unnaturally, they were more concerned with the war in America than the wider war in Europe and beyond. They had contributed men for the campaigns in the Ohio Valley and for the push up towards Lake Ontario, and they had an important stake in the outcome. Nevertheless, they all knew that the key to supremacy on the continent was Quebec. If that city fell to the British forces, the French would be unable to maintain themselves on the continent, and it would only be a matter of time before the English-speaking people reigned supreme. The fate of Louisbourg was of the first importance to them. It was an intensely interesting conversation to Carlisle and gradually, as he saw that all was well with Chiara, he turned his whole attention to his fellows.

It was a flurry of activity over towards where he'd last seen Chiara that caught Carlisle's attention. He couldn't spot his wife through a crowd of other women, all drawn to something that he couldn't see. With the briefest apologies, he strode over, still unsure whether Chiara was involved in the disturbance. When he reached the group, his worst fears were confirmed. Chiara was lying back on a chaise longue, her face white and her eyes tight closed, with a large, officious lady fanning her for all she was worth. He took his wife's hand; it was clammy and cold.

'Step back, if you please, move away,' said a confident voice behind him.

The commotion had attracted the governor's physician, a small, lean man with a competent air. He held Chiara' wrist between thumb and forefinger and held up his other hand for silence. The fanning stopped.

Half a minute passed.

'Do you have a room that we can retire to, Mister Fauquier?' he asked.

Chiara's eyes had opened, and she was able to walk out of the ballroom with Carlisle on one side and Enrico on the other. By the time they had laid her on a bed, she was on the way to recovery.

'I shall be quite well, Edward, if only I can have a few minutes,' she said and squeezed his hand.

The physician beckoned Carlisle out of earshot.

'Is it possible that the lady is expectant?' he asked tentatively.

Carlisle nodded, not trusting himself to speak.

'Three months, or thereabouts, perhaps?' he continued.

'Yes,' Carlisle replied stupidly.

'Then that explains it,' he went on. 'There's nothing to worry about. This is quite normal in many women, particularly in their first pregnancy. I assume that is the case?'

'Yes,' replied Carlisle, still unable to think of anything else to add.

'Then the lady needs rest, nothing more. But I would like to see her again if I may. I assume there is no question of her travelling?'

He gave Carlisle a knowing look. He'd heard the conversation; he knew very well that Chiara was planning to travel on to Halifax in a few days.

'Would a sea passage be unwise?' Carlisle asked hopefully, knowing now what the physician was trying to do.

'Oh, yes,' replied the physician. He winked, a most unusual gesture from a man of his eminence, but it spoke volumes to Carlisle. 'It would be most unwise, I'm surprised you are even contemplating it,' he said in his best disapproving tone, perfectly modulated so that it could be heard by the lady reclining on the bed.

***

Carlisle anticipated an awkward conversation in the morning. However, in the event, a fully recovered, indeed refreshed, Chiara, was open to negotiation. Susan fussed around her in a way that wouldn't have been permitted a day before, and that gave Carlisle hope. Barbara visited, and the two women spoke privately for a while. Then the physician called, and after examining her and talking to Carlton, he gave her his frank advice.

By the time the physician left, it had all been arranged. Chiara and her maid, Susan – who was already on friendly terms with Barbara's maid – would lodge at the Dexter house. A cart would be sent to Hampton for her belongings and *Medina* would sail north without her.

Carlisle was allowed only one modification to the plan. He insisted that Black Rod should stay. With that imposing person to guard her, he could be sure that his brother wouldn't try anything rash. The Dexter house was a massive affair, having been built back from the printer's shop in waves of prosperity, and there was ample room for three guests, no matter how long they needed to stay.

***

CHAPTER FIVE

Night Encounter

Sunday, Twelfth of March 1758.
Medina, at Sea. Cape Henry West-Southwest 26 leagues.

The convoy had caught a westerly wind and was bowling along into the Atlantic under a watery spring sun. With the whole American seaboard to windward – friendly territory for six hundred miles north and south, from Nova Scotia to Georgia – the threat was to leeward, out to sea, where the French privateers lurked waiting for just such a prize as this. That was why *Medina* was leading the convoy today, and *Shark* was bringing up the rear.

'How long do you reckon, Master?' asked Carlisle.

To the consternation and alarm of *Medina's* people, their captain and sailing master were far out on the bowsprit, clutching perilously at the fore topmast stay and staring earnestly ahead, each with a foot on solid wood and the other waving over the netting.

'Any time now, sir,' Hosking replied. 'Ah, can you see the birds now? Petrels, gulls and suchlike, they're attracted to the area where the water temperature changes at the edge of the stream.'

Carlisle could indeed see the birds – hundreds of them – and birds in the open ocean always indicated something new, often a current or shoal water, and there were no shoals here off the Virginia Capes.

'Bowsprit Ho!'

That was Whittle's poor attempt at topmast humour as he tried to catch his captain's attention.

'Broken water ahead sir, perhaps three miles on either side of the bow,' he shouted.

Whittle knew very well why his captain and sailing master were perched at the end of the bowsprit, and he knew there was no danger from rock or reef in this area. It would have been a stretch to have reported the birds from the masthead although he'd been watching them for the past five minutes; but the broken water, he could get away with that.

Carlisle watched eagerly now. It was always a great occasion when he sighted the stream, particularly when it took him in the direction he wanted to go.

'There, you can see the green turning to blue and the line of weed and flotsam, and the ripples. That's the stream, or my name's not John Hosking!' declared the master, his childish delight showing clear on his brown and weather-beaten face.

'We should get well into the flow before we bear away,' said Carlisle, his mind already wandering back to his family problems. 'What course Mister Hosking?'

'Two points to larboard, the course is nor'east, sir. I'm right pleased that we've found the stream before sunset, now there's no excuse for those fellows not following us when we haul our sheets.'

He looked cautiously at Carlisle. He could recognise that almost dreamlike look when his captain wasn't really paying attention to him, yet Hosking took no offence. If he'd had to leave his expectant wife behind in an unfamiliar city, he'd have been distracted too.

'Then make it so, Mister Hosking. You may haul your wind when you see fit. I'll just stay here until we've crossed into the stream, then I'll be in my cabin.'

Hosking made his careful way back along the bowsprit. He was no longer a young man and had no business playing at topmen at his age. He glared at a young able seaman who was waiting impatiently to lay out onto the jib boom to attend to a wooden hank that had parted on the luff of the jib. Young the sailor may have been, but he had no truck with these new-fangled hanks; the old rope grommets never parted, no not if a real seaman saw to their serving. Wood was a carpenter's business, not a sailor's.

'Don't you go swarming out on that jib-boom with the captain sat on the bowsprit cap! You can just wait until he's come inboard,' said Hosking as he gratefully hauled himself onto the fo'c'sle.

Looking for'rard when his feet were firmly planted on oak planks, the master could see Carlisle, staring absently to leeward at the changing patterns of the sea as the frigate nosed into the stream that would carry them far from Williamsburg and his pregnant wife. What devils clawed at his soul, only the captain himself knew.

***

Carlisle paced backwards and forwards across the cabin. It took only six long strides before he had to turn, and each time he did so, he turned with his face to the windows so that he had a grand view of the convoy. It should have been a sight to gladden the eyes of any sea-officer. All seventeen merchantmen – three had left the convoy at Hampton Roads to sail further up the Chesapeake – were following obediently behind the frigate. None of them had missed the turn to the northeast and so far, none had run aboard their neighbour, and not even one had sheered away at the sight of the broken water at the edge of the stream. So compact was the convoy that he could see *Shark* at the rear, keeping to seaward of their charges in accordance with Carlisle's sailing orders.

And yet, Carlisle was deeply displeased. He was concerned about Chiara and felt the married man's guilt when there was any complication in his wife's pregnancy, whether it was in medical or more practical matters. He felt – no, he knew – that he should be with his wife now. It wasn't that he mistrusted his cousin or her husband. In fact, their offer of a home to Chiara – and her acceptance – was the only mitigating factor in this whole sorry saga. It was his own immediate family whom he didn't trust, particularly his elder brother. With no wife, no children and no prospect of either that Carlisle could detect, his brother must realise that the next to inherit when he died would be Carlisle or his

52

progeny, and it was quite clear that Charles didn't want that outcome. Dexter and Barbara would help of course, but Carlisle could see how easy it would be for the small, round printer to be bullied by the Carlisle family. Barbara wouldn't be quite so easy, but it was a man's world, particularly in the colonies, and the wife of a printer was of little consequence against an established and wealthy plantation owner.

It was for that reason that Carlisle had engaged a lawyer to oversee his wife's welfare while she was in Williamsburg. A lawyer could ensure that his written instructions were obeyed: his father and brother were to have no say in the affairs of Chiara or the child. Lawyers were easy to find in Williamsburg; after all, it was the capital of the colony, but he was happy to agree to Fauquier's nominee. As governor *in locum*, he was well positioned to know who carried weight and who did not.

Carlisle examined his actions for the hundredth time. He was sure that he'd done all that he could, short of delaying the convoy's sailing, which would have been unforgivable; there was an invasion force waiting in Halifax for the supplies that they were bringing. Chiara had even seemed quite cheerful when he left, although he knew well the stoicism that had been bred into her. The fainting and nausea had stopped, probably as a result of the twenty-four hours of enforced rest in the Dexter home. Carlton and the governor's physician had pronounced themselves satisfied.

Yes, he'd done all that he could to ensure the comfort and wellbeing of his wife and unborn child. If all went well, when he next saw his wife, she'd have a child to present to him. Curiously he found that he didn't much care whether it was a boy or a girl, there were too many other worries now. If only Chiara had told him of her pregnancy before they left Kingston, he'd have insisted that she stay in Jamaica along with Black Rod and her maid. But now they were all three in Williamsburg. And that was another comfort; if legal arguments failed to keep his family away from Chiara, he knew Black Rod well enough to be confident that he'd take the law into his own hands in defence of an Angelini.

***

The sun was sinking on the larboard quarter, almost exactly to the west on this day so close to the equinox. Carlisle could see the orange ball each time he paced to larboard and watched as it inched closer to the horizon. One bell sounded from the belfry at the break of the fo'c'sle, half an hour into the last dogwatch. He heard the lookouts being relieved, their movements unnaturally loud against the silence of this soldier's wind. He could feel the vibrations of a man climbing the mizzen shrouds being transmitted through the chains, then through the ship's side to make a soft, deep, bass rumble in the cabin. That would be a hand going aloft to check on that troublesome topmast lanyard. It would need to be turned end-for-end as soon as they were on the other tack, but that could be days yet with this steady westerly wind.

Carlisle knew that his mind wandered off to these simpler problems when he was overloaded, and now he felt overwhelmed. If only he could be more philosophical about his problems. There was nothing he could do now for his wife except to write the most loving letters that his limited skill could devise and send them by the most expeditious means. Luckily Dexter's business meant that he had correspondents all over the English colonies, so it would be easy to find the best means of sending a letter from whichever port *Medina* should touch at.

Back and forth he strode, his steps becoming less and less firm until, long after the sun had hurried away to cast its last light on the Ohio Valley and the infinite plains beyond, he found himself dragging his feet, shuffling rather than striding. It was when he tripped over a ring bolt, the same that he'd avoided all the long months of his command, that he decided to turn in. His mind was in that torpid state that comes from extreme mental and physical exhaustion. He turned to shout for the sentry to send for his servant; a new and untried man to replace Black Rod, he remembered with resignation.

Carlisle hadn't even opened his mouth when he heard the lusty hail, apparently from the mizzen top.

'Sail. Sail on the starboard beam.'

There was an immediate hurry of feet overhead, and before he'd reached the cabin door, it was flung open, and an excited midshipman just managed to avoid falling into the cabin.

'First lieutenant's compliments sir, there's a sail five cables on the starboard…'

But Carlisle heard none of this. He pushed past the midshipman and was on the quarterdeck in a dozen rapid strides, looking over his shoulder for the first glimpse of this ship. Friend or foe, nobody knew.

The quarterdeck was illuminated only by the glow of the binnacle light, but it was enough to show Moxon frozen in indecision. He could be forgiven for not ordering any manoeuvre, *Medina* was already, by her captain's orders, in the best position to protect the convoy for this newcomer. What was unforgivable was his failure to order the frigate to quarters. A ship closing in the black of the night must be presumed an enemy until it was proven otherwise and this one was still no more than a ghostly presence, apparently converging slowly – perhaps cautiously – with *Medina*. It was only by the grace of God, and the faint light of the crescent moon showing just above the horizon that the ship had been sighted as soon as it was. The seaman sent to check the mizzen topmast lanyards had happened to look up and see the faint gleam of the sails in the moonlight. The lookout in the maintop had seen nothing.

'Beat to quarters, Mister Moxon,' said Carlisle as steadily as he could. 'Load and run out.'

The drummer was propelled onto the deck by the marine sergeant and started his wild tattoo even before his feet were firmly planted on the deck.

'She's a frigate, sir. About the same size as us.'

That was Whittle. He'd hurried to the masthead as soon as he'd heard the first hail, not waiting for the drum to beat to quarters. The stranger – the frigate as they now knew – should have been just as visible from the quarterdeck as it was from the main top. After all, it was only a mile or so on the beam. And yet, perhaps because of some thickening of the atmosphere near the surface of the water, Whittle had a better view than Carlisle or any of the growing crowd of officers cluttering the deck.

Carlisle could see the frigate now. He could make out the hull as a darker shade against the inky night, and he could see her courses, her tops'ls and stays'ls as lighter patches, almost luminescent in the blackness. She was under all plain sail, so probably this encounter was equally surprising to the convoy and the newcomer. It was unlikely that any of the merchant ships would have seen her yet, and *Shark* almost certainly not, as the sloop would be far astern bringing up the rear. In his convoy orders, Carlisle had stipulated a night signal for an enemy in sight, and according to his ship's standing orders it should be stowed in the main top ready to be raised, two red lanterns arranged vertically. If he ordered it to be lit and hoisted now, probably the officer-of-the-watch in *Shark* would see it and alert Anderson, in which case the sloop should make sail to join *Medina*. However, Carlisle didn't know whether this strange sail was friend or foe, and if foe, whether it was alone and what were its intentions.

'Mister Moxon. Confirm that the night signal for an enemy in sight is ready to be lit. Send a midshipman to check that there is a portfire in the maintop, but it must remain shielded, I don't want to show any light.'

Probably they'd already been seen – if the stranger's lookouts weren't all asleep – but it was as well to avoid giving them a fixed point of reference on this black night.

'She's holding her course,' said Hosking at Carlisle's side. 'If she's seen us, then she shows no sign of it.'

'Starboard battery ready, sir,' reported Moxon, 'and the

portfire is in the maintop, properly shielded.'

'What do you make of her, Whittle?' Shouted Carlisle, directing his voice heavenwards.

'She's not a King's ship, sir, her topmast is all wrong. Could be a Frenchie on his way north.'

Carlisle grimaced in the darkness. Whittle was a good lookout, but he should stick to the facts and keep his opinions to himself. The fact that the tops'ls were unlike a British man-of-war's was interesting, but that decidedly did not mean that she wasn't British. The navy had taken prizes aplenty in this war, and many had been pressed into service before the dockyards had modified them. She could easily be a King's ship on her way to join the Louisbourg expedition, just as this convoy was. The problem was that anyone on the upper deck – and at quarters that was most of the people of the frigate – could hear Whittle's opinion and take it as the truth. It could influence the way that they fought, the decisions that they made, and it was the captain's prerogative – no, his duty – to order those affairs. Carlisle made a mental note to enforce more discipline in reports from the masthead.

'Masthead! Can you see any other sails apart from the convoy?' shouted Carlisle.

'Nothing sir. I can see the first few merchantmen but nothing of *Shark* and the others.'

The stranger could be seen clearly from the deck now. They were on converging courses, and it certainly looked as though *Medina* and her convoy hadn't yet been seen. She was a medium frigate, perhaps the same size and armament as *Medina*, but somewhat higher in the water. She certainly looked French. The range was about seven cables and closing.

'Mister Moxon. Put a shot across her bows. Not too close in case she's a friend.'

Bang! In the few seconds between the order and the execution, Carlisle had switched his attention from gunnery back to the urgent need to identify the stranger. The first shot caught him by surprise, as it always did, even though he'd ordered it.

The night was too dark and the range too great to make out individual figures, but as Carlisle's night-vision recovered from the sudden flash, he could see a change in the shape of the dark mass on her quarterdeck that indicated people moving about.

'The chase is bearing away, sir,' shouted Whittle.

Carlisle could see for himself that the stranger – Whittle's premature use of the word *chase* was another example of how an opinioned hail could change perceptions on deck – had come four or five points off the wind, showing *Medina* her quarter. That was a normal reaction if they hadn't seen *Medina* until she'd fired her warning shot.

'Mister Hosking, bear away and put the stranger two points on our starboard bow. You may set the t'gallants. Let's see if we can get close enough to identify her.'

'Should I make the enemy in sight signal, sir,' asked Moxon, looking like a man desperately trying to be helpful. He was aware that he hadn't covered himself in glory when the stranger was first sighted.

'No, Mister Moxon.'

Carlisle thought of leaving it there with a flat negative but realised that he was doing nothing for the esteem and authority of his second-in-command.

'If we make the signal, then *Shark* will leave the convoy to join us. I want her to stay with the convoy in case we don't return quickly. A single gun won't bring her, but the night signal will,' added Carlisle with his telescope trained on the fast receding sails of the presumed enemy.

'Aye-aye sir,' replied the first lieutenant.

'Sir, the signal's already lit,' said the quartermaster, jerking his head upwards. He'd been shamelessly listening to the officer's talking and grabbed the opportunity to be the first to point out the first lieutenant's failure. There was no love lost between the raw, hesitant second-in-command and the old and wise quartermaster.

Carlisle looked up. The night signals lanterns were designed so that the illumination was directed horizontally with a minimum of leakage downwards. Nevertheless, the two red lights could be clearly seen from the quarterdeck and Carlisle realised that *Shark* – if she were no more than two miles astern – would undoubtedly see them, if the lookouts were awake.

'Douse those lights!' shouted Moxon in horror.

'Wait!' shouted Carlisle. He knew that anything attempted at night could rapidly descend into chaos, particularly if orders were given without thinking.

Carlisle heard a dull thud from somewhere astern. That would be *Shark* acknowledging the signal. His snap decision to keep the signal up once it was lit was vindicated. If he could be sure that *Shark* hadn't seen it, then it would have been worth dousing the lanterns, but once the sloop had been alerted, the sudden disappearance of the signal would create doubt.

'Keep the signal showing, Mister Moxon, but direct it astern.'

The new lanterns could be shielded so that the light showed only through half the compass, there was no value in giving the stranger a point of reference on this dark night.

'Mister Hosking, we'll chase for a while, but I don't want to stray too far from the convoy. Let me know if you lose sight of her and if you see *Shark*.'

Carlisle took one more look around the dim horizon.

'Mister Moxon, would you join me in the cabin?'

***

CHAPTER SIX

The Chase

Monday, Thirteenth of March 1758.
Medina, at Sea. Cape Henry West-Southwest 26 leagues.

The interview with Moxon had taken longer than Carlisle had anticipated. In one sense, it was entirely the wrong time to berate his second-in-command, with a chase in sight and the prospect of the frigate going into action. However, Carlisle knew that if he left it until this incident was over, his remonstration would lose its impact. Tomorrow, with the chase either withdrawn or brought to action, the near disaster of the night signal would be but a memory, whereas tonight it was fresh in both their minds.

Carlisle believed – rather, he hoped – that he'd made an impression on Moxon. That was the easy part, the difficult follow-up was for his first lieutenant to impose some order into the working of the frigate. The problem stemmed from a lack of leadership; the people just didn't believe that Moxon was any sort of a substitute for Holbrooke. He didn't have his predecessor's experience of battle or of seamanship, but neither of those was essential; half the lieutenants in the navy had never seen action and had spent most of their career at fleet anchorages in ships-of-the-line. No, the critical point was that the people ignored him, when they didn't covertly mock him. Carlisle remembered what Shakespeare wrote:

Some are born great, some achieve greatness, and
some have greatness thrust upon 'em.

The lines were written as part of a comedy, but they were a useful way of understanding Moxon's development as a sea-officer. He wasn't endowed with natural leadership, and he appeared unable to learn it. Would he develop it in the stress of storm, fire or combat? Carlisle couldn't guess, but it was perhaps his first lieutenant's only hope of making his way in the service.

The incident with the night signal was caused by Whittle's freestyle reporting. His publicly declared opinion that the stranger was a Frenchman, then his reporting of a chase had led the able seaman in the foretop to expect an order to light the *enemy in sight* signal. His disrespect for the first lieutenant showed in his not waiting for the order but taking it upon himself to light the lamps and hoist them aloft. There were several factors in the chain of events, but they all stemmed from a *lasseiz-faire* attitude that had infected Carlisle's command since Holbrooke had been promoted into a sloop and sent back to Portsmouth with dispatches.

The man who had lit the lanterns would need to be punished. It wasn't a flogging offence, but a week as captain of the heads – a euphemism for the cleaner of the men's seats of ease – would reinforce the point. Moxon, of course, wouldn't be publicly punished nor criticised, but Carlisle's inclination to recommend him for promotion was decreasing by the day.

***

Carlisle lingered in his cabin after Moxon left. How he missed Holbrooke! He remembered how he'd initially despaired of making anything of the young master's mate who'd been wished on him by the man's father, an old sailing master from a long-ago commission.

He could date Holbrooke's turnaround from the first time that he'd been given any real responsibility. It was when he needed someone to systematically keep a tally of the French squadron and invasion force in Toulon Road. From there had come the decision to send him away in an independent command – a small vessel to take dispatches back to Port Mahon – which led to a more permanent command of an armed barca-longa and thence to his promotion to lieutenant. Sadly, he just couldn't see Moxon making that transition. He feared that letting his first lieutenant out of his sight with a valuable vessel and even more precious men would only end in the loss of both.

A knock on the door heralded Midshipman Angelini.

'Mister Hosking's compliments, sir,' he said in his still-accented English. 'We're closing slowly on the chase, she's about a mile on the starboard bow, and *Shark's* in sight on the starboard quarter, about a mile and a half.'

'Very well Mister Angelini. You may tell the master that I'll be on deck directly.'

Shark had done well to close them so quickly, but he'd have preferred that she stay with the merchantmen. When the sloop was within hailing range, he'd have to order Anderson back to the convoy, but he didn't want to lose contact with the chase by waiting for *Shark* to catch up. It was the classic dilemma of the convoy escort commander: to pursue the enemy and reduce that threat before it could do any harm would in the meantime leave the convoy unprotected, and who knew what lay below the horizon?

***

It took a few moments for Carlisle to regain his night vision. He could see the chase – for a chase it now most certainly was – just where Enrico had reported it, and he could barely make out *Shark* with a press of sail hurrying to join his commander.

'Mister Gordon. Can you annoy her at this range?' he asked the gunner, who had been loitering at arm's reach for just such an opportunity.

Gordon was a young man for a master gunner. He'd joined in Port Royal just before they'd sailed, and he hadn't had much opportunity to display his skills, but he came well recommended from *Augusta*.

'Annoy him I certainly can, sir,' he replied, rubbing his hands in anticipation. 'I can't promise we'll hit him and at this range and if we do, we won't do much damage, but at least we may provoke him.'

'Then pray do so, Mister Gordon. The for'rard guns should bear but let me know if you need me to come off a point.'

The gunner jumped down into the waist and ran to where his precious numbers one and three guns waited under the fo'c'sle, invisible from the quarterdeck.

Gordon was able to train his two guns for'rard enough and very soon they came into action, banging away steadily. The master gunner was evidently having difficulty seeing his target in the darkness and was taking his time to allow the smoke to clear. It was too dark to see the fall of shot, so the fine work of adjusting each round to creep closer and closer to the target was just impossible. The master gunner was right; a hit was unlikely.

Carlisle stood alone on the weather side of the quarterdeck, feeling the wind on his check and watching the chase, trying to put himself into the mind of his opponent. He cast a critical eye over the sails but could think of nothing that would make them draw better or give the frigate an extra knot of speed. Hosking watched him warily. The master knew that *Medina* was moving as fast as she'd ever done, and the last cast of the log showed eleven knots.

'Why's she running from us, sir,' Hosking asked, observing the dim outline of the chase through his telescope. The moon had set half an hour before, but the cloud cover was starting to thin and the stars gave a faint illumination.

'I was wondering the same thing, Master. She can't have seen *Shark* yet and perhaps hasn't even sighted the convoy. She probably believes we're a lone frigate on our innocent occasions.'

'Then her captain must be a poltroon,' said Hosking, 'to refuse battle with a frigate of equal force.'

'She's French of course,' said Carlisle, 'and that could explain it.'

Hosking looked sharply at his captain. He'd never heard him damn a whole nation in that way, and he'd often commented at the spirited way in which his French adversaries fought. Carlisle correctly interpreted the look.

'No, Master, I don't mean that all Frenchmen are cowards. But because they're short of merchantmen – most of 'em have been taken by our privateers – they often strip the guns from their frigates to make more space for stores, and they have a more rigorous view of their mission than we do. If it conflicts with the orders he's been given, that French captain – I'm assuming he's French – will certainly avoid fighting us.'

Hosking made a non-committal noise deep in his throat. 'Or he could know all about the convoy and be drawing us away while his friends fill their boots with our merchantmen.'

'It's a risk, sure, but I don't believe it,' replied Carlisle thoughtfully. 'We didn't see a single sail after we cleared the Capes and it's conceding too much to French intelligence to suggest that he knew our departure plans. No, I believe this is a chance encounter. In fact, I'd bet that our friend over there is on his way to the same place as us. He's on passage to resupply the garrison at Louisbourg and is armed *en flute* to cram in as much cargo as possible. He'll keep on running east until we must turn back. But in the meantime, if he doesn't know that we have a convoy to protect, he'll assume that we'll chase him all night.'

'Twilight's not 'till half past five. He has plenty of time to lose us if the sky clouds over.'

Carlisle nodded. He'd imagined it would be something like that, but it was good to hear the exact times.

'Well, there's little more that we can do for now. Let's allow the gunner to bang away while he can. I do believe we're moving a little faster than him,' he said nodding at the dim shape on their starboard bow, 'what do you think?'

'Barely, sir, barely. Unless we can slow him down, we won't catch him before the morning watch.'

'Then let's look to our tacks and sheets, Mister Hosking.'

***

They chased all through the first and middle watches, a long chase with little to show but overheated guns and tired men. It appeared that they scored at least two hits, but at that range, with mere nine-pound balls they couldn't expect much. There'd been no return fire from the Frenchman, tending to confirm the theory that her guns were struck below. In that case, it was a certainty that she was ordered to relieve Louisbourg or perhaps to sail up the St. Lawrence to Quebec. In any case, she was bound for Île Royale or New France.

Shark had moved into hailing range at midnight and Carlisle had promptly sent the sloop back to look after the convoy. At least it wouldn't be a hard beat for Anderson. According to Hosking's calculation, *Shark* would be able to sail a point free on the larboard tack and should be back with her charges before dawn. The convoy must have spent an uncomfortable night, hearing rather than seeing their escort disappear to leeward accompanied by a steady discharge of cannon fire. What they would do if dawn found them alone on the sea was anyone's guess.

***

Eight bells sounded and, as if by magic, a thick blanket of cloud started to snuff out the stars one-by-one. Over to the east there was not even the faintest of a pre-dawn glow; it was hard to imagine that the rising sun would offer any light. It was pitch dark, and the chase had disappeared. The bow guns ceased their monotonous firing, and an eerie silence fell over the deck

'We won't see her again for an hour or two,' said Hosking, hanging his telescope on the hook on the side of the binnacle. There was an air of finality to his action; clearly, the master thought they'd seen the last of the chase. Carlisle agreed. The Frenchman could turn to the north or the south, or he could stand on. With this fresh breeze, in an hour he could be twelve miles away; twenty-four if Carlisle chose poorly and their courses diverged.

'Set a course to rejoin the convoy, Mister Hosking,' he said, trying to keep the resignation from his voice. It had always been questionable whether this chase far to leeward was a wise decision, but now that there was no better than a fifty-fifty chance that the Frenchman would be in sight at dawn, the balance had tipped. He should be back with the merchantmen.

Medina heeled extravagantly as her bows came around to the north. A capful of spray burst on the mizzen chains and soaked the quartermaster and the steersmen. Gone was the silence of the moonlit run to the east; now they were sailing barely a point free, and the lee gunwale was dipping into the black waves.

'A reef in the tops'ls, perhaps, sir,' said Hosking, looking at the bar-taut sheets and aloft at the straining canvas, just visible through the stygian blackness. He and Carlisle were holding onto the larboard hammock cranes to keep themselves from skidding to leeward.

'No, Mister Hosking. I want to be back with the convoy in the forenoon watch. We'll carry this canvas unless the wind freshens. I'll be in my cabin.'

***

The cabin was in darkness, and for a moment he wondered why his lantern wasn't lit. Then he remembered his new man. An experienced captain's servant would have been able to anticipate his master's return. He'd have felt the frigate haul her wind and have guessed that they had given up the chase. From there, it was no great leap of intellect to deduce that the captain would leave the deck to take some rest. Carlisle felt his way to the seat that ran the width of the cabin under the stern windows. It was padded with oakum and covered in a gay chintz that Chiara had chosen in Kingston. The wind was steady, and the waves were regular. If he lay with his head to larboard – the high side of the seat – he'd be able to get an hour of sleep before the sky started to lighten, when he must be on deck. He stretched out his length and, with nothing visible to claim his attention, he fell asleep, his worries about Chiara and his unborn child forgotten with the mental stimulation of chasing the Frenchman.

Carlisle was in such a deep sleep that his servant had to call three or four times before his master woke.

'Sir…sir…sir, the first lieutenant reports an hour before dawn. The wind's steady from the west, and the ship's under all plain sail.'

'Very well, I'll come on deck,' he replied, shaking himself into wakefulness. It was his own damned standing orders that were to blame. If he hadn't ordered that the ship would clear for action and the hands go to quarters each morning before the dawn, he could have stayed asleep if he wished. Yet he knew his orders were sound. Many were the man-of-war that had sailed along happily through the night, oblivious to the deadly enemy just a mile away that had revealed itself, well within gun range, at the first light before dawn. In a time of war, in waters where an enemy may reasonably be found, it was a wise precaution to greet the sunrise with loaded guns run out, ready for whatever the growing light reveals.

***

CHAPTER SEVEN

Dawn Action

Tuesday, Fourteenth of March 1758.
Medina, at Sea. Cape Henry Southwest 65 leagues.

I t was still pitch-dark when Carlisle groped his way up the quarterdeck, but now there was a definite glow to the east. It wasn't enough to offer any illumination, but it was noticeable.

'Good morning sir.'

That was Moxon; Carlisle could just see his outline against the light of the binnacle. And now he could see shadowy figures around the first lieutenant: steersmen, the crews of the four three-pounders, the master, assorted midshipmen. Gradually the day became lighter as the still-invisible sun neared the horizon. To the east, it was just possible to imagine a distinction between sea and sky while to the west, a sullen mist lay over the face of the sea. He was reminded of Genesis:

And the earth was without form, and void; and darkness was upon the face of the deep.

The mist would evaporate with the sun but, for now, it had the odd effect of delaying the light of the rising sun to the west, while to the east, the day moved forward apace.

'Sail Ho! Four points on the larboard bow. Looks like the convoy, sir.'

Carlisle trained his telescope to larboard. He could see nothing but an indistinct horizon, but that was to be expected. The lookout's horizon was probably five miles further than was available to the officers on the quarterdeck.

'I can see *Shark* now, sir. She's ahead of the convoy and to leeward.'

That was right and proper. In the absence of *Medina*, the sloop should be stationed at the head of the convoy on the side closest to the threat.

Four telescopes were trained to windward, all looking for the first sight of their charges. Naturally Hosking wanted an early indication so that he could adjust his course to take the convoy commander's station, presently occupied by *Shark*. A delay of five minutes now could turn into an additional thirty minutes if the convoy was further on their bow than the lookout reported.

Carlisle, too, was watching to windward. The part of his mind that wasn't trying to be the first to see the topmasts pierce the horizon was dimly aware that Moxon alone wasn't staring through a telescope. In fact, the first lieutenant was at the leeward side of the quarterdeck, his hands on the hammock cranes, looking to the east. Carlisle was irritated to see that Moxon should take so little interest in this delicate manoeuvre that the frigate had to execute. He should know by now how important it was that the convoy commander's ship should be the example to all. Otherwise, the merchantmen had all the excuse they needed to wander all over the sea rather than stay in a tight formation.

'I do believe I see them, sir,' said Hosking, 'four, no five points on the bow, just as we rise on the swell.' Probably the master was bluffing, Carlisle thought. He'd calculated that they'd be visible from the quarterdeck at any moment and had taken a risk on their bearing.

Silence. Nobody else was prepared to commit themselves, and as the minutes passed, Hosking was starting to regret his little conceit. Wishart, the master's mate of the watch, nudged the midshipman who hurried away to turn the glass and stream the log. Four bells sounded and the relief lookouts swung out around the shrouds and made their way up the ratlines. The people were at quarters, and the frigate was cleared for action, as she would be every dawn that she was at sea while this war lasted.

***

'Sir,' said Moxon from somewhere behind Carlisle. 'Sir, there may be a ship to starboard, I've just lost her again in the mist.'

Carlisle swung around. The telescope was useless in that reduced visibility, the naked eye was far better at catching shifting shapes in the murk. He studied the grey-white bank for a full minute, but there was no sign of a solid mass within that barrier of moist air.

'Are you sure, Mister Moxon?' asked Carlisle. He was desperate to keep the scepticism from his voice; his first lieutenant needed all the endorsement that he could get from his commanding officer. Yet, there was nothing to be seen. Nobody else had raised the alarm, but that was easily explained because all hands were imitating the quarterdeck and looking earnestly to larboard for the first sighting of the convoy from the deck.

What was the visibility? About a mile, somewhat less in the thicker patches, Carlisle thought. If Moxon had seen something, then it was dangerously close. He gave it another full minute, searching the denser, closer patches of mist, but then he heard Wishart over his left shoulder.

'There they are, just where the master said. Four points on the bow.'

Carlisle turned back to larboard. As he did so, he noticed Moxon still gazing to starboard, intently watching a point right on their beam. He soon forgot the first lieutenant's imaginary sighting; the sooner he could be unloaded on a ship-of-the-line where he could do less damage, the better. And the convoy was indeed in sight, a forest of tiny topmasts breaking the horizon.

'You'll need to come a point or so to starboard, Mister Hosking, I fancy,' he said.

'Sail Ho!' Moxon shouted. There was no doubt in his voice this time. 'Sail a point for'rard of the starboard beam.'

This time Carlisle swung about quickly, and the whole population of the quarterdeck followed him. They were quick, but not fast enough to see the flash of a full broadside that the frigate on their beam unleashed on them. All they saw was the bank of smoke that the moderate breeze pushed back over the deck and sails of the intruder, and they heard the howling of the chain shot as it tore the sails and rigging over their heads. *Medina* staggered; evidently, they'd been hulled, and even chain shot could damage a frigate's light sides.

'Mister Moxon, the starboard battery if you please. Fire as soon as guns are properly pointed. I'll bear away towards that fellow.'

'Aye-aye sir. Gun captains! Run out and stand by to give her a broadside!'

'Mister Hosking. Three points to starboard. Brail up the courses, let's see the enemy!'

Carlisle looked around him. The quarterdeck was full of people and he quickly spotted those he needed.

'Bosun. Chips. I want a damage report as quickly as possible.'

He had a moment to again regret the missing Holbrooke. At a time like this, he needed trusted men around him.

Medina staggered as her first broadside fired. It was a little ragged, but it appeared that all the guns had fired almost simultaneously. He couldn't see the aftermost guns in his cabin, but it looked like a good opening salvo. He spared a moment for a searching look at his first lieutenant. He wasn't sure what he expected, a furious panicked running from gun to gun perhaps, but he was surprised to see Moxon standing alone in the centre of the upper deck. He was looking calmly around him and issuing rapid orders to the midshipmen and quarter gunners. Moxon looked towards the quarterdeck.

'Number twenty-one gun's out of action, sir. One of the chain shot came straight through the gunport and destroyed the carriage. Carpenter's looking at it now.'

Then his cabin would be a wreck, thought Carlisle. That was where his cot swung when *Medina* wasn't cleared for action; and of course, that was where Chiara would have been if she hadn't stayed in Williamsburg.

There would be casualties, but now wasn't the time for him to be concerned with mere flesh and blood; it was the guns, inanimate confections of oak and cast iron that mattered. Carlton had offered to stay behind in Williamsburg to tend to Chiara but thank God he'd resisted the temptation. Apart from the obvious and rightful disapproval of whichever admiral he came under at Halifax, it would have been a criminal loss to those men who were now helpless in the midshipman's berth awaiting the knife and the saw.

Carlisle tried to distance himself from his guns and the ship's damage. His job was to out-think his opponent. What was the Frenchman doing? He could see that it was the same frigate that they'd pursued the previous evening. Why had her commander decided to attack now? Was he hoping that *Medina* would have chased him through the night, drawing further and further away from the convoy, leaving it undefended for this dawn attack? One thing was certain, his guess that his enemy was armed en flute was dead wrong. For reasons of his own, the Frenchman had attempted to give that impression, and he'd fallen for it. Evidently, this was a war-wise adversary and not one to be trifled with

'Mister Hosking. Put me across his bow at pistol-shot range.'

Another broadside of chain shot screamed across the deck. The range was less now, and the French gunners had been out of the mist for ten minutes. They had the range and the shot went high into the tops, shooting away halyards, sheets and braces and tearing rents in the canvas sails. Luckily the slings had not been hit, not yet.

'Nothing below the waterline, sir,' reported the

carpenter, loaded down with softwood wedges and great iron nails. 'My mates are re-mounting number twenty-one gun; it shouldn't take long. Just knocks and dents, nothing to worry about.'

The Frenchman's tactics were clear. He was trying to disable *Medina* to leave himself free to run riot among the convoy. Where was *Shark*?

Carlisle stole a quick look to windward. There was the sloop charging down into battle. It was hard to criticise such aggressive tactics, but Carlisle would have preferred *Shark* to stay with the convoy. She may not be able to stop a frigate, but she could buy time for the convoy to disperse, and that was better done after the Frenchman had dissipated his force on *Medina.*

The starboard battery fired again. The Frenchman was being hit now, hulled, and some of them were between wind and water. Now *Medina* was benefitting from the decision to engage with roundshot. If the Frenchman had made some significant hits in *Medina's* sails in his first few broadsides of chain, then his decision would have been vindicated. He could have disabled *Medina* and bought himself a crucial hour. Now, though, with the British frigate only superficially damaged and closing fast to decide the contest, it was clear that the Frenchman's gamble hadn't paid off. It must be a worrying sight, a decidedly battle-ready frigate and one of those six-pounder brig-sloops bearing down upon them and no friends in sight.

The mist had almost dispersed now, and the eastern horizon was clear from north to south.

'Masthead, do you see anything other than the convoy and the French Frigate?' shouted Carlisle through the speaking-trumpet.

There was a long pause, and Carlisle almost picked up the trumpet again. Perhaps Whittle was wounded or dead, he'd be right in the path of that devilish chain shot. Then he heard the call. Evidently, Whittle had taken the time for a careful all-around scan.

'Nothing, sir. The horizon's clear. There's nothing to windward of the convoy.'

An intelligent response saving Carlisle making a supplementary call.

Surely...surely the Frenchman would break off the engagement before *Medina* set her claws into him. With a frigate pinning her into position and a sloop manoeuvering to rake her stern – for that was surely what Anderson intended – there was no other sensible course of action. Every second the French captain delayed would make his retreat more perilous.

Crash went another broadside and almost at the same moment, another salvo of chain shot brought its hail of parted lines and unmounted blocks raining onto the deck. But still nothing vital had been hit.

'There she goes, sir,' said Hosking. 'She's coming through the wind. Very sensible, she'd never veer in time.'

'Then we'll rake her stern. Mister Moxon. Hold your fire until we see her taffrail. I want a full broadside of roundshot to see her off.'

'Aye-aye sir.' Moxon waved his hat and turned back to his guns. Carlisle noted that he'd barely moved throughout the engagement. He just had time to wonder whether he'd underestimated his second-in-command. The guns were being served with single-minded concentration by the crews. That was, to a great extent, a result of the example of their leader.

The Frenchman's movements were evident now. Those beautiful bluff bows were moving fast into the wind. Her stern galleries were presented to *Medina* within range of her nine pounders. Nevertheless, it was a difficult target, at least half a mile distant and the target's aspect was altering fast while *Medina* was tearing through the water at only a knot or two less than she would with undamaged sails. There was the rub. If the Frenchman could survive this broadside, she'd have two knots over *Medina*, thanks to the damage done by her chain shot.

'Fire when you're ready Mister Moxon.'

There was a breathless pause. Hands shot up all along the line of guns as their captains were happy with their training and elevation. He could see the handspikes being nudged to track the crossing target. There was a wicked symmetry to it, the impersonal air of a deadly fighting machine.

'Fire!' shouted Moxon. The handspikes were whipped away, and the gun captains stepped aside. As soon as they were clear of the recoil, thirteen linstocks were brought down onto the pans of priming. *Medina* shuddered as the broadside was released, eleven nine-pound balls from the upper deck and two three-pounders from the quarterdeck. Carlisle had a flash of recollection: *Vulcain* off Nice two years ago. He'd won that engagement before it had properly begun, with a broadside just such as this, and his opponent was only saved by being in the territorial waters of a neutral nation. This broadside had a similar effect. The stern windows just disappeared, one moment they were there, twinkling in the sun, and the next they were gone. The taffrail was shattered and the mizzen shrouds were cut through in the lanyards. Now, if only the rudder were hit, they'd have her.

'Mister Hosking bring us about. You see the chase, let's catch her!'

They watched eagerly from the quarterdeck, looking for some sign that their adversary was steering wildly, but they looked in vain. Not a shot came from the fleeing Frenchman, but nor did her speed slacken and she was running to leeward as fast as the wind would carry her. Carlisle couldn't blame the French captain. He'd made a bold attempt at the convoy; he'd rolled the dice, but his sixes hadn't come up. Now he was doing the sensible thing and preserving his frigate to complete its real mission. This was opportunism after all, nothing more than private enterprise.

Carlisle looked up at the sails; they were a pitiful sight with hardly an undamaged bolt of canvas. Could he ask *Shark* to run the Frenchman alongside and hold her until *Medina* could limp up and finish her off? He looked again at the frigate and at the sloop. *Shark* was no flyer. Perhaps Anderson could catch her, but by then *Medina* would be so far behind that the most likely outcome would be to lose the sloop before *Medina* could come into action. No, he'd follow for an hour in the hope that some calamity would befall the Frenchman, but then they must disengage and let him be.

***

CHAPTER EIGHT

New England

Wednesday, Fifteenth of March 1758.
Medina, at Anchor. Boston, Massachusetts.

Hosking exhaled in a low whistle.

'I've been in and out of Boston these last thirty years and I've never seen the like of this,' he exclaimed, staring at the mass of shipping in the harbour. Wherever there was space on the wharves, there was a ship: loading, unloading or repairing; double, treble and quadruple-banked. Those that couldn't get alongside were anchored, seemingly scattered at random around the broad, island-studded bay.

'They'll be waiting for the last of the ice to clear before they sail for Halifax,' replied Carlisle, himself in awe of the sheer number and variety of vessels. Whatever errors of strategy had caused the failure of last year's attempt on Louisbourg, this year's expedition wouldn't want for naval effort.

'That cutter's heading for us,' said Hosking, his telescope trained on a small gaff-rigged vessel that had just become visible between Governor's Island and Castle Island, 'It'll be our pilot, I don't doubt.'

As the cutter took a wide sweep to approach *Medina's* starboard side, the frigate briefly backed its main tops'l to take the way off, and the pilot jumped aboard at the waist. The cutter, barely pausing in its progress, sheered away and veered abruptly, the massive boom swinging across the stern and laying her over on her larboard side as she took the first tack in her beat up to the convoy against the fresh easterly breeze.

'I'm to take you to your anchorage, Mister,' said the pilot as he climbed the quarterdeck ladder. He addressed himself to Hosking and studiously ignored Carlisle. 'Just take in your courses now,' he said, and turning to the wheel, 'come up a point, quartermaster.'

Hosking had grown old dealing with pilots of all kinds and he knew this type well, the grizzled New Englander with a chip on his shoulder and an inbred dislike of King's ships and King's officers. A man with an indemnity against impressment and the security of tenure in lucrative employment.

'Hold your course,' snapped Hosking.

The quartermaster stood impassive. He'd had no intention of following the pilot's orders until the master had directed him to do so. Neither had the bosun made any move towards his pipe. The hands at the sheets and braces stood immobile.

'You'll be addressing yourself to Captain Carlisle, Mister Pilot,' replied Hosking, staring hard at the brown-clad figure. 'When he's happy with your proposal, we can discuss sails and steering.'

A range of emotions played over the pilot's face. He dearly wanted to damn both Carlisle and Hosking to hell, but he could see the marine sergeant eyeing him, and he didn't look like a man to be trifled with. And then there was the question of his fee. He'd have no chance of being paid if he didn't have a signed paper from the captain or master. He half-turned towards Carlisle.

'Your berth's off the Dorchester Flats, South Battery west-southwest by five cables. *Now*, will you take in your courses and come up a point?' he asked rudely.

'Your name, sir?' asked Carlisle, returning the pilot's hostile stare.

Carlisle's recent visit to his home colony had brought out the Virginian accent that had been almost lost by his years of service. Now the long vowels came out loud and clear as he addressed the New Englander.

'You're a southerner,' said the pilot. It was a statement, not a question and his face hardened as he said it. Then he turned and spat on the deck.

Carlisle didn't react for a moment, so astonished was he at this behaviour. The rivalry and mistrust between the New Englanders and the Southerners were as old as the founding of the colonies – Plymouth Rock versus Jamestown – but Carlisle had never seen it so openly expressed.

'Sergeant Wilson!'

'Sir!' replied the sergeant, marching the few paces to Carlisle's side.

'Take this man into custody, the gun-deck will do for now. If he chooses to spit again, or if he transgresses any of the ship's standing orders, you may use the bilboes.'

The pilot's attitude didn't soften as he was led away between two marines, with Sergeant Wilson following. He shrugged off the hands that would have pinioned him.

'You'll pay for this, Carlisle, by God you will!' he shouted over his shoulder.

'Sergeant Wilson! The manacles and an armed guard,' ordered Carlisle, his face showing no emotion.

At that, the pilot tried to turn and run back up the ladder, but Sergeant Wilson was behind him and no prisoner had yet escaped his iron grip. The pilot was bundled below without further ceremony, and the last that the quarterdeck knew of him was a muffled curse abruptly cut off and a dull thud as though a body had hit a hard object. On deck, nobody moved. Nothing like this had been seen before on *Medina*.

'Mister Hosking, you know the harbour well, I believe,' said Carlisle in a formal, to-be-recorded-in-case-of-court-martial voice.

'I do sir. I can bring the frigate to her berth,' he replied in an equally clear voice. 'That pilot is not fit for his duty, in my professional opinion,' he added, just for the record.

'Very well, carry on,' replied Carlisle, ignoring the wooden faces of the officers gathered on the quarterdeck.

Carlisle beckoned to his clerk, who had been a mute observer of the sordid drama.

'Mister Simmonds, I'd be obliged if you'd make a

verbatim note of that conversation.'

Carlisle was aware of the enormity of his action, and he knew that he'd have to account for his decision to sail into Boston Harbour without a pilot, in defiance of both civil and naval rules. However, he had enough witnesses who would testify to the belligerent attitude of the pilot, and they were already between Deer Island and Long Island. He could argue that he was in no position to turn back against the easterly wind. In Hosking, he had a sailing master with a strong enough reputation to make the lack of a qualified pilot justifiable, perhaps.

***

Medina approached her allotted berth between the Dorchester Flats and Long Wharf. *Shark* followed close behind, the sloop's Boston pilot still blissfully unaware of the fate of his colleague. The berth was on the north-eastern edge of the man-of-war anchorage, with a host of merchant ships anchored further to the north and east, all waiting their turn to come alongside one of Boston's many wharves.

'There's *Royal William*,' said Moxon, pointing to a great three-decker that dominated the channel, 'but she's flying no flag.'

'Are you sure, Mister Moxon?' asked Carlisle, busy watching the small gap that Hosking was steering the frigate into. 'I'd expected Admiral Hardy.'

'I'm certain, sir. She's just a private ship today.'

'Then there'll be no salute, Mister Gordon,' he said to the master gunner as the anchor fell clear of the cathead. The best bower took the ground, and *Medina* lay back on her cable, the ebbing tide dominating as the furled sails offered no resistance to the easterly wind.

The yawl was brought alongside, and the crew stepped carefully into their seats, anxiously wiping any hint of dirt from the thwarts and gunwales to keep their best rig clean.

'You may hold the pilot onboard for another hour, Mister Moxon, then send him ashore in Sergeant Wilson's custody, with a file of marines. I hope I'll have seen the captain of the port by then.'

Carlisle was certain that there were grounds for legal proceedings against the pilot under at least two specific articles of war – sedition and reproachful speech – not to mention the last article, the so-called *captain's cloak*, that covered all other crimes not explicitly mentioned in the text. Moreover, it was no use the pilot claiming that he wasn't subject to naval discipline. The law had recently been clarified: pilots were subject to the articles while on board a king's ship. Nevertheless, it would be a nervous few days for Carlisle until he was sure that his actions were approved.

Now here was a conundrum. With a three-decker at anchor just a few cables away with no flag flying, and a captain of the port of unknown rank ashore – Carlisle was aware that much would have changed since his first news of the naval establishment at Boston – who should he call upon? He'd just made up his mind that it should be the captain of the port, principally because he wanted to make his complaint about the pilot as quickly as possible before the news had time to leak out, when he saw a uniformed figure on the deck *Royal William* waving him alongside.

His coxswain saw the signal at the same time and with a glance at his captain for confirmation, he pushed the tiller to starboard and brought the yawl in a tight turn towards *Royal William's* entry port.

***

The reason for his summons to *Royal William* had quickly become evident, because the captain of the port was on board, visiting Captain Evans, so both the senior sea officer and the senior Navy Board appointee were in one place. The matter of the pilot caused some discussion; he was a notoriously difficult man with some influence over the other pilots. In this case, though, he'd clearly outdone himself in his rudeness to a post-captain. The captain of the port – a very old and long superannuated post-captain by the name of Pegler, plucked from retirement to bring some order to this growing city's maritime facilities – believed that the pilot could be suspended from his duties for six months without imperilling the co-operation of his fellows. The worst that could happen would be for the pilots as a body to refuse to offer their services to King's ships. Pegler knew, however, that there were twice as many equally qualified pilots who had been excluded from the guild just waiting for the opportunity to break into this closed circle of lucrative employment. A hasty note sent ashore to Pegler's deputy, who also held the post of chief pilot, would ensure that the errant pilot was held in the cells until he could return and issue his sentence.

'Well, I hope that settles the question of the pilot, Captain Carlisle,' said Pegler. 'He has a certain reputation, little of it good. He was a pilot at Louisbourg you know, when we held it from forty-five to forty-eight, and I imagine that he'd hoped to find employment with Mister Boscawen. He may yet; who knows what view the admiral will take.'

Carlisle showed no emotion. He knew there would be pressure to find knowledgeable pilots.

'He'll feel the pinch with no income for six months,' continued Evans. 'Perhaps he'll throw up piloting for good, which would only be to the benefit of the profession. But be warned, he's a man with friends in the port; I'd advise that you don't go ashore alone.'

'I've no need to go ashore at all. I'll just be taking on wood and water and I'll be away to Halifax,' said Carlisle, 'unless Sir Charles left any orders to the contrary.'

'Nothing that I've seen,' replied Pegler.

'And I've a list of bosun's stores, canvas and cordage, if you'd be so kind as to present that to the naval storekeeper,' he said handing a document to Pegler.

'Sir Charles left in *Captain* on the fourteenth,' said Evans, referring to Rear Admiral Hardy. 'He thought a sixty-four would be able to operate off Louisbourg earlier in the season than a three-decker, so he shifted his flag and sailed as soon as he had a westerly wind. We're to wait here until we get news of Boscawen, then we're to meet him at

Halifax.'

'Do you know when Sir Charles intends to be off Louisbourg?' asked Carlisle, eager to get early intelligence of his mission.

'It all depends on the ice. There's a sloop on station, with orders to report when the harbour looks like becoming ice-free. It could be any day now, but it's been a hard winter in the north and the thaw will likely be late. He's in a tearing hurry to establish a blockade to stop the French bringing in supplies, and even more important, to stop them reinforcing the fortress. You know that Colville spent the winter in Halifax?'

'I'd heard something along those lines,' replied Carlisle cautiously.

What news he had was old and unreliable. If he'd commanded a ship-of-the-line his orders would have included a general summary of naval dispositions, but as a frigate captain, he'd been merely ordered to report to Halifax, in as few words as possible. He'd picked up local news and gossip in Williamsburg and Hampton, but he knew how far from the truth such sources could be.

'I wouldn't have wanted the job! The facilities at Halifax are basic, to say the least. It can't have been easy, but Lord Colville appears to have his squadron ready for sea.'

'How many?' asked Carlisle.

'Seven of the line and a fifty, and he has two frigates.'

Carlisle nodded appreciatively. That must have been a monumental effort to prevent that many ships rotting away through the long winter in Halifax.

'We sent almost all of our shipwrights to him in January,' added Pegler, 'They grumbled, but they've been well paid, and the threat of being laid off in Boston persuaded them. Halifax isn't a popular place in the winter.'

'I've had little experience of ice,' admitted Carlisle. 'Most of my service has been in the West Indies, the Mediterranean or the southern colonies.'

'Then you'll learn quickly,' replied Evans. 'Don't be

surprised if your stay in Halifax is as short as your stay in Boston. Is *Medina* in good repair?'

'Her timbers and planks are fine, but we had a brush with a French frigate off the Capes. My sails and rigging were badly cut up. Otherwise I'd have had him!'

Pegler had been examining Carlisle's shopping list while Evans had been talking.

'Then that explains this list, Carlisle. There's enough canvas here for a whole new suit of sails. You can carry out the work yourself?'

'Yes, it's just patching and splicing. No doubt a King's yard would look askance at us, but we bent on a whole new suit of sails after the engagement – there wasn't a bolt of canvas without a hole in the old ones – and all hands have been splicing day and night. We'll reeve new braces, sheets and halyards in slower time and the sailmaker can work on the canvas.'

'Don't leave it too long, Carlisle,' advised Evans. 'I was off the mouth of the St. Lawrence this time last year and we needed every spare sail that we had.'

**

Carlisle dined with Evans and Pegler in *Royal William's* great cabin. It was a far cry from his cabin in *Medina*; grander, more spacious, but it lacked the feminine touches that Chiara had brought to the frigate for their passage from Jamaica. There was a masculine rigidity to the furnishings that reminded Carlisle of an obsessive bosun's insistence on the exact squaring of yards for a harbour stow. He looked down at the carpet – a luxury of which his frigate was innocent – to see that the feet of the dining table were precisely aligned with the pattern. The velvet cushions on the seats looked as though no human body had ever crushed their pristine nap. He felt oppressed by the formal geometry.

Through the windows he could see his boats pulling to and from the wharves, obedient to the note that he'd sent back to Moxon.

It was a long dinner, and the bells of the afternoon watch

came in their due succession. It wasn't until six bells had been struck that they drank the loyal toast and the servants withdrew. Evans had drunk a little more than was wise and Pegler far more.

'Well, what do you think of our chances against Louisbourg this year,' asked Evans. 'We'll surely do better than last year.'

'Aye, it was a shambles,' replied Pegler. 'I saw them all go. I felt the tempest even down here in Boston, and I saw the sad remnants limp back into the harbour.'

'I beg your pardon gentlemen, but I was in Jamaica all last year, and all I've heard has been through the broadsheets. Can you tell me what went wrong?'

'What went wrong?' exclaimed Pegler with a vinous laugh that could probably be heard across the harbour. 'Too few ships arrived, and they were too late in the season to prevent the French from getting a strong squadron into Louisbourg. Poor leadership by the army, disastrously so, and then the hurricane that scattered the fleet.'

'It was a humiliation,' added Evans. 'Back in forty-five, a colonial militia army took Louisbourg as easy as you like, mostly New Englanders. Twelve years later, with a detailed knowledge of the defences, a whole regular British army was sent home! We should never have given it back at the peace.'

'It's a strange place,' said Pegler thoughtfully. 'Nobody in their right mind would want to spend a summer there, much less a winter, and yet it's vital to the security of New France. It's the gate across the St. Lawrence that can be shut at will.'

'And yet not quite a gate,' objected Evans. His few extra glasses – he'd called for another bottle of port only moments before – had loosened his tongue to the extent where he was close to being argumentative.

'Not exactly a gate, I say. It's a hundred and fifty miles of stormy seas to Saint-Pierre, and no fortress can hold that passage, it needs ships! The real value of Louisbourg is that it'll threaten our fleet when we eventually move up the river to Quebec and Montreal. It's a base for a French squadron that could prevent supplies and reinforcements reaching us. We can't invade New France while Louisbourg sits across our supply lines, and the French can't hold New France if we take the fortress.'

'You know what the French call it?' asked Pegler. He looked questioningly at the two captains. Carlisle had a childish urge to respond, *Louisbourg*? but he restrained himself.

'They call it *La Forteresse Maudite*; the Cursed Fortress,' he said in a portentous tone, 'and you can see why. The Boston winters are hard, yet the Halifax winters are harder, much crueller, near unbearable in fact. But the Louisbourg winters! There's that cold current coming down from the north bringing almost constant fogs, hail, rain, frost and snow; every disagreeable circumstance of bad weather that can be imagined. There's little chance of supply until the spring and even on shore, the men are ruined by scurvy and fevers. The Cursed Fortress indeed! Who'll want to garrison it when we take it, I wonder? Not me, that's for sure.'

'Nevertheless, take it we must if we're to send a fleet up the St. Lawrence,' said Evans. 'Anson's agreed that we besiege Louisbourg as soon as it's ice-free, then Quebec in the summer. Montreal must fall when they're cut off from the Atlantic then we can clear the French out of all of Upper Canada before the winter.'

'A fine plan,' said Pegler. 'Yet, if there's no squadron blockading Louisbourg before the end of the month, the French will be running supplies and men into the harbour, and men-of-war with them. That's what will break up a siege, a boldly-handled French squadron operating from the security of the harbour under the guns of the fortress.'

'Then I must make all speed to join Sir Charles at Halifax,' said Carlisle, rising to his feet and finding that he wasn't quite as steady as he'd hoped. 'May I beg one of your boats, Captain Evans?'

***

CHAPTER NINE

The First Lieutenant

Thursday, Sixteenth of March 1758.
Medina, at Sea. Cape Cod Southwest 20 leagues.

*M*edina and *Shark* spent a single night in Boston and sailed the next morning with a friendly south-westerly wind and an ebbing tide. Carlisle, free at last from the desperate headache that Captain Evans' port had given him, and with the self-satisfied glow that came from surviving yet another afternoon of over-indulgence, was abstractedly watching the sailmaker and his party patching the old fore tops'l.

'Aye that's a job and a half,' said the bosun, seeing his captain in a mellow mood.

'Did you get enough canvas out of the Boston yard, Mister Swinton?' he asked.

'I did, sir. Not that I really needed it, but now we have enough to patch up after another fight,' he replied, rubbing his hands. 'They were short of number four canvas but were very free with everything else, although neither the canvas nor cordage is as good as I could wish. More Chatham than Portsmouth, in my opinion.'

Carlisle smiled. He was used to these prejudices. The bosun's home was in Portsmouth, and nothing would convince him that anything good came out of any other yard, certainly not Chatham.

'Eight holes there are in that fore tops'l, sir,' he continued remorselessly, 'and the starboard leech-rope shot through just under the earing-cringle. I'll have the sailmaker replace the whole starboard cloth, or it'll never hold in a blow. I'll be using the best number three canvas from my store, not that stuff from Boston.'

It was strictly true that the sailmaker came within the bosun's empire, being an inferior warrant officer, but most bosuns wouldn't have so emphasised their ownership. Not Swinton, he was a decent bosun, but jealous of his responsibilities and privilege. Anything that belonged to the sailmaker or the yeoman of the sheets naturally belonged to him and let nobody forget it!

Down in the waist, Carlisle could see the first lieutenant apparently being taken on a tour of the main batteries by the gunner. Each group of six nine-pounders had its own quarter gunner, petty officers who were subordinate to the gunner. There was another quarter gunner responsible for the quarterdeck three-pounders and the swivels and yet another who kept the magazine. It was interesting to see that all six quarter gunners were present for this inspection, each looking alternately nervous and pleased as their weapons were inspected. At each gun, Moxon went down on his knees, as though in supplication. But he held a shielded lantern in his hand and was really peering down the barrel to check for rust or signs of the dreaded honeycombing of the barrel, caused by the acidic gasses from the explosion of the black powder; it was the eventual doom of any well-used cast-iron gun. Rammers and sponges, powder horns and linstocks, handspikes and buckets; all were checked by the first lieutenant with the gunner looking on approvingly.

What interested Carlisle was that this inspection was taking place without him having ordered it. Until now he'd had to remind Moxon of nearly every element of his duty, but here he was acting very much at his own initiative and – it could be said – intruding upon the master gunner's own responsibilities and privileges. He couldn't stop himself comparing Moxon with his previous first lieutenant Holbrooke. He knew that Holbrooke would have done something very similar, but he'd have consulted his captain first. It was slightly irritating to see that Moxon felt no need to consult him. His mind ran away to remember the halcyon days when Holbrooke had sailed with him in this very frigate. And yet…and yet something was intruding on his recollection. Was it fair to compare Moxon with

Holbrooke? To treat Moxon in the same way as he'd treated Holbrooke? Moxon was a much older man with greater experience, whereas Holbrooke had been rushed through the ranks with almost indecent haste. Was this in fact what he should expect of a good first lieutenant? For the first time Carlisle wondered whether he'd become too accustomed to a second-in-command with an abundance of intelligence, leadership and fighting spirit, but lacking the experience that would have come with a few commissions to larger ships with senior lieutenants to show the way. Was he guilty of having mothered Holbrooke, of having controlled him too much?

So agitated had he become that he started pacing the quarterdeck, for'rard and aft, turning at the taffrail and the quarterdeck ladder. Hosking could see that he was distracted, could see the intensely thoughtful mask that had descended, and motioned the quartermaster and the midshipmen to move to the leeward side. Evidently, the captain was thinking of his pregnant wife left behind in Virginia. How wrong he was.

***

Up and down paced the captain. The bells struck, the watch was changed, and still he kept his lonely vigil. Over the past two years, Carlisle had come to think of himself as a born leader of men and a brilliant seaman. It was a private conceit that he'd shared with nobody, but the facts provided enough evidence to support the theory. He'd brought an old and under-gunned frigate and her people from the depths of peacetime ennui to a peak of fighting efficiency that had allowed him to beat a much larger French frigate into submission. That had been in the Mediterranean back in 'fifty-six. At the same time, he had, by his own efforts – so he told himself – saved his master's mate George Holbrooke from the otherwise inevitable ruination of his career. He'd nurtured and encouraged the boy and had seen him grow into one of the most notable young lieutenants of his day. He'd been given a new, more powerful frigate in which he'd taken prizes and won sea battles in the Caribbean. Young Holbrooke had prospered under his command and had been promoted and given a sloop. He was now somewhere in the North Sea blockading the French army's supply lines. In his mind, that was all Carlisle's doing. *Fury* and *Medina* would have been nothing without his leadership. Holbrooke and Jackson, his old coxswain, would have been unnoticed without his patronage. Those facts were the bedrock of his self-esteem, the fixed points that justified his view of his own brilliance. That was a very comforting thought, and yet he was starting to see the danger. Had he become addicted to the sort of detailed management that had protected Holbrooke from the consequences of his own inexperience? Would the master's mate have become a lieutenant and now a commander – probably the youngest in the navy – without his captain's protection?

In reality, of course, it had been eight months since he'd sailed with Holbrooke. In that time the young man had taken temporary command of *Medina* while Carlisle recovered from a wound, and he'd sailed for England in his sloop before Carlisle had resumed command. Holbrooke had fought Dutch pirates and French frigates without Carlisle's help, and he'd taken part in a significant squadron action off Cape François. Heaven alone knew what fresh adventures he was having off the German coast, but whatever it was, he was doing it alone.

Carlisle dissected his own motives and performance. Perhaps…just perhaps, he'd become too controlling. It had been a unique experience when he'd lost his old and experienced first lieutenant in *Fury* and in a moment of serendipity had asked for Holbrooke as a replacement. It had forced him into becoming more involved in the management of the ship, in matters that were properly the responsibility of the first lieutenant. Yes, he acknowledged, that was probably the case, but what else could he have done? The ship had to be run, the men had to be led, and there was a war to be fought. He felt justified in filling the void that would otherwise have opened with a raw, untested second-in-command.

Carlisle paused in his pacing. The inspection of the guns had ended an hour ago. The watch had changed and now there was a master's mate on the quarterdeck, a painfully shy young man who probably hadn't even started shaving. And yet the business of the ship went on. The lookouts were changed, he could see Nathaniel Whittle climbing the main shrouds now, apparently looking forward to his thirty minutes perched on the main topmast crosstree. The log was being cast, the quartermaster was watching the luffs and the compass, and the steersmen were moving the spokes of the wheel through their fingers in response to the regular thrust of the waves on the frigate's quarter. All this was going on without his intervention, and that was as it should be. He wouldn't have dreamed of interfering in these minute-by-minute tasks that kept a King's ship at sea. Why, then, did he feel the need to supervise his second-in-command so closely?

By long-standing seagoing tradition, the internal workings of the ship were the first lieutenant's responsibility, and now that he thought about it, it wasn't just a tradition, it was codified in his own printed orders. The first lieutenant effectively presented the ship as an efficient fighting machine so that its captain could use it to fulfil the tasks that his admiral or the Admiralty gave him. It was a sensible demarcation that allowed the captain of a man-of-war to concentrate on his mission, secure in the knowledge that his ship and its people would step up to the mark when he called. He'd been guilty of pushing the boundary of his responsibility down, squeezing his first lieutenant's room for initiative. That, he now realised, was a consequence of having such an inexperienced second-in-command for so long.

Carlisle thought again about Holbrooke, but that was history. They would never serve together again; there was room for only one captain in a ship and Holbrooke would surely be posted in the next year. Posted or found wanting and put on the beach, to languish on half pay for the rest of his days. Was that likely? Carlisle realised with a start that he knew nothing of how Holbrooke had reacted to the demands of command. Had he cast off his dependence on Carlisle? Presumably so, otherwise his few months in command of *Medina* would have been a conspicuous disaster, and that didn't appear to have been the case. Certainly, Commodore Forrest thought well of him and had recommended his promotion to the commander-in-chief at Jamaica. Of course, he could ask Hosking, but it wasn't really a fit subject for discussion between a post-captain and a sailing master. If not Hosking, then the only other person he could ask was his former chaplain, David Chalmers, but Chalmers had chosen to sail with Holbrooke and was three thousand miles away in the North Sea.

Pondering on Holbrooke was an unprofitable use of his time. It was his present first lieutenant who deserved his attention. It was starting to dawn on Carlisle that he may have done Moxon a disservice by treating him in the same way that he'd treated Holbrooke. Moxon had been a junior lieutenant in ships-of-the-line for several years, and his commission as first of *Medina* must have been the answer to his prayers. Here he could be noticed, and he was only one heartbeat away from the command of a twenty-eight-gun frigate! Carlisle could only imagine his disappointment when he found that his captain hovered over him and monitored everything that he did. Carlisle examined his actions over the last four months. Yes, he'd certainly stifled Moxon's initiative, reminding him of every action that he should be taking, just as though he was as inexperienced as Holbrooke had been. And worse, Carlisle had started to believe that Moxon lacked the skills that were needed to maintain *Medina* as an efficient weapon of war. And that, thought Carlisle, was unforgivable.

***

Carlisle paused his walking and gazed astern at *Shark*, now becoming an indistinct lighter patch in the gathering darkness. *Medina's* top light had been lit at some time while he was pacing the quarterdeck. He hadn't even noticed the shielded flame being carried into the top, nor the inevitable sequence of orders that would have set it in motion. Proof, if it were needed, that the business of the ship carried on without his intervention as, of course, it should. The watch was being changed again, and here was Moxon himself, taking the last dog watch to give the regular watchkeepers a break. He watched his first lieutenant covertly. He didn't know what he was expecting, some sort of disrespectful demeanour being shown by his subordinates perhaps, something to validate the private impression that Carlisle had not yet managed to shake off. But nothing of the sort was evident. He seemed to have a relaxed relationship with the off-going master's mate, the man who was most likely to challenge his first lieutenant, relaxed but respectful. The master's mate even removed his hat when Moxon approached him, an unnecessary formality in a frigate. Was it done only because Carlisle was on the deck? No, he could see that there was no ambiguity in the relative status of first lieutenant and master's mate; the younger man was positively deferential to his senior. It may well have been otherwise; he was the senior of the two master's mates in *Medina's* establishment and a candidate for a lieutenancy. He wasn't planning to try for a master's warrant, so only an examination and a commission separated him from Moxon, and of course the years of seniority that the first lieutenant had accumulated.

Yes, now that he bothered to study Moxon, he realised that his experience was matched by his natural authority. Enrico Angelini was keeping the watch with the first lieutenant, and he clearly hung on his every word. Carlisle could even see that the midshipman studiously copied Moxon's actions; he held his hands behind his back in just the same way, and he mimicked the way that Moxon looked from the luff of the mainsail to the binnacle and then walked to windward to see how the jib was drawing. All the sort of things that he'd expect when a first lieutenant was properly respected. Why had he not noticed it before? He was certain that the junior officers and the people hadn't treated Moxon with respect when he'd joined in Port Royal.

Carlisle cast back through the incidents of the cruise. Yes, that was it, the engagement with the French frigate, that was the point where Moxon earned the respect that he now enjoyed. And it had happened quickly, in a matter of days.

Was he, the captain, the last person in the frigate to acknowledge Moxon's qualities? It appeared so. Hard self-analysis suggested that he'd failed to adjust his own leadership style for this new relationship, but why hadn't he noticed this error before? The answer came slowly and reluctantly. In the first days after they sailed from Port Royal, he'd been preoccupied with his wife's comfort, and then, when she'd revealed that she was expecting their child, he'd been consumed with worry about where she should be landed. That concern for his wife had prevented him from considering the integration of his new first lieutenant into the frigates command structure. That and his regret at parting with his friend Holbrooke. He'd been deficient in a fundamental task of command, he now knew.

***

'It all seems quiet, Mister Moxon. Would you join me in my cabin? I believe Mister Angelini can keep the watch for a glass or two.'

'With pleasure, sir,' Moxon replied, removing his hat, then turning to give a few instructions to the midshipman.

Now *there* was another benefit of delegation. Carlisle could see the pleasure on Enrico's face. As it happened, this was the first time that his wife's cousin had been trusted with a night watch alone, and he evidently relished the opportunity.

While his servant fussed around offering drinks, Carlisle sought to put Moxon at his ease. It was odd, now that he thought about it, that he hadn't really had the opportunity get to know his second-in-command. Yet another proof of the disadvantages of bringing a wife to sea.

'Mister Angelini appears to be progressing well,' he said as a way of opening the conversation.

'Yes, sir, he is. He still struggles a little with the language, but the men understand him well enough, and his seamanship is improving.'

'I have the impression that he was a little startled by the amount of professional knowledge that's required of a midshipman in the Navy.'

'In contrast to that required of an ensign in the Sardinian army,' Moxon replied, smiling. 'Yes, although I haven't heard him complain, he appears to positively enjoy accumulating knowledge. In other circumstances, I'd say he'd be ready for the examination in a year or so…'

Carlisle nodded. There was an air of unreality to Enrico's service in Medina. All midshipman strove for a commission – it was the whole point of the rank – but Enrico had perforce to find other motivation. In fairness, nobody could question his zeal, it was just where it was all leading.

'I regret, Mister Moxon,' said Carlisle when they were both seated with drinks, and his servant had withdrawn, 'that I haven't had as much leisure as I would have liked to become acquainted with you.'

Moxon inclined his head in acknowledgement; there was no need to state the obvious reason. Moxon had joined the frigate just days before sailing, and both men were aware of the amount of Carlisle's time that had been taken up with his wife on the passage north.

'Indeed, I haven't really had the chance to acknowledge your conduct in the fight with the French frigate, but I hope you'll accept my thanks even if I'm a few days late. I have, of course, mentioned you in my letter to their Lordships. It's the last letter that I'll send to them as we come under Mister Hardy at Halifax, or Mister Boscawen if we meet him first.'

'Thank you, sir, it was no more than my duty, but I appreciate your good word. Promotions are becoming tighter as the first rush of new ships slows down and, well you know…' replied Moxon, spreading his hands in the universal and eloquent gesture of acknowledgement that nothing is certain in life, except death and taxes.

'You deserve it, Mister Moxon, and I hope I'll have other opportunities to acknowledge your value. However, here we are just days away from joining the fleet, and I hope you'll be able to give me an impression of the frigate's readiness for what will be a hard few months.'

'Perhaps I can bring the latest statements from the warrant officers, sir,' replied Moxon, rising to leave.

'No, no, I've seen those. It's your personal thoughts that I'm interested in. You're much closer to the people than I am, and command opens a gap between the cabin and the wardroom, let alone the mess-decks. I'm asking for your own thoughts.'

Moxon looked slightly uneasy, as well he might, having become accustomed to his captain's aloofness. He was used to being ignored or at best viewed with disfavour. He was a philosophical soul, and all his experience taught him that he should expect nothing better from the god-like entity that inhabited the great cabin.

'Well, sir, the carpenter has put the damage to rights now and our second suit of sails is drawing well. The bosun has finished repairing the rigging and just needs to refresh the gammoning when it's light tomorrow.'

He thought for a moment.

'I won't be quite happy with our spare sails even when the sailmaker has finished patching them. Too many are shot through in the boltropes. I hope we can obtain a new suit in Halifax.'

'We can certainly try,' replied Carlisle. 'They've been maintaining a substantial squadron over the winter, so perhaps they'll have built up a reserve of sails.'

'As for the men, sir, the old *Medinas* are, of course, the

backbone. The new men that we had in Port Royal are well on the way to becoming useful seamen, those with previous service of course. Only the sixteen that we took as landsman volunteers are still a problem, they've formed a clique and I believe they'll jump ship at the first opportunity.'

'Really?' Carlisle was only marginally surprised, although this was the first that he'd heard of any disaffection. It was commonplace for men abandoned by their employers in Jamaica to sign on for a voyage home, and to desert at the first attractive port.

'It's not a serious problem yet. The master-at-arms watched them with great care in Hampton and Boston, the most likely place for desertion, but they'll have more opportunity to run in Halifax. Although where they'd run to in that howling wasteland, I don't know.'

'Do they mess together?' asked Carlisle.

'They did, in numbers seven and nine messes, but I've had them broken up and spread amongst the regular sailors.'

They spoke of the ship, the people, the stores, the training, the guns and all the myriad of subjects that kept first lieutenants awake at night. It was eight bells when they had finished, and it was Midshipman Angelini, knocking on the cabin door to report the change of the watch to the first lieutenant, that broke up the discussion.

***

When Moxon left, Carlisle sat long into the night reflecting on the errors of judgement that had brought him to this turning point in his relationship with his first lieutenant. He'd caught himself just in time, he realised. Another few weeks and the vaguely hostile – no, not hostile, just distant – relationship would have become settled, endangering the effectiveness of Carlisle's precious frigate to the detriment of the King's business.

***

CHAPTER TEN

Halifax

Sunday, Nineteenth of March 1758.
Medina, at Anchor. Halifax, Nova Scotia.

Neither Carlisle nor Hosking had previously been to Halifax but the pilot that brought them in was a naval sailing master, and an old friend of Hosking, quite a different character to the Boston pilot.

'I hope you're not too disappointed when you see the town, sir,' said the pilot conversationally as they passed through the narrows to the west of Cornwallis Island. 'It's not been here long, less than ten years, and we're a bit rustic still. Despite that, there's great energy here and I do believe we have a future in this province.'

Carlisle was surprised at the proprietorial tone of the pilot. He'd heard of sailing masters taking to pilotage, it was reasonably common as a means of eking out a warrant officer's superannuation, but most retired to small towns in England where the living was comfortable but without the cost of the big cities. This pilot had found one of the rare employment opportunities in the gift of the Navy Board.

'You sound as though you like the place,' replied Carlisle, looking at the thickly wooded shoreline dusted with snow, with just a hint of homely white cliffs opening to larboard.

'Your pardon sir,' he replied. 'A cast of the lead to starboard if you please Mister Hosking.'

'We're through the shallowest part now, sir, but there's a tricky turn here with a reef to larboard and a nasty shoal just off that little spit you can see to starboard.'

There was silence as the lead was cast. The light south-westerly breeze was just enough to waft *Medina* into the harbour, but Carlisle could see that the higher land concealed the risk of an awkward fluke in the wind, a squall even, and this part of the passage required all the pilot's attention.

'By the deep, fifteen,' called the leadsman.

The pilot nodded. 'We're right in the centre of the channel now,' he said. 'In just a mile I'll be asking you to come three points to starboard. You may have to veer,' he added, looking at the play of the wind on the main tops'l.

'Now, you remarked that I seem to like the place, sir. Well it's true, I do. The winters are hard and the summers short, but the air is clean, and I have a good position here. I started a family late, and my wife and youngsters are happy. The Navy Board pays me as a master of a third rate, but I don't have to spend years away from home like I would if I were employed as a regular sailing master.'

'You don't fear invasion then?' asked Carlisle.

'There's always a chance. The town was built as a counter to the Mi'kmaq and the Acadians, both in the pocket of the French, of course, but there's been no trouble for a few years now. No, I think we're here to stay, and if you good fighting folk can kick the French out of this continent, then there's a great future for us.'

'One step at a time,' Carlisle laughed, 'Louisbourg first and that's a tough enough nut to crack.'

'You can make that turn now, Mister Hosking,' the pilot said, taking a rough bearing of the north end of the island.

It really was quite eerie, thought Carlisle. With the wind nearly dead astern and the sea reduced to just the lightest of ripples, he could hear every word that was spoken on deck. Moxon was ordering another cast of the lead – a wise precaution regardless of the pilot's confidence – and the thuds, creaks and groans as the bosun prepared the starboard bower anchor for letting go were perfectly clear on the quarterdeck.

'Of course, Halifax is quite different from Boston. It still has the character of a frontier town. The gates are barred at night, and we keep a watch on the walls. They're still mostly wood and earth, but the gun positions are being built up with good solid masonry. We won't hold out against a regular siege, but nor will we be surprised by the natives, be they Mi'kmaq or Acadian.'

The sounds of the ship veering, the tacks and sheets being swapped and the great mizzen yard swinging over to larboard were unnaturally loud. Carlisle looked astern. He could still see the open sea, but it was evident that Halifax was in a sound defensive position. Any attacking fleet would have to negotiate this tricky passage. The pilot made it look easy but in truth it would test the finest navigator if he didn't know it well.

'There's George's Island,' said the pilot, pointing to a small, wooded obstruction in the harbour that blended so well with the shoreline to the north that it was almost indistinguishable. 'The soldiers are putting up a battery, nine-pounders, I believe. They've cleared the trees from the top of the island, and you can see the revetments going up.'

Carlisle looked through his telescope. There was a flag drooping lazily from a pole at the highest point of the island and all around it the bare earth showed. It must be hard work with the frost not yet gone, he thought.

'Now you can see our town, just opening around that headland,' said the pilot with evident pride.

Carlisle's expectations of Halifax had been low, so he was surprised by what he saw. A neat town had been laid out in a grid pattern. Most of the houses were of wood and were built one or two storeys high. Many had gambrel roofs, looking more like barns, but with windows and doors. At least one church spire was visible, and there was a big new hall with its own steeple. The whole was surrounded by a wooden stockade with bastions, and the ground was cleared for perhaps a quarter of a mile beyond the palisade. Carlisle nodded in approval.

The most cursory inspection showed that the business of the town was mostly conducted on the shoreline, where a jetty protruded into the bay. The anchorage was crowded with shipping, loading and unloading to lighters that jostled for space at the single jetty, or run up onto the shingle beach to be unloaded across the shallows. Even at this distance, the town had an urgent air of industry, as though with the easing of winter the inhabitants had set to with a will to make up lost time.

'You can't see the navy yard yet, it's outside the walls just to the north of the town,' said the pilot. 'Now if you'll pardon me for a moment, there's only three cables between the island and the town. It's deep water, thirteen fathoms or so, but the locals have no sense of right and wrong, and a boat could shoot under our bows at any moment.'

The pilot took some rapid bearings and ordered another point to starboard.

'All clear now, sir. If you look past the island, you can see the village further up the bay. Dartmouth they're calling it, and they're building a battery and stockade. It's really just to stop anyone taking up positions on that eastern shore.'

Carlisle looked through his telescope. Sure enough, there were some wooden houses there and the start of a palisade. It was an excellent location to dominate the northern end of the bay and would at least provide a deterrent on that side of the harbour.

'Just two miles to run now, sir,' said the pilot. 'Your number one seems to have it all under control.'

Carlisle looked for'rard to where Moxon was checking the anchor. It needed to be ready to be tripped, and yet there must be no chance of it being let go prematurely. His crew were behaving like real seamen; there was no chatter on the deck and as far as he could see everyone was attending to their business.

'If you look past the town now, sir, you'll see Lord Colville's squadron anchored off the navy yard. I suppose I should call it Admiral Hardy's squadron, as he arrived last week. There's still a frigate careened on the shore but otherwise they're all there.'

The tall masts had been in sight for a few minutes, but the full visual impact of a squadron of ships-of-the-line in this out-of-the-way place could only be appreciated as the ships themselves came into sight.

'Eight of the line. Nine if you count that old fifty-gunner, and two frigates. There are a few sloops and cutters, but they come and go. And there's Mister Hardy's flagship, *Captain*, a sixty-four.'

The sight of eleven men-of-war wasn't so impressive to sea-officers who'd seen the fleet at Spithead, or the squadrons at Antigua and Jamaica, but their presence here, in this bleak outpost of the British Empire was startling in the extreme. Carlisle had been raised in the colonies, so to a certain extent he was familiar with log cabins and makeshift settlements, although Williamsburg was a modern, sophisticated colonial capital with the facilities of a moderate-sized English town. Nevertheless, the juxtaposition of a frontier community clinging to the very edges of the civilised world, and a powerful squadron of line-of-battle ships, took his breath away. He could only guess at the superhuman efforts Colville had made to have these ships so trim and obviously ready for sea this early in the year.

'Your berth is two cables to the east of the flagship,' said the pilot.

Hosking looked meaningfully at Carlisle, who nodded in reply.

'Hands to furl the courses and fore stays'l,' called Hosking, 'brail the mizzen.' There was no need to shout in this stillness.

Medina ghosted towards her anchorage under fore and main tops'ls and jib. They were making no more than two knots, barely creeping forward over the ground against the ebbing tide.

'Mister Gordon, you may commence the salute as soon as the anchor is let go.'

'Aye-aye sir,' replied the master gunner. The smoke from the slow matches was barely dispersed by the light breeze and Gordon breathed deeply of the intoxicating smell. This is what he lived for.

'Hands to the tops'l yards, bosun,' said Hosking, watching the bearing of the flagship.

'What do you make of the tide, Pilot,' asked Carlisle.

'Just the start of the ebb, sir, no more than a knot, perhaps half a knot. There are fourteen fathoms at your berth, mostly good thick mud, and at this phase of the moon, the range is no more than eight feet. Just two cables to go now, sir.'

Hosking exchanged another meaningful glance with his captain. 'Furl the tops'ls, drop the jib,' he called to the bosun.

The bosun raised his call to his lips and blew the short sequence of notes. Nothing more was said, and as if by some sorcery, the tops'ls vanished from the yard and the jib was rushed hand-over-hand down to the jibboom. *Medina* moved slowly under bare poles to her designated berth.

'You'll want to make this perfect under the eyes of Sir Charles,' said the pilot. Carlisle certainly did, and he could see the admiral, his new commander, watching *Medina* from the flagship's quarterdeck.

'Rightly we should let her run on half a cable, but there's a little williwaw coming up the harbour, so I recommend we anchor now before it catches us and pushes our stern away. Nobody will notice that we're a few yards short.'

'Very well, you may anchor, Mister Hosking.'

'Let go!' shouted the master at the top of his voice. There was no value now in silence and a real danger that with all the other activity the group on the fo'c'sle might miss the order.

The anchor fell with a splash into the cold, dark water, dragging the cable behind it.

Bang! The first gun of the salute caught Carlisle unawares as usual, and at that moment the pilot's williwaw – a cold gust of wind funnelling down from the hills – caught the frigate's stern, driving the bows over the cable at the point where the anchor had descended into the mud at the bed of the harbour. Carlisle watched anxiously. Was it enough to drag the anchor?

'Give her forty-five fathoms, Mister Moxon, then hold her on the bits,' called Carlisle.

That should be enough scope to take up the shock of the williwaw. The frigate would certainly run further up the harbour than he'd intended, but she'd be held by the cable, and the tide would soon swing her so that she faced north along with the other anchored ships, as soon as the squall passed.

There was a slight jerk as *Medina* surged against her cable, and a series of creaks and scuffing sounds as her starboard bow overrode the cable. However, her port-lids on that side were closed, and no damage was done. By the time the thirteen guns had been fired, the wind had dropped, and the frigate was already drifting back onto her cable, her bows to the north. *Medina* appeared for all the world a regular part of Hardy's squadron, which of course, from the moment the last gun had been fired, she was.

***

'Welcome to Halifax, Captain Carlisle. Not quite the end of the known world, but we'll be going there shortly.'

Evidently, Sir Charles Hardy was in a good mood. He had every right to be, thought Carlisle. When he arrived in Halifax a week ago, he could have found a squadron rotted from neglect over a hard winter, with ships unready for sea and crews reduced by desertion and disease. In contrast, he was presented with a fighting force that, in the main, was ready to sail and eager to take part in this great endeavour.

'I see you've brought your reports, Captain, but just let me know your frigate's state in your own words.'

'Stored for eighty days, sir, wood and water for a month. She's sound and tight, but my sails were cut up by a French frigate a week ago. They're patched, and my spare sails are good, but I could do with a new suit if one's available. Ten seamen short on my establishment.'

'Well, there are no spare sails in Halifax, I regret, although we may be able to offer a few bolts of canvas.'

Hardy made no comment on the shortage of a few seamen, a deficiency of ten men was barely worth mentioning, and neither man had any illusions about picking up seamen in Halifax.

'I'm not short of canvas, sir, but some of my sails were shot through in the bolt-ropes. My sailmaker's done a good job, but they can't match regular loft-sewn sails.'

'Then I regret that you'll have to make do until the next storeship convoy reaches us. But of course, you'll be sailing long before then. You've seen the squadron,' Hardy said, waving a hand towards the great stern windows, 'Lord Colville insisted that all his captains lived on board right through the winter. I imagine they weren't too happy about it, but it forced them to look to the preservation of their ships, and you can see the result.'

How easy it would have been to use the Halifax yard's embryonic facilities as an excuse for a derelict squadron. Carlisle could appreciate the enormous efforts that Colville must have made through the long winter.

'Colville has already sent a sloop and a cutter to watch Louisbourg. As soon as they report that it's ice-free, I'll sail.'

Hardy looked out of the windows at the ice-rimmed harbour. It would be hard lying in a square-rigged ship off Île Royale while winter persisted.

'I have in mind that you should sail before that. I can give you two days to put yourself in order, but then you must be away. I'll wait for the next report from the sloop, it's *Hawke* I believe,' he said glancing at some papers on his desk to remind himself. 'Yes, *Hawke*, she's been out there two weeks now and must be feeling it. You must brave the ice as she has. I need a ship of your force to watch the French as soon as is humanly possible, a brig-sloop just won't do the job. Let's say Tuesday, and I pray that the weather will break soon.'

Amen, thought Carlisle.

***

CHAPTER ELEVEN

Île Royale

Thursday, Twenty-Third of March 1758.
Medina, at Sea. Off Louisbourg, Île Royale.

It had been a frustrating passage north and east. Just two hundred nautical miles of sea separated Halifax and Louisbourg, and with fair winds, *Medina* could easily have covered the distance in twenty-four hours. Fair winds, however, were hard to find. Instead headwinds, dead calms and a persistent heavy swell from the southeast had made a frustrating time of it, and the planned day's passage had taken more than two days.

Hosking had tried everything, including bringing the frigate dangerously close to the Nova Scotia coast, inside the Frenchman's Bank and the Middle Bank. Nevertheless, the sun was just not strong enough to create an evening land breeze, and the frigate rolled horribly in the swell that built up in the shallowing water. An anxious, moonlit night was spent when the boats were hurriedly manned to tow the frigate off the deadly rocks of Cape Liscomb. Carlisle watched helplessly from the fo'c'sle as the longboat and the yawl strained to pull *Medina's* head clear. The breaking swell made it almost impossible to keep time, and when one oar caught a crab, it put the whole bank of oars out and it was all the rowers could do to keep their seats.

It was Moxon in the longboat who saved the day, calling the timing with one eye on the sea and the other on the oarsmen, taking a long, deep pull whenever the swell permitted, first with the starboard oars, then with the larboard. Wishart in the yawl copied him, calling for a stroke whenever the swell permitted, with one eye always on the longboat. Slowly and painfully, the frigate's head was pulled around and dragged out to sea. With the morning, a breath of wind came from the northwest, a blessed relief that allowed *Medina* to set her sails and creep away from the dreadful, iron-bound coast.

***

'I stand humbled,' said a shaken Hosking, not caring who heard him. 'I brought the ship into danger, and it was only you, sir, you and Mister Wishart and those brave lads in the boats, who saved us,' he said to the exhausted first lieutenant when he climbed back on board.

The moon had dipped to the horizon, saving Moxon's blushes from being seen. He'd noticed a real change in his relationship with both Carlisle and Hosking since the fight with the French frigate, but he was not yet used to hearing compliments. In truth, he *was* pleased with himself. He knew that the boat coxswains, vastly experienced though they were, couldn't have achieved it alone. They were too steeped in the ways of the navy and would have persisted in merely thrashing the water to no good effect, demanding greater and greater efforts from the oarsmen. In a way, it was his relative inexperience that had allowed him to see a better way – the only way as it turned out – of managing the boats.

'Mister Moxon,' said Carlisle from the darkness behind the wheel, 'perhaps before you turn in, you'd ask the purser to serve out a measure of spirits to the boat crews. I believe we could break into the Jamaica rum on this occasion. And then they are to turn in.'

There was a ragged cheer from the boats as the news was passed down to them. *Medina* had been on beer since they left Williamsburg, and not very strong beer at that. The navy's policy was quite firm; beer was to be drunk for as long as it lasted, then whatever spirit was available could be issued – rum in the West Indies, Brandy off Spain or Portugal – or wine in the Mediterranean. For many of the crew, this was their first time out of the Caribbean for years, and they sorely missed their daily tot of rum.

***

Even the worst nightmares end, yet sometimes they are

just replaced by a different quality of nightmare. The ironbound coast of Nova Scotia was replaced by the biting cold and persistent fogs of Île Royale.

Carlisle stood immobile on the quarterdeck of *Medina*. He was bundled in layers of clothing: two wool waistcoats, an overcoat, a boat-cloak and a tarpaulin over all, with numerous mufflers and a thick pair of mittens. Yet still the cold seeped through. It appeared that there were two types of weather off Île Royale at this time of year: a howling, gale that whipped the sea into dangerously steep, curling waves, but with the advantage of crystal clear visibility; or light winds that allowed a thick fog to form, reducing visibility to less than the length of the ship. Either way, it was bitterly cold; of the two Carlisle would have preferred the howling gale for this introduction to Louisbourg. In heavy weather, he at least could see dangers – the surf on the rocky shore, the enemy sail – but in the sort of fog they were experiencing today, it was just blind man's bluff, not unlike his childhood games but with higher stakes.

'Mister Angelini,' he whispered, 'run aloft and tell that damned lookout that he's to cease stamping on the boards of the maintop immediately. If I hear him again, he'll be keeping his watch at the topmast head.'

Enrico disappeared for'rard into the fog. It was a genuine pea-souper, and the foremast couldn't be seen from the quarterdeck, just the shifting outline of the fore tops'l. Carlisle had ordered silence on the deck, not only so that he could hear any sounds from outside the ship – breakers, the creaking of an oar – but also so that no other vessel should hear *Medina*. Carlisle knew that the French, despite the weather, regularly ran supplies into Louisbourg, and it was to be assumed that with the first hints of spring – late though they were in this God-forsaken land – they would re-double their efforts. The failed expedition of last year had taught a painful lesson that had not been lost on the British planners. Admiral Hardy had confided his greatest fear; that a powerful French squadron and reinforcing regiments would make it into Louisbourg before a regular blockade could be mounted.

The British navy's problems were quite different to the French. Every sea-officer knew how difficult it was to maintain a blockading squadron for any length of time in even the most benign weather. Yet to maintain a tight blockade off Louisbourg, they had to keep a squadron on station through all weathers, week in, week out, exposed to the worst of winds from the north and the east.

Hardy's ships, when they all arrived, would carry over three thousand men. The dry provisions – salt beef and pork, bread and peas – weren't the problem, it was water and beer and, in this weather, firewood, that were the critical commodities. Men who came off watch wet and freezing must be able to get warm and dry. Otherwise, fevers set in. And men must have fresh food to supplement the dry, or else the dreaded scurvy took hold of a ship. In more benign conditions, a ship could be expected to stay disease free for six weeks, but off Île Royale before spring had broken the bonds of winter, four weeks could see a ship's company decimated.

That was why Hardy was holding his squadron back in Halifax. Nevertheless, he needed eyes and ears – and a ship that could fight – to watch the French fortress, because he knew that a fast run across the Atlantic for a few transports or frigates armed *en flute* was well within the capability of the French navy.

'Let's go below and have another look at the chart, Mister Hosking, it's a long time since we saw Cape Canso. What I'd give for a landfall now!'

Carlisle took one last hopeful look around the compass, but the fog was giving nothing away. If anything, it had thickened and now the fore tops'l was entirely hidden.

'Mister Moxon, you have the deck.'

The master had two charts, one covering the whole of the Nova Scotia coast and Île Royale, and another showing the detail of the harbour and fortress of Louisbourg. They were good charts, but what he really needed was a survey of the approaches to Louisbourg, preferably showing lines of soundings. Without that he was really groping blindly in this fog. The lead-line was of some use, giving them a general impression of their distance off the land, and they'd agreed that thirty fathoms should be their minimum while the wind was anywhere in the west. If the wind backed or veered into the east, then they would stand off and give themselves plenty of sea-room. Of course, they had no real idea of the currents this close to the land. It was well known that the Atlantic drift turned towards the east in these parts, and that was what brought the fog when it met the cold winds from the north, but its effect was weak and uncertain. Really, until the fog lifted, their best navigation aid was their ears. In these conditions, they should be able to hear breakers at a mile if there was no extraneous noise on the deck, but even then, a mile was dangerously close in the fog, and this easterly wind could have them on the rocks in no time.

'The last heave of the lead found no bottom at a hundred fathoms, sir,' said Hosking, 'we should be at least five miles clear of the land. Other than that, I can say that we're somewhere to the south and east of Louisbourg.'

'If the soundings on the chart are accurate,' Carlisle added, 'if there's not a stretch of deep water running right up to White Head.'

'Indeed, sir. I've only been here once before and had no time for surveying on that occasion, but the Halifax pilot was here in forty-five and has been here since, in the peace. He told me there's nothing more than thirty fathoms within five miles of the shore.'

'Hmph,' said Carlisle. He hadn't yet forgiven Hosking for running his ship dangerously close to Cape Liscomb. It was all very well the master toying with the safety of his frigate, but courts-martial had a habit of blaming the captain for the loss of his ship, while the master escaped with only his reputation damaged.

'The wind seems set in the east-nor'east,' continued

Hosking, 'what there is of it.'

They pored over the charts, committing the details to memory for the hundredth time. When the fog lifted – if it lifted – they both knew they would be able to determine their position by reference to the features of the land. With a bit of luck, the first thing they would see would be the tall lighthouse on the eastern side of the harbour, or the spires and towers of the hospital and the King's Bastion inside the fortress. If neither of those was visible, then the broad Gabarus Bay beyond White Point in the west was quite distinctive, as were the cliffs and coves running away to the east, towards the Gulf of St. Lawrence.

'Then we'll put her about and stand to the south. At this time of year, I expect any Frenchman to be riding the drift like our friend off the Capes. I hardly expect they'll take the northerly route. Perhaps five miles off Gabarus Bay would be about right; that should allow us to beat up to Louisbourg if the fog lifts.'

'Aye-aye sir,' replied Hosking rolling up his charts.

***

The morning watch wore on. The usual routines of the ship had been halted to reduce the noise on deck, and if it hadn't been for the biting cold, the *Medina's* would have been in a holiday spirit. Half of them were enjoying an unexpected make-and-mend, and the other half were looking forward to the same in the afternoon.

Carlisle was in his cabin, going over the books with the purser. It required all his concentration to follow the purser's smooth chatter and to determine where he should probe a little deeper; a cask of beef condemned here, was that properly surveyed by his officers? The sale of tobacco, did that figure look correct for his two hundred men? He realised that he'd never queried the amount. It wasn't unknown for pursers to sell tobacco ashore, in places where it fetched a better price than the victualling board's standard rate. That was all very well and typical of the way that pursers managed to balance their books and turn a profit from their business; all very well until the illicit trade left the ship short of tobacco. The men would stand for many impositions on their way of life, but the loss of tobacco or alcohol, when they knew the purser's tricks better than the captain did, could lead to real trouble.

Carlisle had just determined that he'd personally inspect the tobacco stocks when there was an urgent knock on the door, and Midshipman Angelini burst into the cabin. He saw the start of his captain's frown and had just enough sense to remove his hat, catch his breath and make something approaching a proper report.

'Mister Moxon's respects, sir. He can hear a vessel to windward. The hands are going to their quarters.'

Now that he wasn't concentrating on the tobacco issue book, Carlisle could hear the almost stealthy sounds of men moving about the ship. The first lieutenant must have passed the word to the watch below at the same time as he dispatched Enrico to alert the captain. That was sensible. If there was a ship that near to them, then they needed to be at quarters, but a beating drum would only reveal their presence, and the knocking down of bulkheads that was part of clearing for action was hardly any quieter. Having the hands at quarters allowed Carlisle to strike a blow – if that was needed – as soon as this strange ship came in sight.

'Thank you, Mister Angelini, you may tell Mister Moxon that I'll be on deck immediately.'

He was deliberately not rushing. The ship took its pace from the captain and he judged that the sound of a ship to windward would be heard at a much greater distance than it could possibly be seen. The stranger, with the wind blowing from her to *Medina,* would hear the frigate much later. He had time to adopt a measured pace.

Carlisle walked steadily out of his cabin. The crowd at his door had been kept back by the marine sentry; there were the crews for the four nine-pounders that shared his living space and a carpenter's mate, anticipating an order to clear for action, when he'd knock away the bulkheads to the cabin, leaving a clean sweep of deck for the upper deck batteries.

'Where away, Mister Moxon?'

'It's hard to tell, sir. It's definitely to windward, somewhere abaft the larboard beam.'

After the muted bustle of the crew moving to their stations, there was an unnatural stillness on the deck. Not a man stirred. There was just enough wind for the tops'ls to keep pressing the yards forward, and only the faintest creaking escaped from their junction with the tops of the masts. The men at the guns, those that he could see abaft the foremast, were all looking up at the quarterdeck, poised like statues. Moxon's order for silence had penetrated even the few landsmen that were left among the people.

'There it is, sir,' whispered Moxon, 'nearer the quarter than the beam.'

Carlisle had heard it, the same sort of sounds that *Medina* was making, only these were carried down on the wind to his waiting ears. He nodded in response.

'Mister Moxon, you may turn over the deck to the master. I need you to have the guns ready for instant action. They're not to be run out, that'll create too much noise, but everything else is to be at immediate readiness.'

'Aye-aye sir,' he replied and moved soundlessly down the quarterdeck ladder, quickly disappearing into the gloom.

'Do you hear it now, Mister Hosking?'

'Aye I do, sir, but it seems to me to be moving forward somewhat, as though she's under more sail than we are.'

Carlisle held up his hand again for silence. He stood still; his head cocked to one side to catch the sound. There it was, the sound of a bow-wave and the creaking of rigging. The master was probably correct; whatever it was appeared to be to seaward and moving south faster than *Medina*.

'Come up two points, Master, let's close and see what we've got.'

'Larboard broadside ready, sir,' said Moxon almost in his ear, 'we can run out in a trice as soon as you give the word.'

'Thank you, Mister Moxon. Nobody is to fire until I blow my whistle,' he said, holding the silver instrument in his left hand. 'Whatever's out there is neither going to nor coming from Louisbourg. My guess is she's either a Frenchman coming from the St. Lawrence, homeward bound, or we've made our rendezvous with *Hawke*.'

Moxon nodded. He knew that *Hawke* was on station and waiting to be relieved and he'd guessed that Carlisle was ordered to be the relief. It was slightly annoying that his captain hadn't confided his orders in his first lieutenant, but that was perfectly normal. Most captains preferred it that way.

With the wind only just abaft the beam, *Medina* was making more noise as the north-easterly swell slapped against her bow and sides. Carlisle knew that it was only a matter of moments before they were detected. By the increasing level of sound coming from the stranger, less than five cables were separating the two ships.

Was that a break in the fog bank? No, it was gone, just a shifting of the play of light. Carlisle peered eagerly to larboard. The fog was still impenetrable, a thick, moisture-laden blanket that blocked the sight and muffled the sounds, making it difficult to accurately determine the direction. There it was again. A definite break this time, a thinning of the fog. Now he could hear the clanking of a pump, the dull, monotonous sound of the iron cranks being turned. If a ship had been on station for some time and endured a few gales, then her caulked seams would have opened, and she'd have to pump, regardless of the need for stealth as she groped her way through the fog. Thank heaven *Medina* was a dry ship!

'I see him, sir,' said the quarter gunner, standing beside the larboard three-pounder, still speaking softly. 'Two points abaft the beam. Gone now, but I'd swear I saw a main yard.'

Not a schooner then, nor a cutter, but something bigger, brig or ship-rigged.

'How many decks?' asked Carlisle.

'Just one that I could see, sir.'

Carlisle spared a moment to look at the petty officer who had made the report. He wasn't looking at his captain; he was staring again to larboard, hoping for a second glimpse. Carlisle's inspection took less than two seconds, but what he saw reassured him. The man was probably right. There was a frigate out there to windward, or perhaps a sloop. It didn't help with identification. If it was a frigate then it was almost certainly French; there were no British fifth or sixth rates at sea to the north of Halifax except *Medina*. If it was a sloop, then it must be *Hawke*. She was a brig, and a brief glimpse of a main yard could easily be that of a brig-sloop.

Whatever it was, in a moment *Medina* would be visible from the stranger's deck, and Carlisle was determined to take the initiative.

'Run out the larboard guns, Mister Moxon,' he called in a low voice. No doubt the sound of the gun trucks would be heard and recognised, but there was nothing to be gained in announcing *Medina's* nationality by a loud shout in English.

***

Occasionally nature shows a sense of the theatrical that quite takes the breath away. Carlisle had suffered hurricanes at sea that left humanity humbled, he'd heard that the great falls at Niagara were a sight of almost unimaginable sublimity, but neither, he was sure, could match the dramatic way that the fog bank lifted, as though it were the curtain of a stage. One moment they were staring into an impermeable airborne soup, the next moment a gust of wind had blown it away to leeward leaving a watery sun illuminating their little patch of sea.

There, not two cables distant, was a two-masted brig, her guns run out and an ensign floating lazily at her gaff – a white ensign, St. George's cross with a union flag in the canton – in anticipation of coming under Rear Admiral Hardy's command.

Carlisle glanced at Moxon. The first lieutenant had seen it also, and he waved and smiled in acknowledgement. A white ensign and the unmistakable rig of a British brig-sloop. *Hawke* without a doubt.

'We're flying our ensign,' said Hosking, anticipating Carlisle's next thought. It was all very well *Medina* recognising *Hawke*, but it was entirely possible that they'd take the frigate for a Frenchman, and the sloop looked aggressive and determined, ready for a fight.

'Make the signal for the captain to come aboard,' said Carlisle to Midshipman Angelini.

'Mister Moxon, you may secure the guns.'

***

CHAPTER TWELVE

The Mission

Sunday, Twenty-Sixth of March 1758.
Medina, at Sea. Off Louisbourg, Île Royale.

Just a few hours after they had met, *Hawke* stretched away to the southwest, bound for Halifax and a relief from the constant watch over Louisbourg; *Medina* was alone on the Île Royale coast. The first part of Carlisle's orders told him to guard the most likely route for French reinforcements and supplies to reach the fortress, and that meant patrolling a line from Cape Breton to the northeast to Anse de la Cormorandière to the southwest. As patrol lines went, it was short, just fifteen nautical miles from cape to cape, and the harbour of Louisbourg lay right in the centre.

However, here off Île Royale, the weather determined everything. From the north and east came fog; from all other points of the compass came gales in a never-ending parade of misery, but always, always it was wet and cold. When sails had to be handed or reefed, when the lead had to be heaved, when the sheets and tacks had to be hauled, the men were left soaked by seawater, rain or fog. It didn't matter where the water came from: it was always cold.

***

'Well Doctor, what's the tally today?' asked Carlisle, trying to disguise his own fatigue.

Carlton came daily to update Carlisle on the physical condition of *Medina's* people. Usually, there was not much to say. Once clear of the land and while fresh provisions lasted, there was little sickness in a well-ordered man-of-war. Off Île Royale in March, however, the story was bound to be different. Carlton held a written report, but he didn't need to refer to it.

'I've a full sickbay, sir, and I've had to turn away a few

who shouldn't rightly be back on the gundeck. Apart from the one broken arm who I'll discharge to light duties tomorrow, the others all have fevers.'

'Caused by the cold and wet, I imagine, Doctor?'

'Yes, there are no putrid fevers, not yet, but a few more weeks in these conditions and I can't say that they'll be unexpected.'

'No sign of scurvy, then?'

It was far too early for that dread disease, as Carlisle well knew, but then he'd never captained a ship in these waters.

'No, but you know that these conditions will bring it on quickly,' replied Carlton.

'You're persuaded that it's a disease of the environment?'

'Not exactly, sir, there are many factors: putrefying food in the gut, bad water, hard labour and this mortal damp and cold. It stops the men sweating, that's why a turn before the galley fire is so useful.'

'I'd heard that an experiment was carried out in the last war, and it partly pointed to the diet as being the cause.'

'Certainly. I have a copy of Doctor Lind's *A Treatise of the Scurvy*. He conducted a systematic inquiry, an experiment if you like, when he was the surgeon in *Salisbury*, in the Channel Fleet. It must have been eleven years ago now. The problem was that his conclusions merely suggested that the normal hazards of a sailor's life tended to breed scurvy, and many more sicknesses besides. We already knew that. He suggested that oranges and lemons can relieve the disease, and he may be right. We rarely see it in the Mediterranean, even in winter, or the Caribbean. Oranges and lemons are plentiful in those places, but then the weather is much better than the Atlantic, and the cruises are generally shorter. It's difficult to isolate the various factors.'

Carlisle pondered this for a moment.

'What more can we do? I dread the ship being struck with disease; men dying as fast as sheep with the rot, and nothing that can be done about it once it takes hold.'

'A facetious man would answer that it was necessary to

return to Halifax before another week has passed…'

Carlisle looked at the doctor sharply.

'…however, in practical terms,' the doctor continued quickly, checking off the points on his fingers, 'first, we must keep the galley fire burning day and night and have the petty officers check that the men dry their clothes, then I'll purge any man whose bowels haven't moved in a day; that includes the officers.'

Carlisle nodded in agreement.

'Then we should ensure that the men most exposed to the elements, the steersmen, the topmen, the leadsmen, and so on, are relieved every glass…'

'I've already given orders to that effect,' Carlisle interrupted.

'… and of course, we must look to our water. Is there any chance of refilling while we're on station?'

'None, I regret, or at least none that I know of. Our beer should last another two weeks and then we have at least two months of water. I asked Admiral Hardy to carry beer and water for us when he brings the squadron north, and I reinforced that in a letter that I sent back with *Hawke*. He should be here within a week or two, and let's hope for some fine weather to transfer the water.'

'Then we are doing all we can, sir,' said Carlton, 'and the rest is in the hands of the Almighty,' he added piously.

***

The great cabin was crowded, with Carlisle and all the frigate's principal officers gathered around the small table. They knew that this meeting was out of the ordinary. Not that a gathering of the ship's officers was unusual, but they could see the captain's servant guarding a brace of the best bottles of Madeira, corked and ready to be poured. They each took a glass and held themselves as steady as possible against the unruly motion of the frigate as the thick, reddish-brown liquid was poured. None had yet guessed the cause of this celebration – for celebration it must be – but one of the wardroom legends about Captain Carlisle was his jealous

119

hoarding of the fine Madeira wine that he'd bought when *Medina* called at the island eighteen months before. In all other things, Carlisle was open-handed. He regularly produced sherry, claret and port when his officers visited him in his cabin, but rarely ever the precious Madeira.

'Gentlemen,' Carlisle began once all the glasses were charged, 'today is an important day for me. It's the first anniversary of my marriage to Lady Chiara!'

His officers all looked from one to the other. Only his clerk looked smug. Simmonds knew – of course he knew – but he'd long ago learned that information was power, and it was not to be lightly given away. He'd seen no profit in telling the other officers and had held the secret close. He'd been present at the occasion in the church of St. John in Antigua, as had Hosking and some of the other warrant officers, but it was Simmonds' job to remember the captain's affairs and, in fact, it had been he who'd reminded Carlisle of the anniversary.

'Please join me in toasting Lady Chiara,' Carlisle said. He looked around his assembled officers, seeing the smiles of pleasure, and solemnly sipped from his glass. First Moxon, then the rest followed their captain's lead.

'I remember it well,' said Hosking. 'A beautiful day in a beautiful place. It seems like a different world from here.'

There were reminiscences and anecdotes from those who had been there, the old *Medinas*, the first commission officers. It came as a shock to Carlisle to see how few they were. Only half of the men around him had brought the frigate to the Leeward Islands, and it was not much more than a year ago.

'Fill them up again, Walker,' he said to his servant.

'May I, sir?' asked Moxon.

Carlisle inclined his head in agreement; Moxon evidently had something to say.

'A toast, gentlemen,' he said, turning to the other officers, 'to Captain Carlisle and His Majesty's frigate *Medina!*'

This second toast was quite rightly thrown back in one, they all knew the protocol, and Walker could be seen securing the bottles. There was perhaps a glass left for the captain's supper.

When the lively chatter had died down, Carlisle rapped his knuckles on the table.

'I didn't ask you all here, gentlemen, just to toast Lady Chiara, much less to toast myself and the ship. There's more important business. Mister Hosking, would you unroll the chart?'

It was a chart of Île Royale with a detailed plan of Louisbourg and the harbour in the top left corner; it lacked only soundings. Apparently, all the charts made during the brief British ownership of Louisbourg at the end of the last war had been drawn from surveys by soldiers, army engineers mostly, and they hadn't concerned themselves with nautical matters.

'We're all becoming familiar with the area to seaward of Louisbourg. The captain has asked me to point out the features closer inshore.'

Hosking was a good subordinate; he was letting nothing slip about the mission, that was for his captain.

'The area we're interested in starts in the northeast, here at Cape Breton. It's a rocky coastline for six or seven miles with nothing but a few fishing villages. I draw your attention to these two, the larger and smaller Lorraine, and this one, Baleine.'

He indicated the rocky inlets where the tiny communities sheltered from the Atlantic storms.

'Then we come to the entrance to Louisbourg. You've all heard about its famous lighthouse on the north side of the passage. Well, what you won't have seen, because we haven't been close enough, is the three islands that guard the entrance. The passage is between this one here, Battery Island, and Lighthouse Point, and it's less than a mile wide. There are gun emplacements on either side, so it's a perilous undertaking to enter there!'

Carlisle nodded. 'That's not our business today, gentlemen.'

'Now here, to the southwest of the entrance, you can see the fortress.'

They all crowded around.

'If you'll excuse me, Mister Hosking,' said Carlisle, as he took over the briefing.

'The important point about the fortress, as far as we're concerned, is that the guns are mostly sited to cover the western approach to Louisbourg across this plateau,' he said, pointing to the apparently desolate area of stones and scrub that lay at the landward side of the fortress. 'The face of the fortress that looks south and east to the Atlantic is only covered by secondary batteries. The reason's obvious, it would hardly be possible to land a force on that rocky coast immediately below the walls.'

Carlisle paused to collect his thoughts.

'The French defend the entrance to the harbour with the batteries at Lighthouse Point and Battery Island. Then there are guns to cover the anchorages; Grave Battery on the edge of the fortress and Grand Battery, on the north shore. When they can, they anchor a squadron of men-of-war under the eastern walls. That's what they did in '57, and it's to prevent that happening again that Hardy's squadron is sailing so early in the year.'

He nodded to Hosking to proceed.

'As luck would have it, Louisbourg is neatly in the centre of our area between Cape Breton and *Anse de la Cormorandière*, or Cormorant Cove as we call it. Now we'll turn our attention to the southwestern part.'

From his vantage position, Carlisle was well placed to watch the officers' reactions. He hadn't invited the carpenter or the purser; they would have added nothing to the gathering and would have taken nothing useful away. Carlton was there, the ever-inquisitive doctor, interested in everything and taking nothing at face value. The two master's mates, Wishart and Gilbert, were there also because one way or another he had important roles for them. Carlisle had paused before inviting Enrico. He was nothing more than a midshipman, and a relatively inexperienced one at that, and if he invited him then he should in fairness have included all the young gentlemen in the invitation. It was Enrico's knowledge of soldiering that had swung the argument. *Medina* still had no marine officer even though the new sixth rate establishment included one and Enrico, as a sometime ensign in his Sicilian Majesty's army, had at least some claim to an understanding of military matters.

The bosun and the gunner were showing polite interest, but neither man really believed that they had anything to do besides their specialist tasks. The two master's mates were on the edge of their seats, wishing with all their hearts that whatever plan was to be unfolded, they would play a part. Enrico showed the studied disinterest of the Sardinian nobility, though Carlisle knew him well enough to know that it was just a front. He yearned for the recognition that would come from a successful action in which he had a leading role, just as much as Wishart and Gilbert.

'The shore continues rocky right past the fortress. There's a promontory here, White Point, and then the coast runs away westward into Gabarus Bay. We'll discount the western end of the bay; as far as we're concerned our interest ends here, at Cormorant Cove.'

They could all see the deep gulf that pushed westward into the land, and the chart seemed to show that the shoreline was less rocky than that to the north of the harbour.

'Thank you, Mister Hosking. Now, if I may?'

Hosking took a step back, checking that the chart was securely anchored to the table. All his charts were stored in a roll, and without being forcibly restrained, they'd recoil immediately.

'This is the area we're interested in,' Carlisle said, pointing to the northeastern shore of Gabarus Bay, 'from White Point in the east to Cormorant Cove in the west. Flat

Point breaks the area naturally into two.'

'Isn't that where the New Englanders landed in forty-five?' asked Carlton, 'at Cormorant Cove?'

'They did, Mister Carlton. In the western part of our area. I call it *our area* because, as you may have already guessed,' he said looking at his officers, 'we have a specific directive to determine the state of the French defences to the west of Louisbourg as far as the limit of Cormorant Cove. That's the second part of my orders'

The faces around the table were more sober now. They all understood the weather patterns off Louisbourg: if the wind was in the east, they had fog and a dangerous lee shore; if it was in the west or almost any other point of the compass, they would often have hard gales. Neither offered hope of an easy task in the close confines of Gabarus Bay.

It was the gunner who spoke first.

'That sounds like a tall order this side of summer, sir.'

'It would be, Mister Gordon, it certainly would be, if I had any intention of taking *Medina* into Gabarus Bay. This will be a boat operation.'

What Carlisle didn't say was that he was perfectly prepared to take *Medina* inshore to carry out soundings if that became necessary.

He could see serious faces now. He'd already briefed Moxon and Hosking, so they were impassive, but his warrant officers looked grave indeed. They could see the danger inherent in this enterprise. The fog and the gales would be just as bad for the boats as they would for the frigate. Worse, in fact. Wishart and Gilbert, in contrast, looked keenly interested. They had missed the first flush of promotions at the start of this new war, and until recently they'd both been so obviously less than twenty years of age that it would have stretched the patience of the board to present them with forged credentials. Their best chance now was to distinguish themselves in some desperate enterprise that relied upon their own initiative. This scheme of the captain's had definite potential.

'This evening, the longboat and the yawl will proceed in company to coast along the shoreline looking for signs of defences.'

'Will they be able to see anything, it being dark?' asked the bosun.

'Don't concern yourself on that score, Mister Swinton. There was never a soldier yet who didn't light a fire on a cold evening. There are acres of fuel in those scrubby hills, and any post will be shown up by a roaring blaze. What do you say, Mister Angelini?'

Enrico looked startled to be addressed and for a moment, Carlisle regretted involving him. His grasp of spoken English was still not perfect, and it was entirely possible that he hadn't understood a word of the briefing. Carlisle breathed a sigh of relief when his young cousin replied confidently.

'Certainly, sir. Any soldier on that bare hillside will be brewing coffee and drinking his wine around a campfire. Even in Sardinia, which is just a little warmer than this…'

That raised a laugh of sympathy.

'…even in Sardinia, there would be fires.'

'And soldiers are the same the world over,' added Carlisle. 'There's one other task for the boats. I want to know how far offshore the six-fathom line lies. There's no question of a proper survey, not in the dark with no points to take bearings from, but it should be possible to estimate the distance offshore to the nearest cable.'

The significance of six fathoms was evident to all; it was a safe anchoring depth for a frigate. If naval bombardment was needed to support an opposed landing, then the closer they could get, the better, and an anchored ship with a spring to the cable was a far more stable platform for gunnery than a ship underway.

'I have some ideas for a more detailed survey if we get the weather. That'll be your responsibility, Master.'

Hosking nodded. It would be interesting to hear how Carlisle thought that an accurate survey could be made within the range of enemy guns.

'Now Mister Hosking, what do you think of the weather for this evening?'

Hosking was prepared for the question. Carlisle had been merciless in interrogating him about his weather forecast. He'd have liked to respond with a Gallic shrug of the shoulders, but he knew that wouldn't do.

'It's nor'westerly now, sir, blowing a moderate gale. At some point the wind will veer into the east and drop, then we'll have the fog. But my guess is that won't happen until later in the night. For the last dog and the first, I reckon we may have a northerly tops'l breeze.'

'That will do for us. We'll launch the boats here, a mile or so south of White Point, as soon as it gets dark.'

He looked questioningly at Hosking.

'Sunset's at six twenty, sir, twilight at seven twenty-six.'

'And the moon, master?'

'It's two days after the full, sir. It'll rise just after eight, and it'll set at six bells in the morning. I doubt whether we'll see it though, not with this cloud.'

'Then we'll stand in with the last of the twilight and launch before moonrise, at half-past seven.'

Carlisle studied the faces of his officers again. The warrant officers knew that it would be most unusual for them to be sent on an expedition such as this. The carpenter and the gunner, as standing officers, were far too valuable for the long-term maintenance of the ship. The master and the doctor were equally irreplaceable in the short term. That left the first lieutenant, who already knew the plan, two master's mates and a Sardinian midshipman.

Carlisle didn't intend that Enrico should be sent on the expedition. For one thing, he wasn't at all sure of the status of Sardinia: was King Charles Emanuel still neutral, or had he sided with King Louis? Anything could have happened, and here in the Americas, they wouldn't know for months. For another thing, Enrico was Chiara's first cousin, and Carlisle dreaded having to tell his wife that the young man had been killed, wounded or captured. He'd decided that Enrico would fill the place of a master's mate on the quarterdeck, while Wishart and Gilbert went in the boats. Yes, he'd decided. Then he glanced at his cousin and saw the look of longing in his face. Just for a few moments, the aristocratic mask had slipped, revealing the young man thirsting for adventure; for adventure and for recognition.

'Mister Moxon, would you do me the honour of commanding the expedition?'

'With pleasure, sir,' the first lieutenant replied in what was the closest thing to a rehearsed speech.

'Mister Gilbert, you'll command the yawl and Mister Wishart, you'll second Mister Gilbert.'

Both attempted to look like seasoned stoics, but their beaming faces betrayed them. They were good friends and Gilbert was only a matter of months senior to Wishart, but those few months meant that one commanded and one seconded, an immutable law of the sea.

'Mister Angelini,' he let the uncompleted sentence hang for a few seconds as he studied the young man whose face was set in an aspect of false indifference; a defence mechanism as Carlisle knew well. 'Mister Angelini, you'll second Mister Moxon in the longboat.'

And may God have mercy on my soul if this should all go wrong, thought Carlisle, because my wife certainly won't.

***

CHAPTER THIRTEEN

Gabarus Bay

Sunday, Twenty-Sixth of March 1758.
Medina, at Sea. Off White Point, Île Royale.

The muted bell struck three, half an hour before the end of the last dogwatch and the beginning of the first. The clear weather that the nor'easterly wind brought had extended the period of twilight, and *Medina* had loitered off the coast, not out of sight, but perhaps out of mind until the last afterglow of the setting sun had been consumed by the darkness. The moon hadn't yet risen; for a blessed hour the world was in darkness. It was unlikely that watchers on the shore could see *Medina* under her fore-and-aft sails, let alone the two boats, so low in the water.

'Bring her to, Mister Hosking. Bosun, haul those boats alongside,' said Carlisle in a quiet voice. There was really no need for silence a mile off a windward shore in a two-reef tops'l breeze, but boat operations at night had that effect upon people, Carlisle had noticed. He remembered another dark night when he'd sent boats inshore; at Toulon where his first lieutenant John Keltie had commanded. But Keltie was dead, shot down by a French marksman as he cut away the enemy frigate's colours and he'd been launched over the gunwale into eternity in five hundred fathoms to the east of the Bonifacio Straits. Carlisle shivered at the memory. Then he remembered Holbrooke, who'd commanded the boat at Fort St. Philip in Minorca, and he'd prospered and had been promoted and given the command of a fine ship-rigged sloop. He still missed his friend Holbrooke, but less keenly now that Moxon was growing into the job.

Medina bucked and rolled to the stiff nor'easterly wind. In the lee of the land, the sea was moderate, but the backed jib caught enough of the near gale to make working on deck uncomfortable.

'Longboat's alongside the fore chains, sir,' reported Hosking.

'Very well. Mister Moxon, you may begin embarking your crew.'

'Yawl's alongside the main chains now, sir, just hooking on.'

'Mister Gilbert are you ready?' asked Carlisle. There was no discipline to be lost in a last fussy question to a young master's mate, nothing lost and perhaps a little gained in a slight increase in the bonds between a captain and one of his followers.

The two boats pulled away from the ship's side into the darkness. The wind was fierce, and rowing was difficult, but it would get easier as they neared the shore, and it wasn't worth the risk to show any canvas at this point. If soldiers on the land had seen the frigate – and that was unlikely – they would almost certainly not have seen the low boats moving towards the shore. They'd be in ignorance of *Medina's* intentions.

'Bring her onto the wind, Mister Hosking. Larboard tack, and we'll beat up to the harbour mouth.'

***

It was simple enough to keep station by the light of the gibbous moon, and sure enough, as the boats neared the shore, the waves decreased so that the oarsmen found their task more manageable. Moxon and Enrico sat in the stern sheets of the longboat, jammed into the confined space with the captain's coxswain. Looking for'rard between the two rows or oarsmen they could see the corporal and the marine, carefully shielding their muskets with tarpaulin sheets against the spray that burst over the bows every few seconds.

'Bring her two points to starboard, Souter,' said Moxon to the coxswain. 'Do you see the low cliffs on our starboard bow? I want to be two cables off there before we turn to larboard.'

It was no use talking compass points to the coxswain.

They had no compass in the boat, and even if they did, they wouldn't have dared to illuminate it.

Enrico was guarding a slate under his cloak to record the positions of lights on the shore. To act as a defence against the rain and spray, the carpenter had secured a flap of stout canvas to the top edge using copper rivets, the same that he used to fasten the strakes of a clinker-built boat. The carpenter, unfortunately, hadn't been quite as clever as he'd thought and one of the holes that he'd bored in the slate had been too near the edge and had broken through. Enrico was very conscious that the success of his part of the mission depended to a great extent on keeping the slate dry, so the slate came under the cloak, regardless of the discomfort.

'Bring her to larboard now, Souter. You see that next point, about a mile away?' he pointed just for'rard of the beam. 'That's Flat Point. There's a rock just a cable or so offshore, and it'll be only just visible, so keep us three or four cables off.'

'Aye-aye sir,' the coxswain replied, pushing the tiller away from him so that the longboat would come to larboard in a gentle arc. It did no good to knock the oarsmen off their stroke by making violent turns when they weren't necessary.

The longboat turned west on a parallel course to the coastline. It was almost entirely dark now, and if there were anything to be seen, any campfires betraying the positions of batteries and defensive positions, they would soon be visible.

'Mark seven,' called the leadsman softly, abbreviating the usual report. The splash of the lead hitting the water had been lost in the other sea-sounds, and Moxon had forgotten that he'd ordered the lead to be cast as soon as they left *Medina*. The leadsman had been keeping the reports to himself until he found seven fathoms with the red rag, between the black leather at ten fathoms and the white rag at five, as Moxon had ordered. It sounded simple, watching for the flash as the white cloth slipped through the fingers and knowing that the next marker – invisible in the dark but easily detected by the fingers – meant seven fathoms; Moxon knew it wasn't.

'Edge inshore coxswain,' said Moxon, 'I want to find the six-fathom line. How far off would you say we are?'

'Not more than six cables, sir,' said Souter, 'maybe five.'

It was deeper here than Moxon had expected. Six fathoms offered a good holding depth for a frigate or even a small two-decker, a fifty or sixty-gun ship, and that put the shore batteries within a comfortable range.

'Deep six.' The leadsman's voice floated over the heads or the rowers. How there was space for the bow oar, two marines with their muskets and a swinging lead was a mystery, but the soundings were coming in fast.

Moxon looked over his shoulder. The yawl was following in his wake, perhaps a cable astern. Too far really, but no signal of his would be seen. He just had to hope that Gilbert had the sense to stay close. The only reason for sending a second boat was for mutual support, and that meant they must remain close together. The sky darkened and he looked again, but of the yawl, there was no sign. A bank of cloud, hurrying down from the nor'east had obscured the low moon, cutting the visibility like the snuffing of a candle.

'Easy,' ordered Moxon. The coxswain relayed the order to the stroke. The longboat yawed rather more as the wind caught its starboard quarter and pushed the stern away. 'We'll let the yawl catch up with us.'

'I see a light,' whispered Enrico. 'It's astern of us, at the base of White Point.'

Moxon strained his eyes into the blackness. Yes, there was certainly something there. It looked as though it was higher than the shoreline, perhaps on the slightly elevated rocks of the point. He could see the line of surf where the point and its outlying rocks carried on their daily battle on the frontier between land and sea.

Enrico scrawled a note on his slate under cover of his cloak. He was doing it by touch alone; there was no light in the boat. He started each line two fingers below the last so that there was some chance of it being legible when he returned to *Medina*. Enrico knew that Wishart would be doing the same in the yawl; naturally, without really thinking about it, they were in competition with each other.

'Very well,' whispered Moxon in reply, 'and I think I see another. Four points on the bow, there's a black space between two patches of surf, I can just see a red glow, lower down than the last.'

'Yes, I see it, sir.'

Enrico made his second entry on the slate then returned to his study of the coastline. Even with the moon behind the clouds, he could infer the main features of the land by the white, slightly fluorescent breakers on the shore. The surf, moderate though it was in this nor'easterly wind, outlined the rocky parts of the coast and its points and headlands. The spaces in between were cloaked in darkness, that was where the sandy coves would be.

Moxon still looked astern, hoping for a glimpse of the yawl, but it had disappeared completely. He looked at the sky, but there was no help there. He could see a diffuse glow where the moon should be, but it was impossible to see the extent of the bank of cloud that was obscuring it.

'Blast that damned Gilbert,' he muttered, not quite softly enough to prevent the coxswain hearing him. The last thing he wanted was to turn back to search for the missing yawl.

'Rest on your oars, Coxswain,' he said.

The longboat came to an uneasy stop, rolling hard as the way came off her.

'Mister Angelini, you keep watching the shore while I try to locate the yawl.'

Moxon had thought about this before they'd left *Medina* and he'd given Gilbert strict instructions that the boats needed to stay together. If they were separated, they would immediately aim for a rendezvous off Flat Point, in the centre of the area that they were to patrol. The point was well named, and from seaward, it was difficult to discern, but the wave-washed rock that lay two cables to seaward was constantly battered by the sea, and the surf gave away its position.

Moxon stared astern, but he could see nothing. Then the cloud started to thin, and the rising moon cast its light over the sea. After the near total darkness, it was shockingly bright, revealing details that had been hidden. It seemed to those in the longboat that they must be plainly visible from the shore, however much their reason told them otherwise.

'There's the yawl, sir,' said the coxswain, with an edge of excitement in his voice. 'Two, no three, cables on the starboard beam.'

Moxon had been looking astern, where he expected the yawl to be following him. The last thing he expected was to see it well inshore.

'They'll cop it if there are any Frogs awake this side of the town,' said Souter.

'Keep your opinion to yourself, coxswain,' snapped Moxon. 'Head towards the yawl and let's see how these men can stretch out.'

Was there a reluctance to get the longboat moving? Moxon thought that perhaps there was. It was to be expected. The longboat's crew would reason that their own boat had kept itself out of trouble and was consequently in a relatively safe position. Those fools in the yawl had gone astray in the dark, and it was their own damned fault if they now found themselves in trouble. Why should they put themselves in danger for the preservation of fools?

'Eyes in the boat, damn you.' Moxon almost shouted. He could see the danger; the yawl was only a few hundred yards from the second group of lights that they'd seen. Souter was right; if that was a battery and not just a platoon position, then Gilbert's boat was in mortal danger.

The oarsmen had settled now; they had just needed leadership. They bent to their oars, and the longboat sped over the water into the teeth of the wind.

Had Gilbert seen the danger? He must have lost his

bearings when the cloud passed before the moon. Perhaps he was relying too much on following the longboat, and when that had disappeared into the darkness, he was left disorientated. It was hard to see what the yawl was doing, which way they were heading.

'There are more lights now, sir,' said Enrico, 'some new ones between the two points; and the lights on Flat Point are getting brighter.'

Moxon could see that for himself. Either they saw the same lights from a different aspect, or there was a lot more activity over there. It was a strange feeling, as though he were in an amphitheatre with an audience on three sides, and the sensation only intensified as they pushed further into the shallow bay.

'By the deep, four,' called the leadsman, 'Shoaling fast.' He'd abandoned the abbreviated reports now that secrecy appeared to have been lost.

Now the yawl was becoming more distinct. It looked like Gilbert had turned his bows to seaward. Yes, there was furious activity among the rowers.

Moxon saw the corporal and marine checking their priming.

'Don't fire unless I give the word, Corporal; we don't want to give the French an aiming mark.'

'Amen,' said the stroke oar in what he imagined to be a Sunday church-going voice. He shifted his quid of tobacco from one cheek to the other, managing that facial contortion at the same time as speaking without pausing the regular beat of his oar. He was an experienced man and chosen for that position of honour from which the other oarsmen took their time.

Flash-bang! The sound of a gun followed shortly behind the obscenely bright flash of its discharge. So there *was* a battery on Flat Point. That information alone made the expedition worthwhile, if only they would live to take it back to *Medina*.

Flash-bang! A second gun joined the first. In the

darkness, Moxon couldn't see the fall of shot, but he could tell that they were shooting at the yawl, not at the longboat. Probably they had no idea that the longboat was there.

There was a pause. Only two guns then, and they sounded like four or five pounders, six at the most. Nevertheless, the longboat and the yawl were within easy range.

'The yawl's returning fire, sir,' called the corporal from the bows.

The pinpricks of light were visible now, and the faint pop-popping of the muskets came down on the wind. Had they lost their minds? Their weapons could do no harm to the French at that range, and they were offering a perfect aiming mark to the gunners who would have lost much of their night-vision after the first two shots from the battery.

The boats were only two hundred yards apart. It was a strange experience, rushing through the calm inshore water towards a darkened land with a stiff breeze blowing overhead. The flashes from the battery only intensified the darkness, and the lights of the campfires could hardly be seen. The French on that battery must be reloading frantically, thought Moxon. Any moment now.

Flash-bang! Another shot came from Flat Point, and then another, but from White Point this time. That was a long range for such small guns, but Gilbert's marines continued to provide an aiming mark with their musket flashes.

'Bring her around in front of the yawl at about a hundred yards,' said Moxon, 'then you may have the men pull as hard as they like! Straight out to sea until we're out of range of those guns.'

Souter watched the yawl with an appraising eye, waiting for the moment to start his turn. He'd just started to push the tiller when the yawl broke apart, hit by an unlucky shot from the battery on Flat Point. The yawl's disintegration wasn't graceful, and it wasn't slow. One moment it was a solid object, its oars in urgent motion as it sped to seaward away from its tormentors, the next it was nothing: just a mass of men struggling to survive in the icy water surrounded by broken planks and oars.

'Belay that, coxswain,' shouted Moxon as he felt Souter pushing the tiller hard away from him, to turn the longboat towards the sea and safety. 'There'll be survivors, hard a-starboard and stretch out!'

Something like a gasp came from the oarsmen, but they pulled with a will and the longboat came around in a tight arc and headed to the scene of the tragedy. The batteries hadn't stopped firing, it was likely that they had no idea of their success, and another shot – a six-pounder almost certainly – raised a spout a few yards from the longboat as the oarsmen dug in to slow the boat down.

There were cries for help from overside, men struggling in the grip of the freezing sea and men holding on to whatever they could find to keep themselves afloat. Men in the water, but oh, so few. Of the yawl's crew of eleven, only five were hauled in over the longboat's gunwales, and it was only after her bows were again pointing to the sea that Moxon realised that only Wishart, of the two master's mates, had been saved.

The crew of the longboat dug deep and, encumbered though they were with the exhausted survivors lying at their feet, they hauled at their oars and brought the longboat off the shore and out to the safety of the sea. The batteries were firing blind. Did they know that there were two boats out there? It was impossible to say. The men at the oars stripped off their coats and gave them to the shattered, shivering men of the yawl. Shockingly, there were no injuries. Those who had been wounded, however slightly, had drowned in the few minutes before the longboat arrived on the scene.

The last shots from the shore served no purpose and were a waste of powder and shot.

'By the deep, twelve,' intoned the leadsman. Nobody had told him to stop sounding and so he'd continued to do so, even after the corporal had pulled his grego and

Guernsey sweater off his back to give to the shivering marine who'd sought the companionship of his mates in the bow.

Moxon had just started to consider how he should spend the next four hours before *Medina* was expected to pick them up when he heard another gun, a deeper, more familiar sound. Then he saw the flash to the east. Carlisle had heard the gunfire, deduced that all was not well, and had abandoned his diversion off the harbour entrance. *Medina* had run fast to the west to pick them up.

***

'A sad story,' said Carlisle when he'd heard Moxon's report. 'It appears that young Gilbert, God rest his soul, was out of his depth as soon the yawl left the ship's side, and when he could no longer see your longboat, he lost his head entirely.'

'Yes, sir. Wishart is being protective, of course,' Carlisle nodded, 'but the coxswain of the yawl, who's a steady hand, says that Wishart tried to persuade him to close the longboat, but he was happy where he was. Apparently, he became confused when he had nothing to follow and mistook the surf on Flat Point for the headland past Cormorant Cove.'

'How did he die?'

'He'd started moving for'rard to encourage the marines to fire faster,' replied Moxon. 'He was just amidships when the ball struck. All the casualties were in the centre part of the boat, those in the bows and stern were flung into the water uninjured. The wounded survived only a few seconds and one of the marines, who wasn't touched, died as well, even though there was plenty of oars and planks to hold onto. The freezing water and the shock I suppose. The doctor says all the survivors will do well; he has them wrapped in worsted in front of the galley fire.'

'I'll see Wishart in the morning. But I've entirely forgotten. Did you learn anything?'

'Yes, we did, sir. We know the location of two batteries

between White Point and Flat Point, and we have some idea of the soundings. The batteries are six-pounders, for sure, and well served. Their rate of fire was good and, of course, they were accurate.'

'Then tomorrow we'll consider how we investigate the western part of the area. But you should get some sleep, Mister Moxon. The master will take your watch.'

***

CHAPTER FOURTEEN

Under Fire

Tuesday, Twenty-Eighth of March 1758.
Medina, at Sea. Off Cormorant Cove, Île Royale.

Carlisle woke to the sound of a knock on his cabin door; he could see that it was pitch dark still. Even when he was sound asleep, he was conscious of the change of the watch, the striking bell registered in his brain but didn't wake him. He knew that the morning watch hadn't yet been called, so it was between half-past three and four o'clock. Before the door opened, he was aware of a change in the weather. *Medina's* motion had altered. No longer was her stern rising to the long, lazy swell from the east, but she was now rolling more, and leaning to larboard, so the wind must have shifted to the north. His heart beat a little faster; was this the weather window he was looking for?

'Mister Moxon's respects, sir, and I'm to inform you that the wind has backed into the north with just a hint of west in it. The fog's dispersing. The ship's under single reefed fore tops'l, jib and mizzen.'

This was Atwater, the newly promoted master's mate. With the loss of Gilbert when the yawl was sunk, Carlisle had a difficult decision to make. There was a vacancy for a master's mate that must be filled from within the ranks of *Medina's* young gentlemen. Without a doubt the most suitable candidate was Enrico Angelini, he was older and more mature than the other midshipmen, and he'd picked up enough seamanship over the last year to allow him to discharge the duties. However, there was another factor that had to be considered. Promotion to master's mate implied that the man was a suitable candidate for a commission or if not, to become a warranted sailing master. Enrico Angelini was neither. It was understood that the young Sardinian was serving in the British navy as a temporary

139

measure and that at some point he'd return to his Mediterranean home and take up his commission in the army of his own country. In principle, that was not a bar to him being a master's mate, but it was unfair on the other midshipmen to squander the opportunity. For Enrico, it would be a welcome recognition of his growing nautical skills and no more. For the other midshipmen, it was a vital step on the promotion ladder.

Carlisle had conducted a short service for Gilbert, the four seamen and the marine who had been lost. There were no bodies to bury; Moxon had quite rightly wasted no time after rescuing the living, and in any case, the bodies had almost certainly sunk under the weight of their clothes.

After the service he'd called Enrico into his cabin to discuss his future. As he'd expected, Enrico understood that his Sardinian commission and his religion prevented him being commissioned a lieutenant in the British navy, and he was sensible to the ambitions of his friends in the midshipmen's berth. It was agreed that Enrico would continue to serve as a midshipman.

'Very well, Mister Angelini. My compliments to the first lieutenant and I'll come on deck.'

The fog was indeed lifting, enough to allow the moon to cast a feeble light over the sea. The bowsprit was clearly visible as were the t'gallant masts reaching skywards above the reefed tops'ls.

'Good morning, sir,' said Moxon, touching his hat. 'The wind's north by west and as you can see it's picked up a little. White Point's on our beam, maybe five miles.'

Carlisle picked up the traverse board and studied the log readings and compass courses. The frigate had been patrolling five miles off the land heading southwest from Cape Bretton as he'd ordered. The log showed speeds of four, five and six knots and a steady course. The first lieutenant's estimate of the position was probably correct, at least the distance from land would be reasonably accurate even if the variable currents had set the frigate further to the south than expected.

It was cold. The northerly wind was bringing a stream of frigid air down from the Labrador regions. As Carlisle studied the traverse board, he felt the first drops of hard rain spatter on his hat. It would be sleet, then hail before the morning watch was called, the worst of all weather for men coming on deck after no more than four hours in their hammocks. On the other hand, Carlisle knew that the sleet and hail were the precursors to the fog lifting.

'I believe this wind will serve, Mister Moxon. What time's sunrise?'

'Five forty-seven, sir,' replied Moxon. All of Carlisle's officers knew by now that it was best for them to have the times of the rising and setting of the sun and moon at their fingertips.

'Then we should see the first of the dawn just before two bells. I wish to be two miles southeast of Cormorant Cove at one bell in the morning. Shake the cook and arrange for the men to have breakfast at the change of the watch, then we'll go quietly to quarters at one bell, and clear for action.'

Carlisle had discussed his plan with the first lieutenant immediately after the longboat had been picked up from Gabarus Bay. It was clearly too dangerous to send a boat in to sound the bay, particularly now that the French had been alerted. The artillerymen in those batteries would be aware of their success. Probably some of the bodies had drifted ashore; wreckage from the yawl would undoubtedly have done so. Yes, they would be ready for a second attempt. What they perhaps wouldn't expect is for *Medina* to enter the bay and run the lines of soundings. It was a dangerous plan, but Carlisle had two critical advantages: he knew the positions of at least two of the batteries, and he out-gunned them by a considerable margin. He'd oppose his broadside of twelve nine-pounders and two three-pounders against the French six-pounders. The French had the advantage of firing from fixed positions, and they had presumably thrown up earthworks to protect their guns, but still, Carlisle

141

felt confident that he could hold his own while the work of sounding was carried forward. He'd been waiting for the right weather condition. Daylight and good visibility were essential as was a moderate offshore wind so that if *Medina* should suffer damage to her masts and sails, she'd be carried out to sea rather than onto the shore.

***

Back in England, or in Virginia, the children would be playing outdoors with marbles later in the day. But it was no fine spring day here off Île Royale. The sleet had come and then the hail, with great balls of ice the size of the children's marbles, stinging and bruising where they struck exposed flesh. At one bell the people had trooped wearily to quarters while throughout the ship the sounds of clearing for action competed with the beat of the hailstones on the deck. In all other circumstances, the gun crews stationed under the fo'c'sle and in the great cabin reckoned themselves unfortunate and envied their shipmates in the open air of the waist where the noise of the discharge was less, and the smoke dispersed more quickly. But today they were snug and relatively warm under the shelter of the decks above.

'Stand on, Mister Hosking, and close to a mile off the point. You may start the soundings now.'

This was the master's favourite occupation, surveying an otherwise unrecorded coast. He had an eager accomplice in Mister Angelini, who not only had a masterful hand at sketching a shoreline but had a meticulous mind for recording bearings and soundings and turning them into a two-dimensional representation of the area that they covered. That was what mariners needed, an outline of the coast accurately referenced to a good latitude and longitude, lines of soundings related to conspicuous points on the shore and a view of what the mariner may see when looking towards the land. Of those, the longitude was still uncertain. Hosking was deeply suspicious of the way that the position of Louisbourg had been laid down and he was determined, once the fortress was in British hands, to spend some time on White Point, fixing the longitude by observation.

Carlisle looked over the starboard bow. He could see the sky clearing, and even now the hail was slackening. It would soon turn to sleet, then to big, fat drops of freezing rain and finally, with no warning, it would cease. This was his weather window, and he was determined to make the most of it.

'No bottom on this line,' called the leadsman in the starboard main chains. That wasn't surprising; the hand lead line was only twenty fathoms long, and he wasn't interested in soundings greater than that.

'The ship's at quarters and cleared for action, sir,' reported Moxon formally, removing his hat. 'Larboard battery's loaded with ball and run out.'

'Very well, Mister Moxon. I expect we'll come under fire as soon as we close to less than a mile from the shore. Simmonds will record the positions of the batteries. I'll leave the engagement to you. Use single guns, divisions or the whole broadside as you see fit.'

'You think they'll unmask, sir?'

'I believe they will. It'll be hard for any artilleryman to resist the temptation of an enemy frigate within range of his guns. If they don't, then we'll bombard them anyway. We know where the easterly batteries are, and it will be odd if we can't spot the batteries to the west of Flat Point at five cables.'

'We're just a mile off Cormorant Cove now, sir,' reported Hosking. 'You can see the little group of rocks off the point, *Grande Cormorandière*, they're called.'

'Very well, stand on. You may bring her about on ten fathoms and we'll start our first line of soundings.'

'Deck there,' shouted the lookout from the mainmast head. 'There's something on shore on those low cliffs on the point.'

That was Whittle, enjoying his self-appointed role as the chief lookout. Carlisle wondered how he'd felt in that exposed position when the hail had been pelting down.

He'd forgotten that he'd ordered a lookout at the masthead, rather than at the more protected position in the main top.

He levelled his telescope at the cliffs. Surely that was too obvious a position for a battery. Obvious, but still the best, he decided. A few guns there could dominate Cormorant Cove and the western quarter of the bay, and in any case, once they had unmasked, it didn't matter how obvious the position was. He looked at Moxon who was studying the same point through his own telescope. The first lieutenant bent to speak to a quarter gunner, calling him to the fo'c'sle to point out his first target. *Medina* was pointing directly at the battery so there would be no opportunity to fire yet. Carlisle had a momentary temptation to interfere, to confirm that he wished the target to be engaged, but he thought better of it. He'd told Moxon to carry on with the counter-battery fire; there were plenty of other concerns to engage a captain's attention.

'They've opened fire, sir,' said Enrico.

A spout of water appeared a cable off *Medina's* quarter, and a puff of smoke could be seen over Cormorant Cove. A second gun fired, then there was a pause. Just a two-gun battery thought Carlisle. It's there to disrupt a landing in boats, not to conduct a duel with a man-of-war. What was that artillery commander thinking about, giving away his position so readily?

'By the deep, sixteen.'

Two lead lines were going on the starboard side, but only one was calling the depth, the other was taking a sample of the seabed. A midshipman was recording the result on a slate.

'By the mark, thirteen.'

The ground was shoaling fast. Carlisle glanced at Hosking, who nodded in acknowledgement. They'd already determined that they'd attempt to run along the ten-fathom line. That would give them a margin for error; in her present trim *Medina* drew a touch less than three fathoms.

The French guns were firing rapidly, but there were only

two of them, and they evidently had difficulty following a moving target. Probably they were on a rough-hewn platform of logs that shifted at every firing. If so, then fine adjustment would be difficult.

'By the mark, ten.'

'May I bring her about, sir?' asked Hosking.

'Make it so, master, keep to the ten-fathom line.'

Medina came about quickly under her reduced headsails. Now the land was on the larboard side with Cormorant Cove just abaft the beam.

'Fire!' shouted the first lieutenant, and the larboard after division of guns made a ragged reply.

The smoke from the guns blew back over the quarterdeck, momentarily blinding the captain, the master and all the rest.

'Too low,' Moxon called. He'd positioned himself on the fo'c'sle for that first engagement and had a clear view of the fall of shot. 'Knock those quoins out a touch,' he said to the quarter gunner for the for'rard division.

The quarter gunner relayed the order and watched keenly as the gunners tapped the quoins from side to side with their handspikes and the guns rose a few inches. The gun captains squinted along the barrels, lining them up on the battery. Their target was easy to see now that it had been pointed out. The French artillerymen had tried to cover the disturbed earth with scrub and tree branches, but they were a noticeably different shade of brown to their surroundings, and the shock of the first discharge had blown away some of the camouflage revealing the turned earth below.

Six hands were raised as each gun captain pronounced himself happy with his training and elevation. The quarter gunner paced behind them, checking for himself that they were well-pointed; he raised his own hand.

Moxon saw the quarter gunner's signal. He waited for the frigate's larboard side to start its upward roll and again shouted 'Fire!'

That was better. At least two of the balls had landed

close enough to the battery to give the artillerymen something to think about. With twelve nine-pounders against two six-pounders, it shouldn't be long before *Medina's* weight of shot started to tell.

Medina was creeping forward now under the bare minimum of sail. Hosking and the quartermaster were using all their skills in this fresh breeze, spilling wind where necessary, luffing a little to retard their progress.

'Fire!' shouted Moxon. It was a whole broadside engagement this time, and the range had shortened. As the smoke cleared, Carlisle could see that the French battery had been hit hard. The earth and logs in front of the embrasures had been torn up, and one gun could be seen pointing awkwardly towards the sky.

'And a half, nine.'

'I'll ease her away another two points, sir,' said Hosking. He wasn't asking permission and Carlisle made no response.

'Well done to your gun crews, Mister Moxon,' he shouted above the din of the guns being run out again. 'You may get one more broadside, then you must look for a fresh target after we've turned.'

Medina came off the wind and Carlisle noted that Flat Point was now at least two points on their weather bow. Each of the three miniature capes in this easterly part of Gabarus Bay held a nasty surprise for the unwary in the form of low rocks lying between one and three cables off the southern extremity. They'd be a problem in the fog, but in this blessed clear weather and with a stiff breeze breaking the sea over them, they showed up easily. Nevertheless, they were the determinant of where the frigate could safely navigate.

'Deck there! There's a flagstaff on the shore, partly hidden behind a hill, right on our larboard beam.' Whittle again.

Carlisle scanned the shoreline. It was a small flagstaff apparently rough-cut from a felled tree. It probably marked nothing more than a platoon position, but it was a fair target.

'Mister Moxon, you see the flagstaff?'

As Carlisle spoke, the white Bourbon flag climbed laboriously up the staff. There was probably no block at the top, just a cleft in the pole through which the halyard was rove, and it was in imminent danger of jamming.

Moxon waved back. The target was well in range, just three or four cables, and he could see men moving about beside the flag. There was no sign of artillery.

Carlisle's attention was taken by the flag on shore; he jumped as he felt the wind of a shot screaming across the deck. It miraculously passed without causing any damage and plunged into the sea ahead of the frigate.

'I may question that artillery commander's tactical sense,' he commented to Hosking, 'but I can't fault his devotion to his duty. He's lost half his force, and yet he persists.'

'Fire!' shouted Moxon. *Medina* heeled to the force of the broadside, and again the intoxicating smell of powder invaded the quarterdeck. That was more satisfactory, noted Carlisle. He could see the flagstaff leaning drunkenly to one side, its flag nowhere to be seen, and there were fallen men beside it. He saw the flash of a sword, presumably an officer calling his men into the dead ground on the reverse of the low hill. There was nothing to be gained in standing to be fired upon by nine-pounders, and no glory in the decimation of his command.

'Mister Angelini, take note of the position of that flag.'

Medina had moved into the middle of the space between Cormorant Cove and Flat Point. It was a long range for six-pounders from either of the promontories, and it seemed likely that there would be a battery somewhere in the centre, between the two points.

Carlisle again raised his telescope to study the slowly passing shoreline. There was another feeling of a passing shot, closely followed by a crash. A six-pounder ball had passed through the taffrail and struck a glancing blow on the planks of the quarterdeck, just a few feet to Carlisle's left. A seaman beside one of the three-pounders looked in amazement at the blood seeping out of his shirt sleeve, the result of an oak splinter thrown up by the shot. The rammer he was holding fell from his hands, and his mouth opened and closed without any sound coming out.

'Get him below to the surgeon, Mister Atwater, his mates on the starboard gun may take him.'

***

Medina continued her run of soundings. If there was a battery between Cormorant Cove and Flat Point, it didn't show itself and try as they may, no sign of it could be seen. Hosking edged the frigate a little further to seaward as they approached Flat Point, the centre of the area that they were to survey. The battery that had sunk the yawl was easy to see, it sat right atop the low ground of the point. The engineers that built it and the artillerymen that manned it must have realised the futility in camouflaging the gun emplacements, and the new-felled trees and turned earth stood out clearly against the winter-blackened scrub.

Moxon had a personal score to settle with that battery, and he set about its demolition with a will. After two deliberate broadsides, he let the individual gun captains practice their pointing in their own time. Two shots were all the battery managed to fire before it was overwhelmed by the weight of *Medina's* outraged fury. Long after the last artilleryman must have abandoned the post, the frigate's guns kept firing, reducing the palisades to splinters and levelling the earthworks. It must have been a lucky shot, but suddenly there was a loud explosion and a plume of black smoke issued from a point a hundred yards inland from the battery. They'd found the magazine; Gilbert and his five fellows were avenged.

***

CHAPTER FIFTEEN

The Chase

Tuesday, Twenty-Eighth of March 1758.
Medina, at Sea. Off Cormorant Cove, Île Royale.

Carlisle watched the smoke over Flat Point being dispersed by the keen wind.

'You may follow the ten-fathom line, Mister Hosking.'

Medina had passed the group of rocks that lay offshore; the next real obstacle was White Point with its much more substantial obstacles lying to the south. In fact, so close were the rocks to the point that they formed part of the same structure, though they were lower, their tops barely washed by the waves.

The wind was still a whisker west of north and the visibility was good. *Medina* was on a beam reach with the whole of the North Atlantic under her lee. Carlisle left the navigation to the master and turned his attention to annoying the enemy.

'Lookout!' he shouted with his head tilted up to the main masthead.

'Quarterdeck!' replied Whittle. On the face of it, the lookout's response was unexceptional, but Carlisle knew very well that there was a humorous tone in this case. *Aye-aye sir* would have been a correct reply, but Whittle chose to bounce back Carlisle's hail with a literal equivalent.

Carlisle was aware of the licence that Whittle took, usually on occasions when Carlisle had higher matters to consider than the mild insubordination of an able seaman. He and Whittle had grown up on the same plantation in Virginia. They weren't precisely childhood friends, there was too vast a social chasm between the son of a wealthy plantation owner and the son of one of the poor tenants that farmed scraps of land carved out from the estate. He was aware of the covert smiles of the steersmen and the wooden face of the quartermaster. Nobody else in the frigate had presumed to imitate Whittle's familiarity – yet – but something must be done.

'Souter,' he called in a low tone to his coxswain, whose station was on the quarterdeck in action. 'Run up to the main masthead and tell Whittle that he's to direct his attention for'rard of the beam. I want to know immediately if he sees anything stirring in the harbour or any force leaving the fortress.'

'Aye-aye sir,' replied Souter, 'and I'll remind him of the correct reports for a lookout at the same time.'

Carlisle looked sharply at his coxswain, but Souter's face betrayed nothing.

'And a half, ten,' chanted the leadsman.

***

The shore slipped slowly by; but there was nothing to be seen in the shallow indentation between Flat Point and White Point. Probably any French troops stationed there to prevent a landing had decided that this British frigate wasn't to be trifled with. They'd all seen the fate of the battery on Flat Point.

'If we see nothing better, may I try some random shots at anything that looks suspicious, sir?' asked Moxon.

'You may, Mister Moxon, it'll be good practice for the gun crews. Concentrate on the land on the beam until we turn to seaward around White Point, then you can give the battery there a regular bombardment.'

It was almost like a yachting trip now, if it hadn't been for the cries of the leadsman and the intermittent fire from the larboard battery. Even the keen edge of the wind was blunted by the land close on the beam.

This was the first really clear day since *Medina* had arrived off Louisbourg, and the fortress was clearly visible from the deck. That would allow Carlisle to fulfil another of the items in his orders, to report on the number of men-of-war and merchantmen in the harbour. There'd be plenty of time for that once they'd finished this line of soundings. He trained his telescope over the land where he could just see the highest spires of the buildings in the town. Whittle at the main topmast would be able to see the masts of any vessels in the harbour. He resisted the temptation to call up to him. Partly because he was trying to curb his tendency to repeat orders, and partly because he didn't want to risk another run-in with the able seaman's sharp wit. He'd given his order and must assume that it was being carried out.

Moxon was clearly enjoying himself, pointing out targets to each gun captain and commenting on their accuracy. It was good for the crews to practice this individual shooting; too often it was assumed that naval gunnery consisted merely of loading and firing as fast as possible at another ship so close alongside that it would be impossible to miss. That may be very well for ships-of-the-line, although Carlisle didn't really believe it. He'd seen a fleet action, at Minorca, where the lines were far apart, and greater accuracy might have produced a better result. For a frigate, it just wouldn't do. He needed his guns to be able to hit moving targets at the limit of their range. The rate of fire was important, but less so in the sort of battle of fire and manoeuvre that he was used to.

Carlisle watched as the larboard battery kicked up earth and vegetation on the low, rocky shore. It was mostly scrub with here and there a stunted tree, not good terrain to dig defensive works, and not suitable ground, either, for siege works. The soldiers would have a hard time of it digging their saps in that unforgiving terrain.

'Sail ho! Sail five points on the starboard bow.' That was Whittle, no hint of foolery now.

Carlisle trained his telescope to starboard. At first, he could see nothing. There was a haze over the sea as though the fog was trying to re-assert itself, and now he thought about it, the wind appeared to be wavering a little as though it would soon veer eastwards and bring the mist rolling in. What bizarre weather! A strong northerly breeze with incipient fog! It was unheard of in any civilised part of the world. Then he saw just the hint of a patch of white showing over the haze. It was there and gone.

'Mister Wishart,' he said without lowering the telescope, 'up to the main topmast head and let me know what you make of it.'

It would be a tight squeeze on the crosstree at the top of the main topmast, but it was important that someone other than an able seaman should give an opinion on the newcomer.

'Deck there!' shouted Whittle. 'It's a ship, close hauled on the starboard tack under reefed tops'ls, could be a man-of-war.'

Very likely a man-of-war, thought Carlisle as he tried to get a steady view of the sail that was now showing clearly above the haze. Whatever it was, it was trying to make Louisbourg harbour without putting in another tack. It would be a close-run thing.

'Mister Moxon, cease firing. Sponge the guns, reload with ball and run them out again. Report when you're ready.'

The gun crews had been so engrossed in the pleasant business of bombarding an unresisting shore that they hadn't heard the hail from Whittle. Now they were feverishly preparing for this new encounter.

'Mister Hosking, we'll cut that sail off from Louisbourg. Secure the leadsman if you please. Set the courses, the fore tops'l and the fore stays'l.'

That last order caused a flurry of activity as the men whose stations were aloft for sail handling handed over their rammers, sponges and handspikes to their mates and raced for the ratlines.

Medina came rapidly off the wind as the steersmen heaved the wheel to starboard. The sense of a pleasant yachting trip was gone in a flash. There was a chance that this ship was British, another frigate sent to join *Medina* in watching Louisbourg before Admiral Hardy's squadron should arrive, but it was unlikely. The sail – the chase as

Carlisle now thought it – was approaching from seaward. It hadn't coasted up from Halifax, or even from Boston. Possibly her captain had directed his course around Sable Island to approach his destination with the least possibility of meeting a British man-of-war. He'd be disappointed.

The waisters strained on the tops'l halyards, the stays'l was run out and the coarses set. In a mere few minutes, *Medina* was transformed from a slow lumbering platform for surveying and gunnery into a sleek, speedy ocean predator.

'Both batteries ready,' reported Moxon.

That was good work with half the crews sent away to their sail handling stations.

'Captain, sir!'

That was Wishart at the main topmast head. He must have had an awkward time of it with the halyards running through their blocks right on his shoulder. Carlisle had a moment to be pleased that it was Wishart who was reporting rather than Whittle.

'It's a man-of-war, for certain. A frigate probably.'

Carlisle stared hard through his telescope. Yes, Wishart was probably right, and he had Whittle there to help.

'Could she be the frigate we met off the Capes?' replied Carlisle, using the copper speaking trumpet now that the sounds of the frigate's way through the water had increased so much.

'She could be, sir,' replied Wishart, not wanting to commit himself on the identity of a ship that was still two or three leagues away and seen through a veil of haze.

Could be. That meant that Wishart and Whittle had seen nothing that ruled out the identification. Carlisle hummed a few bars of a tune. He was sure, even if his lookouts weren't. He knew that he had unfinished business with that frigate when she ran away from him off Cape Henry.

The bosun was in the maintop, checking the chains that secured the yard in case the slings were shot away; two of his mates were rigging the boarding nets that had not been needed for their earlier cruise along the coast.

'She's tacked, sir,' said Hosking, a second or two ahead of the next call from Wishart.

Now, what was she up to? There was no doubt of her course and little question of her destination, thought Carlisle. She must be heading for Louisbourg. Her captain hadn't shown himself to be shy before, but now he was positively declining to fight his way through. On his new course, he'd be heading for the Gulf and then up the St. Lawrence. Had he mistaken his navigation? It was possible. He must have caught his first sight of land by now, and if his reckoning were in error, he'd be tacking to correct it. Perhaps Quebec was his destination after all. If he believed that he could get past without a fight, he'd be disappointed.

'Captain sir!' There was a note of urgency in Wishart's voice as it cracked with the strain of shouting over the wind. 'There's another sail beyond the frigate, just to the right. I can't make it out yet,' Wishart paused, 'and another, two more sail to the right of the frigate.'

'Mister Hosking, bring us onto the wind and set a course to round Cape Breton if we can make it on this tack.'

'Aye-aye sir. The wind's veering towards the east and dropping,' he said, wetting his index finger and holding it up to the breeze.

The quartermaster nodded in agreement.

Now that his attention was drawn to it, Carlisle could feel the wind faltering, and the horizon to the east was becoming less distinct. He could still see the frigate, but its outline was starting to become blurred. Of the sails beyond and to right, he could see nothing.

'Damn it all!' he muttered and stamped his foot on the deck before he checked himself. A display of petulance would do no good with half of the ship's company watching him.

'Keep her full and by, Mister Hosking. Our friend out there will be struggling to avoid being set off to Newfoundland, with the east wind and *Medina* dictating his course!'

That was better, show the people that he could laugh in the face of adversity. But it was difficult. He had a moral certainty that this frigate was his old friend. Given that, it was odds-on that the two sails were supply ships for Louisbourg and that they'd had a pre-arranged meeting. Perhaps their rendezvous had been at Sable Island, that remote, uninhabited crescent off land eighty miles off the Nova Scotia coast.

If all that was true – and he had to admit to himself that it was only one of several possible explanations – then he was doing his duty merely by preventing them from getting into Louisbourg. But the weather may yet be on the side of the French frigate. If the fog came in – and that appeared very likely – then they may be able to feel their way into the harbour without *Medina* ever catching sight of them. The ability of the Frenchmen who had grown up on this coast to find their way through thick weather was legendary.

'Captain. Sir, I've lost sight of the other two sails now. I can still see the frigate, she's close hauled on the larboard tack.'

Carlisle looked up at *Medina's* sails. Hosking caught his movement and looked up also. The two men's minds were precisely in parallel.

'What do you think, master?'

'T'gallants? I don't know, sir. There's a risk that they'll carry away, and I'm not sure what we'll achieve by beating the chase to the Cape. The fog will be there before us.'

'You're right,' replied Carlisle. There was no point in charging to the north when in all probability the chase would turn to the southwest before she reached the Cape. After all, Louisbourg was a more likely destination than the St. Lawrence. Or was it?

***

Medina ploughed on into the gathering gloom. It was midday, but the sun was looking decidedly hazy as the wind veered further into the east and lost its strength. The banks of fog could be seen rolling in on the wind. The French frigate persisted as a vague ghostly shape, just five miles to the east, then suddenly it was gone, swallowed up in the grey blanket of fog.

Carlisle paced the weather side of the quarterdeck, trying not to let his nervousness show. It was ten-to-one that the Frenchman would escape, taking his convoy with him. He could already have tacked and may be heading directly towards Louisbourg, the wind was now fair for him. But was that his destination? Carlisle was sure that it *had* been until he saw that his way was barred by a ship of force. The French captain had every right to believe that there would be no British blockade of the port, not yet, not so early in the season, when the ice floes hadn't even stopped coming down the St. Lawrence. There was a slight grinding noise now, as a moderate-sized growler scraped along the frigate's side. It was growing colder again.

'Mister Moxon, see to it that the men go below to get more clothes on, it'll be freezing before too long,' he said, motioning to the advancing bank of fog.

And yet…and yet, that had looked like a very deliberate move when the frigate tacked and headed off to Cape Breton. It all depended on the ships that she was escorting, what was their cargo? After a hard winter, and in confident anticipation of a siege, Louisbourg must be in urgent want of food – flour and rice, beef and pork – to sustain the garrison and population when they must retreat behind the walls. Food, without a doubt, but if they were serious about holding the fortress – and with it the French dreams of empire in North America – they would also need men. Infantry to hold the walls, artillerymen to bombard the siege lines, engineers to improve the defences. If those ships carried food, then it must be offloaded at Louisbourg, nowhere else would do; the terrain of Île Royale was not conducive to overland transport of supplies. However, if those were soldiers, though it may be inconvenient in this harsh climate, they could march across the country to reach Louisbourg.

Of course, he could be wrong about the destination. Quebec needed supplies too, and the French must have few illusions about the British objective after Louisbourg had fallen. Nevertheless, that tack to the north looked too much like a response to seeing *Medina*, and not like a navigational correction. If they had met off Sable Island, then to miss the entrance to the Gulf of St. Lawrence would be a gross error in navigation that even the French navy would blush at.

When he'd weighed up the alternatives, Carlisle was almost certain that those other two ships carried soldiers. Two big transports could bring most of a battalion between them, and if they'd made a fast passage and met their escort for the final leg off Sable Island, then those would be fresh troops, ready for a hard march if that's what it took to reach the fortress. He could set a course to intercept them, and that was his first instinct. However, he'd learned to treat his first instincts with caution. His orders were quite clear. He was to watch Louisbourg and survey Gabarus Bay. If he chased these Frenchmen around Cape Breton and off to the northwest, he'd be leaving the approaches to the fortress town unguarded. If it turned out that they were on passage for the St. Lawrence, he'd look foolish at best, insubordinate at worst, if Hardy chose to interpret his actions as prize-hunting at the expense of his principal task.

Carlisle took two more turns the length of the quarterdeck then stared hard to the east hoping for another glimpse of the frigate, but the visibility was down to less than a mile, and the wind was still dropping. The Frenchman's last sight of *Medina* would have suggested that the British frigate was holding its position off the entrance to the harbour. He turned sharply; his decision made.

'Mister Hosking,' he said in a loud voice so that his officers could hear. They had crept, one-by-one, onto the quarterdeck to be nearby at this critical decision point, 'set the t'gallants, and lay off a course to pass eight miles off Cape Breton. I want to be off East Point before our friend over there. I'll be in your cabin with the charts.'

It was done, the decision was made. If he was correct, then he'd be in the ideal position to intercept the French convoy before it could make Spaniard's Bay or Port Dauphin. If the fog persisted, he would have to think again. If he was completely wrong, then there'd be three more sets of masts in Louisbourg harbour.

***

CHAPTER SIXTEEN

The Trap

Wednesday, Twenty-Ninth of March 1758.
Medina, at Sea. Off Île Royale. East Point, West 2 leagues.

The master's chart of the east side of Île Royale was in French, of course. Carlisle had studied it before, and he knew the general layout of the coast that trended north-northwest from the small, rocky island known as Scatari that lay off Cape Breton. East Point was the furthest extremity of Scatari Island and thus the ultimate eastern extremity of the French possessions on Île Royale. From there a heavily indented coast ran sixty-six nautical miles up to North Cape.

If his theory was correct and the Frenchman had decided that it was too dangerous to make for Louisbourg with *Medina* guarding the entrance, then he had two real options. The first was to land his soldiers – if that was indeed his cargo – at Spanish Bay, sixty nautical miles from his last position before the fog enveloped him. The second was to continue a further fifteen miles up the coast to Port Dauphin. Spanish Bay had no port facilities; that fact had been confirmed by an audacious incursion by the sloop *Hawke* a month ago. At Port Dauphin, however, there was a fort, wharves and facilities for unloading troops and cargo.

How many men would the transports carry? They looked like good-sized, ship-rigged vessels capable of a fast passage from Brest, La Rochelle or Rochefort. The limiting factor in carrying troops was always food and water. The men themselves could be fitted into any spare space for a three or four-week passage, but their provisions for the voyage were bulky and liable to spoil. Probably each ship could carry three hundred soldiers, a whole battalion between them, with the battalion staff in the frigate. That almost certainly ruled out Spanish Bay; they would need the

159

facilities of a regular port to disembark that many soldiers and their equipment.

On his own in the master's cabin, Carlisle stared at the flickering candle that illuminated the chart, trying to put himself into the mind of the French captain. What would he do? Or, perhaps more importantly, what would the colonel in command of that battalion demand that he did? Both men would want to disembark the men as soon as possible. They were vulnerable every day they were at sea, and one British frigate that they'd seen may mean a whole squadron lurking somewhere in the fog. Without a doubt, the colonel would prefer to be put ashore in Louisbourg, but he wouldn't want to fight to reach the harbour. On land, he'd face anything, but at sea he was helpless, and a single broadside could destroy half his force. If not Louisbourg, then would he demand to be landed at Spanish Bay? It was a lot closer to the town and would save at least a day's march, more likely two.

Carlisle looked more closely at the chart and the pencil notes that Hosking had made in the margin. The entrance to Spanish Bay held deep water and was over a mile wide. It was almost made for a frigate such as *Medina* to sail in and destroy the anchored transports. Of course, the French frigate would probably hold the entrance. Yet it wasn't a very reassuring place to disembark a battalion. And when they were ashore, there was no fort, no protected area that could be used to marshal the companies and form them into their marching order. Probably there were few boats, and to disembark a battalion and its baggage would take several boat trips, perhaps more than the ships' boats could achieve in a day. Carlisle instinctively felt that the unknown colonel wouldn't like the look of Spanish Bay, not with *Medina* ready to interfere.

He turned his attention to Port Dauphin. It was, he knew, the second most important French settlement on Île Royale. The gap between the solid land on either side of the entrance was again nearly a mile wide, but a long sand-spit projecting from the north shore constricted the passage to barely a cable wide, and that narrow channel was dominated by a fort. Once through the gut, the transports could anchor in perfect safety, undisturbed by anything less than a determined attack by a moderate squadron. For security, it would be attractive to both the French captain and the colonel. The question was whether the soldier was willing to trade the shorter distance from Louisbourg that Spanish Bay offered against the superior security and facilities of Port Dauphin. He was sure it would be Port Dauphin.

Of course he could be entirely wrong about the French intentions, but he wasn't expecting Hardy and his squadron for two weeks yet, and if he *was* wrong, his absence from Louisbourg would probably not be noticed, even if he felt it necessary to mention it in his report. If he failed to find the French, there would be no engagement, and no harm done.

'Pass the word for the first lieutenant and the master,' Carlisle called to the marine sentry.

***

It was cold here in the Gulf of St. Lawrence. *Medina* was less than forty miles from Louisbourg as the crow might have flown if crows ventured this far out to sea, and the temperature had dropped significantly. Here the waters of the St. Lawrence hadn't mixed with the warmer Atlantic, and the frigid wind still blew from the north and east. *Medina* had been at sea for only a week, yet already the watches were reduced by illness. The galley range was running day and night and even with the stock of wood that he'd taken on board at Halifax, he'd need to resupply in a month.

'Masthead, do you see anything?' called Moxon. It was a measure of the frustration on the quarterdeck that the first lieutenant, usually a man of few words, was induced to make that unnecessary hail.

'Nothing, sir,' came the reply from high above. The lookout was perched at the main topmast crosstree, the highest point that could be achieved while wrapped in enough layers of clothing to prevent him from succumbing to the deadly cold. In warmer weather, a man may climb a dozen feet further, to the t'gallant masthead, but in these conditions, with the feeling leaving a man's fingers after five minutes exposure, it would be foolhardy in the extreme. As it was the lookout had to be relieved every fifteen minutes, and that was putting a strain on the already undermanned watch on deck.

'Can you still see over the fog bank?' asked Moxon.

'Aye sir, I can see maybe a league, but there's nothing in sight.'

Medina was lying-to four miles off the mouth of Port Dauphin. The fog had persisted off East Point and Carlisle had followed the logic of his hunch. He'd decided to move further west and meet the French off their most likely destination.

It was an uncomfortable place in this easterly wind. The high land that led towards North Cape was just ten miles under the frigate's lee, and the fog made navigation merely speculative. The lead-line suggested that they were at least four miles clear of the land, but the surveys weren't encouraging with blank gaps in the lines of soundings. At least the easterly wind was light and there was a little south in it. They could claw off North Cape if they found themselves set too far to the west.

'There's another of those growlers,' said Wishart, the officer-of-the-watch, as a flat chunk of ice the size of the main hatch ground its way down the side.

'You can expect more of the same,' said Hosking. 'The thaw's been late this year and the ice only started coming down last month. There'll be ice like that,' he motioned over the side, 'aye and larger, until at least May.'

They lapsed into silence, the only sound being the casting of the lead and the muted call of the soundings. Even the wind was hushed in this cloistered world of fog and ice.

'Here comes the captain,' said Wishart as he heard the slap of the marine sentry's musket salute from below the quarterdeck rail.

***

Carlisle chose not to speak. By the master's calculation, the French convoy could be approaching the bay in an hour or two. Or they could be feeling their way into Louisbourg as he waited here forty miles to leeward. Well, it was worth playing the game through to its end, he thought, even as his conviction that the French were heading for Port Dauphin started to ebb.

'Mister Moxon,' he said, 'have the watch on deck and the idlers clear for action if you please. Don't disturb the watch below.'

He knew he was taking a risk. If the lookout couldn't see as far as he believed, if the French frigate and the transports should appear from the fog at just a few cables distance, he'd hardly have time to beat to quarters before they'd be at close range. Nevertheless, he had to carefully husband the strength of his men. There was no doubt that they needed their watch below to recruit themselves for another four hours on deck in this unrelenting cold.

The carpenter's crew were removing bulkheads and furniture, making as little noise as possible. That was one of the advantages of a frigate over a ship-of-the-line: the people all berthed on the deck below the guns – perversely still known as the gundeck even though it was entirely innocent of weaponry – and were therefore largely unaffected by clearing for action.

'The ship's cleared for action, sir,' reported Moxon removing his hat. 'The guns are loaded with ball and run out.'

'Very well. Have the watch on deck who aren't otherwise employed stand by their guns, and then there's to be silence on deck. I don't trust this fog, it's liable to lift at any moment. What do you say, master?' he asked, turning to Hosking.

'You could be right, sir. Now that we're losing the Atlantic currents, the water is getting colder and strange

163

things happen to fog when the water or the air changes temperature.'

There were no bells, just a softly delivered report from the quartermaster each time the glass was turned. It was approaching the end of the morning watch and in the world outside the fog bank, the sun was making its slantwise course into the southern sky. Inside the fog bank, it may as well have been midnight.

And yet, so gradually that the eye couldn't perceive it, the fog to the southeast started to change; it was as though some inner light was illuminating it. The visibility was no better, but vague shapes on the frigate's deck became recognisable as familiar objects. And then the miracle happened. First, there was a flurry in the fog to the east; nothing substantial, just a noticeable burst of illumination breaking through, and then it was gone. The quarterdeck held its breath. The next movement was a definite break in the fog, an uneven rent in the curtain that surrounded *Medina*.

'Sail Ho!' came the excited cry from the main topmast head. 'Three sail on the starboard beam. I can see their topmasts about two miles away, sir,'

'Then I believe you may beat to quarters, Mister Moxon,' he said with a smile. 'You can say what you like about a Frenchman, but he's punctual to the minute, and he's done the starboard watch the courtesy of allowing them the whole of their watch below.'

The marine drummer started his tattoo and the quartermaster, taking the hint, nodded to the boy who was huddled in the lee of the binnacle, who ran for'rard, leaping over the train tackles, to strike eight bells.

Sleepy they may have been, but the starboard watch was at its stations in less than two minutes. The men had no need to dress; nobody took off a stitch of clothing when they turned in.

'The ship's at quarters, cleared for action,' reported Moxon.

'Very well. I expect it will be half an hour at least before we engage the enemy. Have the cook serve out breakfast to the men. You may dismiss a man from each gun and each station to fetch it.'

Moxon hurried away to the galley. He knew that the cook had started the breakfast burgoo an hour ago, and it only needed the biscuit and beer to give the men a good, hot meal in their bellies.

The sailing master was waiting impatiently for orders. Another minute and he was in danger of making an unwanted suggestion.

'Bring the ship about Mister Hosking. I fancy we'll see the shore soon and I want to be close enough to cut those gentlemen off from their harbour.'

As though he'd been released by a spring, Hosking bellowed at the bosun, 'hands to sail-handling stations, prepare to come about.'

The bosun lifted his call to his lips and sounded a series of notes. Men left the guns to attend to sheets and halyards, while a smaller number scampered up the ratlines to the tops. The process of tacking was carried out principally from the deck, but all hands knew that the next order, once they were settled on the larboard tack, would be to reduce to fighting sail.

Carlisle studied the unfolding scene. The French must make for the safety of one of the harbours to leeward. If they tried to beat back to Louisbourg, *Medina* would catch the lumbering transports in a matter of hours, long before they rounded East Point. The frigate may stand and fight, but it would be an act of desperation; they'd already felt *Medina's* teeth and knew that she'd be boldly handled. The French were committed, and one way or another there would be an engagement off Port Dauphin today.

***

The fog was thinning fast, and in only a few minutes the enemy ships came into view from the deck. They were huddled close together so that they kept in touch in the fog.

Probably they'd been firing muskets or ringing bells to advertise their positions to each other.

'That's our friend from the Capes,' said Hosking, watching the ships through his telescope, 'and those are troop transports, or my name's not John Hosking.'

Carlisle felt a glow of pleasure. So far, he'd guessed correctly. Now, what would they do next? To him, the answer was simple. The frigate must throw itself at *Medina* and lock the British frigate in close combat while the transports made their best speed to Port Dauphin. There was nothing subtle about it, and it would fulfil the mission, in the best French naval tradition. Most likely it would be the end of the frigate, but that would certainly be acceptable to the colonel of the battalion, and probably grudgingly acknowledged as the correct course of action by the frigate captain.

'There's a boat leaving the frigate, sir,' said Moxon. 'It's stuffed with gold braid; you can almost see it flashing without a telescope.'

Carlisle nodded; it was just what he expected. The frigate might sacrifice itself, but it would be a hollow gesture if the leadership of the battalion should be separated from the soldiers. Yet they were cutting it fine; in fifteen minutes *Medina* and the Frenchman would be exchanging broadsides.

'Mister Moxon, a moment of your time, if you please,' said Carlisle.

This, he knew, could be a desperate fight and it was his clear duty to ensure that his second-in-command knew his plan in case he should be killed or wounded. It was well-understood that the most dangerous place in a sea-fight was the quarterdeck and that was at least partly why the first lieutenant should be stationed in the waist among the guns, so that he had a better chance of surviving to assume command.

'He'll expect us to use the normal frigate tactics, to pummel him with roundshot and then when the time is right to close and board. The problem is that by the time we've taken him, the transports will be through the narrows into Port Dauphin, and there's nothing we can do with that fort dominating the entrance.'

Carlisle paused, watching Moxon's reaction. They'd come a long way in a short time, earning each other's trust the hard way; now Carlisle hoped that his first lieutenant would step up to the challenge of command.

'Then we must be French in this case, I find, sir,' Moxon replied. 'Chain shot?'

'Indeed, Mister Moxon. You have time to draw the ball and re-load with chain. I intend to disable her and have a try at those transports before they slip away for good.'

Moxon turned away to give the orders, but Carlisle stopped him.

'This will be a desperate affair if we do have to close and board, Mister Moxon. Whatever happens, I wish you well,' and he grasped his first lieutenant's hand.

***

CHAPTER SEVENTEEN

The Siboux Islands

Wednesday, Twenty-Ninth of March 1758.
Medina, at Sea. Off Cape Dauphin, Île Royale.

As *Medina* sailed south, the fog cleared, and a pallid light pierced the haze. It wasn't enough to provide any warmth, but it did reveal the scene of the coming action. It looked for all the world like a sandbox; miniature ships upon an ocean painted in shades of grey against a sky of so light a blue as to be almost colourless.

'Yards are chained and puddened,' reported the bosun. 'I've rigged the boarding nets in case we need them, but I see that's not your intention,' he said nodding towards where the crews of the nine-pounders were going through the delicate drill of drawing the round-shot and loading with chain.

'That's right, Mister Swinton, but best be prepared. I expect he'll pepper us with chain shot himself, so have your crew ready to knot and splice.'

'Aye-aye sir,' he replied, 'that I will.'

'The guns are loaded with chain shot,' reported Moxon, touching his hat.

'Very well,' replied Carlisle. 'We have a few minutes. Call the crews to the quarterdeck rail, if you please, Mister Moxon.'

It would be hard to say what had motivated Carlisle to address the crew. He had rarely done so, not even before a battle, but this one would be different to any he'd led them into before and he wanted to be sure that they knew his plan.

The crews came jostling aft, securing the tackles and giving a last blow on the slow match to keep it alight before they left their guns. He'd known most of these men through a commission in the Leeward Islands and Jamaica Squadron where he'd taken them into battle naked from the waist up, now they were in layer after layer of clothing against the killing cold. They didn't at first look like the same men at all. He knew that they'd be shedding guernsey sweaters and gregos after the first rounds were fired – it was hot work serving a nine-pounder gun in action – but for now they looked almost comical. But there was nothing amusing about their faces; they looked like the very model of fighting men, grim and determined.

'You all know our friend over there,' shouted Carlisle so that they could all hear him, 'he's run away from us once, but he won't run this time. He needs to get those transports into port over there,' he said, pointing across the larboard bow, 'and we need to stop them.'

Carlisle was pleased with his phrasing. Keep it straightforward and simple, he thought, that's the way to lead these men.

'Now normally we'd be hammering him with roundshot then boarding him when he's been softened up, but today we don't have time for that. In half an hour those transports will be beyond our reach, and in a day or two the soldiers that they're carrying will be manning those defences on the Louisbourg shore that we found yesterday.'

Was it only a day ago that they were running lines of soundings in Gabarus Bay? It felt like a month at least.

'We have to disable the frigate quickly. I need her yards and topmasts brought down and her sails shredded. I saw you firing at those batteries in Gabarus Bay. That's the shooting that I need. Can you do that for me again?'

The answering roar said all that Carlisle needed to know. The very planking of the deck reverberated as two hundred throats yelled in unison.

'And when we've done that we'll be at those transports. Now, back to your stations and stand by.'

***

'Mister Hosking full and by, if you please. You should be able to weather those islands at the entrance to the harbour, what are they called?'

'The Siboux Islands, sir,' replied Hosking. 'They're laid down on the chart.'

A sudden thought came to Carlisle.

'Can those transports pass inside them? Is there enough water?'

'Now that I don't know, sir. I wouldn't like to try it without knowing the soundings, but in all probability those Frenchmen have better charts than us, perhaps they even have a pilot for these waters.'

Carlisle looked carefully at the islands. He hadn't considered them before; they lay about a mile and a half off the cape at the eastern side of the harbour entrance. Long, low and rocky, they stretched over two miles to the northeast. At first sight it looked like anything bound for Port Dauphin must go around their northern extremity; at second sight too. Surely there wasn't enough water between them and the mainland, was there?

The French ships were just two miles away. The frigate had shaken out her courses and was pulling away from the transports, crossing their track to put herself ahead of them, squarely into *Medina's* path. The boat that had carried the battalion staff under sail now, her gunwale lapping the waves as she sped to return to the frigate. It was the size of a British longboat and would have to be watched if it didn't return to the frigate, thought Carlisle. He remembered that a tender to his first command *Fury*, in the Mediterranean, had turned the battle against another French frigate by boarding her unexpectedly from her blind side. He didn't want the same trick played on *Medina*.

With the wind in the northeast now, yet still nothing more than a light breeze, it was a simple navigation problem for the French transports to slip around the north of the islands and have a dead run into the harbour.

The frigate was in position and furling her courses; she was down to her fighting canvas, just like *Medina*. Perversely, Carlisle was pleased to see the French dispositions; they were doing just what he'd have done in the same situation. The transports hadn't reduced sail. They were staking everything on a fast break for Port Dauphin while the British frigate was engaged. The enemy frigate, meanwhile, was ensuring that *Medina* couldn't ignore her and go for the transports. It was shaping up to be a bloody business.

'Mister Hosking. We'll squeeze them onto those islands. Stand on as you are, and we'll go about when the northern tip is five cables on our bow. That'll force the transports to go to seaward of us and give more time for us to deal with the frigate.'

The Sioux Islands looked menacing, a trap for the unwary mariner and a constant hazard at the entrance to the harbour. Carlisle watched the two transports. Were they shaving the northern tip of the islands too close? It certainly looked as though they were. Or were they trying to fool him? While he was engaged with the frigate off the tip of the islands, could they veer and run down to the southern passage? With a gulp, he suddenly knew that it must be their plan. They were relying on him not knowing that with a squeeze, a ship could pass to the south of the islands. He looked appraisingly at the French frigate.

'Will your chain shot reach her yet, Mister Moxon?' he called.

The first lieutenant jumped onto the hammock crane and squinted into the weak sun.

'Yes, sir, she's just in range,' he replied.

'Then commence firing, Mister Moxon.'

It was long range, Carlisle knew, approaching a mile. Normally he'd have waited until the enemy was at half a mile or less so that the first carefully loaded and pointed broadside wouldn't be wasted, but this was an unusual situation.

'Fire!' shouted Moxon, and the larboard broadside responded in a thunderous broadside.

'Bring her about, Mister Hosking, and be ready to continue all the way around and veer ship if I say so.'

Hosking looked askance at his captain. Why tack now if he was planning to veer immediately afterwards? But Hosking had learned that Carlisle saw opportunities that he often didn't and turned to carry out his orders

Carlisle watched the transports with a cunning look in his eye. If his theory were correct, they'd veer any moment now.

Medina swung through the wind and showed her starboard broadside to the enemy. There was no answering fire; they were squarely on the French frigate's bow, where none of his guns would bear.

'You may fire with the starboard broadside when ready, Mister Moxon.'

He had time for a quick look at the frigate. There was no severe damage yet; he could see some holes in the sails and one or two stray halyards, but nothing to significantly slow her.

'Fire!' shouted Moxon again, and the starboard battery delivered its load of chain shot. The range had reduced considerably, and there were a few yells of triumph as the Frenchman's sails suffered again. He just had time to see the frigate's fore stays'l fall abruptly onto the fo'c'sle, its halyard and the forestay to which it was hanked shot away. That would hinder her manoeuvrability – she'd be slow in tacking and would have to be careful not to put too much strain on the fore topmast stay – but it wouldn't reduce her speed off the wind.

Moxon was resisting the urge to dance with delight, but he did make an uncharacteristic shout, looking down at the guns with pride.

'That's glorious, two broadsides and not a gun in reply. Huzzah, my boys!'

Carlisle looked again at the transports. They were cutting it very fine if they did intend to go south-about around the islands. He wafted away a trail of smoke that had drifted across his eyes and when it was clear, he saw what he'd expected. The two transports were turning to larboard, putting their sterns through the wind and heading south. It was a good move, and by rights it should have caught *Medina* unawares, but now it opened a gap between the transports and their escort, and Carlisle could exploit that.

'Do we have enough way on to veer,' he shouted urgently to the master.

'Aye sir, just about.'

'Then keep your helm to starboard and bring us all the way around. Shape our course for the harbour entrance.'

Hosking looked sharply at Carlisle. Had he correctly understood his captain? The quartermaster, however, had no qualms and with a hand on the steersman's arm, he kept the wheel hard over.

Then Hosking saw the transports and understood.

'Brail the mizzen,' he shouted at the waisters.

That would reduce the wind pressure on the stern.

'Hard a-larboard. Does she answer quartermaster?'

'Aye sir, she answers, she'll come off the wind nicely.'

Carlisle looked again at the French frigate. Her captain had seen *Medina* come about and had brought his own ship hard onto the wind to parallel *Medina's* new course. The Frenchman had been staking it all on a slugging match. It would have given the transports time to get through the narrows. And he knew that if either of the two frigates had been disabled, they'd naturally have drifted to leeward, and only Port Dauphin and its fort awaited them. The fortunes of war had appeared to be on his side until the British frigate fired its starboard broadside and instead of sailing hard on the wind to engage, continued its turn to larboard.

'Make all sail, Mister Hosking. I want to be at the southwestern end of those islands before the transports get there.'

The confusion on the French frigate was evident. She now had to pay off the wind fast without the help of the fore stays'l. The manoeuvre was still possible, but it was slow, and by the time they were heading south, they were in a chase with the British frigate a mile ahead and ready to pounce on the transports as they came through the narrow pass. There was no question of the two transports turning back; from the moment that they veered near the northern tip of the islands they were committed. The transports were now effectively embayed, and the only way out was through the narrow gap between Cape Dauphin and the Siboux islands, and *Medina* could be seen racing for that same gap from the other side.

***

'You see the situation now, Mister Moxon,' said Carlisle, pointing to the transports just two miles to the west.

'Yes, sir. Won't they lie-to on the other side of those islands and hope they can slip through into Port Dauphin when the frigates are engaged?'

'Perhaps, but look at it from that colonel's perspective,' Carlisle replied. 'He'll have seen his frigate already cut about in the sails and rigging. No doubt he'll have been told that she's up against the same British ship that saw her off two weeks ago. I doubt whether he has much faith in a favourable outcome. And if we take or disable the French frigate, the transports will never make Port Dauphin. They could run into that next bay to the east of the islands – Labrador Inlet I think it's called – but there are no facilities there for offloading and the entrance is narrow, just two cables. That'll be his fallback position, but it's not a very attractive one.'

'Then you think he'll make a break for the passage inside the islands while we're engaged with the frigate?'

'I think it's probable.' Carlisle stood in thought a moment. 'Yes, that's what I would do. If he waits, there's a chance that he'll have an uncontested passage, but that's no certainty, and if he's wrong, he'll lose his whole force, and he knows it. He'll shorten sail and wait until we're engaged, but he won't wait to see the outcome. So, we need to deal with that frigate quickly, and that's where you come in, Mister Moxon. Disable her for me, bring down her topmasts or her yards before the transports are through the passage.'

Moxon looked over the taffrail at the French frigate. It was nearly two miles astern now, and the gap was increasing. He raised the telescope to his eye. He could see frantic activity on the foremast and the bowsprit as they hurried to re-rig the fore stays'l. When they achieved that they'd have restored full manoeuvrability, and he'd have to start the process of disabling her all over again.

'Aye sir,' he said thoughtfully, 'the lads will bring down her spars for you.'

***

Carlisle watched the three pieces moving across the coming battlefield. They formed an equilateral triangle with sides of two miles. The Siboux islands were like a knife – a long, sharp knife – penetrating the southwesterly side. The whole triangle moved southwest at a stately five or six knots under the now moderate northeasterly breeze, impaling itself even further on the islands.

There was an optimum time for *Medina* to turn and face the French frigate. It could be calculated to a nicety by trigonometry, but Carlisle didn't have the leisure for that, he'd have to make a guess based on his long years at sea and his experience of previous fights. He'd have about twenty minutes, he thought, to disable his adversary. If he took longer than that the French would win, the transports would be through the narrows and safely at anchor behind the fort. Even two or three well-served guns behind the embrasures would prevent *Medina* from following and render the transports safe from any cutting-out expedition that he could mount. Carlisle desperately wanted to tempt the French colonel to commit to the passage behind the channel, rather than run for the Labrador Inlet. If he saw *Medina* in his way, even if the French frigate was still intact, he'd hesitate, and having hesitated, the northeasterly wind would make up his mind for him. The optimum point for the engagement was where the two islands were separated by a narrow channel. It was coming up fast.

'Mister Hosking!'

'Aye sir,' replied the master.

'I'll be asking you to bring the frigate onto the wind in a few minutes. When I do so, furl the courses as soon as you're on the wind. We'll fight the Frenchman before he can get down to the transports.'

'Aye-aye sir,' replied Hosking. He turned to the bosun to give his orders.

Carlisle took another look at the moving triangle. Not yet, too soon. He wanted to be close enough to the southwestern end of the islands so that he could quickly run down on the transports.

'You're loaded with chain, Mister Moxon?' he asked unnecessarily, betraying his nervousness.

'Chain it is, sir,' the first lieutenant replied with a grin, his white teeth showing through the powder stains on his face.

The seconds ticked by.

'Now, Mister Hosking! Bring her onto the wind.'

Medina swung jerkily towards the wind with rattling blocks and slapping halyards as the courses were furled as fast as they'd ever been. Most of the hands who were strung out along the yards knew that they had to be back at their guns ready to open fire.

With the wind as close to the larboard bow as ever it could be, *Medina* thrust her way into the failing breeze, her speed much reduced but her manoeuvrability greatly improved. Now that the courses weren't obscuring the view, the French frigate was clearly visible four points off the larboard bow. She was coming down on them under full sail in her urgent need to support the transports. Carlisle had time for one quick glance to starboard. The Transports were still steering for the passage between the cape and the islands and as he watched, he saw the leading transport shaking out its courses. They were committing to the passage!

'Send your larboard crews to the tacks and sheets, Mister

Moxon, and stand by to engage to starboard.'

The first lieutenant could see the captain's plan. He was going to turn across the Frenchman's bow and rake him from ahead with chain shot. If that didn't bring down a spar or two, nothing would.

'Remove your quoins,' Moxon shouted to his crews. He watched as the row of muzzles pointed skywards. The captain was clearly planning that this first broadside should be delivered at the closest possible range, and the guns would need to be at maximum elevation for the shot to reach the masts, sails and rigging.

The two frigates rushed towards each other. The Frenchman was intent upon getting past *Medina* and supporting the transports while *Medina* was determined to stop her or render her ineffective before she'd got past her tormentor.

'Mister Hosking bring her about if you please,' Carlisle said calmly, only his clenched fists betraying his state of mind. 'You may fire when your broadside bears,' he said in a moderated shout to the first lieutenant.

Medina came quickly through the wind, but even in that short space of time, the French frigate had moved much closer, so that she was a huge looming presence just two cables off the beam. Her bows were filled with seamen still rigging the new forestay and fore stays'l, her foretop was likewise crowded with men securing the cumbersome rope around the base of the fore topmast.

'Fire!' shouted Moxon.

Medina reeled to the force of the blast. There was a moment where nothing could be seen for the powder-smoke, but the wind quickly blew it away to leeward. The gun crews had no time to admire their handiwork, but the result of that single broadside had been devastating. The fo'c'sle and foretop had been swept clean of people. The scene at close quarters must have been truly frightening because chain shot mangled a body in a way that round-shot rarely did. However, the critical thing for Carlisle was the headsails and the foremast, and they were all apparently undamaged. The chain shot had shredded the sails and decimated the crew, but by some miracle the masts and standing rigging were untouched. The French frigate still bore down upon them.

***

Medina had plenty of way and was moving fast across the Frenchman's bow. The gun crews were working hard to reload the starboard battery, their gregos mysteriously discarded and a few of them were even shirtless.

'Starboard broadside again,' shouted Carlisle. 'Will she stay, Mister Hosking?'

Hosking watched the sails for an infuriating moment.

'No, sir, we'll be in irons if we try that, but she'll veer well enough.'

'Then veer ship!'

Carlisle knew that he'd lost the first round, not by a knockout blow but by failing to achieve his own aim of bringing down the Frenchman's foremast.

'It'll be the larboard broadside, Mister Moxon.'

He'd have to parallel the Frenchman's course, and all his fancy tactics would be reduced to an old-fashioned slogging match as the two ships fought it out broadside to broadside.

'Starboard battery fire!' shouted Moxon, catching Carlisle unaware. Starboard battery! That was a gross breach of discipline, firing without the captain's word, and Carlisle was momentarily angry.

'Begging your pardon, sir,' said Moxon, removing his hat and glancing away on the quarter. Carlisle's anger evaporated. When his larboard broadside captains had started holding up their hands to indicate their guns were ready, and they were intelligently training aft as *Medina* swung off the wind, Moxon had seen the opportunity for another attempt at the Frenchman's masts. Only half of the guns had fired, those belonging to the crews that were faster at reloading and levering the great guns around, but those few had done the business. The fore topmast was swaying dangerously, and, in a moment, it was gone, hauled over the starboard bow with the force of the quartering wind, taking the main yard with it, fractured in the slings. If the Frenchman hadn't already lost his fore stays'l, the situation could have been retrieved, but with the fore topmast went the fore tops'l and the fore topmast stays'l. He was left with no sails for'rard of the mainmast. In seconds the French frigate's bows started to swing inexorably to starboard, into the wind. Faster and faster she turned, her intact jibboom barely missing *Medina's* quarterdeck. And still, the Frenchman hadn't fired a shot.

'Where are the transports?' yelled Carlisle to the quarterdeck at large.

'They're almost in the passage,' replied Enrico, the only officer on the quarterdeck not watching the agony of the French frigate. 'They've come too far to turn back now.'

Carlisle staggered as a blow hit *Medina's* quarter. At least one gun had been fired by the Frenchman; a single shot had hit *Medina*, where he couldn't tell, but there had been no cries of pain.

'Make your course to catch those transports, Mister Hosking.'

'They're hauling their wind, sir,' shouted Enrico. 'They're trying to veer and make the Labrador Inlet.'

'They'll never do it, said the master, 'They'll fetch up on the cape if they're not careful.'

Medina settled on her downwind course and spread her courses. Carlisle watched as the two transports put their sterns through the wind. Whatever Hosking and Enrico thought, it appeared that they'd make it into the Labrador Inlet. They must have an exceptional pilot, thought Carlisle, to so confidently reverse their course off that lee shore. Nevertheless, there they were, long before *Medina* had reached the southwestern point of the islands, running into the narrows under tops'ls, as though they didn't have a care in the world.

***

CHAPTER EIGHTEEN

Poor Bloody Soldiers

Thursday, Thirtieth of March 1758.
Medina, at Sea. Off Cape Dauphin, Île Royale.

There was a sense of anticlimax on *Medina's* quarterdeck. The wind had dropped to a whisper but if anything, it was even colder. The gun crews, sweating in their shirts an hour ago with the exertion of combat, were now hurriedly pulling on Guernsey sweaters and oiled gregos.

'She's ours for the taking,' said Hosking, gesturing towards the stricken French frigate, a mile to windward now and with her stern to *Medina*. 'She'll be unmanageable for at least an hour until they rig a headsail from the remains of the foremast, and even then, she'll be slow in stays, if she can tack at all.'

Carlisle wasted no more than a glance on the frigate. She was no threat and couldn't be until she had a new fore topmast. That would take days to achieve at sea, or more realistically it would require a trip to a harbour with spare spars and the facility to rig them.

'What do you know about the Labrador Inlet?' he asked Hosking, ignoring the master's remark.

'Nothing whatsoever, sir,' Hosking replied. 'Its name is mentioned on my chart but nothing more. It appears to have a narrow entrance, and it probably has steep sides and deep water if it follows the normal pattern in this country, but that's just conjecture.'

'They seem to think they can get in there,' said Carlisle gesturing at the two transports, now well clear of the passage between the islands and Cape Dauphin. They were sailing serenely into what would have looked like the certainty of grounding on a rocky shore if the chart hadn't exposed the concealed entrance to the Labrador Inlet.

'Aye sir, but will they get out again? They'll need a southerly wind and not too strong, and clear weather too. We haven't seen anything of that nature yet.'

'They don't need to get out again,' replied Carlisle. 'That battalion of soldiers, or whatever number there may be, is worth a dozen transports,' he said, looking away from the master.

He was tired of Hosking's attitude and dismayed at his inability to answer simple questions about this coast. He knew he was unreasonable; there were no useful British charts of this area. Once they had rounded Cape Breton, they were into French territory, French for the last hundred and fifty years, and even in the short periods when England or Britain had controlled parts of it, no accurate surveys of the coast were made. Really, he was lucky that they knew the general outline and the names of the capes, bays and islands; most British men-of-war would have no clue.

'I know one thing,' said Carlisle without thinking, 'I'd give a year's pay to have that pilot on my deck.'

Hosking made a huffing noise deep in his throat and busied himself at the binnacle.

To Carlisle, his duty was plain and unlike his sailing master, he understood that *Medina* must influence the land battle if she was to be of any value at all. A French frigate more-or-less was of no consequence to the taking of Louisbourg, whereas a battalion of French infantry, still probably the best trained and best-led soldiers in the world, could make the difference between success and failure. He could see the strategic situation with a clarity that perhaps only Moxon of all the other officers shared. Moxon and perhaps Enrico, who had been brought up in a family that discussed and participated in world affairs. The French frigate – he still didn't know its name despite their two weeks' acquaintance – could run carefully into Port Dauphin or she could keep the sea and make a jury rig as best she could, but either way, she wouldn't be bothering *Medina* for a few days at least. His duty was to make life as

181

difficult as he could for those soldiers.

'Mister Hosking,' he said, not caring to acknowledge the sailing master's mood, 'you may lie-to and warn the cook that dinner will be piped in thirty minutes. Keep a mile clear of the islands and Cape Dauphin and call me if you need to make sail to do so, if the weather closes in or if that Frenchman makes a move towards us. I'll be in my cabin.'

Carlisle motioned to the first lieutenant.

'Mister Moxon, will you join me?'

***

Down in the cabin, Carlisle spread out Hosking's chart of Île Royale. It lacked the detail of the features of the land, but it did show the general route that the battalion would have to take to reinforce Louisbourg.

'You'll leave the frigate be then, sir,' said Moxon. It was a statement rather than a question.

'Yes, unless we determine that we can do nothing against the soldiers, then we can think about making a prize of her. I have to say that it goes against the grain just leaving her unmolested.'

'I'll bet her captain is wondering what we're about,' replied Moxon, chuckling.

The first lieutenant's face and hands were covered in the black residue of powder smoke, and it made his smile appear comical.

'Well, be that as it may, we must do whatever we can to impede those soldiers. Now, what does this chart tell us?'

Even the worst, most minimalistic chart will reveal its secrets if studied with a set purpose, and the master's chart of Île Royale was no exception. Moxon stepped off the distances using his outstretched fingers as dividers.

'It's a good forty-mile march to Louisbourg from the eastern side of this inlet, this Labrador Inlet, as they call it.'

'Yes, Labrador must be their name for this whole lake system at the centre of Île Royale,' added Carlisle. 'Look, from here they could make their way by water deep into the heart of the territory.'

'Little good would it do them, sir. They need to travel southeast to reach Louisbourg. It looks like a decent road and must be well-travelled, probably all these waterways have ferries where they're too wide for bridges, and they won't have to beat their way through brush and bog. If they take the way to the lake, they'll be too far to the west.' Moxon said, pointing to the Labrador lake. 'They must strike southeast, it's the direct route, despite these waterways,' he indicated the network of fingers of the sea that penetrated the northeast coast.

'Of course, the people of this country are all French or Acadians, or they're savages in league with the French,' said Carlisle. 'The soldiers will be able to requisition boats and find food and shelter. Looking at the terrain, I would say that two or three days will see them behind the walls of the fortress.'

For just a moment, Carlisle looked forlorn, defeated by the impossibility of doing anything to prevent the French battalion reaching its destination.

'We could send our boats in tonight, sir. We could burn the transports and any stores that they haven't managed to unload.'

Carlisle could see that even Moxon had scant faith in his own words. The soldiers may be helpless on a ship, in a sea battle that is fought with great guns at ranges that a musket can't match, but in a small harbour with a fort at their back, few ship's boats could pass in, and none would come out again.

'Perhaps if we trace their likely march, sir.'

That was easy to deduce. The land of Île Royale was so broken up by inlets, rivers and lakes that there were few options for a march from the Labrador Inlet to Louisbourg. Assuming the battalion was landed on the eastern side of the inlet – and surely the colonel would insist on that, even if it meant running the transports aground to achieve it – then they must first strike across the country to Spaniard's Bay. It looked like a straightforward march of some ten or twelve miles with a second inlet to cross, called the Little Labrador Inlet. If they spent the rest of this day disembarking, and assuming there were local boats to be had, they could be in the small town on Spaniard's Bay by Friday evening. Again, if there were boats to be had, they could cross the bay and in two more marches – perhaps as little as one – and they'd be in Louisbourg by Sunday evening.

'Once they're past Spaniards Bay, there's nothing that we can do against them, sir,' Moxon said, 'so we have to do something today, or tomorrow at the latest.'

'Yes, then it's the Labrador Inlet,' he said, pointing to the inlet that the transports were entering as they spoke, 'or it's the Little Labrador Inlet or Spaniard's Bay.'

'Spaniards Bay,' repeated Moxon thoughtfully. 'The problem here is that it's almost as quick to march around it as it is to take boats across. If they get even a hint of our presence, they'll surely take the dry-shod route, don't you think, sir?'

Carlisle could see just what the first lieutenant meant. There were rivers to be crossed in plenty and what looked like marshland, but Île Royale had been held by the French for one-and-a-half centuries, and the French genius for engineering would surely have provided safe routes across the country. Moxon was right, there was no point in intervening in Spanish Bay; it must be one of the two inlets to the Labrador Lake. After the battalion had crossed those they would be out of reach of the navy.

Both men stared at the chart, deep in thought. Moxon spoke first.

'As you said, sir, it's too dangerous to attempt anything against those transports once they're in that inlet. They're safe from us there as long as the soldiers are nearby.'

Carlisle nodded. He and his first lieutenant were groping towards the same conclusion.

'It must be this Little Labrador Inlet. It's the only place on their march which is within reach of the sea and where they must have boats to cross; they have no alternative. The river looks about four miles long before it widens into the lake. If we can strip that four-mile stretch of boats, we'll hold them up for days.'

'Certainly, we can do that. We can send our boats away as soon as it gets dark and sweep that river clean of anything that floats. We may even be able to replace our yawl. But is it worth it? What will be the result? A few days longer on their march, before they construct new boats or haul them overland from Spaniard's Bay? What would you do, if you were the colonel of that battalion?'

Moxon considered for a moment. Really, the French options were limited. It was no mean undertaking to move a battalion and even its essential baggage over forty miles of rough ground, and that assumed that they'd leave their larger items and camp followers to catch up as they could.

'I'd send runners overland to Louisbourg and request small boats be sent around, he replied. 'Louisbourg must have dozens of fishing boats large enough to work the banks. They'd certainly be able to make that passage to the Labrador inlets.'

Carlisle looked at his first lieutenant. His reasoning was superb; why hadn't he previously recognised this quality in the man? He knew why, even if he didn't want to admit it to himself. He'd continuously compared Moxon to his friend Holbrooke, and whatever Moxon did, he saw in a negative light. Carlisle shook himself out of his reverie.

A knock at the door revealed Enrico.

'Mister Hosking's compliments, sir, and the French frigate has rigged a fore stays'l, of sorts, and she's before the wind running towards Port Dauphin, well over to the western side of the passage. She's to leeward of us now.'

'Thank you, Mister Angelini, how close will she pass to us?'

Enrico thought for a moment.

'Two miles to the west, sir.'

'Then my compliments to the master and he's to let me

know if she hauls her wind. The hands are at their quarters still?'

'Yes, sir, we're ready for them,' replied Enrico.

The cabin door closed, and the sound of Enrico's rapid ascent of the quarterdeck ladder faded.

'Well, that's cleared out one variable,' said Carlisle. 'That frigate can't beat up towards us now and soon she'll be beyond our reach. It goes against the grain to let her go, and she'd be a good prize, but today our duty lies elsewhere.'

'Yes, sir, there'll be another day,' replied Moxon keeping the disappointment from his voice. A successful action would only help in getting him promoted, and unlike Carlisle, he'd made no prize money yet.

'There may indeed be another day,' said Carlisle, absent-mindedly. 'But for today, we have a plan, Mister Moxon. We'll take or burn everything that floats along that stretch of the lesser inlet,' he indicated the four-mile river that ran from the sea to the start of the lakes. 'Then we'll set a trap for the boats from Louisbourg.'

***

CHAPTER NINETEEN

Take or Burn

Thursday, Thirtieth of March 1758.
Medina, at Sea. Off Little Labrador Inlet, Île Royale.

The French frigate, relieved of its escorting duties and hugging the western shore, had slipped into Port Dauphin under a jury rig. That removed one option from Carlisle's planning; there was no chance of attacking her once she was through the narrows and anchored under the guns of the fort, and without the facilities of a navy yard, she'd be in Port Dauphin for days if not weeks.

Half an hour later, with the French frigate now out of sight, *Medina* had made a show of attempting to pass through the channel between Cape Dauphin and the Siboux Islands. To anyone watching her, it appeared that the frigate's captain had not liked what he saw, and confronted with an unsurveyed mile-wide passage, a foul, rising wind, and middling visibility, he'd lost his nerve. By four bells *Medina* was beating up to the northeast, hard on the wind, leaving Port Dauphin and the Siboux Islands behind. Carlisle hoped that any Frenchmen who cared to follow his progress would believe that he was bound for Cape Breton and thence to the approaches to Louisbourg. To reinforce that impression, he kept the frigate hard on the wind until the land had faded into the light mist. When there was no chance of *Medina* being seen from Cape Dauphin, he tacked and stood in for the Little Labrador Inlet.

The sun had set an hour before and the last glow was fading over the hills of Île Royale. *Medina* lay off the lesser inlet, her longboat alongside, with its mast stepped and its lugs'l ready to be hoisted. The carpenter was fussing around the mountings for a pair of swivel-guns that Moxon had decided were the best armament for the task, while the gunner was stowing combustible packets in every nook and

187

cranny.

'I regret the loss of the yawl now,' said Carlisle to Moxon, 'It somehow doesn't feel right sending you in there without support.'

'After my last experience of keeping two boats together in the dark, I'd almost rather be alone, sir,' replied the first lieutenant, grinning. 'They won't be expecting us, there's no likelihood of a significant military force on this inlet, and I expect we'll be in and out before word gets to the soldiers.'

'Yes, they'll be wholly engaged in disembarking, and it's five miles across rough country from the other inlet. Now you, of course, will have to make your decisions on the spot, but I advise that you sail straight through to the lake. It should only take an hour in this easterly wind, and then sail or pull back, burning as you go.'

'Aye-aye sir, and I'll look out for a replacement for the yawl.' Moxon smiled again; Carlisle couldn't decide whether it was from nervousness or just his usual disposition. 'Well, good luck, and we'll be waiting for you just a mile offshore.'

The two men shook hands, then Moxon swung over the gunwale and down into the longboat. Enrico was already there, and Souter, holding the tiller in one hand and the stern painter in the other. With a few words, the lugs'l yard was hoisted, the painters released, and a strong shove pushed the bows away from the frigate's side. The sail caught the easterly wind and the longboat was quickly lost in the mist and darkness.

***

Carlisle paced the deck for an hour, then went below to his darkened cabin. He lay down on the bench under the stern windows, realised he couldn't sleep but was determined that he wouldn't spend the night pacing the quarterdeck, advertising his unease to the whole ship's company. He called for supper, cold meat and cheese with the very last of the bread from Halifax, now as hard as the ship's biscuit. He found he couldn't swallow it; this was the hardest kind of waiting. There was no diversion to make and no chance of seeing the longboat until it had completed its business, and that would be hours from now, at least into the middle watch and more probably the morning. He called again for his servant. If he sat in his sleeping cabin with the deadlight rigged, he could have a candle and could at least study the charts again; that would be a productive use of this otherwise frustrating and worrying night.

Carlisle heard the soft sounds of the lookout being relieved and the steersmen ending their tricks at the wheel. The longboat had been gone two hours now. If all was well, Moxon should have reached the outlet to the lake and have started his return journey. The channel was less than a cable wide for its whole four-mile length, and that fact was essential to the plan. Any boats along its length would be clearly visible, even in the dark, and Moxon would have noted their positions for his destructive return trip. There was a village at each end of the inlet; that would be where most of the boats would be kept. At the inland end, it would be mostly smaller boats for use on the lake and to ferry people and goods from one side of the inlet to the other. It was that point that the French battalion would march for tomorrow, and that was the critical place to attack. How many boats would there be? It was hard to guess, but probably no more than half a dozen.

The village at the seaward end was another matter. There'd be fishing boats there and perhaps a coasting vessel or two. They'd all have to be destroyed; Moxon had a busy night ahead of him.

***

The change of the watch brought a shift in the wind. A breeze from the south dissipated the mist, blowing it away in tatters to reveal a starry night with a low, waning moon, six days past the full. Suddenly the land became apparent, the rocky tree-topped shore just over a mile to the southwest and startlingly close in this new, naked world. Carlisle sensed the change and went on deck.

'Good morning sir,' said Hosking. Clearly, the master

hadn't left the deck since the longboat had departed on its expedition. He'd been there all through the remaining hour of the last dog and the four hours of the first.

'Good morning, Mister Hosking. This wind is a little fresher.'

'Yes, sir, a prosperous wind for Mister Moxon too. He'll be able to run down to us with no trouble.'

Carlisle resisted the urge to ask if Hosking had seen or heard anything. The master would surely say if he had and asking the question would merely serve to display Carlisle's unease.

'Half an hour to run into the mouth of the inlet, say an hour on a broad reach to make the village on the bay, allow half an hour to investigate anything he sees, he should have been at the bay end of the inlet by three bells in the first,' said Hosking conversationally.

Carlisle didn't respond. He'd made all these calculations himself, and there was no profit in chewing over them with the master.

'He'd have rich picking at that village on the bay. Let's say he'd spend an hour there burning anything he found. We've seen nothing, but there's high land between here and the lake. In any case, he'd have started back two hours ago, if all is well.'

This one-sided conversation wasn't helping Carlisle's nerves. If he lost his longboat, having already lost his yawl, he'd be obliged to return to Halifax to find at least one replacement. His remaining boat – a sixteen-foot gig – was no seaboat, and it was foolhardy to stay out without one. He didn't want to return to Halifax, with nothing to show for his pains but a couple of lines of soundings, a tiny battery engaged – but with no evidence of its destruction – and the loss of his first lieutenant, a master's mate, a midshipman, a boat's crew and two boats. Captains had been replaced for less than that.

Then with a start, he remembered. This wasn't just a matter of lost men and material; one of the crew was Enrico, his cousin by marriage. He'd so carelessly acquiesced to his request to join the expedition without thinking of the effect it would have on his wife if her cousin were lost. And then there was Moxon. A few weeks ago, there'd been no personal contact between Carlisle and his new first lieutenant; he'd have taken the news of his loss with a shrug, but not now. Moxon had insinuated himself into Carlisle's esteem. He'd proved himself an able – no, more than able – second-in-command and, just as importantly, he'd become a friend. Carlisle realised that he most desperately didn't want to lose either Moxon or Enrico.

***

'Deck Ho!' The cry from the lookout pierced through Carlisle's reverie. 'There's a fire ashore, sir, three points on the starboard bow. It looks like it's just behind those hills.'

Hosking shook his head as he lowered his telescope; there was nothing visible from the deck. Yet Carlisle desperately needed to see for himself. A fire so near to the coast could mean that Moxon had completed his work at the lake and was creating havoc at the coastal village that was hidden behind a fold of the hills where the inlet wound its way inland. It could also be the longboat burning, trapped by an alerted village as it tried to make its escape to the open sea.

Carlisle slung the lanyard of his telescope over his shoulder and picked his way for'rard, across the train tackles of the guns that were still cleared for action. He made the long climb up the maintop. God, it was too long since he'd last made that ascent, he thought. He resolved to climb each mast once a week in future, a resolution that he knew, even as he made it, he was unlikely to fulfil.

Carlisle settled himself in the top. The lookout was even higher, at the main topmast crosstree, and that was where he'd have to go himself if nothing was visible from the main top. At first, he could see nothing against the illumination of the moon and stars, but gradually he perceived a dull orange glow to the southwest. It was just as the lookout had said, low down, its source hidden by the small coastal hills.

'Mister Hosking,' he called down to the quarterdeck, 'what should be the bearing of that village now?'

There was a short pause.

'Four points on the starboard bow,' came the reply. 'It's hidden by a point of land to the east.'

That would be the glow that the lookout had reported, and Carlisle had seen. An error of a point in reporting was nothing, particularly at night.

'Make sail to the northwest, Mister Hosking. I want to see into the entrance of the inlet.'

There was a rush of hands to the sheets and tacks, the yards were braced around, the mizzen set and *Medina* reluctantly put her bow through the wind and moved off on a broad reach.

Carlisle watched the shore intently. The orange glow had increased, and it was casting the outline of the hills into silhouette. Gradually the entrance, or the point where Carlisle imagined it should be, started to open. Suddenly the source of the glow came into view, in all its sublime beauty. That wasn't a boat on fire, it was much larger than that. A whole village, or a harbour at least, was on fire.

It was a fascinating sight. No details could be seen, but there was a massive blaze, the light from which showed the entrance to the inlet and the small jetty on the western side. There were buildings alight, and the occasional flare as some sort of oil or tar took fire.

'Captain, sir,' called the lookout in a conversational tone, 'I can see a sail leaving the inlet.'

'Is it the longboat?' asked Carlisle and immediately regretted it. Again, the lookout would say if he thought it was *Medina's* returning expedition, but he was quite rightly reserving his judgement until it should be clear.

'It could be, sir, I'll call when I can see it better.'

Carlisle accepted the implied rebuke. He could see the boat himself now, black hull and black sail against the burning shore. There was no need to stay in the maintop now, so he swung himself into the futtock shrouds and down onto the deck.

'Should I bring her to, sir?' asked Hosking.

Carlisle nodded, not trusting himself to speak in his present state of tension. He was convinced that everyone on deck has noticed his anxiety, not making allowance for the simple fact that everyone else was keyed-up watching the drama unfold.

Medina lay-to on the larboard tack. Everyone was staring at the approaching boat, now half a mile away and running fast towards them.

'There are two boats, sir,' said Wishart, 'the second boat isn't under sail, it's close behind the first.'

'Beat to quarters,' Carlisle snapped.

Two boats could mean many things; it could be the longboat towing a prize, or it could be a determined attack on *Medina*. Moxon and Enrico could be dead or captured, the whole longboat crew with them, and this could be an audacious attempt by a bold enemy to turn the tables on this British frigate.

The drum rolled and the watch below poured on deck, pulling on coats and hats against the cold night. The ship was already cleared for action and it was only minutes before Wishart reported the ship at quarters.

'She's dipping her lug,' said Hosking, 'she's trying to tell us she's friendly. It's the longboat with a capture, for sure.'

'That's to be seen, Mister Hosking.'

Carlisle wasn't lowering his guard at this late point.

***

The longboat – for that is what she was – rounded-to under *Medina's* larboard waist and with relief Carlisle saw Moxon and Enrico sitting in the stern sheets. She was towing another boat, nearly the same length as the longboat but narrower and less sturdily built. It looked a little like their lost yawl, but with a higher freeboard and she was stepped for two masts.

Carlisle rubbed his hands with pleasure at the sight of

such a prize.

'Bosun, sway that boat inboard and put the longboat on a painter, once the crew is on board.'

'Aye-aye sir,' replied Swinton. 'She's a fine-looking craft, locally built by the look of her, but sturdy, as you'd expect off this coast. I'll bet she weighs near enough the same as the longboat.'

'Mister Hosking, once the boats are dealt with, you may make your offing then set a course for East Point.'

He turned to Moxon

'Unless there is anything more that we can do here, Mister Moxon?'

'No sir. There are no boats left on that inlet and the population is stirred up now. As we left, I heard drums and bugles off to the west; I suspect the battalion heard of us and is on the march. It'll do them little good unless they're all swimmers.'

***

'Well, Mister Moxon, I see you had a successful night,' said Carlisle as they settled into his newly restored cabin. The carpenter had wasted no time in replacing the bulkheads and his servant was busy replacing his furniture.

Moxon and Enrico looked strangely sprightly after a day of chasing a French frigate and troop transports, followed by a night of fire-raising on a hostile river.

'We proceeded as directed, sir,' started Moxon, then he realised that formality was out of place in the middle watch in a frigate's great cabin. 'There was no problem in sailing the length of the river, sir,' he continued. 'The village at the seaward end is, or was,' he grinned 'substantial. We noticed only one boat in the water, but six laid up on the shore, presumably for the winter.'

'Were you seen as you passed the village on your way in?' asked Carlisle.

'I don't believe so, sir. If we were, they must have assumed we were coasting traffic on passage for Labrador Lake, because we heard no alarm.'

Carlisle nodded. That was just what he'd hoped. He'd privately told Moxon that he was to return to *Medina* if the alarm was raised on their way into the inlet.

'We reached up the river, sir. The current was less than a knot and it took only just over an hour, I estimate, to arrive at the lake.'

'Were there any boats along the way?'

'Just the one, sir. It looked like a regular ferry berthed under a two-storey house on the eastern shore. Otherwise, the banks were quiet, just the odd cottage, but no substantial boats.'

'It's not there any longer, sir,' interjected Enrico. 'We burned it on the way back.'

'Just so,' said Moxon, grinning at his impetuous second. 'However, the village on the bay was another matter. We burned seven boats there. It was seven, wasn't it, Mister Angelini?'

'Seven, sir,' Enrico confirmed. 'We didn't stove in their bottoms in case they sank before they burned, but they were all well alight and drifting into the lake when we left.'

Carlisle nodded. With no light in the longboat, it would have been challenging to keep an accurate count on that busy night; it was as well that there were two officers in the boat.

'All the boats were in the water, none on the shore,' continued Moxon. 'They looked like lake boats rather than seaboats; they would have easily carried a hundred soldiers between them.'

'Well done,' said Carlisle. 'That battalion would have been over the river in a couple of hours in the boats you burned. They'll have to look further afield now.'

'Well, the country was well and truly disturbed by the time we finished. We had to row back down the river through the mist. We burned the ferry on the way, then this southerly breeze picked up and the mist lifted. We set the sail and ran fast down to the village by the sea. They must have seen the fires because there were people all over the shore. We dispersed them with musket fire over their heads and I set a guard around the boats on the shore. Then we stove in the bottoms and set our incendiaries.'

'Where did you take your prize, Mister Moxon?'

'Oh, that was the only boat in the water at the village. There were some better ones on shore, but we had no time to launch them, so I took that one. Her masts and sails are in the bottom; she looks a good replacement for the yawl.'

'So, what's your tally of boats?' asked Carlisle. He'd have to state the numbers in his report to Admiral Hardy.

'Fourteen burned and one taken,' replied Enrico. 'Seven lake boats, one large ferry, six coastal fishermen and the yawl.'

Strange, thought Carlisle, the prize had already been rated *yawl*, and he knew that nothing he could say would change that now.

***

CHAPTER TWENTY

The Blockade

Saturday, First of April 1758.
Medina, at Sea. Off Louisbourg, Île Royale.

Looking back, Carlisle could pinpoint the start of *Medina's* decline as a fighting unit. There'd been a real sense of purpose in their first week on station. They'd been the only British man-of-war off Louisbourg, and all the frigate's people felt that the success of the coming expedition rested on their shoulders. The reconnaissance in Gabarus Bay had provided action, the chase of the frigate and the transports had been exhilarating and the raid into the Little Labrador Inlet had shown what they could do even against the much-vaunted French army. The let-down, when they returned to the Louisbourg approaches, had been correspondingly severe.

No longer were they the sole watchers of the French fortress. They returned to find *Sutherland*, a fifty-gun fourth rate commanded by the vastly senior Edward Falkingham, and *Boreas*, a twenty-eight-gun frigate. These were the first fruits of Lord Colville's long winter in Halifax. When Admiral Hardy had arrived, it had taken only days to prepare these two for sea, and now he had a substantial force off Louisbourg before the ice had broken at the harbour mouth. This was vindication for Pitt's insistence that a squadron should over-winter at Halifax, in defiance of the sea-officers' advice. Such a feat had never been attempted before in a navy yard that was embryonic at best. Eight ships-of-the-line Colville maintained through that frozen winter, giving Britain that supreme advantage of an early blockade.

***

Carlisle's interview with Falkingham had been brief. He received a letter from Admiral Hardy informing him that he was under Falkingham's command until Hardy himself should arrive off Louisbourg. Any action that he contemplated now had to have the approval of his senior officer.

Falkingham looked to be about fifty years of age, but perhaps the Halifax winter had aged him; it can't have been comfortable living on board a ship at anchor in an ice-bound harbour with few facilities. When Carlisle described his activities over the previous week, Falkingham made no comment; but by his very silence, it was clear that he saw no value in the harassment of the French battalion at the Labrador inlets. He again had nothing to say when Carlisle proposed to interdict the boats that would inevitably be sent from Spanish Bay to ferry the French battalion across the water obstacles between them and Louisbourg.

Falkingham would no doubt have approved if *Medina* had taken the French frigate, that was a tangible naval success that would have been noticed in Whitehall. However, in his opinion a battalion delayed for a few days was not worth leaving Louisbourg unguarded. Worse still, in *Medina's* absence a French seventy-four, *Magnifique*, had attempted to force through the blockade but had turned back for Brest in the face of the fourth rate and the frigate, and the sight of ice still encumbering the harbour approaches. It was likely that Falkingham would use the excuse of *Medina's* absence for not engaging the much larger ship more resolutely.

Carlisle was sent to guard the eastern approaches to Louisbourg – Scatari Island, Cape Breton, and the Lorembec coast. It was a region of small harbours, each with its own fishing village, the fishermen spending the long winter mending their boats and nets, waiting for the ice to break. The area had been cleared of its Acadian and French inhabitants during Britain's three-year ownership of Louisbourg at the end of the last war, and it had never fully recovered. Now even the fishing villages had a forlorn, half-deserted look about them. Nothing moved; it was as though the land had been immobilised by the snow, the ice and the fog rolling in from the Atlantic.

***

As the sun rose *Medina* had looked into Big Lorraine Harbour at the western end of their area, then they'd moved on to view Little Lorraine and finally Baleine. Each tiny community looked abandoned; only the fishing boats drawn high up on the beach gave a hint of the occupation of the inhabitants. Now *Medina* was heading east-southeast into the teeth of a brisk northeaster that had already brought snow and hail and, as it was moderating, it looked very much like it would be bringing fog. The Portnova Islands off Cape Breton were just visible to northeast and Hosking was giving them a wide berth on account of the wicked shoal that lay concealed off their southern extremity. They would have to beat far out into the Atlantic before they could tack and make a board for East Point on Scatari Island. Captain Falkingham had made it quite clear to Carlisle that *Medina's* job – her sole reason for being off Île Royale – was to prevent French men-of-war and supplies reaching Louisbourg. There were two – no, three, Carlisle reminded himself – principal routes that supply ships could take, and two of them passed through Carlisle's area. The first and easiest was for the French to take the southern route across the Atlantic, catching the northeast trade winds from the vicinity of Madeira and following the currents along the east coast of America. That led past the English-speaking colonies and was a notorious haunt of British cruisers. The second was the northern route. It was a shorter distance, but ships had to battle cold headwinds and contrary ocean currents to take the Strait of Belle-Isle and approach Louisbourg from the Gulf of St. Lawrence. It was a brutal passage but happily free from British scrutiny. The third and least likely source of reinforcement and supply was from Quebec and Montreal, and that also meant approaching Louisbourg from the Gulf of St. Lawrence. It couldn't be ignored, but it stretched the imagination to believe that New

France could spare men or produce to support Île Royale.

Carlisle knew that his proper station was off Scatari Island, but there he was exposed to the weather from whichever direction it came. It was a miserable and deeply unhealthy station and he moved southwest every other day on the pretext of watching the Lorembec coast.

***

'Come in Doctor,' said Carlisle in response to the knock at the door. Carlton's daily report had become a depressing tale of sickness and injury. *Medina* had been only eleven days at sea, but they were the most testing that Carlisle had experienced. The coughs and colds and chronic rheumatism that always afflicted sailors in cold weather were being exacerbated by fevers and minor injuries as fingers and limbs, numbed by the cold, contacted hard oak and iron.

'Sickbay's full, of course, sir,' reported Carlton. 'I've sent the normal ailments back to their messes, but I have eight serious fevers and two cases of frostbite. I fear that I'll be removing fingertips and toes soon.'

'Is there anything more that can be done?' asked Carlisle helplessly. He already knew the answer.

'A few days in port, with warmth, fresh food and no watches to keep would help, sir,' he said, as he always did. 'However, if that can't be obtained, then we must keep the galley fire going so that the men can have dry clothes and bedding. That is if they'll make the effort.'

'What do you mean, Doctor?' asked Carlisle.

Carlton had been expecting that question. He had an infuriating way of presenting information only when asked, and he led his listener to pose the right questions.

'Many of the men – no, that's not fair – some of the men would rather go straight from their watch into their hammocks, wet clothes and all, than waste valuable sleeping time standing around the galley range. That means their hammocks get wet, even if they've been dried while the men were on watch. It's the primary cause of the fevers. The men being wet and cold on watch is hardly worth mentioning, they're hardened to it, and it has little effect. The problems start when they spend four hours in a damp hammock in already-wet clothes.'

'Then I'll have Mister Moxon speak to the petty officers.' Carlisle raised his voice and hailed the sentry.

'Pass the word for the first lieutenant.'

Carlisle and Carlton could hear the voices calling the first lieutenant even through the normal noises of the working of the ship beating into a stiff breeze. Moxon arrived breathlessly after a wait of perhaps five minutes. He cut an unpleasant figure, in sea boots and a battered oilskin coat and hat.

'I beg your pardon, sir, I was examining the new turns of gammoning with the bosun. They'll never be as tight as we could achieve at anchor.'

'They'll hold though, Mister Moxon?'

'Yes, they'll hold, sir, and the bosun can take up the slack when we're off the wind.'

'Very well. Now, I understand from Mister Carlton,' the doctor nodded in affirmation, 'that some of the men are turning in without drying their clothes.'

'I regret that's correct, sir, some do.' replied Moxon with a new look of concern.

Both Carlisle and Moxon felt helpless when faced with medical problems. Slack gammoning on the bowsprit was a physical problem that had known and trusted remedies, medical issues were much less susceptible to plain seamanlike logic.

'Then we must find a way of preventing this happening,' said Carlisle, looking from one to the other of his officers.

'It's not quite so easy, sir,' replied Moxon. 'It takes a good half hour to get the everyday dampness out of the clothes, at least an hour if they're wet. There's only so much space around the galley range, and the cook still needs to boil his coppers. It's just not possible to get everyone's clothes dry every watch.'

'Do the men understand the problem, do you think?'

'Oh, I believe they do, but when it's a choice of four hours' sleep or a possible fever, which would take them out of the watch in any case, many choose the sleep.'

Moxon paused to arrange his thoughts.

'I was thinking through this problem just this morning, sir. Normally it's just the men's outer clothing that's wet, their Guernseys, gregos and oilskins. They're naturally reluctant to remove their shirts and trousers and anyway, they're usually just damp, not wet. If we set a routine where the on-watch hammocks and the off-watch outer clothes are spread in front of the range, with a couple of hands to turn them, then I believe much of the problem will be solved. It'll also give the people half an hour in front of the range each watch.'

'That should help,' said Carlton. 'Damp under-clothing in a warm and dry hammock is not nearly so bad as wet clothing in a damp hammock, but can you make it work? The men are very conservative in these matters and can get bloody-minded.'

'It's the carrot and stick, Mister Carlton,' replied Moxon. 'The carrot is the opportunity to spend a half-hour of each watch by the galley fire, the stick is the loss of grog if they turn in wet; with your permission, sir,' Moxon added, looking at Carlisle, 'although I'm hoping that won't be necessary when the men see the advantages.'

'Then make it so, Mister Moxon, and have a petty officer detailed from each watch to supervise. You may make the master-at-arms responsible for this routine, and I'd like a report from you this time tomorrow.'

He turned to the doctor.

'I'd like a report from you also, Doctor. Have your assistant check that the hammocks are dry before the end of each watch; it'll do him no harm to turn out every four hours, like the hands.'

Carlton looked dubious. His assistant jealously guarded his status as an idler, a man who stood no watches and, except for emergencies, spent all night, every night, in his hammock. However, he'd raised this issue, and the first lieutenant's plan was a good one. It would be churlish in the extreme if he didn't agree to a little discomfort for his assistant. He could always take a turn himself; perhaps the change of the middle and morning watches which would be only an hour or two before his usual shake.

***

Medina ploughed her lonely furrow to the east of Louisbourg. Every day brought its fresh crop of sickness. Thankfully there were no malignant fevers, none of the infectious diseases that passed from man to man in the confines of a wooden hull at sea, and so far, no sign of scurvy. The first lieutenant's plan to have the people turn in with no worse than damp clothes, into dry hammocks, appeared to be working, and it had injected a much-needed dose of morale into *Medina's* company. For there was nothing to occupy the men's minds, nothing but this endless tacking and veering, making and shortening sail, frozen by the snow and ice, drenched by the rain and spray and always, always either wind or fog. No French man-of-war had sought to run the gauntlet into Louisbourg, not since *Magnifique* a week ago.

On the fourth of April *Medina* ran right down to the western end of her area, blown by a full gale from the northeast. Carlisle was surprised to see *Sutherland* lying-to off Big Lorraine harbour. As he neared the two-decker, he saw the signal for *Medina* to close within hailing distance. It was a tricky manoeuvre, hailing distance in a full gale was too close for comfort. However, Carlisle acknowledged that it was the only way for a message to be passed between the ships as it was far too dangerous for a boat to attempt to take him across the wind-whipped water.

Medina approached on *Sutherland's* leeward side. Carlisle left the handling of the frigate to Hosking, whom he acknowledged was a better ship-handler than he'd ever be. With infinite care, under double-reefed tops'ls and a fore stays'l, *Medina* edged up towards the larger ship. Carlisle knew that the master, for all his skill, wouldn't be able to hold *Medina* within hailing range for more than a minute, probably not even that long. The two ships naturally had different drift rates, but that was made infinitely worse as one was lying-to with its fore tops'l backed, and the other was surging ahead.

The bosun passed a line around his captain's waist and secured it to a deadeye. Carlisle climbed outboard of the gunwale, standing precariously in the mizzen chains, clinging with one hand to the lanyards.

Falkingham may have been an older man, but there was nothing wrong with his lungs.

'Ice broken up…' Carlisle reeled as a breaking wave slapped into his body, penetrating even his tightly buttoned oilskin and wetting his face.

'Ice broke up in the harbour entrance,' repeated Falkingham, pointing to leeward, towards Louisbourg. 'Go to Halifax…'

Another wave surged up the frigate's side and by some freak shot up through the skirts of Carlisle's oilskin. He was now thoroughly wet.

Falkingham pointed emphatically south, the direction that *Medina* would have to sail to make her offing for a passage to Halifax.

'Tell Hardy.'

Falkingham's meaning was obvious, and in this howling wind there may be no chance of him elaborating his orders for days, and by that time it would be too late. The gale had finally broken up the ice that prevented easy access to Louisbourg. It now needed Hardy's squadron to blockade it against French attempts to reinforce and resupply the fortress.

Carlisle waved in reply and himself pointed towards the south. Falkingham nodded emphatically.

'Thank you, Mister Swinton,' said Carlisle as he was handed carefully back inboard, more than half drowned.

'Mister Hosking, you may veer the ship and set a course

for Halifax. Make a bold offing, if you please, I've no more liking for Île Royale's lee shore than I do for any other. Perhaps we'll have a quiet night tonight.'

***

CHAPTER TWENTY-ONE

News of Ice

Thursday, Sixth of April 1758.
Medina, at Sea. Off Halifax, Nova Scotia.

The northeasterly gale drove *Medina* hard down the coasts of Île Royale and Nova Scotia, so hard that when the gale reached its peak, which it held for twenty-four hours, they ran under nothing more than a storm jib and yet still they made eight knots. It was exhilarating sailing and would have been enjoyable were it not for the cold. The frigate suffered snow, hail and rain in agonising succession, and the quarterdeck was continually awash with the following seas breaking on the taffrail. However, the frigate's people had the inexpressible pleasure of not having to go aloft; all the sail handling, such as it was, could be done from the deck. It wasn't until the forenoon watch on the sixth of April, with the wind moderating and Cape Sambro in sight, that the master hauled his wind, set the frigate's tops'ls and mizzen and made to the west for Halifax.

'What do you make of it, Mister Moxon?' asked Carlisle, his telescope trained on the harbour entrance to the west. The wind was still strong enough to make the frigate lively, and Carlisle was holding his glass against the mizzen shrouds, leaning far out to windward.

'I suspect Mister Hardy has sailed,' replied the first lieutenant, 'I count at least six of the line and a frigate.'

It was a stirring sight. Against the green of the wooded shore a squadron of men-of-war was reaching out to sea on an exactly reciprocal course to *Medina's*.

'Not Boscawen, then. I'd half expected to find him at Halifax by now, but you're right, Mister Moxon, that's Hardy's squadron.'

The details were becoming clearer by the minute as the

distance between *Medina* and the squadron closed at the rate of a mile every five minutes.

'Seven of the line and a frigate,' said Moxon.

'That'll be *Captain* in the van, and I believe I can just make out Hardy's flag at the main,' said Carlisle.

'Bosun, away the longboat crew, best rig for the captain's calls,' shouted Moxon.

Without a doubt, Admiral Hardy would want the latest news from Louisbourg, and even at the tail-end of a Nova Scotia winter storm, the frigate's captain would be expected to come alongside in some style.

'Mister Hosking, half a cable to leeward of the flagship, if you please. I'll be below for a few minutes.'

He'd have to change out of his offshore rig. Thankfully he'd already prepared a report for Hardy, as it had been impossible for Falkingham to send his own report over to the frigate.

As *Medina* approached the flagship, they saw a plain blue signal flag run up on the mizzen topmast head and a puff of smoke from a single gun. That was Hardy's order for the squadron to bring to on the larboard tack. It was followed by a red-and-green swallowtail at the peak of the mizzen yard, the signal for frigate captains to report aboard the flagship. Hardy had only one other frigate, *Port Mahon*, and she quickly bore away to run down from her station a mile to windward of the flagship.

'Bring to as soon as you're on the flagship's beam, Mister Hosking.'

***

Admiral Hardy was all business when Carlisle and Samuel Wallis of *Port Mahon* entered the great cabin. He was clearly in a tearing hurry be off Louisbourg to impose the blockade in earnest; he didn't even offer the two captains a seat.

'Good morning, Captain Carlisle. No report from Falkingham? Well, I hardly expected one. No, don't worry about your own report, my secretary will take it, just tell me the situation in your own words, I need to be on my way.'

Now that was a curious response, it almost sounded as though he had little faith in the captain of *Sutherland*, thought Carlisle. Well, if Hardy chose to be brisk, he'd reply in kind.

'The ice broke at the harbour mouth on the fourth, sir…'

'Did it, by God?' interrupted Hardy. 'That's good news and I didn't sail a day too early. Is that why Falkingham sent you, to tell me that?'

'Yes, sir, he did…' Carlisle wasn't having much luck in finishing sentences today.

'Good, then there's not a moment to lose. Do you have anything else to tell me?'

'The rest is in my report, sir. We ran lines of soundings in Gabarus Bay, and we identified some batteries and destroyed one. The survey is also in my report.'

'Well done, Carlisle,' Hardy said, not looking vastly impressed. 'I expect they'll have moved their guns by now, but it was worth stirring them up. Did you have any casualties?

'I lost a master's mate and four men, and my yawl, sir, although I replaced the yawl with a French boat that we cut out from the Little Labrador Inlet.'

'What on earth were you doing up there, Carlisle?' asked Hardy, looking suspicious. Every flag officer was bedevilled by captains – particularly frigate captains – who happily left their station to chase prizes.

'We prevented a French frigate and two transport from bringing an infantry battalion into Louisbourg, sir. I chased them up to Port Dauphin and stopped them landing there but couldn't prevent them from getting into the larger of the two Labrador Inlets. I sent the longboat at night to destroy all the boats in the Little Labrador Inlet to annoy their march to Louisbourg.'

Hardy looked thoughtful. He knew that he should have been off Louisbourg a week or two earlier, in which case he could have dealt with the French reinforcements out-of-hand.

'You did well, Captain,' he said, this time as though he meant it, 'and I'm sorry to hear about your men. I look forward to reading your report, but for now I need to get this squadron off Louisbourg, and with this foul wind it could take a week. Now, how are your stores?'

Carlisle paused for a moment. He didn't want to be known as a captain who was always looking for excuses to return to port, and he had stores for three months still. Nevertheless, he was running short of wood and still needed that second suit of sails, and fresh water was always welcome.

'I want for nothing except wood and water, sir, and whatever spare sails I can get,' he said, knowing that he was opening the door for Hardy to order him to join the squadron and beat back to Louisbourg.

Hardy barely paused.

'Then you must go into Halifax. I can't have one of my frigates running out of wood for the galley fire in this weather, and who knows when we'll be able to refill our water butts? I wish you good fortune with the sails; there were none in the yard yesterday, but a storeship from Boston came in a couple of hours ago so you may be in luck. Join me off Louisbourg as soon as you can.'

'Then, with your permission, I'll return to my ship, sir, and I wish you a good passage.'

'As you walk out, Carlisle, tell Captain Wallis what he should expect off Louisbourg. I'm sending *Port Mahon* on ahead; he should meet Falkingham a day before we can get there with these old tubs of sixties trailing along. You have ten minutes, gentlemen,' he said, looking pointedly at his pocket watch, 'then the squadron will be filling and standing on.'

***

Medina anchored off the familiar makeshift navy yard. The Boston storeship had warped alongside the jetty and was disgorging her stores in a steady stream of bundles, casks and spars. Swinton had borrowed the master's telescope and was studying some long sausage-shaped masses of canvas being carried ashore on the shoulders of a dozen men.

'Sails!' he said. 'New sails, and some of them look about right for a frigate's tops'ls. We'll have our share of those or I'm no warranted bosun.'

Swinton ran down to the waist, hailing for the gig's crew and the sailmaker as he went. He was going to squander no time in staking his claim to the best of those sails, he well knew how weak their mended sails were and how difficult it was to make new ones from bolts of canvas while at sea.

Carlisle stepped into their stolen yawl as Enrico held onto a port-lid to keep the boat steady. At any other time, in any other naval port, he'd have insisted on the longboat to support the dignity of his rank. However, in Halifax, in April, with the admiral having just left and the longboat urgently needed to embark wood and water, a French-built yawl would have to do.

'To the town quay, Souter,' he said as the boat shot away from the frigate's side.

The boat's crew were in high spirits; they were still dressed in their best rig and they were getting out of the hard labour of embarking wood and water. All they had to do was to row dry for a few hundred yards then wait for their captain to return. They may even get a wet in the tavern close by the quay if Jack Souter could be persuaded to let them go.

Carlisle shook hands with the master attendant. There was no port commissioner in this new naval yard and the master attendant, a superannuated bosun, carried the burden of the station. He looked like a man from whose shoulders a great weight had been lifted. He'd had a trying winter, satisfying Commodore Colville's demands to keep eight ships-of-the-line, a frigate and a couple of sloops from deteriorating, then getting them ready for sea so early in the season. The evidence of his success was easy to see. The anchorage was empty, except for *Medina* and *Arc-en-Ciel*, a fifty-gun fourth rate captured from the French and bought into the service in fifty-six. She'd proved too rotten for the meagre shipwright resources of Halifax to deal with, and now she swung to her anchor awaiting her fate. Her captain, John Rous, was a follower of Hardy's and had sailed with him in the flagship. There was a strong suspicion that Hardy would soon find an excuse to place Rous in one of the other of his ships, at the expense of its present captain.

'Captain Rous will be in *Sutherland* within the month,' said the master attendant with a sly look. 'It was evil fate that made Falkingham's ship the first to be ready to sail, but she was the easiest to get ready, being the only fifty apart from the rotten old hulk over there,' he waved towards *Arc-en-Ciel.* 'He and Hardy don't see eye-to-eye and his reluctance to sail didn't endear him to the admiral.'

Carlisle was less interested than he'd usually have been, even though this talk of who commanded what was the very lifeblood of all post captains.

'I'm sure you're right,' he replied. 'However, what I need is wood and water, and I must be away tomorrow afternoon at the very latest.'

Carlisle had already decided that he wanted to catch the squadron before it reached Louisbourg, as a way of displaying his zeal to his new commander. If they sailed tomorrow and if this northeasterly wind held, he'd every expectation of doing so.

'Water we can do easily, it comes down from the hills in torrents, fresh and cold as you like. There's a good watering place in a cove just to the north of the yard. You'll have to supply your own butts if you want it today, Mister Hardy took all that we had. The storeship has a fresh supply, but they're in the ground tier and won't come out until tomorrow or perhaps Saturday,'

That would be extra labour for the frigate's people, but it would be worth it to get back to sea.

'Then so be it,' replied Carlisle, 'and the wood?'

'Now that we can also do for you, there's as much

firewood as you could ever need stacked in the yard, it's even split and trimmed. Is there anything else you need, Captain?'

'My purser and the bosun and carpenter will no doubt be ashore by now. Were those frigate sails that I saw coming ashore?'

'I really don't know yet, but I'll send word to the storekeeper to let you have whatever you need. I remember you were short of a spare suit when you were last in here.'

'Mister Angelini,' said Carlisle, turning to Enrico, 'take the yawl back to the frigate and tell the first lieutenant what you just heard. I want the wood and water complete before dark. You may also tell him that we'll sail before dinner tomorrow and that the hands may have a run ashore tonight.'

Enrico bounded away; there was indeed no time to lose.

'Now Captain, I have some news for you that you may or may not like,' said the master attendant.

Carlisle froze, his fear must have shown on his face, and the master attendant had evidently heard about his expectant wife in Williamsburg because he hastily continued.

'No, never fear, Captain, there's been no mail, no news for you personally unless there's some in that storeship.'

Carlisle relaxed. If it didn't concern Chiara, it couldn't be too bad.

'When you were here last month, we spoke about that rascal of a pilot in Boston.'

So that was it. Carlisle had barely thought about that incident since he'd sailed from Halifax three weeks ago.

'Well, the captain of the port in Boston suspended him from his duties for six months. It seems that he didn't take kindly to that and spent the next week cursing your name high and low,' he said, easing himself back in his chair.

Carlisle had expected nothing less; there must be more to tell. The master attendant made a wry smile that had nothing of humour in it.

'And then he disappeared! One day he was walking the dockside stirring up trouble, the next he was gone. The rumour is that he took one of the smuggling boats and sailed away. Some say he headed this way, but I haven't seen hide nor hair of him.'

The master attendant looked furtive and lowered his voice.

'Some say he went over to the French.'

Carlisle remained impassive. It was possible, of course. A smuggler would have been able to get into Louisbourg at almost any time, and there was nothing that a frigate or a fifty-gun ship could do to prevent it. But why would he do that? It was commonly believed that the French possession of Île Royale wouldn't last the year, and it would go hard with a New Englander who was caught in the collapse of the French capital of the island.

The master attendant eyed Carlisle carefully. 'Did you know that he'd been a Louisbourg pilot from forty-five to forty-eight? I didn't, but the pilot who brought you in the last time told me.'

'I'd heard it,' replied Carlisle, without mentioning that he'd completely forgotten that fact until now. 'I'll look out for him and bring him to justice if I can.'

He realised how pompous that sounded, but he was keen to end the conversation, unless there was anything else that he should know. The chances of him ever crossing paths with the Boston pilot were slim in the extreme. This talk of deserting to the French was sheer gossip. He'd probably gone somewhere completely different, if he'd left Boston at all.

***

Carlisle had been forced to endure more of the same sort of speculative gossip before he could decently get away from the master attendant's office. When he did, he found that Souter had returned with the yawl, Enrico having been conscripted by the first lieutenant to take the longboat to the watering place. He was just about to order the boat to push off and return to the frigate when he saw two figures running along the shore from the navy yard, carrying a moderate sailcloth sack each. Carlisle recognised those sacks.

'Hold on, Souter.'

The two men were gasping when they arrived at the yawl.

'Mail, sir, letters and suchlike,' the older of the two elaborated, in case his meaning wasn't clear, 'for *Medina*.'

Carlisle gave the men a coin each but didn't wait long enough to see them both, with a knowing glance at each other, turn in the direction of the tavern rather than back to the navy yard.

'You may stretch out for the frigate now, Souter,' said Carlisle.

It's certain that in its whole life on the Little Labrador Inlet, the French yawl had never been propelled so fast. *Medina's* people knew the Captain's wife's situation, and they all loved her dearly. Mail for *Medina* would almost certainly mean news from Williamsburg, and it was only right that they should get their captain back to his ship as fast as possible so that he could read his letters in peace. Besides, he was an open-handed captain, and they firmly expected to be rewarded for making the yawl fly across the smooth water of the harbour. And there was a run ashore tonight!

***

For the first time since he'd been in command of a man-of-war, Carlisle ignored the official letters, dismissed the correspondence for his officers and men with a cursory wave to his clerk, and retired to the cabin window seat with the letter that was in his wife's unmistakable hand.

'*My dearest Edward,*' it began. Apparently, Chiara's confinement was progressing well, and all the right signs and indications – thankfully not explained in detail – were in order. Chiara was well looked after by Barbara and her husband, and the governor's physician visited regularly. All this was a great relief to Carlisle, who was suffering all the usual anxiety of a prospective father; the fear and the guilt of being at sea during this critical time for his wife. He read on.

> *'I have some other news. The first will not surprise you, the second perhaps may. I have seen your brother on three occasions in the city, each time while I was escorted by Barbara or Cranmer. The first time he just looked furious and the second and third he cut me dead. Cranmer did not like the look of him at all and has forbidden me to go out alone. You will know how changed I am when I tell you that I am willingly complying with his wish in this regard. There is something about your brother that I just do not trust.*
>
> *The second concerns your father. He sent a note to Cranmer, asking – requesting permission, mark you – that he may visit me. We discussed the matter and decided that it could do no harm, so long as Cranmer and Barbara were at home. We spoke to the lawyer and agreed that he did not need to attend.'*

Carlisle's heart was racing strangely. He trusted neither his father nor his brother, but of the two, it was his brother Charles that he feared.

Charles had no wife, no legitimate heir and no apparent prospect of obtaining either. When Charles should die, by law the family estate would pass to Carlisle or this child who was yet to be born. It was illogical, for sure, but his brother apparently wanted none of that. As far as Carlisle could tell, Charles would prefer to see the estate became an escheat and pass into the ownership of the colonial government. That degree of irrationality could lead his brother to desperate measures.

His father, on the other hand, must surely have a change of heart at some point as he came towards the end of his life. He couldn't possibly relish the thought of his hard-earned estate passing out of the family.

Carlisle read on.

> *He visited yesterday. I would not go so far as to say that it was a pleasant social call, there is too much in the past that must be mended, but it was certainly a step in the right direction. He offered me any help that I might need, he pressed me to accept money, and he offered to deal with any issues that may arise to cause me concern, which I took to mean your brother. After fifteen minutes of this, I claimed fatigue and retired, as I had agreed with Cranmer, and left him and Barbara to talk to your father. They believe he is ready to bury the hatchet, as they say in these parts, and to acknowledge his grandchild when it should be born. It was too early for a really frank discussion, but he will visit again next week, and Cranmer agrees that we should raise the subject of your brother's antagonism.'*

Carlisle realised that he was sweating, even trembling slightly. He read the rest of the letter with only half his concentration because all else was merely chatter. Very amiable chatter and much appreciated, but it paled into inconsequence beside this news.

His brother's attitude continued to worry him. However, if his father was willing to use his influence – after all, he still owned the estate outright until he should die – then perhaps his brother could be brought to some sense.

Then, of course, it raised the exciting possibility of Carlisle himself inheriting, or his child doing so. His brother didn't look well, and he *was* ten years older than Carlisle. Perhaps…

***

CHAPTER TWENTY-TWO

Boscawen

Wednesday, Seventh of June 1758.
Medina, at Sea. Off Louisbourg, Île Royale.

*M*edina caught sight of Hardy's squadron off Cape Canso. They'd made hard going of it against the persistent northeasterly wind. It would be bringing fog to Louisbourg, but here at sea, away from the banks, it merely brought rain, sleet and snow. If this was all the progress that a well-found squadron of men-of-war could make, Carlisle wondered how long Boscawen's invasion fleet would take to reach Louisbourg; and they weren't even at Halifax yet. Carlisle had hoped to be sent on ahead of the squadron, but he found that Sir Charles had already dispatched *Port Mahon* to warn Falkingham of their imminent arrival and he wanted to keep a frigate with the squadron.

***

For two months Hardy's squadron blockaded Louisbourg; two hard, cruel months when winter seemed reluctant to release its grip on the frozen country. The line of battle, eight ships combatting the elements day after day, patrolled from Cape Breton to Gabarus Bay. Their only relief came when a ship or two was detached to Port Dauphin or further south as far as Cape Canso. However, these were infrequent forays because Hardy knew that his main task was to prevent a French squadron making its way into the harbour. Above all other factors, it was the presence of French line-of-battle ships in Louisbourg harbour that had caused the failure of the 1757 expedition. It was to prevent that happening again that Colville had over-wintered in Halifax.

Hardy's squadron may have been the point of the spear that Pitt and Anson had thrust towards Louisbourg, but it was nevertheless a small part of the British effort to bring down the French fortress. Hawke was off Brest, Rochefort and La Rochelle, preventing men-of-war and supplies from setting off across the Atlantic, while Osborn was in the Mediterranean, watching Toulon.

In February Osborn had fought a battle off Cartagena to prevent de la Clue and Duquesne combining their forces and breaking through the straits to join the Brest squadron and ultimately to relieve Louisbourg. It was a dramatic affair; *Orphee* of sixty-four guns was captured by three British ships, and the captain of *Oriflamme* of fifty-six guns ran his ship aground to avoid capture. The eighty-gun *Foudroyant*, de La Galissonière's flagship at Minorca in 1756 and now Duquesne's flagship, tried to outrun the British but was doggedly pursued by the seventy-gun *Monmouth*. The chase stretched into the darkness. By the light of the moon, *Monmouth* caught the French ship and after a bitter battle forced it to surrender. In taking the massive French flagship *Monmouth's* captain, Arthur Gardiner, wiped out the personal disgrace that he'd felt ever since the battle of Minorca, but at the cost of his own life, as he was killed in the fighting. Later in the year the French commander, de la Clue, made one more effort to break out of the Middle Sea and then abandoned Louisbourg to its fate.

Nevertheless, as Sir Charles Hardy was discovering, even with an overwhelming force off the harbour entrance it was impossible to completely seal off Louisbourg. The Île Royale weather favoured the French, whose pilots knew their way into the harbour in even the worst fog, and if they couldn't make Louisbourg, then Port Dauphin and Spanish Bay were only a day's sailing to the northwest. Shortly before Hardy arrived, *Sutherland* and *Boreas* chased the French fifty-six, *L'Apollon,* armed *en flute*, into the harbour but were unable to catch her. A few days later, the frigate *Diane*, also armed *en flute* was less fortunate as she ran into *Captain* and was taken.

More disturbingly for Hardy, a French squadron of four

ships of the line – *Enterprenant,* a seventy-four, *Bienfaisant,* *Capricieux* and *Célèbre,* of sixty-four guns, with two frigates and two other ships sailed from Brest and slipped into Louisbourg with apparent ease on the twenty-eighth of April. There they joined *Prudent* of seventy guns, making a squadron that couldn't challenge Hardy's but would later have a significant effect on the length of the siege.

***

Yet for those two months, it was always the weather that was the real enemy. Colville and the master attendant had done their best over the winter, but Halifax wasn't Portsmouth, and the squadron that Hardy commanded was tired before ever it started its long vigil. Even with herculean efforts, it had been difficult to provide enough naval stores at Halifax to ready eight ship-of-the-line for sea, and even now their hulls, masts and rigging showed signs of make-do-and-mend. Seasoned oak was in short supply and twice-laid rope was a common sight. Even pitch, so close to New England where it was sourced, was rationed. Their crews had suffered over the winter and disease set in within days of their arrival off Louisbourg, the same sickness that *Medina* had experienced a month before but made worse by the winter on board ship that their crews had already endured.

There was no resupply off Louisbourg, and Sir Charles had issued a general order to forbid foraging parties, for fear of the Native Indian allies of the French. When wood ran short, the men suffered the cold even more. The fresh food was quickly consumed and by early May, the first signs of scurvy started to be seen in the squadron. *Northumberland* suffered the worst, a cruel reward for Lord Colville's diligence through the winter, but all the ships were affected.

A sloop brought the news that Boscawen had arrived in Halifax in early May, having taken 11 weeks from Portsmouth via Madeira, the Canaries, Bermuda and Sable Island. However, there was no sign of the land forces commander, General Amherst, even though his brigadier-generals and their regiments were assembling in Halifax and had started training for the harsh environment that they were soon to be thrown into.

Then, flying before a westerly gale, the same sloop brought the news to Hardy that Boscawen had sailed on the twenty-eighth of May. He'd waited for Amherst but eventually decided that he must proceed to Louisbourg without him. The fleet had been delayed by contrary winds, but overnight the wind backed allowing them to sail the next day. Miraculously, Amherst arrived that morning. A hundred and forty-three transports, twenty-one ships of the line, two fifty-gun ships and nineteen smaller vessels sailed with three brigades embarked, a battering train of eighty-eight guns and fifty-two mortars. In total, the French defenders of Louisbourg would face some fifteen thousand soldiers – almost all regulars with the addition of four companies of American Rangers – and twelve thousand sailors and marines. It was the largest joint expedition that Britain had ever mounted and a testament to Pitt's determination that the critical theatre of this war would be America; not Europe, not the West or East Indies, and not West Africa.

***

On the second of June the watchers in the batteries and entrenchments around Gabarus Bay awoke to the awesome sight of nearly two hundred vessels making their stately progress to anchor barely more than a mile from the French positions. It seemed like the end of the world had come. Companies of soldiers were rushed hither and thither as the French commanders tried to guess where the British would make their landing. In 1745 it had been Gabarus Bay; that seemed the obvious choice again, despite its exposure to the sea. It was only a few miles from the fortress and allowed the British artillery to quickly take advantage of that fatal flaw in Louisbourg's defences, the high land that overlooked the fortress to the west. And yet there was a persistent rumour that the British army would be landed along the Mira River to advance from the north. True, the Mira River allowed the troops to be landed in a place free from the persistent Atlantic swells that broke along the shoreline, but it was an indirect attack and carried the risk of losing momentum among the rocks, streams and bogs of the inland Île Royale. And then it would play into the hands of the French Indian allies and the force of irregulars that the French hero Charles Deschamps de Boishébert was gathering in Quebec, experts in the very type of warfare that the terrain was well suited to.

***

It was a young colonel, temporarily promoted to brigadier-general for this expedition only, who persuaded Boscawen and Amherst to make the landings in Gabarus Bay. James Wolfe was afire with enthusiasm and energy, and he felt that a landing on the Mira River would take too long. After all, both the admiral and the general had orders from Pitt that as soon as Louisbourg fell, the force was to re-embark and move on to Quebec. Pitt felt that both objectives were achievable in one year, even in the short campaigning season that this far northern part of America offered.

Despite Wolfe's enthusiasm, the French fears of an immediate British landing were alleviated by the weather. It blew strongly for the week after Boscawen and Amherst arrived, and every planned date was abandoned as each morning revealed the proposed landing beaches being pounded by the swell.

***

Medina's longboat ploughed through the disturbed waters of the bay in response to a signal hung out in *Namur*, Boscawen's flagship: *Captains report on board*. Carlisle had been lucky so far; he had a full sickbay but still no infectious diseases, unlike Colville's *Northumberland* where they were dying by the day. It was an unlucky ship. Commodore Colville had performed extraordinary acts of determination in preserving the squadron in Halifax over the winter, but

221

when Boscawen arrived, he'd been stripped of his broad pennant and reduced to his substantive rank of post-captain on the dubious grounds that Boscawen had brought post-captains with him who were senior to Colville. Perhaps his depression had been transmitted to his people, but whatever the cause the ship was barely a functioning part of Hardy's squadron, so sickly were its people. It was well known that Lord Colville was entirely dependent upon his naval pay and regarded his followers in *Northumberland* – his officers and his servants – as his family, and yet they were dying as fast as the seamen.

Carlisle's boat crew were still in the best of health. Their combined efforts at the oars brought the longboat to the mighty three-decker's entry port ahead of the boats of most of the other captains that had been summoned.

***

There were few soldiers in the great cabin of Namur, this was a principally naval meeting, and Carlisle still didn't know its real purpose. There were insufficient chairs, but it was a sign of Carlisle's growing seniority – there were captains of third rates who were his juniors now – that he was shown to a seat only a row behind the front rank.

Admiral Boscawen opened the meeting without any preamble. He offered no refreshments and had the manner of one who wanted to get straight down to business. Carlisle had not met Boscawen or even set eyes on him before, but the admiral was recognisable from his common description. He was a tall man who held his head at an angle, the result of an old neck wound and the cause of his nickname of *Wry-Necked Dick*. He was also called *Old Dreadnought*, a name that he'd won in his many engagements through nearly forty years of service.

'I'll come straight to the point, gentlemen,' he said, 'after one preliminary comment.' He looked around the audience of some twelve or so sea-officers. 'What I am about to tell you is of the utmost secrecy, as you will appreciate in a few moments.'

He nodded to a lieutenant who unrolled a large chart against the starboard side of the cabin, behind and to the right of Boscawen.

'If the weather serves, which it should, we land tomorrow at Gabarus Bay. You gentlemen will be taking your ships inshore to support the landing with a preliminary bombardment and counter-battery fire.'

So that was it, thought Carlisle. *Medina* would have a ringside seat for this historic event. A dangerous ringside seat.

'Captain Rous, you'll command this division at the east of the landing area. Yes, the landing will be between Cormorant Cove and Flat Point, as you can now see. You'll have *Squirrel* to keep you company.'

Rous was a lucky man, thought Carlisle. He'd commanded *Arc-en-Ciel* through the Halifax winter and when his ship was found unseaworthy – she was the only one of Colville's original squadron to be left behind at Halifax – he'd been brought to Louisbourg with Hardy, just waiting for an opportunity for a ship. When Falkingham was taken ill, he'd been posted to *Sutherland* with indecent haste.

'Captain Medows, you'll take *Diana* and *Shannon* under your wing and anchor off Flat Point.'

Carlisle tensed; he knew what was coming next.

'Captain Carlisle, I'm giving you the Nova Scotia Province snow *Halifax;* you're to cover the west end of the area, right off Cormorant Cove. You know the soundings there, I'm told, and with *Medina* and *Halifax* you should be able to get close enough to support the landing.'

Cormorant Cove! Right under the battery that they'd bombarded back in March. I wonder what changes the French have made in that time, he thought.

Boscawen continued.

'The landing will be in three divisions. Wolfe's brigade on the left will land here, at Cormorant Cove. Mister Whitmore's brigade will land at White Point on the right and Lawrence will land in the centre, in the area around Flat

Point. There will be a diversion to the east of Louisbourg, just to keep the enemy guessing, but the real landing will be here, in Gabarus Bay. That's where our main force will be employed and it's where we must prevail.'

Boscawen paused.

'Now this is the most secret part. It is intended – *intended*, I say – that the only landing will be at Cormorant Cove. Whitmore and Lawrence will go through all the motions of landing, including sending the boats inshore, but Wolfe's brigade will be the only ones to land. That said, if Lawrence sees the opportunity, he may land at Flat Point to support Wolfe.'

Carlisle swallowed nervously. His frigate was being placed at the critical point of the assault. All these months of planning to assemble the most massive naval and military expedition that Britain had ever launched, and he was commanding the very point of the naval spear.

'Wolfe will have the cream of the soldiery under his command, including Major Scott's band of marksmen and irregulars. It is they who will find a way ashore at Cormorant Cove.'

Carlisle studied the dispositions. The chart was quite familiar, and the lines of soundings were mostly those that *Medina* had run in March. It seemed like a year ago when really it was not three months. A master's mate, four seamen and a marine had died for those lines of figures on a chart; he just hoped they hadn't died in vain.

'You'll be issued with your orders before you leave, and later today General Amherst has promised that you'll be visited by the brigadier-generals you'll be supporting. That'll be Whitmore for you, Captain Rous, Lawrence for you Captain Medows and Wolfe for you, Captain Carlisle. I wish you all the best of fortune, for tomorrow is the day.'

Boscawen left the cabin abruptly, leaving it in no doubt that he wasn't expecting either suggestions or questions. Perhaps that was his style, thought Carlisle, or possibly this expedition was so complicated that he could spare no more than that bare twenty minutes to brief the covering force. Either way, it was effective, there really was nothing to comment on or to question. The only variable left was the weather.

***

Eight bells sounded at the end of the first watch. A light breeze from the north blew in the face of a moderate swell from the southeast. *Medina* was moving carefully towards her new anchorage off Cormorant Cove, followed by a distinctly nervous-looking *Halifax*. The snow's twelve guns were lightweights but would be vital to cover the final stages of the landing as she could get closer inshore than *Medina*. She was a provincial vessel and the attitude of her Nova Scotian owners could only be guessed if they had seen where her temporary proprietors were taking her.

'By the deep, nine,' called the leadsman.

The master looked questioningly at Carlisle.

'Stand on to seven fathoms, Mister Hosking.'

Medina crept forward under her tops'ls and headsails. There was dead silence on deck. Everybody remembered the battery above the cliffs and had no doubt that the French had rebuilt it; they wouldn't have wasted this prime opportunity to dominate the western end of the bay. The question was; had they replaced the guns with six-pounders or had they up-gunned, perhaps to the real ship-smashing twenty-four pounders?

'By the deep, eight.'

Stillness on the quarterdeck. None of the officers looked at each other, but all concentrated on the soundings and the looming bluffs. It was like being inside a goldfish bowl. Without a doubt the French gunners had seen them, but would they hold their discipline and keep the battery masked until the landing started?

'And a half, seven.'

'You may anchor now, Mister Hosking,' said Carlisle as calmly as he could.

Medina's way carried her on another fifty yards, and she

anchored in seven fathoms of water just three hundred yards off the point that protruded south from Cormorant Cove. She lay back on her cable, her head to the north. The ghostly presence of *Halifax* glided past to anchor half a cable further inshore.

'I'll pass the spring now, sir,' said Moxon. 'A double spring, just in case.'

Both men knew the danger that Moxon was obliquely referring to. The spring was a stout length of line that was secured to the anchor cable close to the point where it disappeared into the water. The other end was led through the after-most gun-port and for'rard to the capstan. It allowed the frigate to be turned so that its broadside could face in the desired direction. If the ship was lying head or stern to the enemy and the spring was shot through, then she'd be unable to engage. A second spring was a wise precaution.

'They're holding their fire, sir,' said Moxon, conversationally.

'Well they may. If they start a duel with us now, they'll be obliterated before the landing. They'll be under firm orders not to unmask before the boats are almost on the beach. Our job then is to destroy the battery.'

'I wonder whether they recognise us, or even if there's a battery there at all. We'll know when it gets light even if they don't unmask.'

Carlisle didn't reply; he was thinking his own thoughts. It was an uncomfortable position, to be anchored within range of the battery, waiting for the dawn. In any other circumstances, the French would have opened the engagement as soon as *Medina* came within range, but frigates weren't their target today. The French commander was also waiting for the dawn and preserving his precious guns until they could do the most damage to the boats.

'Boat approaching from astern, sir,' reported the quartermaster.

'That'll be Commodore Durell,' said Carlisle hastily

before an alarm could be given. 'He has to give Boscawen his assessment of the surf on the beaches before the assault can go ahead. He's delayed it twice already.'

The boat pulled strongly past *Halifax* without any kind of greeting. Carlisle could just make out the lean figure of Durrell sitting tensely in the stern sheets and looking fixedly ahead. He passed down *Medina's* starboard side and disappeared into the darkness.

'What time will it be light, Master?' Carlisle already knew the answer, but he wanted to engage Hosking who was becoming withdrawn. The master, like everybody else, knew that a well-aimed salvo of grape or canister would clear *Medina's* quarterdeck like a broom sweeping dead leaves, and they were within range of grape, if a little distant for canister.

'Nine minutes past four, sir, but it'll start to get light at five bells in the middle.'

'Then send the hands to their quarters at three bells, Mister Moxon, and ensure that the frigate remains cleared for action until then. The hammocks must remain stowed; the men will have to sleep on the deck.'

Hosking patted the stout barricade of hammocks in their netting above the gunwale. They were proof against canister but at that range grapeshot would go straight through.

'Aye-aye sir,' replied Moxon. 'The guns are run out. The men prefer to stay at their stations rather than go below.'

'Then I believe I'll try to catch some sleep,' said Carlisle, carefully positioning himself in the chair that had been lashed to the taffrail. His cabin, of course, was an extension of the upper deck and with the bulkheads removed it was nothing more than the aftermost part of the nine-pounder broadside, with no trace left of its more peaceful function.

The north wind blew gently over the deck raising barely a whisper in the rigging. The swell lifted *Medina* rhythmically as it passed under her on its way to break on the rocks and sand of Gabarus Bay. Neither disturbed Carlisle as his exhausted body surrendered to the sleep that it craved.

***

CHAPTER TWENTY-THREE

Wolfe's Gamble

Thursday, Eighth of June 1758.
Medina, at Sea. Off Louisbourg, Île Royale.

That would be a story to be told around the mess-deck tables in future commissions; the captain of *Medina* sleeping soundly under the very noses of the French guns.

'Three bells in a few minutes, sir. The first lieutenant thought you'd like to know,' said Enrico as he gently shook his captain's shoulder. Some kind soul had spread a blanket over Carlisle during the night, and it was wet with dew, but at least he was reasonably dry underneath.

Carlisle instinctively looked over to the southeast, but there was no hint of the dawn yet, and the anchored invasion fleet was still invisible.

'Send the men to their stations, Mister Moxon.'

'The ship is cleared for action, sir, and the quarters are manned, guns run out, loaded with ball.'

Carlisle looked questioningly at Moxon; that report was almost too glib.

'The men have been at their quarters for the past hour, sir. Nobody fancied sleeping below so they've been dozing beside their guns.'

Carlisle walked for'rard to the quarterdeck rail and was met with a crowd of upturned faces. Not a word was said; the men didn't need telling that the French were only a couple of cables away.

'Very well, Mister Moxon. It's a little early, but you may hoist our largest ensign on the staff, and we'll have a couple of union flags at the mastheads.'

The largest ensign was enormous, its hoist was the length of the ensign staff, and its fly reached almost to the waterline. *Medina* hadn't broken it out since their visit to

228

Boston, the makeshift nature of Halifax had seemed an inappropriate place for such ostentation. In any case, it was a horribly expensive piece of adornment and not to be exposed lightly to the elements. There was a visible stirring on the main deck as it flew proudly from its staff above the taffrail.

***

'The sky's just starting to lighten, sir,' said Hosking, looking over the anchored fleet to the southeast.

It was, Carlisle realised as he followed the master's gaze, and it revealed an awe-inspiring sight. Something approaching two hundred vessels were anchored to seaward of *Medina,* creating a forest of masts that obliterated the horizon. But that wasn't the most impressive feature. There were hundreds of boats upon the water. Longboats and yawls, whaleboats and flat-bottomed bateaux from New England and hired fishing boats, every kind of waterborne craft that could be scraped together to support the expedition. Carlisle was aware that specialised flat-bottomed landing barges were being built in England after the difficulties experienced at Rochefort the previous year, but they hadn't been ready for Louisbourg. It was indeed a makeshift flotilla, but nonetheless, its sheer size was impressive. There were boats under oars and boats so stuffed with soldiers that they had to be towed, boats flying the flags of company commanders and boats in which the soldiers were all standing for want of space on the thwarts.

Carlisle looked at the western end of the anchorage. He could see the transport *Neptune* half a mile offshore; she was the closest ship to *Medina* and *Halifax*. *Neptune* should be showing a single lantern on her seaward side. It was invisible to Carlisle, of course, but more importantly invisible to the French at Cormorant Bay. That was where Wolfe's brigade would be gathering in about a hundred boats. Wolfe's force was deliberately the smallest of the three, to complete the deception and buy the vital minutes that would be needed to put the brigade ashore.

***

It was growing lighter as each minute passed. On *Medina's* quarterdeck they heard a burst of cannon fire over to the east, from the area of Flat Point, and a few moments later they saw Durell's longboat racing towards the flagship from the shore. The commodore and his boat crew had suffered an exhausting night, being sent back for another look at the beaches before Amherst would consent to the landing. That cannon fire, now ceased, must have alerted the whole coast.

'It's five minutes to four, sir,' reported Moxon. 'The spring's holding us well, and our larboard broadside's ready to engage the French guns.'

Medina well knew the position of those French guns, if they hadn't been relocated since their first visit in March.

'Very well, Mister Moxon. When I blow my whistle, you may commence the bombardment.'

Carlisle looked at his watch in the dim and covert light from the binnacle. Two minutes to go.

Suddenly, there was a crash of gunfire from their larboard quarter. *Halifax* was warming the bell, or more likely, her commander's watch told a different story to Carlisle's. Well, the cat was out of the bag now. Carlisle lifted his silver whistle to his lips and blew a single blast.

The larboard broadside erupted in fire and thunder. This was no hasty broadside, but the fruit of an agonising middle watch as the gun captains obsessively adjusted the quoins so that their first shots should reach the French battery on the low cliffs to the south of Cormorant Cove. In the growing light the fall of shot could be easily observed as the earth was torn up around the supposed position of the battery. Fifteen minutes they had been given to bombard the shore before the boats started their assault. *Medina* was to silence the battery while *Halifax*, closer to shore, was to break up the *abatis*, the jumble of felled tree and implanted stakes that lined the beaches.

Carlisle spared a moment from watching *Medina's* fall of

shot to assess the effectiveness of the snow's fire. As ordered, she was firing grapeshot to break up the obstacles on the beach and appeared to be having some success. Great rents were appearing in the abatis, and some of the roundshot was reaching the earthworks behind. It must be uncomfortable for the French defenders, waiting for the assault while being bombarded from close range.

Still, there was no answer from the French battery, even though the ground in front of its presumed position was being churned up again and again. With only one broadside being able to bear on the target and no need for sail handling, Moxon had as many extra hands for the larboard battery as he could ever wish for. The rate of fire was superb, and the starboard battery gun crews were heaving with a will to help their opposite numbers.

'The boats are starting to move,' said Hosking. It was a measure of his tension that he omitted the normal *sir* that he invariably used when addressing his captain.

They were indeed. Wolfe's boats were pulling hard towards the shore; the brigadier's own boat was in the lead with its distinguishing banner flying bravely. Surely now the battery would unmask, thought Carlisle.

Closer and closer the boats drew to the shore. The first wave had already pulled past *Medina*, ignoring her entirely in their haste to reach the beaches. The soldiers looked fixedly ahead, each cradling his musket and lost in his own thoughts. The tension was palpable. Amherst had issued a general order that no musket was to be discharged from a boat. Each soldier was to set foot on land with a loaded weapon ready to charge the enemy, and so far, the discipline was holding.

The boats were in the first line of surf before the French guns opened a murderous fire from the cliffs. Carlisle thought that if he'd been the French battery commander, he'd have left it a little longer until they were committed and had no means of escape.

Halifax shifted target to the heights to avoid firing on

Wolfe's men and the two vessels kept up a hot fire on the battery that had now been unmasked. This was more-or-less as Carlisle had imagined it. The battery had preserved itself intact to pour down its fire on the boats; *Medina* and *Halifax* hadn't been fired upon – yet.

The boats were well into the surf and making hard work of it. Carlisle watched helplessly as one boat, poorly handled or just unlucky, was overturned fifty yards from the shore. Then a second boat broached and rolled over. He could see red-coated soldiers struggling in the sea. There would be bodies washed ashore when the tide turned.

He could still see Wolfe's boat and could even make out the brigadier, waving his cane and urging the rowers on. He was heading for the centre of the beach just below the French battery and was in grapeshot range. Soldiers were falling in the boats; there were missed strokes among the oarsmen as the French fire took effect.

Medina and *Halifax* were engaged in a bizarre three-way engagement, pouring their own fire into the French battery, which was, in turn, hammering the boats, from whom not a shot had been fired in reply. Inevitably it was the soldiers who were taking the brunt of the casualties.

This was a critical moment. Carlisle knew from his meeting with Wolfe that the brigadier had been given the authority to withdraw if the landing didn't look feasible. Carlisle could see the danger posed by a well-organised defence, a dangerous surf and growing British casualties. Would Wolfe keep going?

'Hammer them, Moxon,' shouted Carlisle, pointing at the French battery. It had evidently been reinforced since March, and there were now at least four guns firing on the boats. They were nine or twelve pounders, not the six-pounders that *Medina* had silenced before.

Wolfe's boat had a signal staff, and Carlisle knew the signal for a withdrawal. It was a red flag replacing the brigade colours, and he saw it now as the boat slewed awkwardly around and started heading back out to sea. The others followed. Those that had not reached the surf managed the manoeuvre with ease, but those that had almost reached the beach were in trouble. Another boat, timing the turn badly, overturned. There was no saving the soldiers, not in that surf and under that fire. Those that weren't drowned would struggle ashore, and if they were lucky, they'd be taken by regular French soldiers. If they were unlucky the French allies, the native Mi'kmaq and the Abenakis, would find them first.

The whole flotilla had turned. Carlisle couldn't imagine the anguish that Wolfe must be feeling at this first reversal. He'd liked the brigadier-general when he'd met him a few days ago. He'd been impressed by his enthusiasm and his humanity and was distressed to witness his failure. Presumably, with the landing at Cormorant Bay abandoned, the plan to land the army along the Mira River would be revived, with all its attendant delays.

***

Medina's guns were still firing and having an effect, as the French fire seemed to have slackened, although they were still harassing the retreating boats.

'Sir, can you see those three boats over to the right?' asked Enrico, breaking in on his captain's thoughts. 'They've turned back again, towards that small beach just on the starboard bow.'

Carlisle looked through his telescope. Enrico was right. Three of the boats had indeed turned around again. It was difficult to see, but it looked as though they were filled with the irregulars and rangers, the troops who were supposed to spearhead the storming of the beaches. Now that he looked more closely, it appeared that the tiny cove – it was only a hundred yards wide – was not covered by the battery on the bluffs, nor by the smaller gun emplacements to the east. He could see an officer standing on a gunwale, waving frantically towards Wolfe's boat, but the brigadier hadn't yet seen him, and the whole force was pulling lustily back towards the ships.

'Mister Moxon,' Carlisle called urgently, 'your starboard broadside can see that beach, I believe. Start bombarding it immediately.'

There was a disciplined rush to the starboard guns. It was at times like this that Moxon thanked God that he'd spent so many hours drilling his gun crews. The starboard guns were already loaded and run out; it was a matter of moments for the train tackles to be freed and the guns pointed.

'Fire!' shouted Moxon, as soon as he saw the gun captains' hands go up.

The soldiers in the three boats hardly flinched as the nine-pounder balls flew over their heads to embed themselves in the sparse abatis and earthworks. Amazingly, the French defenders appeared to have ignored this small beach. It was almost entirely undefended – the earthworks were unmanned, and no French guns swept the landing.

Carlisle trained his telescope at Wolfe's boat which was between the frigate and the small cove. He saw the brigadier turn angrily towards him as *Medina's* balls flew over his head, then he saw him turn again to look in the direction that the balls were travelling. In an instant, Wolfe realised what was happening. He waved acknowledgement at the officer who was trying to attract his attention, then he spoke to someone in the boat. The red flag came down with a rush, and the brigade colours flew proudly again as Wolfe's boat turned towards the smaller cove. Brandishing his cane, Wolfe turned his face once again to the shore.

One by one, the other boats realised what was happening. Soon nearly a hundred boats were surging towards that tiny space of sand and shingle wedged between two bold cliffs, that one place that the French had failed to adequately defend.

'Mister Moxon, fire at the heights above that cove. Haul in the spring to bring your broadside to bear properly.'

The starboard guns had been trained as far for'rard as they would go to reach the cove. Now, to reach the heights to the west, the frigate would have to be turned.

The scene was one of utter confusion. The shape of the attack, the boats organised by battalion and company, each following its own flag, had been irretrievably lost. Now it was a free-for-all with every boat racing its neighbour to reach the new landing site. The surf was less than on the larger beach, but Carlisle could see that the landing had other equally severe problems to overcome. As the first boats ran ashore, the others behind them had to force their way between the earlier boats to find water shallow enough to disembark. The latest boats had no hope of reaching the beach, and they just secured to those that were before them while the soldiers leaped from boat to boat to make the shore. This was the result of all the training that Wolfe and the other brigadiers had insisted upon while they were waiting in Halifax for Amherst to arrive. They'd spent many hours – no, days – drilling the companies in embarking and disembarking from boats in all conditions. Now, in the chaos of this tiny landing area, the soldiers arrived ashore mostly dry, mostly with a loaded musket ready to fire and all eager to get at the enemy that had been firing at them so far without them being able to respond.

Historians would say that Wolfe was lucky, Carlisle guessed, but it wasn't luck that gave Wolfe's brigade the confidence to seize this opportunity when it was presented. That was the result of careful preparation and training. Ultimately, a man makes his own fortune.

***

Medina's starboard battery was shooting well. No stray shots were landing on the beach; each ball was carrying to the cliffs above. Carlisle saw the first soldiers start to climb the path leading to the summit and blew a long blast on his whistle – cease firing – and the starboard battery fell silent. He wasn't actively aware that through all this the larboard guns had continued to pound the French battery on the southern side of Cormorant Cove. Wishart was commanding to larboard while Moxon was engaged to starboard, and he appeared to be making an excellent job of it.

Crash! Carlisle turned to see a large portion of the taffrail fly up in splinters. The battery must have realised that it could do nothing useful against the soldiers that were shielded from its fire and had turned its fury on *Medina* and *Halifax*. Now it was a real duel, the sort that the *Medina* understood. Many of the men on the upper deck – the gun crews, the quartermaster, the steersmen – had stood with Carlisle as he'd bombarded Fort Royal at Grenada and knew that this was a much less dangerous situation.

Now that Wolfe's men were advancing on the heights the starboard broadside could no longer fire in support and Moxon turned his attention to the larboard battery.

Carlisle was almost certain that they'd silenced one of the guns, but it seemed that at least three were still firing – all twelve-pounders, he guessed – and they were concentrating their fire on *Medina*. *Halifax* had still not been engaged, and she was continuing to fire at the battery. *Medina's* gunners' blood was up, and they were keen to get back to the French battery, to silence them for good.

'Do you see that French column, sir,' said Enrico, pointing to the ridge that led up from the originally planned landing beach to the heights above the left side of the smaller cove. 'They're rushing to counter our landing, sir,' he said urgently.

Trust a soldier to recognise a move like that, thought Carlisle, for at heart that's what Enrico remained, he was only a sailor by courtesy and for want of a war that his own country was engaged in.

'Thank you, Mister Angelini,' Carlisle replied with studied calmness. He realised that he'd been guilty of losing the bigger picture, of being caught up in this inconsequential duel between his frigate and the French shore battery. Those French soldiers that he could see hurrying up the slope, *they* were the reason for *Medina* to be in this position.

'Mister Moxon,' he shouted above the din. 'I'm going to spring the head to larboard. Engage that column as soon as the starboard broadside bears. Leave the larboard side to Wishart.'

The bosun heard Carlisle and needed no further orders; there was a rush of idlers and marines to the windlass. The larboard spring was heaved in, casting the bows further and further to the west. Whether those French soldiers saw their doom, Carlisle would never know, but they were in long grapeshot range and as soon the for'rard guns would bear, they opened a deadly fire upon them. Carlisle was almost sorry for them as he saw the white-coated figures bowled over to lie still upon the rocks and brush.

There was another crash, from for'rard this time. A French twelve-pound ball, better aimed than the others, had smashed through the capping above the number six gun-port. The gun crew was scattered, the sponger and loader were bleeding from splinter wounds and the train-tackle man had been dashed against the mainmast in a bloody ruin, not moving and unlikely to move again.

Moxon shouted for idlers to carry away the wounded. Carlisle could see that the man who'd been hit by the shot was still alive and he was carried below also, although it was scarcely believable that it would do him any good.

The French column had disappeared behind a fold of the land, and there were no more targets for the starboard battery. Wolfe's men were pouring up the slope and the low cliffs behind the cove. It was a land battle now and there was little that *Medina* could do to help except look for French movements within range.

Carlisle was a mere spectator now as this bloody little duel with the battery continued. *Medina* was taking hits regularly but still had only one gun out of action. Moxon and Wishart were running from gun to gun, adjusting the training and elevation, leaning on handspikes, knocking the quoins to make every shot tell.

Then it happened. Carlisle heard the flat sound of an explosion that was shielded by the land. He looked at the battery and could see a column of smoke rising a short distance behind it. Then there was another explosion and an answering cheer from the gun crews. A shot from *Medina*, or perhaps *Halifax,* must have reached the powder magazine behind the battery. The firing from the battery stopped abruptly, either for want of powder or for lack of enthusiasm.

***

CHAPTER TWENTY-FOUR

Lighthouse Point

Wednesday, Fourteenth of June 1758.
Medina, at Sea. Off Louisbourg, Île Royale.

If it wasn't summer, it was at least spring, or what passed for spring as winter grudgingly relaxed its icy grip over Île Royale. The light westerly wind brought no fog, no rain and no snow, and the half-moon showed fitfully through the overcast sky.

'Easy, Souter,' said Carlisle, 'we need to keep the boats together.'

Medina's longboat was rowing along the Lorembec coast, heading southwest towards the entrance to Louisbourg harbour. The details in the boat could be easily seen, but the shore half a mile on the starboard beam was indistinct, a smudged impression of rocks and forest, except when the moon found a gap in the clouds. Then the sea and shore were revealed in a silvery light and Carlisle silently cursed the moon.

He was leading a flotilla of ship's boats. Five of them, including his own, had guns mounted in the bows and each carried two files of marines armed with muskets. They were deployed in a crescent formation ahead of the main body of the flotilla. The main body, the reason for this clandestine expedition, consisted of ten of Boscawen's largest boats, all heavily laden to within inches of their freeboard. The two largest, borrowed from the two-deckers, carried a monstrous twenty-four pounder gun slung underneath the boat. The next two each carried an eight-inch mortar stowed in the bottom of the boat, followed by another two each carrying a royal, the smaller five-and-a-half-inch mortar, still mounted on its wooden baulk. The remaining boats carried the twenty-four pounder gun carriages, the baulks for the larger mortars, the equipment to disembark and re-mount

239

the weapons, a small amount of shot, shell and powder and the myriad of implements required to service a battery.

Carlisle looked over the stern. His entire flotilla was visible even when the moon was obscured, and he wondered whether they would be seen from Battery Island at the entrance to the harbour.

After the euphoria of the initial landing at Cormorant Cove, the siege had slowed down. Amherst appeared to be in no hurry to move his guns within battering range of the fortress, and those who advocated an early assault, without the formality of a protracted siege, were disappointed. Amherst was immovable despite the entreaties of Wolfe, his vigorous subordinate. Having established himself ashore, he was determined to keep his casualties to the minimum, because his orders from the King and from Pitt still stated that he should attack Quebec in 1758, and for that, he needed an intact army.

In the first few days after the landing, the French had withdrawn inside the walls of Louisbourg, and within a week they'd abandoned their batteries on the north shore of the harbour and on Lighthouse Point, overlooking the entrance. They'd retained the guns on Battery Island and those in the Grave Battery, facing the sea across the rocky shore in front of the fortress walls. However, for Amherst and Boscawen, the lessons from the 1745 siege were clear; a British battery on Lighthouse Point could command the central part of the harbour and could silence the guns on Battery Island.

Amherst was a good judge of people and he knew his officers well: their strengths and their weaknesses, those who fretted at inaction and those who cherished an idle life. He had selected Wolfe to take a strong force north-about around the harbour to establish himself at Lighthouse Point. Wolfe had accomplished the task in thick fog on the twelfth of June, unmolested by the French men-of-war in the harbour, who suspected nothing, even though Wolfe's men could hear the routine activity on the ships. When the fog lifted, the French saw that their abandoned positions on

Lighthouse Point had new owners. A force of British infantry and irregulars were digging positions that the retreating French had filled in only days before. However, infantry and irregulars were all very well, but they couldn't hurl shot and shell at Battery Island and the anchored ships; for that they needed guns, and, in this terrain, they could only be delivered by sea.

***

Carlisle was pleased to have been given this mission. It was a mark of the trust that Hardy had in him, it allowed Moxon to command *Medina* for a day, and it gave Carlisle some variety in this endless blockade and siege. And yet it was a complex task. He'd had to write the orders for the gathering of twenty boats off Big Lorraine harbour, three miles northeast of the entrance to Louisbourg. He'd visited the transports that carried the guns and mortars and confirmed the arrangements for slinging them into or under the boats. A day had been spent gathering together a crowd of carpenters and bosuns and agreeing on the equipment – and more importantly the highly-skilled people – that would be needed to disembark the guns at the cove. Then he'd personally briefed the officers in charge of each boat, ensuring that they understood the signal system that he'd devised, how they were to be formed for the passage and what they needed to do in the event of a French sortie. Finally, and this was a point that he won against Hardy's reluctance, he'd rowed the distance from Big Lorraine to the cove the night before so that he'd be more able to recognise the land as he approached it at the head of his small flotilla.

This was only the first instalment of guns, ammunition and equipment for the battery on Lighthouse Point. Carlisle knew that over the next days and weeks, as the men under Lieutenant Colonel Hale sweated to prepare the gun emplacements and the revetments, further boat convoys would bring more and more guns until the battery would be capable of suppressing the French guns on the island only a thousand yards away across the harbour mouth.

***

The rocky coastline of Lorembec slipped by to starboard. Carlisle had impressed on the escorting boats that they must not pull ahead of the cargo boats. It would be all too easy in the darkness for the force to lose its cohesion, and Carlisle knew well how quickly a French sloop-of-war could decimate his fragile command. He couldn't see them, but *Hawke* and *Halifax* were patrolling off the harbour, hidden in the darkness so that the French weren't alerted. Then also there was a danger from Battery Island itself. It was long range for the French twenty-four pounders, but their gunners had been preparing for just this test ever since Britain had returned Louisbourg to the French in 1749. They would know the range, and they would have established training marks so that they could bombard the approach to the cove even in the dark. Hale's men had already endured days of harassing bombardment from that battery, and they knew well how accurate the French artillerymen were.

Carlisle looked astern. He couldn't count the boats – they were too indistinct even when the moon peeped through the clouds – but he could see that a good number were following obediently. He could see nothing of the escorting boats; they were disposed on the wings of the convoy and the rear, while Carlisle's boat led from the front.

'Rest on your oars, Souter,' said Carlisle. 'When that boat,' he pointed to the leading gun-carrier, 'is abeam, place your bow on his stern and I'll jump across. You know what to do Mister Johnson?'

'Aye-aye sir,' replied the lieutenant from *Namur* who'd been appointed his deputy. 'I'll station the gunboats in an arc around the cove and wait for your signal to come and take you off.'

'Very well. I hope the task will be completed before dawn.'

Embarking the guns had, of course, taken longer than Carlisle had anticipated, and had caused an hour's delay in setting off. Now he ran the risk of dawn finding the ship's boats still clustered in the cove and vulnerable to French bombardment. Usually a few ship's boats wouldn't be of any great consequence in a grand operation such as this, but Hardy had pointed out that the fleet had lost a hundred already in landing the army at Gabarus Bay. Every man-of-war was short of at least one boat. The loss of these fifteen of the squadron's heaviest workboats would be felt severely over the coming days when the navy would be required to carry more and more guns and mortars to Lighthouse Point and to resupply the powder and shot and the provisions for the soldiers.

The black shape of the heavily laden longboat pulled steadily past them. It was interesting to see how slowly the boat moved even though the exertions of the rowers were evident. That vast bulk of a mortar was a ponderous weight to be moved by mere muscles. Yet move it did, and Souter had to be careful in nosing up to its stern with the vulnerable rudder hanging off the transom.

Carlisle made the jump and found his shoulder clasped by the master's mate in charge of the boat. The coxswain barely flinched as he fell forward against him, all his concentration was on keeping his boat moving steadily across the darkened sea.

'Thank you, thank you,' said Carlisle. He'd forgotten the man's name; he wasn't prepared to admit it, and this was no time for formal introductions.

Medina's longboat sheered off to larboard to take its station to seaward of the cargo-carrying boats and was soon lost in the gloom.

Carlisle peered into the blackness on the starboard bow. They were heading for a tiny cove just over a thousand yards to the northeast of Lighthouse Point. It was at the extreme range of the French guns on Battery Island, and it provided a sandy beach for unloading.

'Hand me the lantern,' he said tersely to the master's mate. Those were the only lights that he'd permitted in the flotilla. Each boat carried a shaded lantern that, when shuttered, couldn't be seen at ten yards. He withdrew the brass shutter just enough to allow a sliver of light to escape. It was the smallest of lights imaginable, but on this dark night, its intensity was shocking. Carlisle checked his watch and replaced the shutter. He'd worked the winds and tides and the likely speeds of the boats to determine an approximate passage time. If all the calculations had been correct, then the cove should be half a mile on their starboard bow. Too soon to show the signal yet.

The boat rowed on in silence while Carlisle counted the seconds for ten minutes.

'You may show the signal now,' he said.

The master's mate stood and held the lantern high. He deliberately opened the shutter for two seconds, closed it for another two then opened it again. Three flashes of two seconds each. That was the signal that Hale was waiting to see.

Nothing, no response from the shore.

'Make the signal again, if you please,' said Carlisle tensely.

The master's mate rose and repeated the signal, three exposures of the light for two seconds each. No response.

'Begging your pardon, sir,' said the coxswain. 'I just saw a light on the larboard beam, but it's gone now.'

'Are you sure?' asked Carlisle. The coxswain nodded in reply.

Carlisle paused and looked covertly at the coxswain. He appeared a steady man, not one to be taken by flights of fancy. Assuming he was correct, then the light could be nothing to do with them. It could be a party of soldiers on the foreshore between Lighthouse Cove and their own cove. Or it could be that he and Hosking had overestimated the speed that these laden boats could row, or they'd miscalculated the tide. He knew that he had to get this right. If he took these boats into the wrong cove or, heaven forbid, if he led them onto the rocks that guarded this coast, the mission could end in disaster. Fifteen boats lost, the guns and mortars on the bottom of the sea, and at least another few days before it could be attempted again.

'Sir!' said the master's mate urgently. 'I can see breakers on the starboard bow, not more than a couple of hundred yards away. You can hear them, just about.'

Carlisle looked across the coxswain's shoulder. Yes, he could see breakers. There were breakers all along this iron-bound coast, but unless his navigation was wildly in error, they could only be caused by the outcrop immediately to the east of the cove that they were searching for. He'd turned his flotilla towards the shore too soon!

'Hard a-larboard, coxswain.'

He thrust the lantern at the master's mate. 'Shine it lantern astern now and hold it there.'

The lumbering longboat turned ponderously to larboard. Carlisle looked anxiously behind but could see nothing. The light from his pre-arranged signal had destroyed his night vision. For a few seconds he was effectively blind. However, he knew he must continue to shine that light to indicate to the following boats that he'd turned. Hopefully, they would all see the signal – it could hardly be missed – and follow obediently.

'Close the lantern now,' he snapped after two minutes. That should have been enough time for the other boats to have seen the signal.

'I can see that light again, sir,' said the coxswain. 'Just where it was before, if we hadn't turned.'

Was the coxswain mocking him? Probably, Carlisle thought, but he knew very well that he was safe. Remarks thrown around in the stress of a mission such as this could hardly be followed up with any dignity.

Carlisle could see the light too.

'Make the signal again,' he said in a level voice. There was quite enough excitement in this boat without adding to it. 'Keep making it. If the French are awake, they'll have seen us by now.'

'T'other boats be following us now,' said the stroke oar in a west country burr.

Carlisle was on the cusp of telling the man to mind his own damned business, but it would have been crass; he was offering some useful information.

'Eyes in the boat, stroke, stow it!' said the coxswain mildly, without any real conviction. The west countryman just grinned and kept up his stroke, steady as a metronome.

Carlisle could see the signal now, and as the moon appeared through a fleeting gap in the cloud, the enormity of his error became apparent. If he'd persisted on his course, they'd soon have been in the surf of a rock-bound bay to the north of their destination. Even in this unusually calm weather it would have been a miracle if all the boats had escaped. He'd most certainly have lost some of the guns and probably some of the men. He could feel the sweat trickling down his back at the thought.

'Belay the signal now,' Carlisle said. 'Watch for the cliffs on either side of the cove.'

Carlisle took the lantern from the master's mate and shone a beam of light on the boat compass that had been secured to the stroke oar's thwart. The signal on shore was bearing west-northwest. When it came a point further on their beam, at northwest-by-west, he'd turn and steer the boat's bow at the signal.

'I can see the cliffs to the left of the signal now,' said the master's mate. 'They're low, and there's a surf breaking on them.'

Carlisle nodded but said nothing. He was concentrating on the right moment to order the boat to turn towards the signal. It wasn't an exact science. The longboat was rising and falling to the constant Atlantic swell and in the past few minutes had started to pitch as the surge met the shallower water. His compass was also a very approximate instrument, not damped as well as the ship's instruments that were mounted in their sturdy binnacles, and there was no way of sighting towards the mark.

Ten more strokes, Carlisle thought to himself, then I'll order the turn.

The coxswain could feel Carlisle's tension, and he too watched the signal intently. Some blessed soldier understood the importance of his task. Since he'd first seen the boat's light, he'd kept his own lantern flashing as regularly as a Trinity House light.

'Bring her to starboard, coxswain,' said Carlisle. 'Make the signal to the boats.'

The cliffs to the right of the cove were visible now, lower than those to the left and with their own rim of breaking waves. Carlisle could feel the longboat pitching as the surf ran under her keel. God, this looks dangerous, he thought. The hundred-yard entrance to the cove appeared much smaller at night, and the space of relatively smooth water between the two bands of surf looked ridiculously narrow. His orders to the boats were for them to enter the cove one-at-a-time, and he was glad he'd insisted upon it. There really was no room for error and two heavily laden longboats making for that entrance together could easily result in one or both being wrecked on the rocks.

There was dead silence in the boat as it entered the cove; even the stroke oar looked impressed at the gravity of the situation. For the first time in several minutes Carlisle looked astern. He didn't really know what he expected to see, but another fortuitous break in the cloud showed a spectacle that any navigator could be proud of. There was a string of longboats, not in a straight line, but at least all heading for the same point, neither too close to the one in front nor lagging. On either wing he could see his gunboats, resting on their oars, guarding the precious convoy from seaborne attack. Of *Hawke* and *Halifax*, nothing could be seen. They were obeying their orders and keeping out of sight to avoid alerting the French defences.

Carlisle relaxed and smiled to himself in the darkness. He could leave it to the master's mate and the facetious coxswain to run the boat onto the sand at the head of the cove. The other boats with internal cargos would undoubtedly follow. The last two, with their under-slung twenty-four pounders, would be more difficult. However, Carlisle was comforted by the knowledge that the navy had been taking guns ashore in this fashion for generations. On a sandy beach, they became awkward monsters that required a lot of brute force to shift from their fathom deep resting place up the beach and onto a carriage, but the squadron had been scoured for the right expertise, and it was all there in the boats following behind him. Two of the boats were carrying an array of spars and baulks of timber of a size and shape agreed by a team of carpenters and bosuns. They would be rigged into sheers to manhandle the ponderous loads, but none of that required the direct intervention of a post-captain.

The longboat ran up the beach and willing hands dragged it higher, using its momentum and the surf to best effect so that it rested far up the debatable territory between saltwater and dry sand.

The stroke had jumped out of the boat as soon as his oar became redundant. Carlisle looked at his face for the first time. He was an old man, old by naval standards, in any case; he must have been in his sixties at least.

'That was a good job, sir,' he said, smiling confidentially and knuckling his brow as he offered his arm to help Carlisle out of the boat. 'It'll be a good yarn to tell one day, and the telling of it'll earn me a tot or two.'

***

CHAPTER TWENTY-FIVE

Fire in the Harbour

Monday, Twenty-Fourth of July 1758.
Namur, at Anchor. Gabarus Bay, Île Royale.

Louisbourg's short spring turned to full summer and the soldiers sweated in their woollen uniforms. Sailors volunteered for the siege works in their hundreds, and a strong contingent of Cornishmen, miners all, bolstered the ranks of the army's engineers. To the west of the fortress the sappers crept forward, digging their parallels closer and closer to the walls. Their batteries were now placed so near the defenders' positions that there was no question of missing.

To the east, Wolfe's guns on Lighthouse Point had silenced Battery Island, and under its merciless bombardment, the French navy had shifted its remaining ships to the shallow water to the north of the fortress. The governor of Louisbourg had already rejected one demand for capitulation, preferring to wait until the conventions of military honour had been satisfied, and a *practicable breach* had been made in his walls.

The commander of the French ships had made repeated demands that they be allowed to escape, to preserve this significant squadron to fight another day, but the governor knew that it was only those ships that prevented Boscawen's squadron sailing into the harbour and battering the poorly defended northern walls.

Relations between the French governor and the commander of the French naval forces had never been good and under the stress of siege they deteriorated. Conceding to pressure, the governor agreed that *Aréthuse* may make its escape. This was a blow to the morale of the defenders because it was only this brave frigate, of all the French naval forces, that had made a significant contribution to the defence of the fortress. Its shallow draft had allowed it to anchor far to the western end of the harbour, close to the encroaching British. The frigate's continuous bombardment of the advancing lines had substantially slowed the progress of the siege works. Daring sailors, under continuous fire, had taken it in turns to direct the frigate's fire from the dangerous peak of the main topmast head.

Aréthuse slipped away at night, passing through the sunken blockships and suffering the fire of Wolfe's batteries on Lighthouse Point. Despite being hit in the stern by British twenty-four-pound balls, the gallant frigate reached Bayonne safely, and its precious dispatches were hurried away to Versailles.

Aréthuse left just in time. On the twenty-first of July *Célèbre*, anchored close to the quay at Louisbourg, was hit by a mortar bomb that ignited powder charges stored on the poop deck. The wind carried sparks to the sails of *Entreprenant* and *Capricieux,* both of which rapidly began to burn, and soon repeated explosions rocked the town and the harbour. The French naval commander, the Marquis des Gouttes, now had only two ships-of-the-line remaining, *Prudent* and *Bienfaisant*, and their time was running out.

***

'Take a seat, Captain,' said Boscawen as Carlisle was ushered into the great cabin on *Namur*. It was like no other admiral's accommodation that he'd ever seen. Every flat surface was covered: charts, maps, plans, documents, drawings, lists, books; every kind of document that was needed for the planning of a campaign littered the table, the benches, the chairs and even the deck. Sir Charles Hardy was already there and looked as though he had been for some time. A staff officer – a soldier Carlisle noted – swept aside a sketch of the harbour entrance to make a space for him. He and the other soldiers and sea-officers tactfully withdrew as the Admiral nodded in their direction. Evidently, this was to be a private conversation, just the two admirals and himself. Carlisle quelled a momentary nervousness. There was nothing in his conduct or *Medina's* that warranted censure, so it must be something else. Chiara perhaps. Had Boscawen or Hardy heard news of his wife, bad news? No, it couldn't be that. Hardy, as his immediate superior would have told him himself; Boscawen was far too elevated, and far too busy, for that kind of interview. Then it must be some special sensitive duty, Carlisle's heart beat faster.

'You know the general situation, Carlisle. Louisbourg must fall soon but the French governor, de Drucour, is being obstinate. Every day he delays his capitulation, Amherst loses more men.'

'As do we,' interrupted Hardy. 'My squadron hasn't recovered from the late spring; I know that Colville's men are dropping like flies.'

'Quite, Sir Charles,' said Boscawen showing no hint of annoyance at the interruption. Evidently, these two men had a good working relationship. 'These soldiers have their own notions of right and wrong. Apparently, there hasn't yet been sufficient destruction and bloodshed for Monsieur Drucour to surrender the fortress and retain his honour.'

Boscawen looked away. Was he mourning the useless loss of life, Carlisle wondered, or was he preparing the next part of his speech?

'Now this part is a secret, although in God's name, the French must have guessed it,' he walked closer to Carlisle and Hardy so that he didn't need to raise his voice. 'My orders, mine and General Amherst's, state that we must endeavour to carry our forces up the St. Lawrence to Quebec before the end of the season.'

Carlisle had heard that rumour, but he was surprised to hear that it was still being spoken of as a real possibility. Here they were at the back end of July and Louisbourg's walls were still standing, yet the joint commanders were considering the capture of Quebec in the next... how long? Three months maximum before the bad weather set in again.

Chris Durbin

'So, you see, we must end this affair as soon as possible. The soldiers won't do it, they're moving at a snail's pace, all except that youngster Wolfe. I find there's a theatre to these sieges, as formalised as a Greek tragedy, and our friends in the army are reluctant to forego any act or scene of the play.'

So that was it, thought Carlisle. Boscawen was trying to move the siege along at a faster pace than the army thought quite proper.

'Louisbourg's weakest point is its side facing the harbour.' Boscawen didn't use a map, presumably assuming that Carlisle was aware of the geography of the fortress and its surroundings. 'It's always been their weakness and that's why they tried so hard to have a strong squadron in the harbour before we arrived.'

Hardy was trying not to look smug. It was his early arrival – facilitated by Colville's masterpiece of organisation and willpower in maintaining the squadron in Halifax over the winter – that had prevented the French from carrying out their plan. Hardy, and of course Hawke in the Channel and Osborn in the Mediterranean. In a moment of clarity, Carlisle glimpsed the entirety of Pitt's plan, the moves and countermoves that would culminate in a final battle for New France.

'They're down to two of the line now, not a tactically useful force but one that is preventing Drucour from surrendering: *Prudent* and *Bienfaisant*. If we can take, burn or in any other way destroy those two, then we may be able to shorten this siege by a month. Then there is a possibility – and only a possibility – that we'll be able to move up the St. Lawrence before the weather beats us again. Then, if the French have any sense at all, we can end this war a year or two earlier than otherwise.'

Boscawen seemed satisfied with his speech, perhaps – no, certainly – he'd delivered it a few times already. He paused for a moment. He then nodded significantly at Hardy and made a curious motion with his right hand, his fist clenched with his thumb pointing upwards in the manner of a Roman emperor deciding the fate of a gladiator. Hardy nodded in reply.

'Ye'll be wondering why you're here, Carlisle,' said Hardy, 'other than to hear a pair of admirals give you their view of the world.' Hardy smiled as for just a moment Boscawen looked like a man caught acting a part.

Carlisle inclined his head cautiously. Hardy's statement seemed to require an answer.

'I had wondered, Sir Charles.'

Boscawen broke in. 'We'll be cutting them out tomorrow night,' he said, 'or rather you will, you and two commanders. You'll lead the expedition.'

'And if you're wondering why you're here and they're not,' added Hardy in his forthright manner, 'it's because the commanders are already well known to the admiral, whereas you,' and he bowed to his superior admiral, 'are known to Mister Boscawen only by reputation. In an enterprise such as this, reputation is an insufficient recommendation, but now you *are* known.'

***

'Then, if you'll follow me,' said Hardy.

They rose to leave the great cabin. Boscawen shook hands with Carlisle, but it was clear that his mind was elsewhere, perhaps planning the next move after the cutting-out expedition.

Hardy led him to what he assumed must be the captain's day-cabin, although the geography of these three-deckers was a mystery to Carlisle; he'd only been on board two before, Byng's *Ramillies* after the Battle of Minorca and *Royal William* in Boston. At that moment Carlisle remembered that it had been Boscawen who'd signed the warrant for the execution of Admiral Byng. Did he know that Carlisle had been one of Byng's captains at Minorca? Almost certainly so, he assumed, although the admiral had shown no sign of knowing it. Perhaps the command of such a huge proportion of Britain's naval power gave him a comfortingly thick skin where it came to the matter of personal relations.

'Much of the planning has already been completed,' said Hardy. 'I regret that you're something of an afterthought. Let me explain.'

An afterthought! That was a strange way to introduce the commander of an expedition to the plan.

'There will be two divisions, of course, one for each of the ships to be cut out. The commanders of those divisions have already been appointed, and today they carried out a reconnaissance of the harbour. Their report is encouraging; it can be done with a reasonable degree of risk. Perhaps you know the two gentlemen? Commander Balfour of the *Aetna* fireship and Commander Laforey, presently without a ship.'

Carlisle shook his head. 'I have not had that honour,' he said stiffly.

Hardy looked sharply at Carlisle.

'Now look here, Captain,' he said, emphasising Carlisle's rank. 'I recommended you to Boscawen because you've shown that you're prepared to roll your sleeves up and crack on with things. You've done well in similar situations, at Lighthouse Point, at St. Philip's in Minorca and in the Caribbean.'

Hardy glared hard at Carlisle.

'Yet there's a dozen, no three or four dozen other post-captains who would give an arm or a leg to take this command. I selected you as the best person for the job, but if you choose not to take this command, then you may leave now.'

Hardy had a reputation for straight-talking and Carlisle had seen flashes of it before, but this was the first time that he was on the receiving end of one of his famous blasts. He managed not to stammer in his reply.

'My apologies, sir. Of course, I'm honoured to take this command, and I'll be delighted to meet these two gentlemen.'

Hardy nodded, and his face lost its grim aspect. He was mercurial, this Rear Admiral, and his anger dissipated as fast as it grew.

'Very well,' he continued. 'Now, as I was saying, there will be two divisions, each of around twenty-five boats.'

Carlisle was starting to see where he came into this plan. An expedition of that size and of such importance merited a post-captain to command it. It seemed that the truth of it had only dawned on Boscawen and Hardy after the two commanders had reported from their reconnaissance.

'Each ship-of-the-line will provide two boats and each frigate one. *Northumberland* only will be exempted due to the sickness among Colville's people. The cutting-out crews will be primarily composed of seamen armed with pistols, cutlasses, tomahawks and boarding pikes. There'll be a few marines in case there's any organised resistance, but there must be enough seamen to bring those ships out. You'll be in overall command of the expedition, Carlisle, and you'll have *Namur's* longboat with two guns and as many marines as she'll carry, along with signal lanterns and a means of displaying them. You'll coordinate the efforts of Balfour and Laforey, re-allocate boats as you see fit, and ensure the success of the enterprise.'

Carlisle thought for a moment. He knew nothing of these two commanders. Now was the time to get Hardy's opinion.

'Can you tell me anything about Mister Balfour and Mister Laforey? I regret our paths have never crossed, nor have I heard mention of their names.'

'Certainly. I interviewed them and I flatter myself that I know their characters. Balfour is the older, perhaps a little older than you,' he said, looking at Carlisle appraisingly. 'I've known him for several years; you could call him something of a follower of mine.'

That's worth knowing, thought Carlisle; Balfour's been given this opportunity to prove himself in a most public way by his mentor. The prospects for promotion had started to close off in a Navy that was near its maximum size, and this would be a real chance for him to shine.

'He's had *Aetna* for two years and is aching to be posted.

He's energetic and bold and he'll dare anything. He may need a restraining hand. His division will board *Bienfaisant* the sixty-four.'

'Thank you, sir.'

'I only met Laforey yesterday. He had the sloop *Hunter* on Lake Ontario until we were kicked out of there. He's been on Boscawen's staff waiting for employment such as this. I would say he's as much younger than you as Balfour is older. He'll take *Prudent*, the seventy-four. Oh, and he was with last year's expedition to Louisbourg, so he knows these waters well.'

Don't we all, thought Carlisle but wisely kept his peace. So, both of his divisional commanders came with the personal recommendations of the two admirals. Carlisle just hoped that they would live up to their mentors' expectations.

'The batteries will fire continuously once your flotilla is underway, to try to keep the enemy's attention on the land. If you are detected before the boats reach their objectives, it will be for you to decide whether to continue with the boarding, but I have this point to make.'

Hardy paused for effect and stabbed the air with his finger.

'It is of the utmost importance that those ships are brought out or destroyed. To that end, casualties are to be expected. Do we understand each other, Captain Carlisle?' he asked with a certain formality.

'I understand, sir,' replied Carlisle, his eyes never wavering from the admiral's. He was being given the authority to press home the attack even at the cost of a high number of casualties.

'Then I'll give you the rest of today to lay your plans. There's a cabin here if you need it. I know that your first lieutenant – Moxon, isn't it? – is a safe pair of hands while you're gone. I'll send Balfour and Laforey in to see you when you're ready. Tomorrow forenoon at two bells the commanders of each of the boats will gather in the great cabin. Admiral Boscawen will introduce you, and then the show is yours. In the meantime, if you need anything, ask Captain Buckle.'

And with that Hardy was gone, back to his responsibilities for maintaining the blockade of Louisbourg harbour while Boscawen's main force attended to supporting the siege.

***

Carlisle was nervous. He'd never commanded anything on this scale before. The Lighthouse Point expedition came close, but it had been an essentially logistic operation; there was no expectation that they would have to fight. But tonight, he'd have to take fifty-one boats – fifty-two counting his own – and six hundred men into action with every expectation of taking casualties and with a fleet and an army waiting for news of his success. He tried to look as though he did this kind of thing every day.

He watched the flood of people entering the cabin. Each boat was commanded by a lieutenant, a master's mate or a midshipman, and some had a second in command. With Balfour and Laforey he had a total of fifty-five officers, each of whom introduced himself before taking a seat. There were young men and old men, some shockingly young and some old enough to be their fathers. Some men were clearly looking forward to the night, and there were others who were failing to keep the concern from their faces. A few of them Carlisle recognised but most were entirely unknown to him.

He'd been pleasantly surprised by his two immediate subordinates. Both Balfour and Laforey were the type of sea-officers that Carlisle liked; they were open to advice and eager to engage with the enemy, like greyhounds in the slips, as Shakespeare would have had it.

When all the officers were seated, a flag lieutenant opened the door and nodded significantly at Carlisle.

'Gentlemen,' he said to the rows of expectant faces.

As one, they stood for their commander-in-chief. One

midshipman at the back pushed over his chair with a clatter and blushed bright red. He was probably the youngest officer there and Carlisle at that moment hoped with a surprising intensity that he'd survive the night.

Boscawen stood aside and to Carlisle's surprise, he saw General Amherst's tall figure stoop under the lintel and walk with a deliberate pace to the curtained stern windows. They were followed by Hardy, who winked conspiratorially at Carlisle. Carlisle could only guess what that wink meant, but it could have meant, *look who I've brought to meet you and enhance your career prospects.*

Boscawen was brief. He introduced Amherst who said a few words about the importance of the mission, then he spoke himself and introduced Carlisle. Then, as swiftly and mysteriously as they had appeared, the two joint commanders of the Louisbourg expedition trooped out again leaving the gathering of sea-officers with the feeling that, just for a moment, the Gods had come down from Mount Olympus to address the mere mortals.

***

Carlisle's briefing was short. Flanked by his two divisional commanders, who looked suitably deferential, he described his plan for attacking the two ships. Stealth, of course, was the key. No weapon was to be cocked or half-cocked until they were on the enemy's deck or until their presence was detected. The two divisions were to pass through the entrance simultaneously, following Carlisle's boat that would show a red light astern. Carlisle would take the well-defined route past the sunken blockships. The French had been in such a hurry to get the job done that the scuttled ships' masts were visible above the surface. He described the signals that the divisional commanders were to make and the signals that he'd make. Finally, he emphasised the need for speed, stealth and aggressive action when they boarded the ships.

'Then, gentlemen, I'll leave Captain Balfour and Captain Laforey to each brief their own divisions. I'll offer you this final thought: *Prudent* and *Bienfaisant* are the last elements of French naval power in these waters. When we have taken or burned them, the governor of Louisbourg will have no hope left. His fortress must fall in the following days, and we will have struck a mighty blow for our cause.'

***

CHAPTER TWENTY-SIX

Cutting Out

Tuesday, Twenty-Fifth of July 1758.
Medina's Longboat. Louisbourg Harbour, Île Royale.

When Boscawen's squadron arrived, Sir Charles Hardy shifted his flag from *Captain* to the much larger *Royal William*. The three-decked second rate had been rebuilt from a first rate only the previous year at Portsmouth and fitted out for an admiral and his staff. It was from *Royal William's* lofty poop deck that Sir Charles looked down on the boats of the squadron mustering on its seaward side, away from prying French eyes.

Balfour and Laforey had already taken their leave, each rowing over to the anchored third rates where their own divisions were forming.

'Well, Captain Carlisle, I wish you the best of fortune,' said Sir Charles as they walked together towards the entry-port, 'you have the weather for it.'

Even Hardy was nervous. There was something cold-blooded about setting off on an expedition such as this. There was no knowing whether their plans were known to the enemy, and it would be a bloody business if the French crews were alerted. Grapeshot would sink the boats at four hundred yards and canister would decimate the crews at a hundred. Cold shot dropped into a boat from a two-decker would complete the carnage and those few men who survived and found a foothold on the tall sides of the ships would be met by swivel-guns and boarding nets, pikes and muskets. It would be surprising if half of the force returned to the squadron.

Carlisle looked out at the dark water. There was a light westerly wind and wisps of mist flitted across the surface of the sea. Only the closest ships of the anchored squadron were visible; the rest were lost in the darkness. He knew that the moon would rise in an hour – a moon just five days past the full – and by midnight, if it could penetrate the mist, it would start to illuminate the flotilla. Carlisle looked at his watch. Ten o'clock, they should be away.

'Thank you, sir,' he replied and felt Hardy's hand reaching for his.

The pipes wailed as Carlisle caught hold of the manropes and descended to his boat. Souter ordered the bow shoved off and the longboat moved away from the ship's side and soon disappeared into the blackness.

'*Prince Frederick*, Souter,' said Enrico from the other side of the coxswain. His main job was to manage the communications with the flotilla. He had three shuttered lanterns: a white for signalling, a red-over-green to show at the stern and a spare in case either of the first two failed.

Enrico also had under his nominal control the means of communicating with the flagship. In the for'rard part of the longboat, resting on baulks of timber that lay directly on the keelson, there sat a short, squat twelve-pound coehorn mortar, the least of its very ugly tribe, attended by two artillerymen in their blue uniforms. It had only six shells and six charges. Each shell was fused for three seconds so that at maximum elevation it would burst high in the air and be seen by the flagship in Gabarus Bay. A single burst would indicate success while two bursts would tell the admiral that they had failed and were withdrawing. The whole apparatus, including the shells, weighed less than four hundred pounds and a short trial had confirmed that it wouldn't immediately break the back of a longboat, nor would it drive the boat bodily underwater. Carlisle was sceptical. How would the shell-burst be distinguished from all the others that were being lobbed into the fortress? It was all very well to say that the other mortars were fused to burst close to the ground, but Carlisle had seen many bursts well above their targets. The boat's crew, moreover, were frankly alarmed. They eyed the mortar and its uniformed attendants with dislike and suspicion.

They rowed the few hundred yards to where three vertical top-lights showed the position of the two-decker. The twenty-five boats were clustered in the darkness on the seaward side of the ship, and Balfour's boat was immediately visible holding water on the outer edge of the cluster.

'Give him two flashes, Mister Angelini', said Carlisle.

Enrico held up the white lantern and opened and closed the shutter twice. There was an answering light and as Carlisle's boat crept slowly past, Balfour's moved into position on the longboat's starboard side. Balfour waved at Carlisle and turned to adjust his own shuttered lantern, a green light for his own division. Carlisle could see the whole mass of boats dissolving now and organising themselves into two columns following their leader.

'*Invincible*, Souter,' murmured Carlisle. Laforey's division was waiting for them to seaward of the seventy-four and they moved onto Carlisle's larboard side, following the red stern light of their leader.

The flotilla had a long row ahead of it, along the eastern end of Gabarus Bay and past White Point. Then they would have to row past the French batteries on the seaward side of the fortress and the remaining guns on Goat Island before they could turn north and then west past the sunken blockships and into the harbour. The French positions on Battery Island had been suppressed by Wolfe's guns on Lighthouse Point. Otherwise, the expedition would hardly have been possible.

Navigation was easy while the British batteries continued to throw mortar shells into the fortress. The glow of individual burning buildings enhanced by the flashes of exploding shells were the simplest possible landmarks, showing through the thin veil of mist that covered the water. At eleven o'clock, just as the flotilla was approaching Goat Island, the three-quarters moon showed briefly and indistinctly between the eastern horizon and the base of the low cloud before rising further and losing itself in the mist.

Their next head mark was Lighthouse Point. They had just made the turn to steer northwest towards the flashes when the steady tempo of its cannon, howitzers and mortars increased to a furious rate. This was the diversionary bombardment that Amherst had promised. Looking west across the burning town, Carlisle could see the batteries on the hills above Louisbourg contributing to the display. With all that light and flame, it would be almost impossible for the French defenders to see this stealthy attack from the mist-shrouded sea.

The flotilla rowed steadily through the masts of the sunken blockships. They were intended to be an obstacle to ships-of-the-line, not shallow draft boats, and with only a few scrapes and bumps both divisions followed Carlisle's longboat through into the harbour itself. It was inevitable that his force would lose some of its cohesion as it negotiated the blockships, but Carlisle had emphasised the need for the boats to return to their stations as they made the turn towards the west. Carlisle's greatest fear was that one division would reach its objective minutes before the other. The noise of boarding would inevitably alert the second ship with potentially fatal consequences for the attackers.

Laforey's boat was starting to pull ahead. He was between Carlisle and the French ships, and this was no time to be flashing lights in that direction. However, there was so much noise in the background that Carlisle risked a hail.

'Captain Laforey! Your Station,' he shouted. There was an answering wave from Laforey's barge which was close enough for Carlisle to see the rowers rest on their oars while it dropped back. The boats following Laforey started to bunch up, but that didn't matter. All that concerned Carlisle was that he should throw his force at the two French ships simultaneously.

Laforey was back in his proper station now. The Grand Battery on the north shore was the next head mark.

'Easy to larboard, Souter,' said Carlisle. 'Use the battery

as your leading-mark.'

The longboat started to turn. Carlisle could see that Laforey had anticipated the manoeuvre and had, in fact, dropped a little abaft the flotilla leader's beam so that he wouldn't shoot ahead again.

'There they are, sir,' whispered Enrico, pointing away on the larboard bow.

It was difficult to make out the ships against the glow of burning buildings and the flash of guns and mortars, but now that he knew where to look, Carlisle could see the two hulls silhouetted against the background lights. He'd have to stand on for another cable before he could be confident of passing to the north of the shallows around Battery Island.

'Come to larboard again,' Carlisle said, and Souter pushed the tiller away from him to bring the longboat on its final approach.

Balfour's division was having to pull heartily now to hold their position on Carlisle's flank, while Laforey's oarsmen again rested on their oars.

'There's something in the water ahead, sir,' said Souter, peering into the darkness. 'Boxes or bales perhaps.'

There was a bump as the longboat shouldered aside something heavy and soft. Souter pushed his hand into the water and brought up a mass of dark vegetation. He sniffed it, then tasted it.

'Tobacco, sir,' he grinned. 'The harbour's full of bales of 'baccy, and some of 'em have split open. It's like the Sargasso Sea in there!'

This must be flotsam from the ships that had burned in the harbour, thought Carlisle. Well, it was no real obstacle to the boats.

They were just five cables from the ships now. The bombardment from the British guns had intensified with shot and shell from the Grand Battery and from Lighthouse Point whizzing over the flotilla. Carlisle looked at his watch in the light from the stern lantern. Fifteen minutes past one.

They were a few minutes later than he'd hoped, but that didn't matter.

'Mister Angelini, three flashes to starboard.'

He was releasing Balfour first as *Bienfaisant* was further away than *Prudent*. She was anchored to the northwest of the town, almost into the Barachois, the salt lagoon that extended Louisbourg harbour to the west.

There was an answering flash from starboard and Balfour's barge instantly increased its speed. Carlisle had deliberately kept the pace of the whole flotilla down so that at the assault they would be able to increase speed without going so fast that the splashes from the oars would give them away. He watched as Balfour's twenty-five boats rowed rapidly past, following their leader's light past the burned-out hulks of the *Entreprenant*, *Célèbre* and *Capricieux*, stark reminders of the vulnerability of even the most potent line-of-battle ships when confined to a restricted harbour.

'Three flashes to larboard, Mister Angelini,' Carlisle ordered.

Laforey had clearly been waiting for the signal. He must have seen Balfour's boats move ahead and was naturally keen to get moving. He knew very well the perils of arriving at his objective after it had been alerted.

It was a race now. There was no restraining the two divisions as they sped towards the unsuspecting French ships.

***

With the boats on their way, Carlisle could only watch as they pressed home their attacks. He held his position between the two ships, waiting for any indication that he'd have to intervene, to reallocate his force or to lend the weight of his few marines to an attack that was losing momentum.

There was fighting on the deck of *Bienfaisant*, that much was clear, but it was impossible to see who was winning. If the attackers were on the deck, then Carlisle was confident that they would carry the day, he knew that getting up the ship's side was the hardest part.

There was less noise over to larboard on *Prudent*. It looked as though Laforey had achieved complete surprise and he could see British seaman swarming unopposed over the gunwales. She looked to be aground, which was hardly surprising as she was close to the north of the Grave Battery, the only substantial defence on the harbour side of the town, and it was low tide.

'Stretch out now, Souter. Put us alongside the ship on the starboard bow,' he pointed to *Bienfaisant*.

It was a strange scene, lit by the fires from the shore. The British batteries were still blazing away, and Carlisle knew that they would do so until he gave the signal. As they drew closer, he could see people running up the masts of the two-decker, loosing the sails. There was a rhythmic thumping sound that he couldn't place until he realised that it must be a group of seamen chopping at the two colossal anchor cables. A third rate's anchor was fastened to a twenty-inch hemp cable made up of three separate ropes laid up in opposite directions to the individual strands. The best axeman would take a dozen or so strokes of a sharp, heavy axe to get through. Probably two strong men were working on each of those cables, hewing away from opposite sides.

'Pull us right under the stern, Souter.'

The side of the ship was festooned with boats secured by painters. A single unattended yawl was drifting away on the wind and tide.

'There are men swimming,' called Sergeant Wilson, 'shall we fire at them, sir?'

'Let them go,' replied Carlisle. Best of luck to them, he thought. They'd be prisoners soon enough and, in any case, the marines needed to preserve their first carefully loaded rounds in case they were required on either of the ships.

A face appeared over the taffrail, a hand waved and then it disappeared. Ten seconds passed and then Balfour looked over at the boat.

'She's ours, sir!' and at that moment Carlisle heard the

signal that they had agreed, three loud cheers from the three hundred attackers.

'Then take her over to the east end of the harbour, Captain Balfour,' Carlisle shouted in reply. 'You'll need to tow her in this wind. If you can't anchor, then put her aground.'

The wind was indeed dropping, and the mist was lifting; it had never been thick enough to be called fog. The moon appeared briefly between some clouds in the east. It went as quickly as it came, then re-appeared to sit like a pale witness to the battle.

'We've lost a few men, sir,' shouted Balfour.

His force may have suffered casualties, but he didn't look unhappy. If there were any justice, Boscawen would give him his step to post-captain within twenty-four hours, and their Lordships would surely confirm it. Cutting-out expeditions were commonplace, but Carlisle couldn't think of another example of a successful cutting-out of a third rate; merchant ships and sloops were the usual prey.

At that moment, there was a loud crash overhead. The Grave Battery had realised what was happening and had opened fire, hitting *Bienfaisant's* high stern with its first salvo. Probably they hadn't yet understood that *Prudent*, anchored right under their guns, was also under attack. Carlisle looked to see what damage it had done, but it was just one more hole in a badly scarred ship. She'd been under the guns of Lighthouse Point and the Grand Battery for weeks, and her battered upper works showed the evidence.

'Get under way as soon as possible, Captain Balfour,' Carlisle shouted back. 'I'll go over to *Prudent*.'

Balfour's face disappeared over the taffrail.

'To the other one,' he said to Souter, 'and have those men put their backs into it!'

It was eerily quiet on board *Prudent*. Carlisle hadn't yet heard three cheers from Laforey's men, but evidently the boarding had taken place.

The longboat sped across the harbour, pushing aside

bales of tobacco and ignoring the French swimmers, some of whom clung to floating bales, resting before continuing towards the shore.

'Take us alongside, Souter,' said Carlisle. 'Sergeant Wilson, bring your men and follow me.'

He entered the ship through a lower deck gunport, sword drawn. The ship may have been in British hands, but it didn't necessarily follow that all resistance had ceased. There could be pockets of Frenchman determined to fight to the last. He hurried up the ladders to the upper deck.

The ship was clearly under new ownership, but there was an air of stealth about the way that the seamen moved. Men were climbing the rigging to set the sails, but they did it without haste and in small numbers.

'The ship is ours, sir,' reported Laforey, saluting.

Carlisle waited. He wasn't going to ask the obvious questions: why were they not underway and why had they not given three cheers as a signal?

'Problem is, sir, she's firmly aground, and there's a battery only two hundred yards away.'

Carlisle could see the Grave Battery firing away at *Bienfaisant*, the shot hurtling close past the ship's stern. Evidently, the battery commander hadn't yet realised what was happening under his very nose.

Carlisle moved his weight from side to side, testing the level of the deck. The ship was listing a few degrees, and she wasn't moving the way a vessel with water under her keel would.

'You're certain, Captain Laforey? She can't be moved?'

'I'm certain, sir,' he replied, deferring to Carlisle for the next step.

'Then we'll burn her. Get your combustibles up from the boats; these marines will help.'

'Excuse me, sir. We have some prisoners, and there's a British deserter among them,' he said, pointing at a group of men in the waist. 'Could your marines guard them? My men know where the combustibles are.'

'Why are there so few?' asked Carlisle.

'That's all that were on board, sir,' said Laforey. 'No more than a hundred and fifty, and we killed less than a dozen. Some seem to be in hiding below decks.'

Most likely a large proportion of the French seamen would be manning the walls of the fortress, thought Carlisle. De Gouttes would have been lucky if he'd been left with half of his full crews.

'Sergeant Wilson, guard those prisoners,' Carlisle said, indicating the group of men clustered against the starboard gunwale.

'Now let's burn this ship.'

Laforey was all energy. He sent men to the middle gundeck to set the combustibles. Others he sent to the bases of the masts.

Crash! The first shot from the Grave Battery tore through the gunwale and passed close to the tightly packed mass of prisoners. Those Frenchmen were going to be a problem, Carlisle thought. A damned nuisance to guard, and a dead weight in the boats; they'd be prisoners in a day or two anyway.

'Those men have the choice of swimming for it or coming with us in the boats,' said Carlisle, pointing to the Frenchmen. 'But the deserter comes with us. Which one is he?'

One of Laforey's lieutenants pointed to a man standing apart from the other prisoners. He was being guarded by a British seaman with a pistol and a cutlass.

'That's the deserter, sir,' he said.

Carlisle looked at the man who was staring sullenly at the deck. At that moment, the deserter looked up, and a flash of recognition passed between them. The prisoner roared and smashed his fist into the seaman's face. The seaman's pistol went off with a bang and a flash, the ball harmlessly embedding itself into the deck, but his cutlass was snatched by the deserter. He ran at Carlisle, intent only on killing. Carlisle just had time to raise his sword against the inexpert but overwhelmingly powerful overhead stroke. Their blades clashed and Carlisle's was forced downwards. The man raised his arm again for the killing blow, his face a mask of hate. The cutlass quivered slightly at the top of its arc, then the man's eyes opened wide in a surprised stare. He still looked amazed as he was forced to the ground by the power of Sergeant Wilson's bayonet through his chest.

The sergeant pulled the dying man onto his back.

'An old friend of ours, sir,' he remarked without emotion as he wiped his bayonet on the man's shirt.

Carlisle was shaking. It took all his self-control to master himself. Yes, he knew the dying man; it was the pilot from Boston. So it was true. He *had* deserted to the French. After all, he was a pilot for the whole of this coast from Boston to Newfoundland; he'd have been greeted with open arms. When *Prudent* was taken, he must have realised that only a noose awaited him when he was recognised, and the thought of killing the man whose actions had brought him to this pass was too attractive to ignore.

'*Où est le maître du vaisseau de guerre?*' Where is the ship's master? asked Carlisle, scanning the crowd of prisoners.

A middle-aged man in a blue frock uniform stepped forward, looking concerned at being singled out, yet defiant in the face of his captor. He was so much like a master in the King's service that Carlisle wondered how he hadn't already picked him out. Hosking in a French uniform.

'This man,' he said, indicating the dead pilot, 'where did he come from?'

The master looked scornfully at the body.

'*De Port Dauphin, en avril,*' he replied. '*un anglais, mais il connaissait bien la côte.*'

He'd come from Port Dauphin in April! So that was why the frigate captain was so confident in altering course away from Louisbourg when he found it guarded. That was how the French transports knew the Siboux islands so well and were able so easily to evade *Medina*. The pilot must have persuaded the Boston smuggler to take him to meet the

French convoy, probably at Sable Island. Most likely he'd been planning for some time to defect, his brush with Carlisle must have merely precipitated his flight.

***

Carlisle took a few moments to recover, but there was too much requiring his attention to dwell on his narrow escape. He saw that the destruction of *Prudent* was in good hands. There were already wisps of smoke curling up from below decks and an intrepid group of Frenchmen were jumping into the water from the main chains, clutching anything handy that would float. The remainder were being herded into the largest of the boats and put to the oars by the marines. Sergeant Wilson, apparently unconcerned by having only minutes before saved his captain's life, oversaw the proceedings with a magisterial detachment.

'Captain Laforey, you don't need all your men now. Any that aren't engaged in burning the ship or securing prisoners are to row over to assist Captain Balfour. It's getting too dangerous on this deck anyway,' he said as another shot from the battery smashed into the ship.

They both looked over to the northwest, past the shattered remnants of de Gouttes' squadron. The moon was now bright enough to show that *Bienfaisant* was underway and would pass close to the north of *Prudent*. However, the slight breeze barely gave her steerage way, and the few men that could be spared from working the ship were insufficient to make much progress towing.

'Aye-aye sir,' replied Laforey. 'The last prisoners are going now. Any that have hidden below decks will have to shift for themselves.'

Carlisle didn't wait to see his orders carried out. He found a spare halyard hanging over the stern and lowered himself down into the longboat.

'Mister Angelini. When we're clear of the ship, I believe we can bring the boat's crew aft and fire a single shell from the mortar.'

***

CHAPTER TWENTY-SEVEN

Louisbourg's Fall

Wednesday, Twenty-Sixth of July 1758.
Bienfaisant. Aground. Louisbourg Harbour, Île Royale.

*P*rudent burned all through that short summer night, a stark warning to the Louisbourg defenders that there would be no relief from the sea and that the soft underbelly of their town and fortress was now open to attack by the British navy. As the fire reached her gun decks, thirty-six and eighteen pounders fired randomly into the town and harbour, deterring any French attempts at saving her.

The westerly wind failed entirely as with the last burst of the oarsmen's energy *Bienfaisant* was run aground at the eastern end of the harbour. Her main and foremast went by the board as the soft mud brought her to a halt. She'd be quite safe there, well out of range of the French batteries and covered by the British Grand Battery and the smaller gun emplacements around the eastern shore.

As the full light of dawn illuminated the decks of the shattered ship, Carlisle surveyed the scene. It was strangely quiet. There seemed no need to man the pumps as the ship was firmly aground, although that would change with the turning of the tide. The batteries had all fallen silent; Carlisle guessed that Amherst was allowing Drucour to consider his predicament, and *Prudent's* guns had, at last, ceased their chaotic explosions.

'My glass, Mister Angelini,' said Carlisle, more in hope than expectation. However, Enrico was nothing if not meticulous, and he'd preserved the essentials through the last half-day of turmoil. With a flourish that was lost on Carlisle, he produced his captain's telescope from an oilskin bag.

'*Prudent's* burned down to her lower deck,' he observed

to Laforey who was standing beside him. The contrast between Laforey and Balfour was almost comical. Each had carried out his duties in an exemplary manner, yet Balfour had been lucky and now commanded – perhaps only temporarily – a third rate ship-of-the-line, while Laforey was reduced to the role of a bystander, a mere provider of manpower and runner of errands to his more fortunate colleague.

'Captain Balfour!'

'Sir?' he replied, turning from the work of directing his lieutenants to sort through and cut away the tangle of masts, yards and rigging that cluttered the deck. It was important to save anything that could be used as a jury rig to get the ship out of the harbour and back to Halifax. The French – now British – ship had suddenly become very dear to Balfour.

'You will command *Bienfaisant* until you're given new orders by Mister Boscawen. I regret that I can't put that in writing, but Captain Laforey, I'm sure, will stand witness to your orders.'

Balfour positively beamed. It wasn't a promotion – Carlisle didn't have that in his gift – but it was a positive step in the right direction.

'You're to endeavour to make the ship tight and to move her out to an anchor berth, that is to be your first concern. I'll leave you with all the officers and men that were in your division.'

'Aye-aye sir.'

'Mister Laforey, you'll send your division back to Gabarus Bay. They may follow my longboat out of the harbour. I don't expect we'll be bothered by the enemy; they have other things on their minds. I hope you'll join me in my longboat, and we can report to Admiral Hardy together.'

That cheered up Laforey. He didn't have a captured ship to command, but he knew that he'd done well, and he was being allowed to carry the good news to the man who could most influence the next step in his career.

'Your division will take all the wounded and as many of the prisoners as they can fit into the boats. We'll leave in an hour. Pass the word for my coxswain.'

'Here, sir,' said Souter from close behind Carlisle. He had a drawn cutlass in his hand and two pistols in his belt. In truth, he'd barely left his captain's side since the incident with the deserter. He felt that it should have been *his* role to save his captain from a cutlass blow, not Sergeant Wilson's, and he was determined that it wouldn't happen again. Two of the boat's crew stood behind Souter cradling a large bundle of stained white cloth and grinning broadly.

'What's that, Souter?' asked Carlisle, pointing at the bundle.

Souter nodded at the two men who, with a flourish, unrolled a huge white flag adorned with gold fleur-de-lis.

'*Prudent's* ensign, sir,' said Souter, 'it didn't seem right that it should be still flying, her having become a prize, if only for a while.' Souter knew very well that he and his men deserved a reward for capturing an ensign.

Carlisle looked with new respect at his coxswain. It must have taken some presence of mind to think of that detail in the turmoil of leaving a burning ship. It was a hugely important trophy of war that would have pride of place in a cathedral back in Britain. He briefly examined the ensign, with its white background torn by shot and stained by smoke, its gold adornments ripped and tattered. Laforey was watching with a wistful look. The French royal ensign was the most tangible evidence of his success, and he was clearly disappointed that his own men hadn't thought to secure it.

Carlisle touched the fabric, feeling the material and thinking his own thoughts of the blood and sweat that had been expended for such a trivial thing.

'Be so kind as to present this ensign to Captain Laforey, Souter, and when we're back in *Medina* remind me to consider you and the men who secured it.'

***

It was a long and slow pull back to the squadron anchorage at Gabarus Bay, and every yard of it had to be rowed because the sailing rigs had all been left behind in the ships the day before. The crews of the boats were exhausted after their labours, and the boats themselves were encumbered by prisoners and those of the wounded who could be safely moved.

The marines stood to their muskets as they passed Battery Island and Goat Island, but never a shot came from the French positions and there was no sign of the defenders other than an ensign hanging limply from a staff.

It was late in the forenoon when they rounded White Point and saw the squadron and all the transports and supply ships, hundreds of vessels – a still mighty armament – spread out before them. It was time for Laforey's division to disperse, and each boat turned towards its own ship, the crews too tired for even a last cheer.

'*Royal William*, Souter,' said Carlisle. 'Larboard side.'

As a relatively junior captain, Carlisle would have chosen the starboard side, the less formal entry to a flagship, for day-to-day business, but today he wanted to emphasise the point that he and Laforey were returning in triumph. He guessed that Boscawen and Hardy would already have moved on to planning the next phase in the downfall of Louisbourg and may even now be engaged in surrender negotiations. The mortar shell of last night would have drawn a line under the episode as far as the senior leadership was concerned, and it would be all too easy for the night's exploits to be understated. Even the taking of a third rate and the burning of another could be overlooked when mighty fortresses fell.

Carlisle stepped in through the entry port to the full ceremonial that was the right of a post-captain in command. As he was ushered away to meet the admiral, he could see that half the sideboys were being hurried away and the bosun's calls were being stowed. Laforey, as a commander without a command, was entitled to nothing more than a doffing of hats by the small number of lesser officers that would remain to greet him, and he'd have to wait on deck until Hardy and Carlisle had met. Laforey lingered near the entry port to see his precious trophy brought safely on board. The remaining sideboys stared as Enrico and two of the boat's crew carried the anonymous canvas-wrapped parcel into the flagship.

Sir Charles was in a good humour. He offered Carlisle refreshments at the same time as quizzing him on the night's events.

'So *Bienfaisant* is safe in the northeast harbour?' he asked.

'Yes, sir, safely aground when I left her, but she'll be floating by now. Balfour's men were busy rousing out the two spare bower anchors; there was enough undamaged cable to lay out at least one of them. She wasn't taking much water, but it would be as well to send him a good carpenter and his mates as soon as possible, and a bosun to sort through the shambles on deck.'

'Dismasted then?'

'Yes, sir,' replied Carlisle. 'She lost her main and foremast when she took the ground, but they would have had to come down in any case, they were both shot through.'

'And *Prudent* is burned, I gather.'

'She is, sir. I took a good look as we rowed out of the harbour and she's burned down to the lower gun deck.'

'Could nothing be done to bring her out?'

'No, sir,' replied Carlisle firmly. 'She was hard aground under the Grave Battery, and we couldn't have waited for the tide, not with the French guns only a cable away. Laforey did well to board her without being seen, and it was perhaps half an hour before the French on shore realised what had happened. When they did, there was nothing for it but to burn her and withdraw.'

Carlisle paused.

'I gave Laforey the order to burn her, sir.'

Hardy nodded thoughtfully. Evidently, he'd have dearly

liked to have taken two French third rates rather than taken one and burned another. It seemed such a waste to have four burned-out hulks resting on the Île Royale mud.

'Then perhaps you would give me a general impression of the conduct of the two officers. Commander Balfour first, I think.'

Balfour is Hardy's protégé, Carlisle remembered. The admiral would be looking for the strongest possible recommendation of his conduct so that he could apply to Boscawen for Balfour to be posted, perhaps to the immediate command of *Bienfaisant*. Laforey was Boscawen's man, and it probably mattered little what Carlisle had to say. A French third rate burned under the guns of a battery was enough evidence on its own to warrant any reward that was in the commander-in-chief's gift.

'Captain Balfour performed to my highest expectations, sir,' he replied formally. 'He overcame stiff opposition in boarding *Bienfaisant*, which he accomplished with only a handful of killed and wounded.'

Hardy said nothing and Carlisle realised that he was expected to elaborate. The admiral's secretary's pen was poised in anticipation.

'In my opinion,' said Carlisle tentatively and saw the answering look of approval, 'and on the strength of his performance in cutting out a French third rate under fire,' he continued more confidently, 'Captain Balfour is ready to be promoted to post-captain.'

Sir Charles allowed himself a brief smile.

'Let the record show Captain Carlisle's comments,' he said to his secretary, who's scratching pen could be clearly heard in the stillness of the cabin.

So that's how it's done, thought Carlisle, that's how a commander-in-chief is manoeuvred into transforming a commander into a post-captain. No doubt Balfour would hear the word from Boscawen within the day, and his promotion would be confirmed by their Lordships within a couple of months, as soon as a letter could reach Whitehall, and a reply could be received. He had himself been manoeuvred, of course, but he comforted himself with the knowledge that the promotion was well deserved.

'Now, your opinion on Commander Laforey,' said Sir Charles. It was evident by the careless way that he said it, that Hardy understood this next report was a mere formality. Boscawen had brought Laforey on this expedition – shipless as he was – specifically so that he was on hand when an opportunity such as this arose. He may not have taken his ship, but he'd destroyed an enemy third rate, again under fire, and even without his connection to Boscawen he'd have stood a good chance of being promoted.

His secretary turned over a leaf in his notebook and dipped his quill, ready to record Carlisle's words.

'Commander Laforey displayed great skill in boarding *Prudent* unobserved and good judgement in setting her on fire when it was clear that she was fast aground.'

Carlisle knew the form of words now.

'In my opinion, Commander Laforey is ready to be promoted to post-captain.'

'Very well, Captain,' Hardy looked over his shoulder to ensure that his secretary was recording the conversation, 'I'll expect your report tomorrow, which will no doubt include the form of words that you used today. My secretary will give you a transcript for your convenience. Meanwhile, I'll send these notes over to Mister Boscawen immediately. He's busy negotiating a surrender and I wouldn't want this recent gallant action to slip his mind.'

'Commander Balfour, of course, is still in *Bienfaisant*, but Laforey came on board with me. May I present him, Sir Charles?'

Hardy looked as though he had better things to do with his time. He'd spoken to the expedition's leader, why would he need to speak to a subordinate in whom he had no interest?

'Yes, please,' he replied with all the grace he could

muster, 'I'd be delighted.'

The secretary went to the cabin door and a few seconds later, the cry of 'Pass the word for Captain Laforey,' could be heard echoing along the decks.

In fact, Laforey was only a few steps away, nervously waiting in the hope of a meeting with the admiral. Hardy and Carlisle may have been convinced of his imminent elevation, but as a junior commander with no ship, he needed all the reassurance he could get.

Hardy meant to keep this short.

'Welcome Captain Laforey. I've heard all about your exploits, so there's no need to elaborate. My sincere congratulations on destroying *Prudent*. It's a pity you couldn't have taken her, but at least she's burned.' Hardy was not the most empathetic of people, and Laforey turned a shade paler at the last sentence.

'However, as I said, my sincere congratulations,' Hardy continued. Even he knew when he'd been insensitive, albeit usually after the event. 'I shall mention you appropriately in my report.'

'I believe Captain Laforey has something to show you, sir,' said Carlisle, looking meaningfully at the startled younger man.

'Indeed, I have, sir,' said Laforey. Carlisle realised that in his confusion Laforey may really have forgotten.

The secretary opened the cabin door and Souter and two of his boat's crew proudly brought in the canvas-wrapped bundle. The light started to dawn on Hardy. They unwrapped it and spread out – as far as it would go within the confines of the cabin – the huge French royal ensign.

'Now that is magnificent,' said Hardy, his austere face breaking into a delighted smile. He stroked the fabric, examined the gold fleur-de-lis and measured the breadth with his outstretched hands. Laforey held his breath.

'Pass the word for Captain Evans and the bosun. I shall have this flown from the maintop underneath one of ours. That'll show the soldiers! What do you think Carlisle, is that legal and decent?'

'Decent? certainly, sir. Legal? who knows? but as there are no admiralty clerks for a clear two thousand miles, I believe we can do as we choose.'

***

Drucour and his officers had hoped that they may enjoy the same generous terms of surrender as had been offered to the British garrison of Fort St. Philip in Minorca. However, Amherst and Boscawen – and most of the population of Britain – were more influenced by the previous year's massacre at Fort William Henry at the south end of Lake George, where the surrendered British garrison had been attacked by the Indian allies of the victorious French. It was being called *the massacre at William Henry* and the name of Montcalm, the French commander of the siege, was anathema.

The British general and the admiral were in no mood to compromise. They knew that Louisbourg couldn't survive a direct assault and that is what it would be subjected to in the next day or two if the French governor didn't accept terms. It was late in the afternoon, and then only with the intervention of the civilian controller of finance that the French military men were persuaded to accept the terms that amounted to an unconditional surrender.

The next day, thirty minutes later than the appointed time of eight o'clock in the morning, because the French had difficulty in clearing the rubble, three companies of grenadiers entered the fortress of Louisbourg through the Dauphin Gate and took possession.

At midday Drucour surrendered the fortress, to the sound of the French drummers beating the *générale*. The terms of the surrender were indeed onerous. The soldiers all had to surrender their weapons and were considered prisoners-of-war, to be transported to Britain until the peace. Any civilian who had taken up arms was similarly treated. The remainder of the civilian population was to be taken to France. The whole of Île Royale and Île Saint-Jean were handed over to British rule.

The men of the Cambis Regiment, regular soldiers of the French army who had only arrived in Louisbourg in early June, smashed their muskets and burned their colours in disgust.

Well may the inhabitants of New France have quaked, because this was undoubtedly the beginning of the end.

***

CHAPTER TWENTY-EIGHT

News from the South

Saturday, Nineteenth of August 1758.
Medina, at Anchor. Halifax, Nova Scotia.

Carlisle breathed deeply of the clean air. Even after two days at sea, he hadn't grown used to the sheer joy of being away from Île Royale and Louisbourg. If anything, the frigate's life had grown worse since the capitulation. Before, there had been a sense of purpose. Afterwards, it was the anti-climax of a battle won, the day after a marriage feast with the house to be put straight.

Since the capitulation his ship had been employed on errands, and much of the time he was short-handed having been mulcted of men for working parties ashore. It hadn't taken Amherst and Boscawen long to determine that the season was too far advanced to risk an ascent of the St. Lawrence; Quebec and Montreal would have to wait another year. They had settled down to the task of making Louisbourg defensible and habitable for the garrison that would have to stay there over the winter. Ships and marching columns had been sent the length and breadth of Île Royale and Île St-Jean to round up the French and Acadian inhabitants for evacuation, some to France and some to French Louisiana. Carlisle wanted none of it. His thoughts were only on Chiara and Williamsburg.

The vast fleet was ready to sail back to Britain by the middle of August. The British soldiers – those that were not remaining in Louisbourg – had been embarked; so too had the French prisoners and the civilians. Carlisle made a farewell call on Sir Charles, who had said good things and made vague promises for the future. In truth, there was little that Carlisle needed. He could be moved into a ship-of-the-line, but he wasn't at all sure that he wanted that, not yet. He found that he valued his independence too highly and, in any case, he'd not yet made enough in prize money. Sometime, for sure, and it would be better to make the move before this war ended and ships became scarce.

He'd also called on Lord Colville who for a short while, as a commodore, had been his superior. But Colville was now substantially the same rank as Carlisle although significantly senior. He found Colville's ship, *Northumberland* in a sad state. His crew had never recovered from the fevers and scurvy that had afflicted them after a winter in Halifax. Since he'd sailed from there in April, he'd buried a hundred and fifty men out of a complement of five hundred and twenty, and they'd left behind at Louisbourg another sixty who were too sick for the transatlantic passage.

Carlisle had always known that *Medina* should be sent back to Jamaica when he was no longer needed at Louisbourg, but he still thought it a stroke of luck when his orders arrived, signed by Boscawen himself. It was always possible that a man of Boscawen's seniority could justify keeping *Medina*. After all, he was the senior naval lord on the Admiralty Board, and a member of parliament to boot, and every admiral was perennially short of frigates. In the end, it was the rumour of a French frigate patrolling off the Carolinas to pick up the tobacco trade that swung the balance, or so Carlisle guessed.

Medina had been ordered to Halifax, to take on stores, wood and water and then to escort some transports and supply ships to New York. Then on to Hampton to pick up a convoy for ports in the southern Colonies and the West Indies. That was the second stroke of luck. With fair winds and no diversions, he could be in Hampton for the birth of his child. Once there and so remote from naval authority, nothing would cause him to sail before the birth, convoy or no convoy.

✳✳✳

The same pilot boarded *Medina* off Cornwallis Island. Carlisle was pleased to see him, his air of friendly competence put the whole quarterdeck in a cheerful mood.

'There's your convoy, Captain,' he said as *Medina* approached her anchor berth.

Carlisle tried to count them, but the confusion of masts in such a small space made it impossible. There were at least twenty store ships and troop transports, all substantial vessels and each a tempting prize for any French privateer. But there were no French ships off Nova Scotia now; the overwhelming concentration of British naval power had persuaded them to make their living elsewhere. It should be an easy passage, at least as far as New York.

'Let go!' shouted Hosking. The best bower plunged down to the muddy bottom and *Medina* swung with her bows to the westerly wind.

'Away the captain's crew,' shouted the first lieutenant, 'away the gig.'

Carlisle was in a tearing hurry to be on his way south, so he'd given up the longboat and the yawl to speed the embarkation of the necessary stores for their long journey to Jamaica. The gig, small as it was, would do for this most informal of naval ports. In any case, he was calling on his old and rustic friend the master attendant, and *he* wouldn't recognise formality if he saw it.

***

'There's mail for you, Captain,' said the master attendant. 'I've already sent it over to your ship, not knowing that you'd come ashore so quickly. You must have passed my boat on the way.'

He saw the look on Carlisle's face. The Louisbourg ships hadn't had mail for months and to hear that the mail was now on his ship, waiting for him to return, was clearly infuriating.

'We can keep this short, sir, as I'm sure you're busy,' he continued tactfully. 'You can see your convoy; there are twenty-four of them, all ready for sea whenever you're stored. The masters know to look for your signal to call on you. You're first in line for victualling stores, wood and water and anything that we have in the naval line. There's fresh food too, and they know to expect your purser. Can I help you in any other way?'

Carlisle tried unsuccessfully to hide his haste, but he simply couldn't just turn around and leave. It was undignified, and in any case, he had his own news to give.

'You remember that we spoke about the Pilot from Boston, who fled after he was suspended?'

'I do, it's believed he defected. In fact, I've heard rumours that he joined the French squadron in Louisbourg. He didn't cross your path a second time, did he?'

Carlisle grimaced. 'He did, a second and a third time,' he replied, and told the story, in all its sordid detail.

'Well, that puts an end to that,' said the master attendant. 'I'll send word to Boston so that they can strike him off the pilot's list. What a curious end for a bad character, and a lucky escape for you.'

***

Carlisle lost no further time in returning to *Medina*. In his cabin, his clerk had already sorted the mail. There was a pile of official correspondence that he'd already opened, there was a heap of personal letters for the officers, and another smaller pile for the men. It was surprising how many of the seamen corresponded with family or friends. More astonishing still; with no official means of sending personal letters, their correspondents found the means to direct their messages to a specified ship so far from home.

Carlisle glanced at the official letters. They were all from the Navy Board, except for one from Admiral Cotes in Jamaica. He skimmed it quickly. It was just routine, new orders for anchor berths in Port Royal and Kingston and a reminder to restrict gun salutes to the first arrival on station, nothing that required his immediate attention. He didn't expect anything from their Lordships. If they felt the need to address a frigate's captain, they'd do it through the appropriate admiral, unless the frigate was under Admiralty orders.

'Thank you, Simmonds, you may distribute the private

letters and leave the official mail for an hour, until after your dinner. There's nothing there that will change our immediate fate.'

Simmonds took the hint and left Carlisle alone in his cabin, alone except for a half-dozen letters from Chiara, all neatly dated on the cover so that he knew in what order to read them.

Impatient for the latest news, Carlisle ripped open the letter with the most recent date, the twenty-fifth of July.

> *'My dearest Edward. I will start the way I have started each letter since we have been apart, to assure you that I am in good health and that my confinement is progressing well. The physician is pleased and confidently expects the happy event in the second week of September, with the normal caveat that the baby will come when it is ready, not before and not after.'*

That was what Carlisle wanted to hear, and he could feel his pounding heart slowing as the news sank in. The second week in September. Yes, he should be in Hampton by then, if his convoy behaved itself. It was a curious coincidence that this latest letter had been written the day that he'd taken or destroyed the last remnants of the French squadron in Louisbourg Harbour. If he'd failed, would it have given the defenders fresh courage to prolong the siege? Possibly, and if so, he wouldn't be contemplating arriving in Williamsburg before his child was born. *The Lord moves in mysterious ways*, he remembered from his Sunday school. He read on.

> *'You will have followed the development of my relationship with my father-in-law…'*

So, it was father-in-law now, was it? Previously Chiara had only been able to bring herself to refer to him as *your father*.

> *'He is a frequent visitor now, although both*

Dexter and Barbara are careful to be in the house when he calls. I am not at all sure how effective Dexter would be, but Barbara would be a tiger in my defence. She is so protective! I think Joshua is not blind to their concerns, but he has never mentioned it. He refers to his grandchild now. Or when he forgets, he slips into calling it his grandson, a common error for a prospective grandfather, I am told. He is ever so humble whenever he visits. I do believe that he is growing on me (I hope that is an appropriate English expression).'

Chiara had committed some hilarious errors in English idioms, and more than a few malapropisms. Carlisle could smile at those, but it was her inability to use contractions that made her letters awkward to read. Did they use contractions when writing in Italian? He'd ask Enrico.

'Your brother, however, still scowls whenever he sees me, and Dexter places himself between us when we should chance to pass in the street. However, the physician says that from next week, I should really be confined, and not merely in the conventional use of the word. I will be shut up in this charming house thinking of you and sewing clothes for our child-to-be…'

Carlisle finished reading the letter then worked his way forward from the oldest. Apart from the lack of contractions, Chiara really was the best of letter writers. She was careful to repeat the news from earlier letters until she'd confirmed that they'd been received, and every letter was dated.

It was good news, of course. The only concern was his brother, and Carlisle decided that he'd take firm action when they arrived at Williamsburg. It sounded as though he may count on the backing of his father, and if necessary, he'd instruct the lawyer to apply to the court for an order to prevent his brother contacting his family. It should be easy;

his brother wasn't a man with any notable friends, and his conduct had become notorious.

***

CHAPTER TWENTY-NINE

Unfinished Business

Saturday, Second of September 1758.
Medina, at Sea. Off the Virginia Capes.

H e was a lucky man, Carlisle thought as he tapped the hard oak of the quarterdeck rail and looked covertly around to confirm that nobody had seen him. The set, expressionless face of the quartermaster suggested otherwise.

He'd delivered his convoy safely to Sandy Hook and the fair summer winds had wafted *Medina*, alone now, on past New Jersey, Delaware and Maryland until they were only a day's sail from Cape Henry.

Eight bells found Carlisle still on the quarterdeck. The men of the last dog had been turned out and were swapping idle banter with their oppos from the first dog. Whittle had just taken his place at the masthead and Carlisle, looking upwards, could see him scanning the horizon. Whittle must be almost as keen to reach Hampton as Carlisle was himself. It appeared that someone had spoken to him about deference to his captain – probably Souter – and since they'd left Halifax, he'd behaved much better, no longer playing on his long, long association with Carlisle. He'd speak to Moxon. Whittle should have some leave while they were in Hampton. He could spend a week at his home and recount tall tales of his exploits.

Carlisle was still watching Whittle when he saw the able seaman's body stiffen. He passed his hand across his eyes and then stared fixedly to windward.

'Sail Ho!' he shouted. 'Sail right to windward, eight points on the larboard bow.'

Carlisle grabbed the copper speaking trumpet.

'What do you make of her Whittle?'

There was a pause. Carlisle thought quickly. On the face

289

of it, the sail could be almost anything. A casual merchant ship from the Caribbean or from Europe; or a slaver, a Guineaman from West Africa. And yet it was unlikely. The war had been raging for over two years; there were few innocent merchant ships sailing the seas alone, particularly here, where the wealth of the Americas was focussed and the hunters congregated. Carlisle waited impatiently for Whittle to respond.

'It's a ship, sir,' he shouted. There was another pause as Whittle stared hard to windward. 'Just one; it could be a man-of-war.'

'Beat to quarters, Mister Moxon.' Carlisle didn't need to look over his shoulder, by now he knew his first lieutenant well enough to be certain that he'd be there. 'Clear for action.'

He knew deep in his bones that a French frigate was approaching them fast from windward. How long before the French captain realised that the sail his lookout had sighted wasn't a fat New York merchantman, bound for the Chesapeake? How long before he hauled his wind and escaped to the east?

All around he could hear the frigate being prepared for an engagement. Bulkheads were being knocked down, furniture was being struck below, boarding nets were being rigged and yards chained. The people were going to their stations in a disciplined rush. Behind, he could hear the marines forming into ranks under the stern eye of Sergeant Wilson; down in the waist, the nine-pounders were being cast loose and the gun-ports opened.

'She's a man o' war for sure, sir,' shouted Whittle in an almost casual voice. 'A frigate I'd say.'

'Bring her onto the wind, Mister Hosking, as hard as she'll go.'

Medina's easy motion ended as she came up two points. Now she was butting into the southerly tops'l breeze with the chase five points off her bow.

'Set the t'gallants.'

She must have seen who we are by now, Carlisle thought. When will she turn away? With the weather gauge and the whole Atlantic to windward, she could easily hold *Medina* off until dark, then she could make her escape. If that were a Frenchman on the lookout for the tobacco trade, he certainly wouldn't willingly tangle with a British frigate. This just didn't make any sense.

'Captain, sir, can I come down?' shouted Whittle.

He'd done this before, remembered Carlisle, when he had something to say that couldn't easily be conveyed in a shouted conversation.

Carlisle nodded to Moxon who sent up a relief. Whittle slid down the backstay and arrived with a skip on the quarterdeck.

'It's him again, sir,' he said breathlessly. 'It's that same French frigate, the one we tangled with hereabouts and the one we beat up north.'

Carlisle's heart beat faster. That changed the equation. Assuming it was the same captain, he had a point to make. He may not even have recognised *Medina*, but any British frigate would do. Carlisle knew how the Frenchman thought, he recognised his own determination, his own pride in the face of all logic.

'You're sure, Whittle?' Carlisle looked at him almost sternly. His next move would depend on the certainty of Whittle's identification.

'I'm certain, sir. He carries his fore tops'l very high, higher than ours or any frigate I've seen. I'd recognise him anywhere.'

They'd last seen the Frenchman five months ago when he'd limped past them into Port Dauphin, his fore topmast and main yard shot away. Since then he must have carried out rudimentary repairs and slipped past the British blockade back to Brest or Rochefort. Now he was off the American coast again, eager – no, *desperate* – to prove himself. Carlisle was as sure as he could be; this Frenchman wouldn't run.

'Bear away, Mister Hosking, put us before the wind.'

'I beg your pardon…' started Hosking in surprise.

'You heard me correctly the first time, master, bear away,' he repeated angrily. Then his face softened. This was no way to lead his senior officers.

'Mister Moxon,' he called down to the waist, 'Mister Hosking, would you join me for a moment? Mister Wishart can handle the ship.'

They stood together against the taffrail.

'This man won't run, particularly if he's recognised us, which I must assume he has. However, I want him to think we don't choose to fight. We'll run north until the light starts to fade, then we'll turn and take him on. I fancy we'll be better in a night engagement than he'll be. We've spent long enough blundering around off Île Royale, after all.'

That brought a smile from the sailing master. It was probably true as well.

'You may pass the word so that the people don't think we're shy.'

***

Medina ran north, her t'gallants and stuns'ls speeding her through the water at nine, sometimes ten knots. The French frigate – after all this time Carlisle still didn't know her name – crept closer, and now she was only three miles astern. God, she was fast, thought Carlisle. She had a real look of determination as her forefoot clove the sea, and the broad spread of canvas rose and fell as each crest of a swell passed under her.

The sun had set fifteen minutes before and there was only another forty-five minutes or so of light left. Carlisle analysed his motives in wanting a night fight. He always felt better when there was a complicating factor in an engagement: rocks and shoals, tricky currents, back-eddies of wind. However, none of those things was available to him a hundred miles northeast of Cape Henry and the only advantage that he could give *Medina* was darkness. Every fibre in his being rebelled against a fair fight, a slugging match between opponents of comparable capability. He knew that even if he won – and that was the toss of a coin – he'd have a butcher's bill a fathom long and his precious frigate would be so battered that she'd need a navy yard to refit. And of course, he may be killed or wounded himself, and he so much wanted to see Chiara and his child. Was that the real issue? Had impending fatherhood made him more careful of his own safety? He shook off the question, leaving it unanswered.

Carlisle looked down at the waist. The gun crews were relaxed, and they appeared confident, swapping jokes and the sort of barbed comments that men throw around as they wait to go into battle. How many would be laughing still in two hours? He took one more look over the taffrail at the advancing Frenchman. That ship must be moving at least a knot faster than *Medina*. Even if he wanted to escape, it would hardly be possible now.

'Mister Moxon. I'll speak to all the officers, master's mates and midshipman, if you please. Bosun and gunner and Sergeant Wilson as well.'

They came hurriedly aft led by the gunner who evidently had not been at his station in the magazine. He'd been fussing around his guns, no doubt. Carlisle waited until they were all gathered.

'Gentlemen, we'll turn and fight as soon as it's fully dark,' he looked over the larboard quarter to where the last glow of sunset could be seen, 'and I expect that will be about two bells.'

As if on cue, the ship's bell struck once, half an hour into the last dog. Carlisle smiled. A good omen? His officers clearly thought so as they grinned back at him in the fading light.

'That's our timing then, half an hour to go. She's faster than us, in case you hadn't noticed,' more smiles from his officers, they'd all seen the Frenchman eating up the gap between the two ships, 'but our gunnery will be better; faster and more accurate. Mister Gordon, can you leave the magazine to your mate?'

'I can, sir,' he replied, rubbing his hands in anticipation. If it weren't for the warrant and the pay that went with the rank, Gordon would gladly be a quarter gunner again, free to point his guns and hurl death and destruction at the enemy. Every minute spent in the magazine at action took a year off his life, he could swear, and frequently did.

'Then you're to be on the waist with the first lieutenant. You're to point the guns in the first phase of the engagement.'

They all drew closer, listening to their captain and nodding in appreciation as the plan became clear.

'But remember, gentlemen, there never yet was a plan that survived the first shots. Be alert and listen to my commands. I intend that we'll sail into Hampton Roads tomorrow with that gentleman in our wake, flying our colours!'

***

Slowly, so slowly, the light diminished. First, the residual orange glow faded from the southwestern horizon, then the brighter stars and the planets came out, one-by-one. Soon the lesser stars showed and then the first trace of the milky way appeared. The Frenchman could be seen quite clearly by the starlight, just two miles astern, and that was all the illumination that Carlisle wanted. The moon would set soon and wouldn't rise again until well into the morning watch, and he intended that it would be all over by then.

'Are you ready, Mister Hosking?' asked Carlisle.

'Ready, aye ready,' replied the master.

'Then haul your wind, larboard tack.'

The sail handlers were ready for this move, and they ran aloft to furl the stuns'l. As the steersmen moved the wheel deliberately to larboard, *Medina* came smoothly around until she was heading west-southwest with the wind on her bow and her bowlines twanging taut.

Carlisle watched the Frenchman keenly. What he should do – what all the logic of single-ship actions dictated – was to come a point to larboard to pass close under *Medina's* stern and deliver a raking broadside that would knock half the fight out of her at one blow. Yes, her bows moved to larboard and she veered her mizzen in preparation. That was what Carlisle was looking for, a sign that the Frenchman was committed.

One mile separated the two ships. The Frenchman came another point towards *Medina*, she was aiming for a very close pass.

'Mister Moxon, you may commence firing as soon as your shot will reach her.'

There was a pause, the gunner ran from gun to gun, adjusting elevation, motioning for the handspike men to nudge the guns left to follow the crossing target.

Usually, Carlisle would have saved the first broadside until they were so close that none of the carefully loaded guns could miss. However, today he was determined to upset any pre-conceived notions that his opponent may have. He had trust in his gun crews and knew that the second broadside would be as good as the first; that was partly why he'd brought the gunner up from the magazine.

Half a mile now and closing fast.

'Fire!' shouted Moxon. *Medina* Staggered to the recoil as the whole broadside hurled its load of cast iron into the night. Carlisle had just enough time to cover his eyes to preserve his night vision. When he looked again, he saw the Frenchman alarmingly close, but he'd taken hits. There was a piece of gunwale missing, and it looked like one of the gunports had a jagged enlargement. That was one gun less, he thought.

'Now!' shouted Carlisle. 'Bring her about Mister Hosking.'

This was where training and long, long months at sea paid off. There was barely a man in *Medina's* crew who was not a competent seaman, and the frigate could perfectly well be tacked without the gun crews leaving their stations. The bosun was on the fo'c'sle and bowsprit with the cook, the cooper and half a dozen others, and as *Medina's* bows nudged into the wind, they flattened the jib out to starboard by brute force, hauling with all their might at the stiff canvas.

There was a blinding flash as the French frigate fired a broadside into *Medina*. They were so close – less than pistol-shot – that every gun should have hit its target. However, the French gunners had been expecting to aim at an unprotected stern with a crossing rate of around eight knots, the speed of their ship. However, what they saw instead was the whole of *Medina's* larboard broadside as the frigate's bow passed through the wind, with a combined crossing speed of perhaps twelve knots. The British guns were already re-loaded and run out.

Carlisle saw a shot hammer into the gunwale alongside number four gun, bringing down two men in a shower of splinters, and he reeled as the remainder of the shot smashed against the ship's side. However, eight-pound shot, even at that range, could barely penetrate *Medina's* timbers, which is what Carlisle had intended.

Medina's bows passed through the eye of the wind, and the frigate paid off fast onto the starboard tack. Now the tables were turned, and *Medina* was passing under the French frigate's exposed stern. It was too much to ask of the French captain that he should react sufficiently fast to avoid this blow. That was the advantage of keeping the initiative, thought Carlisle, he could dictate the shape of the battle and his crew were ready for his next move.

'Fire as you bear!' shouted Moxon.

Carlisle had time to notice, before his guns obliterated it forever, the name of the frigate, painted in bold white lettering across the stern. *Yvette.*

The larboard broadside fired again, in twos and threes as *Medina* passed across the Frenchman's stern. The French captain, seeing the danger, had started to turn his ship to starboard, trying to set up a broadside-to-broadside contest, but too late. *Medina's* round-shot tore through the weak structure of the stern and hurtled along the frigate's upper deck, felling men and overturning guns.

Hosking continued the tack, bringing *Medina* onto the Frenchman's starboard quarter. The Frenchman had brailed his courses and was under tops'ls only, slowing down to avoid overshooting the British Frigate.

Medina was now to windward, just where Carlisle wanted to be. There would be no slugging match, regardless of the French Captain's wish.

'Lay me alongside, Mister Hosking, put our bows on his quarterdeck. Away Boarders!' he shouted.

'Aye-aye sir,' Hosking replied. 'Bear away, quartermaster.'

The quartermaster elbowed aside the lead steersman and took the wheel himself. He spun it a few spokes to larboard and watched the relative position of the Frenchman as *Medina's* speed increased. Closer and closer they came.

The starboard gun crews left their stations and gathered on the fo'c'sle under the urging of Moxon, crouching low behind the gunwales. The larboard gunners feverishly reloaded in the hope of another broadside before the two ships met. The bosun and his mates were aloft with grapnels ready to bind the two ships together as soon as they touched.

Closer and closer. The two ships were almost touching when a belated broadside from the Frenchman tore into *Medina*. This time, at a range of only a few yards, the balls penetrated the oak planking and timbers. Carlisle saw two men down from among the boarders, smashed into a red pulp by an eight-pound ball. But it was only a partial broadside, *Medina's* raking attack had disabled half of the Frenchman's battery and in any case, the time for gunnery was almost over.

'Fire!' Shouted the gunner who had taken control of the battery when Moxon left to head up the boarders. *Medina's* larboard broadside had only lost one gun and its load of grapeshot cleared wide swathes through the men on the Frenchman's deck. The swivel guns were firing too, and the marines on both sides were adding their deadly musket fire to the carnage.

Crash! There was nothing gentle about the two ships coming together, and Carlisle saw men thrown off their feet. The grapnels flew and with a shout of, 'Boarders follow me!' Moxon led the charge onto the French quarterdeck.

'Keep the sails set as they are Mister Hosking, keep pushing our bows against her.'

With that, Carlisle drew his sword and sprinted for'rard to join the boarders.

**

In the end, it was an anti-climax. The French captain had made too little allowance for the inexperience of his crew. He'd lost his seasoned veterans, his experienced seamen, when his ship had been refitted in Rochefort. The replacements were all that the port admiral could spare, and they were an unimpressive crew: coastal fishermen and landsmen for the most part, perfectly adequate for preying on merchant ships but found wanting when faced with an enemy frigate. When asked to think and respond quickly in the heat of battle, they had simply frozen, and when their captain and the sailing master were cut down by *Medina's* grapeshot, they had no fight left in them. Carlisle reached the quarterdeck just in time to see his coxswain hauling down the ensign and the French first lieutenant, bleeding from a dangerous head wound, kneeling uncertainly among the wreckage of his guns, his sword dangling uselessly by its gold knot from his wrist.

**

CHAPTER THIRTY

A Happy Return

Sunday, Third of September 1758.
Medina, at Anchor. Hampton Roads, Virginia.

*M*edina's arrival at Hampton Roads in the forenoon
watch was a very different affair to the previous
time they'd visited. The frigate and her prize had
been seen from Cape Henry and the word had passed
quickly. The pilot cutter had left her warps dangling from
the bollards on the jetty, and yet they'd beaten the horde of
local boats by only a whisker. The merchants of Hampton
and the James River had suffered badly from the
depredations of *Yvette* and her ilk. They'd lost ships and
cargoes, and they'd been frustrated by the navy's response.
Every ship the navy could muster had been off Île Royale
throughout the summer, and the French commerce raiders
had filled their boots.

'Moxon will be enjoying this,' said Hosking, smiling at
the thought.

The first lieutenant had been given the prize to bring into
Hampton. It would look well on Carlisle's report and in the
broadsheets and might even result in Moxon's promotion
to master and commander – if there was a sloop available.

They anchored in the same berth that they'd left six
months before. Since then, spring had turned to summer –
reluctantly off Île Royale – and now the days were
shortening again, and autumn was around the corner.

There was no word of his wife at Hampton and Enrico
came back from the shore with the unwelcome news that
there were no carriages and no horses available that day. The
innkeeper promised that he'd have the same carriage that
he'd hired in March available, but not until the following day
when it had been returned by its present hirers.

'Pass the word for my coxswain,' he called, and paced

his cabin in frustration until Souter was found.

'Souter. Here's a chart of the James River. How quickly can you get me to here?' he demanded, pointing to a bend on a winding creek that thrust northwards from the river opposite Hog Island. 'Princess Anne's Port. It's less than a mile from Williamsburg. About thirty-two land miles of river from here then another four of Archer's Hope Creek.'

Souter studied the chart for a moment. Truthfully, it conveyed little to him, but he could see that once they'd rounded the southernmost point of the peninsula, just past the village of Newport News, this southerly wind would give them a comfortable run up the river.

'How strong's the stream, sir?'

Carlisle thought for a moment; it had been a long time since he'd taken a boat out on the James.

'About a knot and a half on the ebb, half a knot on the flood,' he replied.

Souter had his own mental reckoner for speeds, times and distances. It worked well but would never pass Trinity House.

'Bottom of the tide in an hour, sir, then it'll start to flood. Six hours, maybe seven in the longboat,' he said definitely. 'If we leave now, we may just make it before night. I'll get the boat manned right away, with your permission, sir.'

'Very well, Souter. I want to be underway in twenty minutes. Pass the word for the doctor as you leave.'

***

There was just enough east in the wind to round the point close hauled, then Souter eased the sheets and the big lugs'l bore them away up the river. The crew took their ease, lounging on the thwarts and staring out at the passing scenery. There were plantations all along the river on both sides. Each house, with its attendant cottages and slave huts, was separated by the green of marshes and fields, and the whole was threaded by narrow creeks.

The last stretch of the river passed in silence except for the lapping of the water as it parted against the longboat's bow. Hog Island came into sight to larboard, and Carlisle pointed out the marker that showed where Archer's Hope Creek emptied into the river.

'Furl the sail, lads, drop the mast,' said Souter. 'Look lively with the oars, we've a bit of pulling to do now.'

The sun was setting across the river as the longboat threaded its way past the mudbank that guarded the entrance to the creek. There had been some dredging work here, and the channel was well-marked with straight poles. Now that they were out of the river, they started to lose what little help the last of the flooding tide had given them and they were pulling against the current. The creek wound its tortuous way through swamp and tobacco fields, watched only by egrets and turtles at this late hour. The wind dropped to the faintest whisper. In the stillness, a church bell could be heard three miles away in Williamsburg. Carlisle's thoughts drifted to the opening verse of a new poem; *Elegy Written in a Country Churchyard.*

> *The curfew tolls the knell of parting day,*
> *The lowing herd wind slowly o'er the lea,*
> *The ploughman homeward plods his weary way,*
> *And leaves the world to darkness and to me.*

Thomas Gray had captured the very essence of his mood in iambic pentameter.

'Excuse me, sir,' said Souter, breaking in on Carlisle's reverie, 'what's the name of this place that we're heading for?'

'Williamsburg,' replied Carlisle sharply, 'the capital of the Virginia colony.' Didn't these men listen at all?

Souter lapsed into silence, aware that he'd been admonished.

'I believe Souter was referring to the name of the landing place, sir,' said Carlton, smiling to break the tense mood.

'Oh, of course. Princess Anne's Port, although some are calling it College Landing now.'

Carlisle felt a fool, churlish even, and elaborated to cover his embarrassment.

'It's the southerly landing place for Williamsburg. There's another that you can reach from the York River to the north.'

'Who's this Princess Anne?' asked Davies, the stroke oar, not caring much for the captain's privacy nor for his mood. He was enjoying the feeling of the ship's discipline falling away as they threaded their way into this unknown, silent land.

'Anne of Denmark, I imagine,' the doctor hurriedly interjected to save the captain having to reply. 'She became our Queen Anne at her coronation.'

There was silence as Davies digested this information.

'Then she wasn't English at all,' he said in a challenging tone, keeping his stroke.

'She certainly was,' replied Carlton, falling into the trap. 'Her husband was Danish, but her father was King James the second, and she was sister to Queen Mary. You don't get much more English than that.'

Another pause while Davies thought and the whole boat waited.

'Then she was a Catholic, 'cos her father was. How come she was Queen of England?'

Carlton was beginning to learn what the boat's crew already knew, that explaining anything to Davies was an open-ended contract.

'Yes, James was a Catholic,' replied Carlton patiently, 'but Anne was brought up a protestant…'

'Over the hills and far away…'

The bow oar, knowing Davies of old, burst into song to put an end to the history lesson. It was an old marching ballad that British armies had adapted to the circumstances and belted out in campaigns for at least a hundred years. Davies, pleased with what he saw as a win over the doctor, took up the tune in a firmer voice.

> *'Queen Anne commands and we'll obey,*
> *Over the hills and far away.'*

Then the whole crew took up the song in lusty bass voices, grinning with pleasure, while Enrico joined in the refrain and a few words of the verses whenever he could guess what was coming next.

> *'Over the hills and over the main,*
> *To Flanders, Portugal and Spain,*
> *Queen Anne commands and we'll obey,*
> *Over the hills and far away.'*

Davies knew a surprising number of verses, some martial, some sentimental, speaking of battles and love, regiment and family. The longboat raised a strong bow wave that lapped against the mud banks and marsh plants, and the sounds of the crew's lusty singing could be heard far into the countryside on this most silent, watchful of all evenings.

> *'Over the hills and far away…'*
> ***

With the last of the light, Souter brought the boat gently alongside the jetty, under the looming warehouses and factories that lined the shore. They had not been challenged at any time on their journey. That was a testament to the British navy's mastery of the sea. The possibility of a French raid just didn't occur to the people of Virginia. Would the inhabitants of Brittany or Bordeaux, the river towns of the Loire or the Gironde feel so secure? Carlisle doubted it.

'You'll have to pay your dues in the morning,' called a surly watchman from the shadows.

'Sod off!' replied Souter.

'We're for the city,' said Carlisle picking up his bag. He

suddenly realised that he hadn't given a thought to the longboat's crew's comfort and he turned guiltily to his coxswain.

Souter knew very well why his captain was distracted, and he was determined that a small matter such as the well-being of his boat's crew shouldn't add to his cares.

'Davies, you pick up the doctor's bag and Mister Angelini's, I'll bring along the captain's,' said Souter firmly. 'The rest of you, wait here until I get back, I won't be much more than an hour. Keep a guard on the boat and don't stray. If that damned watchman offers to interfere,' he continued in a rising voice, 'you may press him. He'll make a fine captain of the heads.'

The sound of running feet receded into the blackness behind the warehouses.

***

They walked briskly into the city, past the church, brightly lit for evensong and along Duke of Gloucester Street. The printer's shop came into view. Dexter was burning a small fortune in candles, Carlisle saw, as his storefront stood out from the others with its bright lights spilling onto the road.

'You can leave us here, Souter,' said Carlisle. 'Here's something for the men's comfort,' he said, handing over some coins. 'The ale-house that we passed will give you a room and no doubt they have a keg or two, in case the King's navy should pass by.'

Davies saw the coins before Souter could hide them, a surprising number of coins. He smacked his lips; there'd be no wasting them on a room, not if he had anything to do with it.

'Thank you, sir, thank you,' replied Souter. 'We'll await your word tomorrow then. And good luck, sir.'

Carlisle approached the door to the printer's shop. He was strangely nervous. The baby wasn't expected for another week or two, but Carlton had warned him that it could very easily and without any danger have warmed the bell, or it could be late. He found the whole subject frustrating in its uncertainties. He raised the brass knocker, but before he could drop it, the door opened softly inwards.

'Edward!' exclaimed Barbara in surprise. 'I was expecting the apothecary. Oh, my word, my word. Chiara said you'd be here, how did she know? How did you know…?'

'What's the news?' interrupted Carlisle, almost afraid to ask.

'News?' asked Barbara looking confused. 'Oh, you don't know…'

'My ship arrived at Hampton this morning. I know nothing. What news?' he repeated with a pleading look.

At last, Barbara smiled. It was all clear now, the fates had conspired to bring Carlisle back to Williamsburg at the perfect moment. 'It's a boy!' she exclaimed, 'born but an hour ago and they're both doing well.' She embraced her cousin as a soft wailing sound reached them from the rooms beyond.

***

Chris Durbin

HISTORICAL EPILOGUE

The Seven Years War in Late 1758

The fall of Louisbourg sounded the death-knell for New France. Although Pitt, the Prime Minister, was disappointed that the fortress fell too late in the season for an ascent of the St. Lawrence, he knew that it was only a matter of waiting for the following spring. Quebec could only be supplied by running the gauntlet between Newfoundland and Île Royale or by the long and dangerous passage of the Strait of Belle-Isle.

On land, the left flank of the attack had made little progress, being beaten back from Fort Duquesne on the Ohio in July while the centre had similarly been turned back at Fort Carillon on Lake Champlain.

Nevertheless, 1758 was a success for Pitt and for Anson, the First Lord of the Admiralty, and it laid the foundations for decisive action in 1759.

The French lost a quarter of their navy trying to hold Louisbourg, and they didn't recover their strength for the rest of the war. In contrast, by the autumn of the year the warships that had been ordered in Britain in 1755 were coming into service, and the British navy was poised to reach its peak. The French naval commander, des Gouttes, who had fallen out so badly with the governor of Île Royale, was vilified in France; so much so that his patent as Marquis was publicly burned by the Paris hangman.

Pitt knew that of all the things he needed to win this war, political support was both the most important and the most difficult to acquire. When the House of Commons resolution to thank Boscawen and Amherst was proposed by a Tory, normally in bitter opposition to Pitt's Whigs, it led to a surge in political support for the prime minister. Pitt's reputation and political power went from strength to strength and with it his ability to wage war.

***

306

Where Fact Meets Fiction

The Siege of Louisbourg happened much as I have described it. The ships and people are real except for *Medina* and her crew and some of the characters in the ports along the way.

***

Jean d'Olabaratz, whom we met in the prologue, is often confused with his father, Joannis-Galand, and consequently the record of his resupply voyages to Louisbourg is contradictory. What we know is that after the successful voyage to Louisbourg, at some time in 1758, he left Rochefort in *L'Aigle* bound for Quebec. The British blockade of Louisbourg forced him to take the more difficult northerly route around Newfoundland and through the Strait of Belle-Isle. *L'Aigle* ran aground near Gros Mécatina, and two months later a pair of rescue vessels sent from Quebec collided and were also wrecked at the same place. However, D'Olabaratz was determined to reach Quebec. He loaded what he could salvage of his cargo into a snow that he requisitioned from French seal fishermen. Sadly, the snow proved rotten, and it foundered off Île Saint-Barnabé on the St. Lawrence. D'Olabaratz and what remained of his crew reached Quebec months late and with no provisions for the garrison.

***

Medina, of course, was not anchored off *Anse de la Cormorandière*, or Cormorant Cove in English, for the landings on the eighth of June; that was *Kennington*, a somewhat smaller frigate than *Medina*. You can find Cormorant Cove easily on a modern map; it's called Kennington Cove in honour of that fine ship. I hope that Maximillian Jacobs, the captain of *Kennington* for the siege of Louisbourg, would be happy with the liberties that I've taken.

***

There was indeed a French army reinforcement unit

whose transport ships failed to reach Louisbourg and had to be landed far away near Port Dauphin. It was a battalion of the Cambis Regiment, but it happened later than I have suggested in my story. I often wonder what would have happened to Wolfe's assault if a regular battalion such as the Cambis had been in reserve behind Cormorant Cove on the eighth of June.

***

The cutting-out of *Prudent* and *Bienfaisant* happened as I have described, except there was no post-captain on the scene. Commanders Balfour and Laforey operated co-operatively without any over-arching command. It was just too good a story to leave Carlisle out. Both commanders were promoted the next day. George Balfour was given *Bienfaisant*, the ship that he captured at Louisbourg. Some years later, he commanded *Conqueror* at the Battle of the Saintes. *Bienfaisant* gave another twenty-five years of active service under the British flag before being paid off to a new life as a prison ship in Plymouth. John Laforey was given *Echo*, a frigate of twenty-two guns and he went on to hoist his flag as Commander-in-Chief Leeward Islands.

***

OTHER CARLISLE & HOLBROOKE NAVAL ADVENTURES

Book 1: The Colonial Post-Captain

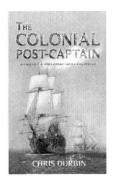

Captain Carlisle of His Britannic Majesty's frigate *Fury* hails from Virginia, a loyal colony of the British Crown. In 1756, as the clouds of war gather in Europe, *Fury* is ordered to Toulon to investigate a French naval and military build-up.

While battling the winter weather, Carlisle must also juggle with delicate diplomatic issues in this period of phoney war and contend with an increasingly belligerent French frigate.

And then there is the beautiful Chiara Angelini, pursued across the Mediterranean by a Tunisian corsair who appears determined to abduct her, yet strangely reluctant to shed blood.

Carlisle and his young master's mate, George Holbrooke, are witnesses to the inconclusive sea-battle which leads to the loss of Minorca. They engage in a thrilling and bloody encounter with the French frigate and a final confrontation with the enigmatic corsair.

***

Chris Durbin

Book 2: The Leeward Islands Squadron

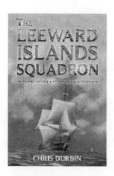 In late 1756, as the British government collapses in the aftermath of the loss of Minorca and the country and navy are thrown into political chaos, a small force of ships is sent to the West Indies to reinforce the Leeward Islands Squadron.

Captain Edward Carlisle, a native of Virginia, and his first lieutenant George Holbrooke are fresh from the Mediterranean and their capture of a powerful French man-of-war. Their new frigate *Medina* has orders to join a squadron commanded by a terminally ill commodore. Their mission: a near-suicidal assault on a strong Caribbean island fortress. Carlisle must confront the challenges of higher command as he leads the squadron back into battle to accomplish the Admiralty's orders.

Join Carlisle and Holbrooke as they attack shore fortifications, engage in ship-on-ship duels and deal with mutiny in the West Indies.

***

Book 3: The Jamaica Station

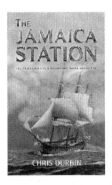

It is 1757, and the British navy is regrouping from a slow start to the seven years war.

A Spanish colonial governor and his family are pursued through the Caribbean by a pair of mysterious ships from the Dutch island of St. Eustatius. The British frigate *Medina* rescues the governor from his hurricane-wrecked ship, leading Captain Edward Carlisle and his first lieutenant George Holbrooke into a web of intrigue and half-truths. Are the Dutchmen operating under a letter of marque or are they pirates, and why are they hunting the Spaniard? Only the diplomatic skills of Carlisle's aristocratic wife, Lady Chiara, can solve the puzzle.

When Carlisle is injured, the young Holbrooke must grow up quickly. Under his leadership, *Medina* takes part in a one-sided battle with the French that will influence a young Horatio Nelson to choose the navy as a career.

***

Book 4: Holbrooke's Tide

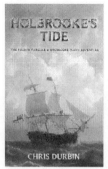

It is 1758 and the Seven Years War is at its height. The Duke of Cumberland's Hanoverian army has been pushed back to the river Elbe while the French are using the medieval fortified city of Emden to resupply their army and to anchor its left flank.

George Holbrooke has recently returned from the Jamaica Station in command of a sloop-of-war. He is under orders to survey and blockade the approaches to Emden in advance of the arrival of a British squadron. The French garrison and their Austrian allies are nervous. With their supply line cut, they are in danger of being isolated when the French army is forced to retreat in the face of the new Prussian-led army that is gathering on the Elbe. Can the French be bluffed out of Emden? Is this Holbrooke's flood tide that will lead to his next promotion?

Holbrooke's Tide is the fourth of the Carlisle & Holbrooke naval adventures. The series follows the exploits of the two men through the Seven Years War and into the period of turbulent relations between Britain and her American colonies in the 1760s.

***

BIBLIOGRAPHY

T he following is a selection of the many books that I consulted in researching the Carlisle and Holbrooke Series:

Definitive Text

Sir Julian Corbett wrote the original, definitive text on the Seven Years War.

> Corbett, LLM., Sir Julian Stafford. *England in the Seven Years War – Vol. I: A Study in Combined Strategy:* Normandy Press. Kindle Edition.

Strategy and Naval Operations

Three very accessible modern books cover the strategic context and naval operations of the Seven Years War. Daniel Baugh addresses the whole war on land and sea, while Martin Robson concentrates on maritime activities. Jonathan Dull covers the French perspective.

> Baugh, Daniel. *The Global Seven Years War 1754-1763*. Pearson Education 2011. Print.

> Robson, Martin. *A History of the Royal Navy, The Seven Years War*. I.B. Taurus, 2016. Print.

> Dull, Jonathan, R. *The French Navy and the Seven Years' War*, University of Nebraska, 2005. Print.

Sea Officers

For an interesting perspective on the life of sea officers

of the mid-eighteenth century, I'd read *Augustus Hervey's Journal,* with the cautionary note that Hervey was by no means typical of the breed. For a more balanced view, I'd read *British Naval Captains of the Seven Years War.*

Erskine, David (editor). *Augustus Hervey's Journal, The Adventures Afloat and Ashore of a Naval Casanova*: Chatham Publishing, 2002. Print.

McLeod, A.B. *British Naval Captains of the Seven Years War, A View for the Quarterdeck.* The Boydell Press, 2012. Print.

Life at Sea in the Seven Years War

I recommend *The Wooden World* for an overview of shipboard life and administration in the Georgian navy.

Rodger, N.A.M. *The Wooden World, An Anatomy of the Georgian Navy.* Fontana Press, 1986. Print.

The 1758 Siege of Louisbourg

Hugh Boscawen, a descendant of the famous admiral, has written a detailed and authoritative account of the siege. Johnston has covered the French perspective.

Boscawen, Hugh. *The Capture of Louisbourg 1758.* University of Oklahoma Press, 2011. Print.

Johnston, A. J. B. *Endgame 1758.* University of Nebraska Press, 2007. Print.

***

THE AUTHOR

C hris Durbin grew up in the seaside town of Porthcawl in South Wales. His first experience of sailing was as a Sea Cadet in the treacherous tideway of the Bristol Channel, and at the age of sixteen he spent a week in a tops'l schooner in the Southwest Approaches. He was a crew member on the Porthcawl lifeboat before joining the navy.

Chris spent twenty-four years as a warfare officer in the Royal Navy, serving in all classes of ship from aircraft carriers through destroyers and frigates to the smallest minesweepers. He took part in operational campaigns in the Falkland Islands, the Middle East and the Adriatic and he spent two years teaching tactics at a US Navy training centre in San Diego.

On his retirement from the Royal Navy, Chris joined a large American company and spent eighteen years in the aerospace, defence and security industry, including two years on the design team for the Queen Elizabeth class aircraft carriers.

Chris is a graduate of the Britannia Royal Naval College at Dartmouth, the British Army Command and Staff College, the United States Navy War College (where he gained a postgraduate diploma in national security decision-making) and Cambridge University (where he was awarded an MPhil in International Relations).

With a lifelong interest in naval history and a long-standing ambition to write historical fiction, Chris has completed the first five novels in the Carlisle & Holbrooke series, in which a Colonial Virginian commands a British navy frigate during the middle years of the eighteenth century.

The series will follow its principal characters through the Seven Years War and into the period of turbulent relations between Britain and her American Colonies in the 1760s.

They'll negotiate some thought-provoking loyalty issues when British policy and Colonial restlessness lead inexorably to the American Revolution.

Chris lives on the south coast of England, surrounded by hundreds of years of naval history. His three children are all busy growing their own families and careers while Chris and his wife (US Navy, retired) of thirty-seven years enjoy sailing their classic dayboat.

***

Fun Fact:

Chris shares his garden with a tortoise named *Aubrey*. If you've read Patrick O'Brian's *HMS Surprise*, or have seen the 2003 film *Master and Commander: The Far Side of the World*, you'll recognise the modest act of homage that Chris has paid to that great writer. Rest assured that Aubrey has not yet grown to the gigantic proportions of *Testudo Aubreii*.

***

FEEDBACK

If you've enjoyed The Cursed Fortress, please consider leaving a review on Amazon.

This is the fifth of a series of books that will follow Carlisle and Holbrooke through the Seven Years War and into the 1760s when relations between Britain and her restless American Colonies are tested to breaking point.

Look out for the sixth in the Carlisle Holbrooke series, coming soon.

You can follow my Blog at:

www.chris-durbin.com

***

Made in the USA
Las Vegas, NV
09 November 2020